Central King

TESSERACTS NINE

NINE

NEW CANADIAN
SPECULATIVE FICTION

Other Books In This Series

TESSERACTS NINE

NEW CANADIAN SPECULATIVE FICTION

EDITED BY

NALO HOPKINSON
AND
GEOFF RYMAN

EDGE SCIENCE FICTION AND FANTASY PUBLISHING

AN IMPRINT OF HADES PUBLICATIONS, INC.

CALGARY

Edge Science Fiction and Fantasy Publishing
An Imprint of Hades Publications Inc.
P.O. Box 1714, Calgary, Alberta, T2P 2L7, Canada

In house editing by Kimberly Gammon
Interior design by Brian Hades
Cover Illustration by Colleen McDonald
ISBN: 1-894063-26-0

EDGE Science Fiction and Fantasy Publishing and Hades Publications, Inc.
acknowledges the ongoing support of the Canada Council for the Arts and the
Alberta Fondation for the Arts for our publishing programme.

Library and Archives Canada Cataloguing in Publication

Tesseracts nine : new Canadian speculative fiction / Nalo Hopkinson
and Geoff Ryman, editors.

ISBN 1-894063-26-0

1. Science fiction, Canadian (English) 2. Fantastic fiction, Canadian
(English) 3. Canadian fiction (English)--21st century. 4. Short
stories, Canadian (English) I. Hopkinson, Nalo II. Ryman, Geoff

PS8323.S3T499 2005   C813'.08760806   C2005-902177-2

FIRST EDITION
(y-20050405)
Printed in Canada
www.edgewebsite.com

Contents

Canadian identity?
No, thanks.

by Geoff Ryman

Nationalities don't exist. They're an invention to help us stop thinking and imagining. Englishmen? Shy, formal and snobbish, with bad teeth. Brazilians? Samba, football and favela violence.

Nobody in their right minds wants a national identity. Canadians are lucky they don't have one.

A strong national identity means that people think they know three or four things about you. They would almost rather die rather than give up that knowledge, however easily won. They'll fight a war over it.

Having a strong national identity is of no use to a writer. People don't conform to the supposed national humours, and characters certainly shouldn't. The hero of Machado de Assis's great novel *Dom Casamuro* is a dour, fragile, shy Brazilian.

What writers DO need is to live in a country that is accepted as a universally relevant venue for stories.

When you are a writer with a passport from a universal venue you can write about any character in any kind of story you like — comedy, war, romance, or a finely judged study of personal grief. People come to your story with fewer deadly fixed ideas. You can use the everyday life around you as a convincing background, confident that people won't read it as local colour. This saves having to do research on, say, which hand people eat with. When your country is universal, you get not to be exotic.

Yes, a young Cambodian has a formal way of talking to his uncle. But that doesn't even make it past translation. "Hello, Uncle," covers it. (This is NOT an invitation to start writing about other countries without a lot of thought and effort or time living there. Otherwise what will come out will probably be the national identity.)

India is on its way to becoming universal, shedding images of poverty and mysticism. So is China, escaping every lotus-blossom, cruel-poverty, and red-guard stereotype.

The UK is an interesting case of a country that WAS a universal venue, which has the odd effect of meaning you tell any story you like about England so long as you set it before 1945. Otherwise it's Hugh Grant or James Bond.

First among the universal venues is the United States of America. You can have stories about shy Americans, good Americans, corporate bastard Americans, intellectual Americans, action hero Americans, or loser Americans.

Yes, Americans do have to struggle against a particularly imprisoning national identity. But even people who see Americans as ignorant and aggressive can still watch and identify with American stories. Last year I was surprised to see American and British movies playing in Aleppo, even though both countries had just invaded Syria's neighbouring Baathist state. Young students' bookshelves were lined with American and British writers.

What outsiders monolithically know about Cambodia is the Khmers Rouges. The first thing Westerners want to hear from a Cambodian is about what happened to them or their families under the Khmers Rouges. We almost won't let them say anything else.

For some reason this makes it difficult for Cambodians to write about anything else even for each other. You get few Cambodia stories about, say, the two clever women I met in a provincial capital who had set up a designer handbag shop.

You can be trapped in someone else's eye. What the rest of the world wants to be told about you controls what gets published. Worse, a strong national identity can sometimes reach inside and control what you are able to imagine.

I started out writing Canadian stories. I was a teenage Canadian living in Los Angeles, CA. What came out was filtered through that other country's down-home sensibilities. The most shuddersome first line of my many awful pieces of writing was "Whenever I think of Meadowvale, Ontario, a harmonica seems to play." Rural idylls, freezing landscapes, honest isolated farmers, rabid foxes, oh, and autumn colours, lakeside cottages, airplanes that could land on lakes, moose, sanded beans, Christmas at the United Church.

I turned to SF because it was universal.

Like the USA, SF has earned the right to be a locale for war stories, romances, comedies, tragedies and any other kind of story. It is our own universal venue and makes the usual national categories irrelevant. Does anyone in SF care that writers like Candas Jane Dorsey, Robert Sawyer or John Clute are Canadian? Are there any anthologies of specifically American SF or fantasy?

So why are we doing a specifically Canadian one?

Certainly NOT to help create a strong national identity.

We do have an interest in keeping Canada as universal a venue as possible. It's a paradox, but the more you write about a country, the less you write about its nationality. The more Canadian stories that get published or filmed, the more universal Canada becomes.

Nationalities don't exist, but languages do. English is not a specifically American, British or Canadian language, but it must feel like a wall of exclusion to writers of other languages. So, Tesseracts Nine includes translations of work originally written in French. This is not done to lay claim to French as part of a Canadian identity. It's done to help SF become even more universal by getting good stories from as many sources as possible.

SF has the equivalent of a national identity and it, too, is a prison. We have SF stories in Tesseracts Nine, but we also have tales of Christian miracles, pagan magic, bizarre events that have no explanation and stories as literary as anything by Donald Barthelme.

Contributors to Tesseracts Nine have almost nothing in common. A language perhaps. Not a genre or a geography. Certainly not a greater sense of cold or big empty landscapes; no particular politics or ways of being, or even a delicious post-modern Gallic sensibility. What Tesseracts Nine proves is that there is no such thing as Canadian fantasy and SF.

Which paradoxically, can only make it better.

From Fugue Phantasmagorical

by Anthony MacDonald and Jason Mehmel

Introduction: Embarking

You stand upon a boat as it wiles its way downstream. The breeze slips by your nose, scent reminding you of something; an old memory from youth that you can't place, can't forget. You've paid your toll to the boatman, got your ticket, and you'll have a souvenir to keep with you when we're done.

We are your tour guides, your travel-mates as we go from place to place. Please, leave your conscious luggage behind; on this trip, you'll only need the carry-on bag of your dreamstate.

We see a speck on the horizon, the current pulls, and we approach him, inexorably. And he's casting about in the water for fish, and he's panning for gleaming gold, and he's drinking from a chalice made out of love, and he's swimming with the water making his own currents around him.

Who is this?

Hermes Trismegistus. Artist. Mystic. Priest. God. He's been all of these things, depending on who's watching. He's got multiple passports; here they call him Thoth, though he still takes care of their words and all its associated luggage. He stood on the muddy bank of the Nile, sandy liquid lapping at his feet, long before the birth of Christianity at the death of Christ. He stands now, watching the stream of information go by, drowning the unwary. Who knows where he'll stand tomorrow?

He has his own passport for our boat; he should, he's the captain. As far as paper trails are concerned, those mundane documents detailing our presence here - bills, pronouncements, certificates and contracts - they are burning in his hand. They return to the ash from whence we come, and each piece of this immolated life touches the water and is swept away. He lives in a well-dug bolt-hole of anonymity, only emerging long enough to be remembered, if never known. What company he has are those who search him out, to whom he doles out a sip of mystery, a morsel of wisdom.

In his home, his cabin, he is surrounded by constant work. Over there, a painted canvas partially done, the panoply of colours making one feel as though truth were to be communicated, were the work finished; a truth of human love and sorrow. Over on the desk, lie sheets of paper, covered with phrases. Reading them gives an electric bolt of understanding; electricity ungrounded though, for a few lines are yet needed to complete the text, to finish its purpose to the reader. In a third corner, to complete this triangulation of creation, he sits, one hand holding a bow, the other embracing the strings of a cello, and as hair passes over string, pulling, scraping, its notes reverberate within the air, within ourselves, and we feel the electric thrill of *knowing*. Here, with all this about him, Hermes joins our crew.

Lemmings in the Third Year

by Jerome Stueart

I've always preferred my Rodentia frozen, tagged, weighed and placed in plastic bags; it unnerves me now to be interviewed by them. The lemmings, four of them, carry notebooks and an inkwell that looks like a dark blue candelabra. They have followed me out onto the tundra, unsure why I am here. Since it is their job to observe me and ask me questions, they come so they won't miss the one vital piece of information that they have been looking for all along. But I'm not in a talkative mood.

The tundra is quiet. I would have expected that, really, back home in the real Ivvavik National Park, the real northern coast of the Yukon Territory. I would have expected the passive look of the Beaufort Sea as it gives in to blocky chunks of ice which grow in numbers like a scar forming on the sea. I can still see the grass underneath a light snow. I expect that too. The vastness of the Arctic is amazing, breathtaking, and all this you can read about in books, see on television specials, even visit.

"What are you thinking about, Kate?" one of them asks me, breaking the silence. They have scratchy, tiny voices, not like Alvin and the Chipmunks, but more like carnies operating a Ferris wheel for the sixth day in a row, people who smoke a lot. Lemmings chitter.

"I'm thinking about home," I tell them. I open the videophone that David gave me before we left. It was working here when we first crashed, but it's not picking up a signal anymore. I've lost the window. You can't see it out there in the sky overlooking this flat, coastal plain, but there is a window our plane came through that is completely invisible. It is only several hundred feet off the ground, we guess.

"Home is Las Vegas," one of them says.

I laugh. "Yeah. You guys would fit in well there, especially in a casino, or maybe even your own show." I wish I could mark the air with a dye — so I'd know where the window is. I pick up a stone and think about throwing stones up one after the other until one of them disappears — but that's several hundred feet. Couldn't make that if I tried. Besides, there's a chance that any window we came through has closed or moved on. And that we are here for a long time. Like the ice freezing up behind you — we may be here until a lead opens in the air to take us back home, away from this land of speaking wildlife.

"She wants to go home," one of the females says. "She wants to give her research back to her people."

The wind batters my blue parka and drives black hair back into my face.

"No one," I laugh, "would believe our research right now. It wouldn't make a difference to them." They watch me punch the small buttons on the videophone. These are still so new, I don't know how to operate it like David would.

"Research is factual. It has to be believed," one of the males says.

"How can research be unbelievable?" a female asks.

I look up at the sky. From the sea to the mountains in the distance it is all one flat colour.

"All right," I say, and put away my phone. I take a big breath. This one is going to be a tough one. "It's time you learned about the scientific method."

I hear them scratching something on notepads behind me. Every once in awhile there is a glub sound of a paw dipping into the ink and coming out again.

The day hadn't started off well. I had lived in a cabin for the last few months with two other scientists and a pilot who was trying to fix our plane. Except he had no parts.

Because, *surprise*, there were no stores for aviation spare parts in this place.

Dr. Claude Brulé, the lead scientist on this expedition, had abandoned science altogether for theatre. I no longer saw him in the cabin as much, as he stayed now with a polar bear that lived in a cabin farther inland. The polar bears here were decidedly friendly and had a non-aggression pact with most of the animals, except the seals, but even that depended on when the seals were selling the bears something and when they were not.

The bears were putting on a play for us. Actually they were putting on a play before we got here, but Dr. Brulé had been helping them with direction since about last week. He'd always had a fondness, he said, for Shakespeare.

Dr. Kitashima and I lived in the cabin together. He was full Japanese, spoke English much better than I spoke Japanese. My father never spoke much of his own language around us girls. So I didn't pick up much. I did study Japanese in college a bit, but didn't speak it well enough to impress a native of the island. He didn't say so, but I knew that he'd rather I not speak any Japanese at all. He said I spoke it like a man.

Rather than abandon what we came here to do, Dr. Kitashima and I had been trying to conduct our experiments on *this* tundra. We had this belief, or I had until today, that one day we would get back and that in the meantime, science would be what would keep us sane. That if we concentrated on our work we would be able to think our way through this, figure out another way to get home. At least, he told me once, we would pass the time.

Our pilot, Ernest Stout, had a tent set up by the plane, but eventually, as winter set in, I knew that he would join us. His dog, River, had started to talk to him for the first time and he didn't know what to do.

It was strange. I couldn't explain how strange it was. We had watched movies in North America all our lives with talking animals. I had read books when I was a child — *Watership Down*, fairy tales, *Charlotte's Web* — and none of them prepared you for all the animals talking. I hadn't heard a mosquito yet, but I was willing to bet that they had some language too. The only reason that the bears, lemmings, ungulates, walruses, and birds (for the most part) spoke English was because the bears learned it first. And they taught it to everyone else.

They all spoke with a southwestern twang.

"Do you mind if we continue our questioning?" one of the males asked me. They all clambered on top of one of the huge wooden desks inside this cabin, dragging with much effort, their inkwell. At one point I had named them, but I was so embarrassed about doing that that I refused to talk to them as individuals.

"I really have a lot to do," I lied. What is there to do in a place you can't escape? There were no research centres, no universities, no schools to get into, no professors to impress, no jobs to interview for. There were no other humans in this place that I'd seen, and the animals all acted as if we were the newest thing. For awhile, we had many bird visitors — kittawakes mostly, nosing around, wanting to know what kind of disturbance we would make to the environment.

I shuffled some papers on the desk, picked up my own pen and begin writing a letter to my long lost boyfriend, David, whose worst nightmare had happened. He had lost me, just as he suspected he would.

He said, "If I let you go to the Arctic, do you promise to come back and get a degree here in Vegas?"

I couldn't tell him yes. I never wanted anyone to control my decisions, box me in. Well, now I had the whole world to move in, free and unencumbered by any other person but one bear biologist, one botanist and one pilot.

Dear David, I am doing fine. How are you? I wrote.

"Will you be eating us soon?" one of the lemmings asked me.

I looked up. Two of them were poised to write, one of them was approaching my elbow, and the other looked horrified aside the inkwell.

"I'm not going to eat you," I told them.

"But we're highly nutritious," one of them said.

"We have plenty of food," I gestured over to the back room that housed a huge supply of seal, and some vegetables that the bears traded for. "I'm not the big enemy this time."

"Do you enjoy eating lemmings?"

One of the females tapped his shoulder, "We know they do."

"We've never said that," I said.

"You enjoy meat?" she asked.

"I do eat meat, yes," I said. "But—"

"You will enjoy us. The bears like to dip us in gelled seal fat. I think that's what I would like. I've heard it is very tasty."

I shuddered. Researchers in the Lemming community were basically sacrificial lambs. They came and did the surveys to determine who would be their big predator in the fourth year, offering themselves as food after the data was delivered back to their community. All this data was compiled in the second and third year and a major enemy was predicted. I'd never seen if this was effective. I'd heard from the bears it was not. According to them, the lemmings became paranoid by their own data and panicked in the third year, and bred like crazy to survive the coming "holocaust," making the fourth year a feast for all predators. It was a terrible cyclical event, but it happened. Lemmings on our side of the window had spurts in population as well. It had never been a crisis, as far as I knew.

But then, I wasn't a lemming.

"I want to be cooked on that beautiful blue flame," one of the females pointed over to our small gas hot plate, which we hadn't used in awhile since we were running out of fuel and wanted to conserve it. It would be a nine-month winter.

"You can't," I said coldly. I waved the pen at them threateningly. "We aren't going to use that very much anymore."

"But I get a request," she demanded.

"Sorry. I'm not even going to eat you. You might as well pick another subject to interview."

They were undeterred. "Did you come here specifically for lemmings?" a male asked.

Dr. Kitashima came in the door and I felt as if I were saved. "Doctor," I said, "what have you heard?"

"Mr. Stout believe the landing gear completely out of commission. Will not be able to fly the plane without it." He took off a stocking cap and placed that on another desk. He went to the removable panel in the floor and took a rake that leaned against the wall and raked the coals beneath the wood, nestled just down a few inches into the ground. It was not the best heater, but it worked.

I'd already heard some of that news, yesterday. But I didn't want to believe it.

I looked away. I told myself that I could be as stoic and as practical as the next scientist. I could make do with what we had, live a life here in the Arctic, watching plays put on by bears, talking to lemmings who are doomed, shooing away nosy birds and foxes. I certainly didn't want to be the weak and emotional one on this expedition — the one who couldn't pull her weight. No reason to accuse me or fulfill their expectations.

"You have remained busy?" he asked.

I hoped he didn't really listen to my voice. There was a catch in it. "I've been working on reports." I stuck the letter to David underneath another pile of papers.

He smiled. "Good. That will pass the time."

He was short like me and his face looked like a windshield after it was broken. He seemed much older than he actually was. I thought he was fifty or so. Really no need for him to look as old as he did. Despite his sometimes annoying habit of treating me like his research assistant, I got along well with him.

"You have been talking to our friends," he said to me, indicating the lemmings.

"I don't really want to—," I started to say, but one of the lemmings interrupted.

"We are in the midst of an interview," he reminded me. "Did you come here for lemmings?" he asked me again.

I ignored them, getting up and moving to where Dr. Kitashima stood. I started telling him how these lemmings were driving me batty.

"Are you perhaps avoiding the question?" one of them asked. "We've had that happen before." He turned to the others. "I would put, yes, she has come for lemmings."

"You can't put that!" I said. "I didn't confirm."

"You confirmed by your avoidance."

"That's not research," I told them.

"We hypothesized that many subjects lie and avoid. This just proves our hypothesis is a true one."

I blew up. "If all your data is skewed to answer your hypothesis then why go do research at all? Why not stay in your lab and make up whatever you want?"

They were quiet for a moment.

One of them said, "When data relies on the answers of individuals isn't there always a margin for error due to the unreliability of interviews?"

"If they are unreliable — why would you do them?"

"How else will we collect data?" they said.

"Look, I don't have all day to explain to you how research is done. But I'll tell you this — there are other ways to calculate threat in a closed system besides interviews. What am I saying?"

Interviews — we'd never *tried* interviews before now. No one — no animal could tell us what they were thinking. And, come to think of it, if they had been able to, we would have solved a lot of the mysteries of how animals communicate, what they are thinking; what a boon to science! 'Course, that's called anthropology.

I walked over to them. "Okay, what you are doing is more of a psychological survey. Now, that's not my field. But I do know this: surveys have a large margin of error and that error margin rises when you are dealing with personal questions. You are asking predators if they are planning to eat you. Now let's think about this: why would a predator tell you he was going to eat you?"

"They all tell us they will eat us."

"So how do you determine which one is the most threatening in a given year?"

"We go by intuition — in the way that the predators answer the questions."

"Intuition? That's not scientific."

"But it has been accurate for generations."

I said, "Wait. You are telling me that the questions are a front — a disguise — for you to assess each predator through nonverbal cues?"

They conferred among themselves for a moment in Lemming-speak. It was a high-pitched chittering.

One of them looked up, "We cannot answer the question without skewing our results."

I was ready to throw something. "You are a walking, talking *insult* to science!" I said.

Dr. Kitashima swept the floor around me, asking me to lift my feet one at a time.

"Perhaps this is opportunity."

"What opportunity?" I snapped at him.

"To spend time. Teach them about science. Real science. Help them see."

He swept the cabin methodically, in rows, until the dust was in one pile and then, without another word, swept the pile out the door.

That's why we are here, now, the five of us, me and my team of protegés, approaching on our bellies a snowy owl nest. In the distance, a snowy owl sits. It's a female, as they alone incubate the eggs. Males are usually gathering food. This is about the distance that we need to be. She can probably see us, but that doesn't matter because my point will still come through.

"All right, let's stop here."

"Why don't we go up to her?" one of them says.

"We don't want to alter the results of observation. A scientist has to keep objective distance at all times. She doesn't want to influence the results of her research. Of course," I pause to remove a small rock from underneath me, "there is a theory that every observer has an effect on the thing she is observing. The Heisenberg Principle."

They scribble on a notepad and repeat, "Heisenberg Principle."

"But we're going to forget that," I say. "We are going to maintain our distance. The first thing you have to learn is how to observe." I look at the owl through my binoculars. She looks sedated.

"Okay, what is the owl doing?" I ask. "Observe her and tell me what you see."

They look for a few seconds. A female says, "She is looking for us."

"What makes you say that?" I ask.

"She is looking straight at us," she says.

I look through the binoculars, "No, actually she looks like she's asleep."

"She is faking," they say.

"You don't know that. You have to go by what you can see."

"She is stalking us," they say.

"No, you are missing the point. You can't make up things — you can't interpret the data you don't have. You have to look at what she's doing and just write that down. Can we do that? Can you just write down what you see?"

They scribble for a few moments, looking up at the owl periodically, and then return to scribbling. One of them even draws a nice picture of the owl.

"That's very good. See, now this guy over here has drawn a sketch to go with his observations. That's very cool, uh ..." Suddenly I want to name them again. "Are you Luxor?" I ask.

"I'm Orleans," he says. I'm embarrassed because I named them after casinos, but I wasn't feeling quite myself that day — a little excited, a little unprofessional. But now they were colleagues and not subjects, so it was different.

"Orleans, yeah. Okay, Orleans here has drawn a picture," I say again.

"It's a very nice picture," Mirage says. "Should we all draw pictures?"

"Well, pictures are nice," I prop myself up on an elbow. The wind whistles under my hood. "But not necessary. Just writing down notes of what you're observing is the important part."

Bellagio says, "She's awake! I saw her move."

"Good," I turn back and look through my binoculars. "All right. Now, look at what she's doing."

"She's cleaning herself," Mirage says.

"She is," I confirm. "Good, write that down." They proceed to write down this information.

"Why is this important? It doesn't tell us if she will eat us?" Luxor says.

"Animal behavior is an indication of their patterns, their habits. If we know the routine of this owl we can then predict behavior," I tell them, feeling a bit like a professor instead of a graduate student.

"How long before we know if she will eat us?"

"Well, Mirage, you have to observe her over time. Like a long time. Like a really long time."

"A couple of days?" asks Bellagio.

"Well, some of these can last for months or years. Depends on funding."

"Funding?" they ask.

"Not important here," I say. "We have to watch this owl and find out what she's like, what she does, what her habits are. Habits don't lie like statements about your habits can."

"Like when we caught you lying," Luxor says.

"I wasn't lying," I sigh. "Okay, it's true I came here to observe lemmings. I'm a biologist. I want to do this for a living. I was going to do just what we're doing now."

"Look at us through binoculars?" they ask.

"Yes, basically. Yes."

"What's basically?"

"That's not important."

"You would have snacked on us," Bellagio says.

I look back at the owl and she has something in her mouth. It's a lemming.

"You guys better see this," I say.

They all hum in chorus and breathe in, and then a world of scratching on notebooks.

"Well, we're done here," they say.

"What?" I look back as they start to leave. Bellagio has the audacity to cross over my back. "Where are you going? You're not done."

"We observed her eating a lemming. That answers our question." Luxor wipes his hands on his fur, smearing it with ink.

"You don't know how often she does that," I say to these science neophytes. "You don't know if the lemming was days old."

"But she was eating her. Clearly, she has the appetite and the habit," Bellagio turns to go.

Mirage stops, "But we don't know how often this owl does that, or if all the snowy owls follow her pattern. Kate is right. We have to stay and watch longer."

Good job! I think.

Orleans and Luxor are off, crossing the tundra. "I have a better idea," says Orleans, "we'll just ask her."

"That won't give you real data!" I call out after them. It gets lost in the wind. "This is not part of the scientific method! Wait!" But they are heedless.

"Men," I say.

"Males," Mirage and Bellagio say, but they aren't as upset as they need to be. They say it in a dreamy sense. "They *always* have the confidence."

"Listen," I tell them. "That's an owl. What's to stop her from eating them?"

Mirage titters, "Wouldn't it be wonderful to be swooped up by an owl? Feel that rush of excitement, even as the talons surround you!" She clasps little paws in front of her and her eyes are wide.

I underestimate their death wish.

I stand up, brush off my coat and walk quickly to catch up to the two others in my team. Back home, in Las Vegas, I was in charge of the Mendor Lab. Diane Mendor really ran it, but when she got engaged, she became wrapped up in a lot of other things, and I just naturally took over. This feels like a lab all over again, a bunch of young grad students who think they know what they are doing, blustering right into a big pit. Live and learn.

Orleans and Luxor have scampered right up to the owl, but the owl is not reacting to them in the way I expect. She sees me, obviously, and this alarms her. Even though I'm shorter than the average human, there is no average here to work from, so I look tall. I've always wanted to be tall. Perhaps I stretch a little when we get up to her. I've also only seen dead owls this close. I know a fellow student who's going into zoo science. She visited an owl sanctuary in California. Said they scratched a lot, and they were flighty. I wonder what owls here are like.

This one has her feathers ruffled, but she's not hissing. She's not moved off the nest either, but I can't tell if she's upset or excited to see us.

"Hello," I say to her. "My name is Kate."

"Well, these *are* nice. Thank you very much, Kate," she says, eyeing my lemmings.

"They're not for eating," I say.

"We're here to ask questions," Luxor announces, pulling out his notebook.

"Ah, I already had a team asking questions. I told them everything I knew," she says, but her tone of voice is cheeky. She swivels around and pulls out a lemming from her nest. "You might recognize this one."

The lemmings chitter among themselves, some high-pitched squeaks, which are either terror or delight, or maybe both. They obviously know the lemming.

Mirage turns to me, "He was a colleague." But it's a fact, not much emotion. I haven't gotten used to facial expressions yet.

"The agreement, you know," says the owl.

"Of course," says Luxor.

I say, "What do you mean, the agreement? These are my lemmings."

Orleans looks me square in the eye and damned if he didn't put his little paw on his hip, "You won't be eating us. You told us that."

"Well, I might. I might just get a hankering for lemming in the middle of the night," I say, with a little jealousy on top of my voice. "Listen," I turn to the owl, "these are my lemmings and I'm training them to do things differently. So you can't eat them. They're experimental."

The owl blinks, "Dear, why do you want to change a good system?"

She knows. She knows the lemmings are basically naïve and knows that their questions don't amount to anything. She's taking advantage of them.

She nestles her wings close to her, "Feel free to ask me any question you wish — for the agreement," she adds firmly. She doesn't look at me.

"Luxor, Orleans. You guys come home. I'll talk with you."

They aren't listening. Luxor has a notebook out, is flipping back through small pages. Orleans has the inkwell and props it up between the two of them.

Luxor looks back at me to show me how this is done. "Now," he says, turning to the owl, "about how many lemmings do you eat in a given day?"

"About two," she says, without pause.

"And how large is your territory?" Luxor asks.

"It is squares 45-53 on the *loo-tow* field."

Luxor beams, as much as a lemming can. "Well now, that's a large area. And you only eat two lemmings a day? Do you have a mate?"

"I do," says the owl.

"And how many lemmings does he eat?"

"He eats two a day as well, on average. Although, lately he has been flying off into other squares." She turns to her right. "He could be anywhere right now."

"Exactly," said Luxor. "And if you had to predict your appetite in say a year's time, would you say that you would on average eat the same amount of lemmings?"

The owl thinks, blinking, and then widens her eyes, little explosions of yellow. "Well, I don't know. Let me see. A year's time. Why, just thinking of that makes me terribly hungry. You know, anything can happen in a year's time."

Without warning, she lunges forward and gobbles Orleans up, slapping her beak against the inkwell. A squirt of red and inky black runs down the owl's feathers. Luxor and the others are entranced. I move forward and grab the owl by her throat and place a hand around her legs just above the talons — I don't want to be scraped. I squeeze until the owl's beak thrusts open. She must be in shock because she doesn't try to resist, and I turn her head towards the ground and shake her, trying to make her gag by pressing her throat. Nothing is coming out. The owl has swallowed the lemming whole, but I know she can regurgitate. I've seen them do it. And with the size of Orleans, there should be a lot more ripping and tearing before she swallows. She's just trying to make a point.

So am I.

The lemmings are clapping behind me, and I can't tell if they are clapping because of what I am doing to save Orleans, or if they are cheering for the "beautiful" death of their colleague.

The wings of the owl slide open like a fan, and she's big enough that when she flaps, she can get a lot of pull. I stand and she is flapping against my face and gagging.

"Cough him up," I say like a gangster, but nothing is coming out.

The wind bites my face and ears, and I have the owl now shoved down towards her nest, hoping that by gravity something will come out. The wing is cradling my face like a palm, reaching around my neck, quivering.

Finally, a body slips out of the owl onto the grass. It's covered in gunk. It's actually two bodies and for a moment I don't know which lemming is Orleans, but they both look still.

I push the gasping owl away from the nest. She squawks about the "agreement, the agreement."

I rub my eyes and begin wiping away the gunk to figure out who is who. I've seen small rodents mangled in traps before, traps that misfire, spring on a leg, clamp down on the body of a mouse and by morning the mouse hangs divided by the metal mesh. It's bothered me before, but not like this.

One of them is barely moving and I pick up Orleans and I wrap him in my scarf and place him in my pocket, the only warm spot.

"We have to go back to the cabin," I tell them and I don't listen to their protests and I don't check on the owl, even after I see her stumbling out of her nest in my peripheral vision.

The cabin is full of scientists and a seven foot tall polar bear. All of them see me come in and I go straight to the desk.

"Something happened," I say. My lemmings jump up on the desk. The cabin is warmer than outside, but you can still see everyone's breath. I think I see concern in Dr. Brulé's eyes. He's reacting to something I'm giving off, something on my face.

"One of the lemmings," I tell them and unwrap Orleans and lay him on the table. He's still. "Can I have the first aid kit?" I ask.

I've never patched up a rodent before — not a lemming, not a rat, not a mouse, not even the flying squirrels I studied in California. If they were injured, they died. If they were dead, we catalogued them. We put them in frozen bags until we were ready to take down notes. We thawed them a few days later with all the other dead animals and we wrote down how they died, where they died, how much they weighed. We sexed them, measured their molars to tell age, and we put them in a large black garbage bag because we had everything important we needed from them.

Dr. Brulé helps me. Dr. Kitashima stretches out the scarf like an operating blanket.

"We were interviewing a snowy owl and then she ate him. He was moving fifteen minutes ago," I say to Brulé.

"He has some deep wounds," Dr. Kitashima says. Some of the gunk we wipe away from him keeps returning from the open beak marks near his tail. There are two cuts on either side of his face too, and I can't tell if the blood is coming from his neck or his cheek. Cheek would be a flesh wound, neck would not.

Luxor, who rests his arm on a cup of water, says, "We have the data. This is what happens."

"Well," I tell him, "I didn't want to *let* it happen. I'm sorry."

I pull off some bandages and I cut a tiny square to wrap around his hind end — almost like a diaper. I'm thinking that if I can stop the bleeding, he'll be okay.

"Someone will have to go back and stay with the owl," Luxor says. "If we don't, she might get upset and that will ruin all our data so far. This might spark a revenge cycle and increase her numbers of lemmings eaten per day. Revenge factors are difficult to measure."

Dr. Brulé gives me a look like he's doing the best he can but it's not going to work. Neither of us have seen Orleans move. He's gone limp in my hands even as I raise his tail to wrap the bandage.

"If he's dead now," Bellagio says, "we can take him back as an offering to the owl, and maybe save the data."

I snap. "I'm not interested in saving the *data*! God, he's your colleague! You weren't even the envoy to the owls. You were *my* envoy." Dr. Kitashima can't feel any pulse at all. He has sensitive fingers, worked with small seedlings and plants all day. I watched how tender he could be growing things. "This wasn't going to happen," I say to Dr. Kitashima because I don't know who I'm supposed to say this to. How I'm to account for this.

Both doctors stop for a moment, helping me find my composure, not condemning me for my outburst. I respect that. Then Dr. Brulé takes out a syringe with a dose of stimulant in it, I'm sure. He injects this into the lemming, and we wait.

My sister had a hamster when we were little. It had escaped and ended up in the inner workings of the dryer. We found it when the smell from the dryer turned sour. She cried for days. I was stoic. I offered to buy her another hamster, a generous offer, I thought. She wouldn't speak to me, ran off to her room. I didn't understand why she was so upset. Later she almost went into veterinary work; I went into biology. She owns two cats and a dog, a budgie, and several fish. I have no pets.

Orleans does not recover. "He was only in there for a few minutes," I say.

Dr. Brulé moves around to my side of the desk. "Owls have a narrow throat, Kate. He was probably crushed, at least suffocated in that amount of time. It's possible that there's a lot of internal damage. I don't know."

I look up at the ceiling. It's a high ceiling, made for bears to walk around in comfortably. The one here now just watches. He fills up the room in my mind, like a supernatural being — if I believed in them. Talking animals have that supernatural quality, the kind that makes me think I am living in a fairy tale. I'm sure the bear doesn't understand the sanctity of life. I don't think I understand that anymore.

If animals talk, then they can't just be eaten as food anymore. They aren't part of a food chain anymore than humans are. If everything talks — where do you draw the line on feeling for them as individuals? God, I was slipping into subjectivity. They warn young graduate students about getting attached to the animals in the lab.

Don't name them. Don't pet them.

Don't ever let yourself get interviewed by them, either.

Luxor writes in his notebook. Bellagio and Mirage walk over to the body. Bellagio picks up the scarf ends and starts to drag the body off the desk. Inevitably it will fall on the floor with a heavy thump. It's all senseless. This whole place is senseless.

Mirage stops her. "Wait," she says, and she goes over to the body and looks down at the face. She sniffs his face, and then backs up and looks at his ink-stained body. She traces her hands across the stains as if she is reading the last marks. He's become a notebook himself, I think. She says, in the quietest voice — I can barely hear it at all, "He had very good penmanship."

I want to scream, but Dr. Kitashima says instead, "How long did you work with Orleans?"

Mirage looks up at him slowly. "We catalogued data and research in the libraries for a season. He had good penmanship there too."

Luxor says, "He was brave."

"He was efficient," Bellagio says. "And he drew nice pictures."

Mirage stands up and walks over to the inkwell. A small notebook rests against it. It's obviously Orleans's. It has blood on it. "We have his notes," she says. She begins reading.

"Snowy Owls eat two lemmings per day. She doesn't predict that she will be increasing or decreasing that amount. I believe, of course, that she's lying."

No one speaks. Mirage looks at all of us, her small eyes, all pupil and dark, stare at each one of us in a glance. She closes the notebook, and sets it against the inkwell, carefully, as if the weight of it will tip the inkwell over.

Luxor looks grave, and when he speaks, his voice seems loud. "I concur. I believe she's lying too."

I just notice that her fur is turning to its winter coat, not all in one place, not like a white patch, but as if every tenth hair has changed to white. A subtle change, a gradual one. I look over at Orleans, now eternally brown, except for the ink scratches, and a black, ink-stained front claw.

"It's a shame," Mirage says.

"Yes," Luxor agrees. "Kate should have let the owl finish. Now the data is skewed."

"No," Mirage says, "It's a shame anyway."

She walks back to him. "She was lying. You both knew that. Why do we trust data from lying subjects?"

"We've always known they lied. That's what makes it accurate."

She looks at me. "No," she says, "that makes it a waste of time."

She steps down off the table onto a stack of books until she is on the floor, and Bellagio and finally Luxor follow her, down to the floor and out a small hole in the wall. Like a little procession, they leave. I think, there you go, Ms. Future Scientist, lead them away from this. She makes me want to smile, but I can't.

I take a paper towel and wrap Orleans in it, but I don't put it anywhere. I just sit at the desk for awhile. Dr. Brulé makes tea for everyone. Dr. Kitashima opens a notebook and writes something I'll never read. The scratching sound of his pen makes my eyes blur and I look up and see the great white mass of the polar bear looking down at me. I get shocked every time, thinking they will eat us. Can I really trust them when they look like this?

He just stares for a few moments like I imagine God would stare — a god with big teeth, and black gums, who makes me feel small and insignificant, a god that stares incomprehensibly, maybe unable to think of anything to say, any excuse to give for such a mixed-up world. Here the whole natural drama plays itself out like it always has, except *now* I'm privy to all the voices, all the person-alities, all the individualities of each player, each animal or bird that is stalked, chased and killed. I get the privilege of talking with them over tea before it all happens. I get to see their beautiful sketches of snowy owls. That's either all wrong, or the way it should have been all along. I don't know which is better.

The bear leans over the desk and fills my vision now with his face, and blows his breath through his nose at me, a puff of smoke. Bears believe you can read a person's thoughts in their breath — the breath that we see coming out of our mouths in the winter. Those are thoughts and feelings unexpressed, they think.

I sigh back as an answer to him, and my breath sneaks out as a flat line of smoke. He looks at it, closes his eyes and moves away. I hope I said something right.

It's October now and Luxor, Bellagio and Mirage have been back to their community of lemmings, not far from our cabin. They have handed back their research. Not only the research on which predator would be the most destructive, the most costly to the community, but also about the recommendations they have based on the evaluation and gap analysis they conducted on their own research methods. Honourably, they have completed the mission of any scientist — human or lemming. They have concluded research and it's up to the community to make decisions. Having returned, they stay in our cabin now.

"We would have sacrificed ourselves anyway," Luxor shrugs.

"This way we get to learn more about research," Bellagio says. They are all almost completely in their winter coats now. They line the railing on the cabin deck and we all look out onto the snow-swept plains, erased in the half-light of early winter, until they are blue, merging with the frozen sea.

Mirage turns to me and asks the question I have been thinking about now for months, "What do you do, though, Kate, when you don't have a community to give your research to? We have no purpose for our research anymore. We can learn. But what does it do?"

I have a cup of coffee in my hand. I don't know where the coffee comes from. Somewhere south of here. The bears trade for it. It's not the same as coffee from home — it's more bitter, a bit spicier, a darker flavour. But it's hot and it's good and it's my coffee now.

"You do it for yourself," I tell them.

She nods, hums a little and then they chitter for a few moments. And then, soft as twilight, the darkness sweeps over us, silent, like a bird with black wings.

Principles of Animal Eugenetics

by Yves Meynard

Kelly stood on the platform and watched the train pull out, gaining speed; a slow arrow of tarnished metal shot from a tired bow. Above his head, the sky was a luminous grey: rags of clouds moved swiftly in front of a featureless haze.

The platform was of varnished red bricks; on the sides of the pit in which moved the trains, the earth had remained raw, and was now stained thoroughly by years of exhaust and grease. The tracks glimmered as if someone had been oiling them, polishing them, inch by inch, lovingly, with a chamois cloth. Kelly could almost imagine the little man — it would have to be a man, and he would have to be little — walking crabwise along the tracks. He would hold an ivory coloured cloth high up in one hand, bringing it down swiftly to buff a narrow section of the rails, then returning it to its absurdly high position, waiting for the next defect to be spotted, to pounce upon it and erase it from the perfection of the track.

There was no one else on the platform. As an envoy from Centrality, Kelly had naturally been alone in his compartment aboard the train; in his wagon, he'd had a glimpse of an old man and a young woman travelling with her baby daughter, but otherwise it was empty. The train had come to a stop at this station; Kelly had gone out of his compartment, which was next to the exit, and climbed down without encountering anyone.

Kelly picked up his heavy suitcase — the handle was slicked with his own sweat, grown cool and greasy — and made his way to the stationmaster's office, passing along a gigantic poster of Sebastian Bloom. The poster was hardly new: it was flaking along the edges, and a corner of one sheet had peeled in the middle, opening a geometric gash in Bloom's face.

There was a sign, thin white letters on a black background, which was overlaid with rust in one corner. "OFFICE." The sign hung perpendicular to the wall, like a pub's. Underneath it was a wooden door with a rectangular pane, obscured by a pale yellow fabric. To the right of the door, a window opened into the wall. There was a rotating drum beneath — for the stationmaster to pass something to the clients without having to risk bodily contact? The room beyond the window was dark, although a tall narrow rectangle of light to the left indicated that at least one room of the station was lit, and presumably occupied.

Kelly rapped on the window a few times, but there was no reaction. He went to the door and knocked, setting down the heavy suitcase with a huff. After another wasted minute, he tried the knob. It turned.

The room was very small; to the right, a doorway led to the window booth; there was a closed door in the far wall, leading deeper into the house. In the room itself Kelly could see no furniture, except a shelf set high on the wall, holding a row of unidentifiable knickknacks. The floor was bare wood, shiny from varnish. In Centrality such a floor would have been called delightfully rustic, but here it was simply, and starkly, crude and inelegant.

Kelly risked a call to the stationmaster, unwilling to enter the strange house. He heard a series of noises, and after a while the door opened, and out came a dark-haired man, wearing a Railroad Collective uniform, which was rumpled and buttoned crookedly down the front. The stationmaster passed a hand through his hair, disarranging it further despite his best efforts.

"Pardon me there, didn't hear you, sir. Heard the 7:46 train going by, but it usually never stops ... I'd forgotten you were coming. Straight from Centrality, heh?"

"Yes," said Kelly. He waited, expecting the stationmaster to offer more in the way of an apology, but the man remained silent. Kelly noticed the stationmaster's hair was thin, the scalp very pink underneath it. From the man's flesh rose a smell reminiscent of cloves; for some reason Kelly found it disgusting.

"I haven't been met in the way I expected."

"Really, Sir? Was there anything special you required? 'Cause I wasn't told."

Kelly sighed, but strove to contain his impatience. The people who lived here, so far from the hubs of organization, were not like the city-dwellers he had dealt with all his life. He must exercise diplomacy; learn to accept laziness and inefficiency as normal modes of life.

"I guess I thought someone would greet me at the platform — but no matter. At any rate, I need to be conveyed to town."

"Well, Sir, everybody here walks, you know. It isn't far. Besides, the only car in town has been brokedown for two months now, and won't run again for a while."

Kelly started to sigh, then stopped himself.

"Well then, is there someone to carry my suitcase?"

"No one here but me, Sir. No one."

"Well, couldn't you…"

The stationmaster looked vastly astounded. "No, sir, I will say I can't. My duties end at the instant of half past seven; and besides, it looks much too heavy for me. Could have one of the boys move it, in the morning, if you like."

Kelly restrained his anger. Provincials held scrupulously to their schedule when it suited them. After all, they had the excuse that these were orders, issued from Centrality. As a representative of the government, he could expect nothing more than meticulous adherence to the rules. He might have tried to invoke some higher regulation — a moment's reflection would bring to mind several such directives, useful to a man in his line of work — but he did not want to make an enemy of the stationmaster. This was something he could not afford at this early stage in the investigation. So he swallowed his humiliation and said, "Never mind. I'll carry it myself. It's not that heavy."

"As you say, Sir." To Kelly's eyes, the stationmaster looked, not smug, but relieved — at what Kelly could not guess. He took the handle of the suitcase and with a subliminal grunt lifted it up.

Kelly exited the office, and closed the door. Just beyond the small brick building, a walkway extended at right angles from the track and came upon a dusty road. The town was to his left, perhaps ten minutes' walk distant. Kelly followed the roadway, toward the town.

He could see a door and two small windows at the back of the stationmaster's house. Through one of the windows, Kelly saw something that made him pause and approach the house.

He was looking into the kitchen. A table with a red-and-white checked plastic tablecloth stood close to the window. At the table sat a young woman, dressed only in a large pale-blue sheet she had wrapped around herself, one breast hanging nearly free. She was cutting her long hair with small blunt-ended scissors, without perceptible plan or pattern, just broad ragged swathes. The cut hair fell into a plate. Every few seconds the young woman reached for the plate with her free hand, picked up a thick lock of hair and crammed it into her mouth. She chewed mechanically, the strands of hair that protruded from her mouth grew shorter and shorter until they vanished, and then she swallowed.

Kelly stared numbly for a while, then suddenly the door to the kitchen opened and the stationmaster came in. His voice came muffled through the window; he yelled at the young woman and pulled her out of the kitchen, she still clutching the scissors in one hand. Kelly had not been seen; he decided to return to the road and set out toward the town.

The sun would be going down in about an hour and a half; though already, because of the overcast sky, the day seemed faded, on the verge of ending. Kelly felt the unease, like the pre-echo of depression, steal over him. There was at the back of his mind the awareness that he was being tested; that the Bureau would base its evaluation of his future, in large part, on what happened here, during his first real mission. He did not like the assignment at all, but when it had been offered him, he had known better than to refuse it.

He was about to reach the outskirts of the town when he met the dog.

He could not tell what breed it was. He did not like and did not understand animals, and knew very little about them. He forced himself to note the features of the dog. It had a long muzzle, but a fairly stout body. It was neither large nor small; it was a dirty brown in colour, with black pointed ears. Its forehead bulged out noticeably.

"Stranger," said the dog.

Kelly had been forewarned; the report he had been given to read had dwelled on this. Yet he had not truly believed the story, and now that he saw it had all been true, it came to him as a bad shock. He found that he had stopped dead in his tracks. Sweat ran down his forehead in rivulets, stinging his eyes.

The dog took two paces forward, sniffing. It did not look hostile, but to Kelly's eyes it definitely did not look friendly. Dogs could smell emotions, especially fear; this he knew. He forced himself to speak.

"My name is Kelly." Then, absurdly, but he felt he must add something and didn't know what to say, he added "How do you do?"

The dog looked up, blinked. "Kelly," it said. Its pronunciation was good, but not human. Its jaw and lips and tongue moved in complicated ways that did not seem to accord with the sounds they produced. "I-am-very-well-thank-you. My name is Leaper."

The dog's bulging forehead was large enough to house a brain capable of higher cognitive functions. Experiments of this kind had been performed in the labs of Centrality, several times. Kelly had viewed films of Mister Chee, an augmented chimpanzee. In one, he had been signing with his trainers, arguing about a movie they had just seen. Kelly recalled that the chimp had won the argument. The difference here was twofold: this was a dog, not an ape, and it was actually speaking.

"You belong to Doctor Jonas, yes?" said Kelly.

"Yes. I'm Leaper. You're Kelly. Why are you here?"

"I've come to see the doctor."

"He won't see you. He doesn't cure people anymore."

"No, I'm here to talk about his work."

"He won't see you."

"I'll call on him in the morning, anyway."

The dog snuffled; a canine shrug? Kelly found he could not resist asking it the question that was foremost in his mind.

"Tell me, how is it that you can talk? Doctor Jonas gave you a big brain, but a dog's mouth isn't made for talking."

"Sugary," said the dog.

"Pardon?"

"Sugary."

Kelly thought there was annoyance in the tone. Suddenly understanding dawned on him. Without pause for reflection, he said, in what he realized a second too late was a condescending tone, "You mean *surgery*."

Leaper sneered, showing off its teeth, and emitted an unpleasant growl. Kelly grew alarmed, but the dog turned away, stalked off through the grasses at the side of the road, and vanished from sight.

A fine beginning, Kelly thought to himself. *You've already insulted one of the natives.* It came to him an instant later what it was he had thought, but he could not erase the idea from his mind. With something of a shiver he went on his way and entered the town.

It was quite a small place; three streets running roughly east-to-west, and two perpendicular intersecting avenues. Doctor Jonas' laboratories were situated a short distance from the town itself, in a shallow valley screened by a stand of trees. Despite having perused a map of the environs Kelly found he was having some trouble orienting himself.

Not far distant he saw the town's single inn, a tall building behind which stretched fields running up to a low hill. He strode over to it, pushed the door and entered. A bell rang as the door swung open and once more as it closed. The lobby was carpeted in dark red, the walls were heavily varnished wood. The aroma of toast drifted in from what must be a kitchen beyond an open doorway screened with a flimsy plaid sheet. A fat woman officiated behind a counter.

"Good evening, Madam; my name is Kelly. You have a reservation for me."

The woman sighed, opened a black ledger and, after much leafing through pages, found his reservation. She took a day's payment in advance, gave him a key attached to an enormous metal prop, like a small dumbbell sawn in half.

His room looked out over the back of the inn, the fields and the hill. The bathroom was appallingly small and the toilet made a constant hissing sound. Kelly laid his suitcase on the bed, tapped out the code on the lock-pads, and lifted the lid.

He took out his shaving kit and a bottle of shampoo, and put them on the narrow edges of the sink. Left inside the suitcase were a pair of binoculars, several books, his gun, and wireless equipment. It was the latter that accounted for most of the suitcase's weight. Kelly took out *Principles of Animal Eugenetics,* re-closed the suitcase, then put it underneath his bed. There were two brass false locks on the case, to discourage casual snoopers. More persistent ones would find that keys could not open the suitcase. The lock-pads were inconspicuous, and the coded sequence was twelve digits long. If a determined person tried to pry the suitcase open, he or she would set off the explosive charges embedded along the contours of the lid. The Bureau had strong feelings about private property, for all that this smacked of heterodoxy.

Kelly opened the book at the page he had marked with a torn-off magazine subscription coupon. For twenty minutes he read, stretched out on the bed. The words hovered teasingly beyond his comprehension; he could understand the gist of the arguments, but not the details; and some of the leaps of logic he could not justify. In the end he put the book on the nightstand and rubbed his eyes. Theory might not be too much use. What he truly understood, anyway, was practice.

He had seen the ultimate results of the chimpanzee experiments. Theory failed to account for them, but they could not be rationalized away. He remembered the final film on Mister Chee: the camera making its way into the chimp's room, all the red on the walls, words written in blood, the script at first tiny and controlled, but growing larger and wilder as the lines went on.

You're hurting me every day and every night. You're forcing me to be bad I don't want to be a bad person but you make me make me and you showed me God and he saw inside my mind and Yes YES IT HURTS THE LADI OUR GUIDE SEESE INTO MEE OH GOD I

The last words were indecipherable, great looping letters fading into meaningless patterns, arabesques of blood splattered across the walls. The self-mutilated corpse was lying on the bed, clothes all torn away except for the neatly tied striped cravat. The right nether hand clutched a shining knife blade; both upper wrists were slashed open, tendons and bone exposed.

Doctor Jonas had gone much further than the scientists of Centrality. There had been rumours for a long time about his activities; reports had been accumulating in the Bureau offices in Centrality. If the rumours were correct, the augmented dogs had been functioning for more than a year, without any anomalies. And giving them speech! Whatever eugenic method Jonas had discovered, it was invaluable.

Eventually, letters had begun to be sent to Dr. Jonas, inviting him to visit the capital and make a presentation of his work. He had never given any response. Now it was Kelly's task to get the information from him. Sending an enforcement squad would have been stupid: the doctor must not be scared off, and so a single agent had been sent to him. Bureau doctrine was clear and based upon long experience: scientists had to be coddled, otherwise they would not co-operate and became worse than useless. Knowledge was a dangerous thing, and the wielders of knowledge dangerous persons.

Kelly felt hunger; he went down to the lobby, and asked if it was possible to get some food. The fat woman morosely sat him at a table in a small dining room decorated with old photographs, and served him a cold ham sandwich. Kelly was alone in the room.

"Are there many other guests?" he asked the woman as she returned, bringing a bottle of beer.

"Nah. Only you."

He could not get any more out of her. Munching the last of his sandwich, he examined the pictures. They seemed about twenty years old or so, were not labelled, and presented groups of people standing stiffly at attention, perhaps overwhelmed by the notion of posterity. Kelly's eye was caught by one face that seemed familiar; it was, in fact, the stationmaster, in the photograph a younger man still in his middle-to-late thirties. Standing next to him was the same young woman he had seen at the house wrapped in a sheet and eating her own hair.

Kelly swallowed and examined the photograph again. Of course, it could not be the same person. Yet he had kept a very clear mental picture of the young woman in the station house — he had earned high marks in Eidetics during his Bureau training — and he was positive the features were almost exactly the same. A daughter, probably. Still... uncanny.

Kelly finished his beer and went back up to his room. The sun had set. Kelly looked out the window onto the fields, now grey under a cobalt-blue sky. From far away came a howl, then a chorus of howls. There were animals on the top of the hill. Kelly opened his suitcase, got out the binoculars. The animals looked like dogs; it was growing dim and they could not be seen clearly, though the top of the hill was bare of trees.

The howls came again, but they were articulated this time, and Kelly after some time was able to make out the words. "Sugary," they sang, "Sweet, sweet sugary."

In the morning Kelly went out of the inn, sauntered down into the valley, and presently arrived at the door of Doctor Jonas' house. He rang the bell and waited for the door to open.

Doctor Jonas looked like a banker. To be precise, he looked like the painting of a banker in a book Kelly had read when he was young, before the species had become extinct. Like that archetypal banker, Doctor Jonas was partially bald but kept a thick fringe of very dark hair; like the image, his ample jowls were closely shaven and his eyes were blue. He wore the kind of jacket the upper class had favoured in the pre-revolutionary days; in Centrality this would have been sufficient provocation to get him arrested. Here, in a town in the middle of nowhere, within the Doctor's own house, it was no worse than a subtle insult, and probably not even that.

"Good morning, Sir. I am sorry, but I no longer take patients. I advise you to see Dr. Duckett, who is a fully qualified—"

"Actually, Doctor Jonas, I don't come as a patient. I wondered if I might have some words with you."

The Doctor's bland face showed almost no trace of emotion. "Are you from a newspaper?"

"No, sir. My name is Kelly; I am an envoy from Centrality. I've just arrived, and I'm eager to speak with you."

"Well, in that case... Please step inside."

The Doctor led Kelly along a thickly carpeted corridor into a sitting room. The furnishings were massive, ostentatious; again this was the pre-revolutionary bourgeois style, but it was offset by a large portrait of Sebastian Bloom that dominated the room.

"Please make yourself comfortable. Something to drink, Mister Kelly?"

"Thank you, no."

There was a soft padding across the carpet and an augmented dog entered the room. This one was pale in colour, bigger but lankier than Leaper had been. It had the same bulging forehead.

"Mister Kelly, this is one of my charges. Her name is Cotton. Say hello, Cotton."

"Hello, Mister," said Cotton. Kelly nodded and mumbled a reply. Then the dog took a step closer to Kelly, sniffed loudly while pointing her nose toward his crotch and added, "You smell like you just had sex."

"Cotton! I've told you not to do that! Go away; bad dog!"
Cotton hung her head and slunk away. Doctor Jonas' face
had ever-so-faintly coloured. "I apologize, Mister Kelly.
That was Cotton's idea of a joke — her sense of humour
is not exactly like ours. She likes to make rude comments
and embarrass people, and I haven't quite been able to get
it out of her."

"No matter." Kelly made a gracious gesture. He did not
at all feel like laughing. He set out his first bait. "Doctor
Jonas, I hope I need not tell you how much Centrality holds
you in esteem. These dogs you have eugenically altered
are a splendid achievement. It was thought you might like
to come and give a conference at the Academy of Sciences;
if there is any time that is convenient to you…"

"Thank you, but no. I am not ready at this time to present
my findings fully."

"If you'll allow me to ask, why not?" Kelly altered his
intonation to put a subtle nuance of threat in the question.

"Such things are complicated to explain," said Doctor
Jonas; his tone seemed to say that he was aware of the
menace and considered it hollow. "I can tell you I will need
many more months of work, perhaps as much as two or
three years, before I am ready to give a conference."

"In that case, will you allow me to visit your laboratories?"

Doctor Jonas made a sour face, but got up and led the
way without speaking. Kelly followed him through the
corridors of the house, down into the basement. He kept
careful note of their journey, paying particular attention
to windows.

The Doctor pushed open a heavy door and ushered Kelly
in. "This room holds initial subjects." A strong animal reek
dominated the room. There were about a dozen animals
of various kinds held here; four rabbits in small wire cages,
five dogs in larger enclosures of steel, three chickens and
one parrot in birdcages hung from the ceiling.

A girl was hunched in a corner, making *tck-tck* noises
with her tongue. The Doctor called: "Lydia!" She rose from
her crouch and turned to face the two men, smiling ingenu-
ously. Kelly could see behind her a glass box full of white
mice.

"Hi, Daddy. I was looking at the mice." She spoke and carried herself as a little girl of seven or eight would, but she was at least twenty years old. The impression of youth was amplified by her clothes: a thin blouse and skirt, shoes of shiny leather, and bare legs. Her right ankle was twisted out of shape and the flesh of the foot was cramped by the shoe.

"This is my daughter Lydia, Mister Kelly." Lydia dropped a wobbling curtsy. "Don't you have something to do, now, dear?"

"Can I go and play in the yard with Jeremiah?"

"Yes, dear." Lydia skipped out of the room. Doctor Jonas immediately made a show of his apparatus, opening drawers full of scalpels, curettes and clamps, pointing to generalized anatomical charts pinned to the walls. There were thick ledgers full of breeding data, tables of reagents with scrawled notes in pencil. Kelly dutifully watched and noted. He knew, with the feeling of an important puzzle piece falling into place, that he had probably witnessed the main reason why the doctor had worked on augmenting animal intelligence: to compensate for his daughter's feeble-mindedness.

After a time he interrupted Doctor Jonas' patter and said: "Doctor, this is certainly interesting, but in fact it is merely the basics. I have some familiarity with eugenetics, and I'm aware that there is more — much more — to it than breeding charts, mutagenic chemicals and supplemental vivisection. I would very much like to see a work in progress, if I may."

The Doctor's face pursed itself again, and with his full banker's assurance, he said, "No, I'm afraid you may not. I do not show my 'works in progress'. I only show finished experiments. I regret that I cannot show you more than I have."

As he was being walked out to the door, Kelly assayed the second bait.

"I have been authorized by Centrality to make you an offer, Doctor Jonas. They are willing to give you large laboratories, fully equipped with the latest in technology, whatever you may want to work with. And a very respectable salary, and very good lodgings — for yourself and anyone else you need with you. How does that sound?"

Doctor Jonas showed him to the door. He spoke with overt contempt in his voice. "I regret that we do not understand one another, Mister Kelly. I have no wish to leave this town. My laboratories are amply sufficient to my purposes and I do not need the latest in technology. Good day."

Kelly bowed — a deliberate pre-revolutionary ritual, a pale attempt to keep face somehow — and left. He felt his face must be burning with shame. He had pressed too hard; Doctor Jonas had become utterly obdurate. Had he completely ruined his chances?

He returned to the inn, asked for his key, and went up to his room. He sat down on the bed, unsure of the proper course of action. Should he communicate with the bureau now, or wait? To call now was to admit defeat: like a child too stupid to understand anything about life. But not to call was to let the situation stagnate. In the end that was worse.

Kelly pulled the suitcase from beneath the bed, pressed the lockpads, opened the lid and unpacked the wireless equipment. The quadrangular antenna he positioned on the nightstand, while the generator and receiver he lay on the bed. To connect the generator, he had to disconnect the lamp from the room's single electrical plug.

He put the earphones over his head. He adjusted the tuning dials and rotated the antenna until he finally heard the carrier-tone. He depressed the pulse-key seven times, then seven more, then sent out his name by Morse code. Presently above the hum of the carrier-tone came a thin, higher-pitched whine, in pulses brief and long. Kelly wrote down the dots and dashes, but he knew the code well enough to interpret directly.

KELLY REPORT

TALKING DOGS CONFIRMED, he replied. CONTACTED DR. JONAS. REFUSED ALL OFFERS. HOSTILE. ADVICE?

YOU MUST GAIN INFO. USE WHATEVER
MEANS NEEDED. WE AWAIT RESULTS.

WILL COMPLY, he said, his finger heavy on the
pulse-key.

The Bureau agent in the wireless office in Centrality,
hundreds of miles away, did not reply. Kelly listened
for a minute more to the blank carrier tone, then he shut
down the wireless and put it back into the suitcase. *We await
results.*

Kelly withdrew from the suitcase a small unmarked
metal cylinder, with a rubber valve on top. Squeezing the
valve released a jet of narcotizing gas, effective on all forms
of mammals. He slipped the cylinder inside his left jacket
pocket and his lockpick's tools in the right-hand one. The
Bureau wanted results, and Kelly would have to provide
them or face demotion.

He opened the door of his room. He had turned off the
lamp two hours ago, and prepared himself by the sparse
moonlight that came into the room. Now he slid out of the
room, and drew the door shut behind him. He crept down
the staircase, paused at the bottom of the landing, alert for
the slightest noise. He felt a childish pang of guilt: guests
were supposed to turn in their keys at the desk when they
left.

Kelly made his way to the front door. There was a chain-
bolt, but it hadn't been set. He unlocked the door and
slipped out.

It was about half past one. The air was chilly; Kelly's
breath made faint plumes of steam. He made his way out
of the town, through the fields, past the stand of trees, down
into the valley, to Doctor Jonas' house.

He felt sure that at least one augmented dog would be
on guard. He kept the canister of narcotizing gas in his left
hand as he crept toward the house, making frequent pauses.

He almost lost his chance; the dog also had been silent,
and Kelly was surprised when it rushed him, making a

sound that was both bark and shout. The jet of gas struck the dog's muzzle off-centre, but the effect was strong enough to slow down the animal; Kelly was able to dodge its jaws. The dog landed heavily on its feet and hesitated. Kelly got off another blast, squarely into its nostrils. The dog shuddered and collapsed. Its mouth worked, and disjointed words came out. "The lady," it said, and "cause the doctor — even if — bite, bit, bitten — no dog good dog..." Its breathing came regular and slow now; it would wake up after six or seven hours.

Kelly was about to leave it and move on, but something nagged at his mind. There was something wrong about the dog... Then he figured it out. The dog's forehead did not bulge. It encased a brain no larger than normal. Things were getting stranger; but he could not stay here, next to the dog's body. He had to go on.

Kelly made his way to one of the rear windows without further problems. Working quickly, he got it to open and stepped inside the house.

There was a heavy silence. The corridor was in darkness but Kelly knew his way; he shone a pencil-light briefly around him to check, then set out for the laboratories downstairs.

Kelly had noted two doors next to the one Doctor Jonas had ushered him through that morning. These were most likely to lead into the interesting rooms. He sidled up to the first one, and set to work picking the lock.

After less than a minute he felt the last tumbler slide into position. He pushed open the door and entered the room. He shone his pen-light onto the walls. There were anatomic charts and breeding tables here as in the room Jonas had shown him, but these appeared more complete. Somewhere there must be a journal, a diary of experiments, or maybe even a monograph. Kelly opened the doors of a large armoire and felt a row of leather spines under his fingers.

He grinned, and at that moment the lights came on.

Kelly whirled around, his hand reaching for the gas canister. Then he relaxed, tried to appear friendly. It was the doctor's simple daughter.

She was smiling at him; Kelly put his finger to his lips and went *sssh* comically. Lydia muffled a giggle and copied his gestures. Kelly went past her, closed the door and whispered in her ear, "What are you doing here, Lydia?"

She whispered back, "I don't sleep much, I'm always up before Mister Sun is. What are *you* doing here? Your name's Kelly, right? Cotton told me."

"Yes, my name is Kelly. I'm playing a game, but it's a very serious game and you mustn't spoil it, okay?"

"I won't. What's the game?"

"Well, I bet myself I could get into the house and get out without your daddy finding out. I had to be very careful, and now if you tell him I was here I'll lose the game. You understand?"

"Yes. You're playing spy."

For a moment Kelly wondered if the imbecility was a careful act; but if it was, he had lost everything already, and it cost him nothing to go on with the charade.

"Yes. That's it. Spy. Now will you help the spy get back to his home so he can finish the game?"

"Only if you do something for me. And if you do that, I promise I won't tell anyone anything."

"All right. Whatever you want."

Lydia lay down on the floor, rumpled up her blue nightgown, pulled her underpants down to her knees. "Rub me, please." Kelly hesitated, taken aback. "My wee-wee," she said, impatient. "Please. Like this."

Numbly Kelly knelt at her side and began to massage her. Lydia shut her eyes and smiled. Soon she started to clutch at his left arm and to buck her hips.

Kelly felt soiled by the act; Lydia had a mature body, but still it felt like forcing a child. He turned his gaze away, accelerated the back-and-forth movement of his fingers along the girl's cleft, to bring her to climax as quickly as he could.

Lydia gripped his left arm fiercely; she began to moan through clenched teeth, then her whole body shook. And Kelly felt the girl's arm against his grow burning hot, and for a second or two it seemed that it had lengthened, like squeezed putty, and reached farther along his back than was physically possible.

Then she was coiling up on her side, panting, bringing his moist right hand to her mouth and kissing it.

"Are you happy, Lydia?" he made himself ask.

"Uh-huh."

"So you won't tell? I can go and finish my game?"

"I promise."

Kelly did not dare to continue his examination of the room. He went out, leaving Lydia still on her back, half-naked, scratching at her legs and smiling idiotically. He made his way back to the window he had eased open. He felt a knot in his abdomen, a vague nausea of shame.

He managed to return to the inn and back to his room. He went into the small bathroom with its hissing toilet, ran the water in the sink and scrubbed his hands, trying to wash the smell of Lydia's body off his fingers. Then he sat down on the toilet's closed lid.

He had failed, and must accept his failure. Depression seized him, a wave of gloom colouring all his thoughts. There was a flicker of impotent rage toward the Bureau. Doctor Jonas was too important an individual to warrant only an inexperienced agent! When he passed in front of the review board, come what may, he would make that complaint heard.

He was too good at Eidetics: once again, an image of Lydia rose unbidden in his mind. He saw again her half-naked body, his hand caressing the cleft between her legs. He had turned his head away. He had turned his body to the side, and his head even further, so that he was looking at her bare legs and feet. He felt a small shock, his training asserting itself. He summoned up the image of Lydia he had absorbed at their first meeting. He had noticed then she had a deformed foot; but tonight, he had seen that both her ankles and feet were perfectly normal.

It might be that he was confused, that tension and fear of failure had impaired his functioning. Somehow he thought not. Kelly shook off his inertia. His incursion into the house would probably have consequences; he could not trust Lydia to remain silent. He must return to Centrality at once, present a detailed report, convince the Bureau to send a full task force and salvage this mess. If he argued his case well he might still save his position.

Kelly pulled his suitcase from beneath the bed, unlocked
it and once more arranged the wireless equipment. He sent
out a message.

> AGENT KELLY REPORTING.
>
> ACTIVITIES OF DR. JONAS BEYOND WHAT
>   WAS EXPECTED. INDICATIONS OF
>   VERY ADVANCED EUGENETICS.
>
> ADVISE BUREAU SEND CLASS B TEAM TO
>   INVESTIGATE.
>
> AM RETURNING TOMORROW MORNING
>   TO PRESENT FULL REPORT.

At this late hour, there would be no reply from the
Bureau officials. The technician on duty acknowledged
reception of the message and Kelly signed off.

He repacked his equipment then, and went to bed. There
would be a train to Centrality at 10:28; he would be at the
station by a quarter past ten.

In the morning he rose, ate a meagre breakfast, and
announced his departure. The proprietress grumbled, and
demanded payment for the two days originally booked.
Kelly paid her, went to fetch his suitcase and set off for
the station. She watched him leave, standing in the doorway, and Kelly got the impression she knew something.
He told himself he was becoming paranoid.

He was at the station by ten past ten. He went to the
stationmaster's office, stated that he must board the 10:28
train. The stationmaster threw a set of switches on a large
board; panels swung out from signposts, requesting the
train to stop when it reached the station.

"Tell me, Sir," said Kelly. "I was lunching at the inn yesterday and noticed some photographs on the wall. You're
in one of them, aren't you?"

"Yes, Sir. Those were taken not long after the Revolution."

"There was a woman with you in the photograph; a
brown-haired woman, dressed in a light suit. May I ask
who she is?"

The stationmaster's face darkened. "That was the wife, sir; she's ten years dead."

"My condolences," said Kelly. "I didn't know."

"Yes, well, I have work to do now, Sir, if you don't mind."

Kelly left the stationmaster at his duties and went to sit on a bench. His observations were starting to form a pattern, but it was not yet complete. Still, it reinforced his conviction that the situation was too much for an inexperienced agent.

The train seemed slow in coming. Again, the day was overcast, and the station was bathed in a weak grey light.

Kelly stood up, walked back and forth, suitcase in hand.

He heard footsteps close to him and turned around. It was Doctor Jonas and Lydia, accompanied by a large dog. Kelly recognized the animal: it was the one he had anaesthetised the previous night.

"Good morning, Mister Kelly."

"A pleasure, Doctor Jonas. Miss Jonas."

The Doctor reached inside his bourgeois' suit and brought out a handgun.

"Mister Kelly, I must ask you not to move."

Kelly felt the burn of adrenaline flooding his muscles. "I will remind you that I am an agent of Centrality. You are committing a serious crime even by threatening me." He noticed that Lydia was smiling delightedly, cocking her head to the side. The dog had pulled back its lips, showing off dark yellow teeth, and was tensing up.

"Spare me your revolutionary bluster, please," said Doctor Jonas.

"You will be seen, Doctor. The stationmaster or the other workers will see you. Put the gun away now, and I won't report this incident."

"The stationmaster and the others support me. No one will interfere."

Bloody pre-revolutionary lumpen. Kelly wasn't really surprised. They'd have to revere whoever came closest to an aristocrat in their shitty excuse for a town. Kelly let the pulse of rage at his betrayal fade away. He did not have time for sentiments; he must consider his options. Doctor Jonas held the gun confidently; Kelly believed he would not hesitate to fire. At this range, there was hardly any possibility of missing. He must gain time. He might well use the arrival of the train as a diversion. In the meantime, if the others shifted their positions, it might be possible to grab hold of Lydia and use her as a shield. The dog, however, might be the most serious opponent.

"What is this about, Doctor?"

"It is about your visit of last night. Jeremiah didn't much like being gassed, and Lydia told me you'd read my experimental diaries. You have seen too much, Mister Kelly, and I can't have you making a report about it."

"So you'll kill me? The Bureau of Intelligence will send out people after me, and you will find yourself in grave trouble. I'm only a minor agent, but the Bureau cares for its own."

"Oh, I wouldn't simply kill you. I know your superiors expect you back in Centrality. And they will see you, tonight; you will give them a confused, incompetent report, which will convince them I am not to be disturbed yet. I may be forced to vanish, but at least I will have time to do so."

Lydia had been staring at Kelly throughout the conversation. Now she nodded, as if finally satisfied. "I can do him, Daddy," she said.

"Go ahead, dear," said Doctor Jonas. Lydia started to undress. "Please take off your clothes, Mister Kelly."

"Why?"

"Just take them off."

The dog growled. "Nice dog, Jeremiah," said the girl as she pulled off her gown.

"Lydia," said Kelly. "We're friends. Tell me what's going on." He would have to do something desperate soon. Three of his fingers uncurled from the handle of his suitcase and made contact with the frame.

"I have to play you, Kelly. So that means I have to take your clothes. It's the first time I get to be a boy."

"Take your clothes off," repeated Doctor Jonas, waving the gun.

"If you shoot me," said Kelly, "you'll damage the clothes. You don't want that." His fingers were pushing the lock-pads unobtrusively, one at a time, very slowly.

Doctor Jonas hesitated; his forehead was beaded with sweat. Obviously, for all his determination, he had qualms about shooting a man in cold blood; Kelly's argument about the clothes would only worsen his reluctance.

Lydia was now completely naked. She frowned in concentration, then relaxed. She began to grow taller, her torso flattening, her shoulders bulking up. Her face altered as well, its planes shifting, hair sprouting over the cheeks and on the upper lip.

"I had guessed," said Kelly, surprised at the calmness of his voice, "but I couldn't be sure. I must admit she's the most impressive example of eugenetics I could imagine. Were you aiming for shape-changing abilities when you altered her? Or is this an unforeseen consequence of an attempt to increase her intelligence?"

"That doesn't concern you, Mister Kelly."

"You intend to pass her off as myself. But she's too slow-witted to do it."

"She will be well advised. Jeremiah is the best of my dogs, and probably more intelligent than yourself. I have no fear." Doctor Jonas mopped his bald forehead.

Kelly thought he heard the noise of the train, still far off. Lydia had by now almost exactly copied his features. He had to keep talking, to gain the brief time he needed. He was afraid, but there was no other way out.

"You do know that she's been fucking the station-master?" Doctor Jonas flinched. Kelly went on. "He got your daughter to copy his dead wife. I saw her yesterday, as I arrived. She was cutting her own hair, and eating it. Re-ingesting her own cellular tissue, I suppose. Shape-shifting has to be subject to conservation of mass. Which means that Lydia can't copy me accurately." Kelly's fingers kept pressing the lock-pads. It wasn't the unlocking code he had been entering, but another one, designed for a slightly different purpose.

"She can do the face. Only the face matters." It was Jeremiah who had spoken. Doctor Jonas' eyes shifted back and forth from his daughter to Kelly.

Lydia's features had now firmed and matched Kelly's to near-perfection. The moment had come. Kelly took a short step towards her, holding forth his right hand, palm forward, letting the suitcase swing toward the front of his body. "Lydia," he said, "don't do this. We're friends, aren't we? Remember how nice I was to you?"

Doctor Jonas, his face white, pointed his gun more sharply. "Don't move, Kelly!" As Kelly had expected and hoped, Jeremiah stepped forward, growling, to interpose itself between Kelly and his mirror image; and at that moment Kelly's middle finger pushed the last lock-pad, and the code set off the explosives embedded in the suitcase's lid.

The force of the blast threw him backwards, close to the edge of the platform; he spun sideways, slamming his limbs into the concrete, almost glad, for a few seconds, to surrender to the energies of the bomb and let them do what they willed to his body.

His ears hurt, and all sounds were muted now. He felt nothing in his left arm; he risked a brief glance at it, saw a mangle of flesh that had been his hand and might yet be saved, if he could get medical attention. The blast had been directed outward, away from him; but the left side of his body was still badly burned.

Leaning on his right hand, he raised himself to his knees. He saw Jeremiah's body, nearly torn in two, lying on the ground. Next to the dead dog the metamorph lay writhing and screaming; her cries of pain seemed to come to him through thick cotton. Fragments of the suitcase and its contents had imbedded themselves into her. Kelly could see her burned flesh twist and flow like thick mud. It seemed to have lost all cohesion, to drape itself at random on her bones. The face, his face, was losing its definition, becoming a blank mask with two holes for the eyes and one for the screaming mouth.

Doctor Jonas had been mostly spared by the blast; he stood staring at the scene. Kelly got to his feet, rushed tottering to him and slammed his right fist in the Doctor's face. The Doctor reeled back; Kelly seized the gun in his hand and wrestled it free almost without effort. Doctor

Jonas looked at him uncomprehending; Kelly raised the gun and shot him twice in the head.

Kelly looked around, but there was no one else on the platform. He strode over to Lydia; her flesh was still heaving and boiling, oozing blood and lymph. He emptied the gun into her, trying to hit the heart; her body convulsed after each shot. The last bullet seemed to hit a vital organ: the body grew suddenly rigid, then went limp; the flesh sagged.

Kelly strode down the platform; Sebastian Bloom's huge, peeling face gazed at him from the poster on the wall. He heard a tinny screech all around him, saw the train pull into the station, finally come to a stop.

A cloud of steam rose from the engine. Kelly hobbled toward the train, but now the pain had begun. His whole left side felt seared, and his arm, his arm, his hand! He faltered, almost fell, forced himself to go on. Surely the conductor must see him; there was no one on the platform, no one looking out of the empty train.

He called out, weakly: "I am an envoy from Centrality. In service to Sebastian Bloom. My name is Kelly. Help me. I'm wanted in Centrality. The Bureau..."

It seemed to him he had clawed his way into the train, was sitting in a compartment, tended by a worried steward who said: "We should call a doctor right now, Sir." And Kelly was saying, "No. Not here. They want me dead here. The next stop. Or maybe wait to Centrality. Call ahead. You have wireless equipment? Call ahead. Call the Bureau of Intelligence..."

And it seemed to him too that he was still at the station, kneeling on the platform, his life running out of him, his arm a spike of burning pain, and the train was leaving the station, ignoring him, pulling ahead, faster and faster, and now he did see the little man walking along the tracks, holding a chamois cloth in one hand, buffing the rails, buffing the rails, erasing every least speck of tarnish from the gleaming metal, while the train sped off into the distance. The little man raised his head to smile at Kelly, and his face was Kelly's own.

Mom and
Mother Teresa

by Candas Jane Dorsey

Mother Teresa came to live with my mother in the fall of 2001. The famous nun had been touring around the war zones of the world, but she was much frailer since her nearly-fatal heart attack a few years before and perhaps she felt it was time to tackle problems of a different nature — no less serious difficulties of the human condition, but in a more peaceful milieu.

My mother was a healthy eighty-two at the time, a healthy, fat, sedentary, angry widow who looked fifteen years younger than her age and charmed strangers with her clear thoughts, her delightful conversation, her grasp of world events, and her vigour. I found her less charming as I extracted her from her agoraphobic denial patterns and drove her to her doctor's appointments, grocery shopping, and visits with friends, listening non-stop to her fears, her complaints about how difficult my mild father had been really, her catalogue of how little help she got from anyone or how alone she was. She often telephoned me to just run her out to — somewhere — in my lunch hour, and the resulting trip usually took three hours or more. My boss had had me in for two little talks already.

My mother's adult years of desultory attendance at the nearest United Church had not served to erase her Scots Presbyterian childhood with its message of duty, sacrifice, and unhappiness, but the reality these reflexes were based on was a long time ago. When she opened the door that day and found a little, spry, sari-clad Catholic nun on her doorstep with a suitcase, I must credit my mother for reacting according to the training of her parents and grandparents. She invited the little woman in and offered her tea and the second-most-comfortable bed in the house.

"I don't drink tea," said Mother Teresa. "Thank you for your hospitality. Thank you, God, for providing this plenty. Nice house. Does anyone else live here?"

"No," said my mother. "My husband died a year ago. I miss him so much, though it was a terrible struggle taking care of him for the last few years. I just couldn't do anything. It was a nightmare time..."

"Plenty of room," said Mother Teresa. "I think I'll just sleep here in the front verandah. It's cooler anyway, and I don't like a lot of clutter around."

"Would you like some lunch?" said my mother. She had just been starting to make egg salad sandwiches.

"Lovely," said Mother Teresa. "How about if you make a lot more of those?" She was already on the telephone. Before the sandwiches were finished, there was a knock on the door, and two young nuns ushered in about two dozen orphans. You could tell they were orphans, my mother told me later, because they were all dressed alike and their last names were alphabetical by age: Anderson, Ben-Adhem, Carnegie, Daillard, Endicott, Feinberg, Griffon and so on, to Singh, Taillenen, Underwood, Versailles, Wooster, Xander, Yung ... there was no Zed orphan.

The orphans stayed for lunch. My mother opened several cans of Campbell's cream of celery soup and used up the last of her milk making it wholesome. She thawed out another couple of loaves of white bread from the downstairs fridge and opened cans of sardines for sardine salad. The older orphans helped her chop onions very fine and one spooned in the mayonnaise, licking the spoon afterward with frightening eagerness. By adding water to the four litre jug of orange juice in the refrigerator my mother was able to give them all orange punch. Mother Teresa said grace, then doled the punch out in the Royal Doulton cups that the grandfather and grandmother that I never met had rescued from the forest fire by burying them (the cups, not the grandparents) in the North Ontario woods and digging them up after the fire had gone through.

The orphans were all pretty careful, and the young nuns washed the dishes and put them back exactly where they came from. My mom appreciated that.

"Now," said Mother Teresa briskly, looking at the orphans, "where shall we put you all?"

It was at that point that my mother left the first message on my voice mail.

It was a hot, "Indian-summer" day, and Mother Teresa decided that the cool basement would make the best dormitory. She hobbled down the stairs step by step, my mother following her anxiously. "Be careful on those steep stairs," my mother said. The young nuns followed unobtrusively, then all the twenty-five orphans in single file alphabetically.

"This will do when we get these things out of here," said Mother Teresa. She began to pull boxes of papers and family antiques out of the corners, and organised the orphans into a kind of bucket brigade carrying the useless stuff outside to the yard. After they discovered that one of the windows hinged up the work went a lot faster, with a few orphans in the yard to receive the boxes and stack them by the garage.

Any box that held anything useable Mother Teresa waved aside and the nuns unpacked it. The old set of dishes my parents hadn't used in the ten years since they moved into that house, the family silver plate, various linens and laces emerged from their newspaper or old-sheet wrappings and were stacked in corners or taken upstairs. After the basement floor was washed down and the soapy water swept into the drain, linens from my mother's upstairs closet were carried down. The orphans, who had been joined by a couple of men in olive green outfits driving a three-ton cube van, started handing in through the window, in pieces, bunk-bed frames of a faintly military nature, and thin sturdy mattresses with striped ticking. Mother Teresa was deft at putting these together, and orphans and nuns followed her lead. Mother Teresa had to resort to her nitro pills at one point, but she didn't make a big deal of it. Soon the basement was transformed into quite a capable dormitory, with bunks stacked three up and clean white sheets hung as curtains to separate the age groups and genders of children. Each orphan had a towel and washcloth and the first shift were taking their baths.

At this point my mother, having left several increasingly frantic messages for me at home and at work, was out in the yard trying to cover the stack of trunks and boxes containing her family history and photographs with a large sheet of six mill plastic my father had used for a paint dropcloth in 1973 and which had been stored in and moved with the garage contents ever since. That's why she was the one to see the bus draw up to the curb, and two other nuns, both older and a little wearier, more street-savvy looking than the two inside, start unloading the families and homeless single men and women.

My mother went in and found Mother Teresa on the telephone. "Excuse me," she said, " but I really think..."

"Good, there you are," said Mother Teresa. "I'm glad you are so capable, and have this many resources here. It makes my job much easier. Now that you've finished outside, perhaps you would help Sister Sophia and Sister Rosario settle the new families in? One family in the back bedroom, one in the middle bedroom. I've had them move your things into the study, because I'm sure you'll want to keep on with your work in your spare time. Really, you have all you need in there — it's a lovely little set-up. Very cozy. I've moved the little desk out to the porch for my office. Once we get everything going, we'll need places to do the administrative work. Right now, though, we should put the men in the living room, don't you think? They're used to sleeping rough. The women — we'll have to figure something else for the women. Especially the ones with children."

"I have to use the phone," said my mother.

"I'll be done soon," said Mother Teresa. "Oh, your doctor phoned. He said to tell you your EEG tracing was normal, all the tests were normal. Your blood pressure was upper normal but he said he thought that was white coat syndrome. He advised you to keep taking the Atavan, and to try to eat less cream and butter. Lose a little weight. The bone density scan was remarkably good, especially for a woman your age. Good. I recognised that you are a woman blessed by God. Is there a car here?"

"Yes," said my mother. "I haven't been able to bear to sell my husband's car yet. He put so much money into that damned old thing when we needed — I mean, he loved that car so much. I'm sure it's a valuable antique, or at least a classic. I don't know how on earth I can get what it's worth. When they see your hair is white, they think they can take advantage of that. I just don't know how I can — with my arthritis, and my vision — it's a nightmare time..."

"Yes, the vision is a problem," said Mother Teresa, "I'm taking into account that you can't drive, so I think it will work best if you give the keys to one of the soldiers. Sergeant Fortunato perhaps. He drove the half-track we used in Palestine to get the disabled children out of the hospital there. By the grace of God, he knows his way around old vehicles. Someone has to pick up the tents and arrange for delivery of groceries. Do you have one of those bank card things? Perhaps you'd better go with him."

It was at this point that my mother barricaded herself in the study and began to phone me on the speed dial, one number after another, until finally someone at the office told her I had gone to the Minister's Office. She actually phoned me there again, despite the fact that after what happened last time I had begged her not to endanger my job that way. The message wasn't clear, but the panic-stricken tone was both familiar and demanding. I had to explain to the Assistant Deputy Minister that if Mother called there after all that they had said last time, this must be an emergency. She said that the last four calls from my mother hadn't been much of an emergency, and that working out this Action Request for the Minister was an emergency too, especially given his problems with bad publicity lately, but I told her that the Minister already had everything in his briefing book that the office needed to answer the letter, and I was sure it was serious. I wasn't convinced myself, but I presented my case firmly, then left while they were still looking for the briefing book. That was actually the last I saw of my job, but by the time I heard that my boss had fired me, I had figured out that I wouldn't starve if I — what do they say? — pursued other options. I learned a lot from Mother Teresa, even if I am more interested doctrinally in Buddhism.

When I arrived at my mother's house I almost didn't recognise the place. The marquee was already up on the back lawn, joined to the porch of the house on one side and the garage on the other by striped awnings, and the tent city was being erected on the large, long front lawn. The ramshackle picket fence that the landlord wouldn't fix was already half-dismantled so that the provisions could be unloaded into the marquee where a sort of summer kitchen had been set up with half-oil-drum barbecue stoves borrowed from the local Lions and Shriners Clubs. The pieces of the fence were going in on top of the briquettes to make a roaring fire in each stove, and people were wrapping potatoes in tinfoil, filling huge pots with water from the hose and putting them on to boil, and cutting up carrots and celery.

A troupe of neat-as-a-pin orphans worked alongside a few soldiers, several young sari-clad nuns, and two homeless men. One of them, I found out later, had been bottle-collecting in the alley (it was the day before the recycling pickup) when Mother Teresa engaged him in conversation, and discovering that he had been in a residential school, suggested that his experience could help the orphans avoid pitfalls in the system and protect themselves from the unscrupulous among their caregivers. As he carried cases of canned goods and sacks of potatoes out of the truck, he was giving the orphans laconic advice: "Take a friend along when you go to confession," was the one phrase I heard, and only heard the context later, so as I walked by I had the odd impression he was repeating some Martha Stewart homily he'd seen in a woman's magazine at the supermarket from which the groceries had come.

"Where shall I put all this day-old fruit we got for free?" one of the orphans said to a small woman standing at the top of the back-porch steps.

"Take it inside; the girls are making fruit salad for everyone and then canning the rest," she said, and I realised with shock that I was seeing the famous Mother Teresa.

My shock had a guilty element. Okay, I can confess it now, but if you ever tell my mother, I'll deny I said it: I actually was the one that told a friend of mine that if she needed to billet anyone for this ecumenical conference she was organising, I was sure my mom had space. After all, when my mother was a kid, her family housed the student ministers for the little rural church they'd helped build. Also, I thought it would bring her out of herself, and, I confess, distract her from her attempt to get the same level of service from me as she had had from my father. When my pal said "What about Mother Teresa?" I thought she was kidding, and I said, "Sure, that would be perfect!" I had no idea Mother Teresa really was coming to our little city and I certainly figured if she did she'd stay somewhere else, somewhere holy and Catholic and conventy. I have never told my mother about this, and I am really not kidding when I say I never want her to know. I figure having to work with her every day is karmic punishment enough.

Anyway, it's too late to change things. It was already too late when I showed up on the lawn, though my mother has never let me forget that she called me for help and instead I immediately got drafted into helping make the fruit salad and Mother didn't find out I was there until two hours later when she finally gave in and came out of her room to take a painkiller and an Atavan.

"But, Mom," I say to her over and over, every time she brings it up. "I knew where all the knives and stuff were. It made perfect sense. I just couldn't say no to a greater need."

From under the folds of the sari covering her abundant white hair, my mother looks at me reproachfully. Luckily, usually, before we get any further, one of the younger nuns comes in and says, "Excuse me, ma'am, there are some new women here; do you have any more clothes?" or "Excuse me, missus, but I'm wondering if you would mind if we gave these talking books you've finished with to that blind woman who's running the tent city?" and she has to bustle off and help with something. Anyway, by the time our day is over I'm ready to leave for my apartment with the other nuns I've got staying there with me, we're both too tired to argue after a hard day's work helping Mother Teresa.

My mother doesn't much like the sari, but since she's become so much more active, she's lost so much weight that none of her clothes fit anymore. Besides, the homeless women, the formerly homeless women I mean, are getting a lot more wear out of all those outfits than she ever did.

Fin-de-siècle

by E. L. Chen

He slips into the room, a shadow creeping into shadow.
- Nick? she says. Oh, Nick, I was so scared. I had the
nightmare again.
- It's okay, he says. I'm here.
- Don't leave me again. It's so lonely here without you.
- I have to, he says. How else are we going to eat?
He draws a baby's bottle from the inside pocket of his
trenchcoat and parts her lips with the rubber nipple. She
flinches as the first hot spurt of blood hits the back of her
throat. He strokes her hair.
- Oh, Grace, he says. You'll never know what we've
become.
He presses his lips to her forehead. She closes her eyes
in contentment and suckles.

- Jerusalem, Athens, Alexandria.
Libby chants the names under her breath like a child's
skipping rhyme as she walks down Queen Street West. It's
an old trick from her youth to distract herself from the
cacophony surrounding her. After the two-month retreat
at Meg's farm and recording studio, being in the city again
hurts her preternaturally sensitive ears.
- Vienna, London, Unreal.
She adds New York to T. S. Eliot's list of mythic cities.
New York is Toronto, squared: twice as tall, twice as narrow.
Batman's Gotham City — a dark, claustrophobic, art deco
dystopia. Although the last time the band played there,
Times Square had been surprisingly clean, and most of the
seedy sex shops replaced by bright and shiny brand-name

franchises. Mayor Giuliani has apparently put it on the road to redemption.

As for her hometown, it's ready to be added to the roster. No one refers to the city as Toronto the Good anymore. Now that Libby's back from recording the new album, she notices the sounds that never bothered her before: the purr of tattered posters peeling from construction hoarding, the monotone hum of her old haunts in the Annex, the smog that drones in the horizon like a church organ. And everywhere she goes, she only hears restless boredom — not only in the conversation of passers-by, but in their heightened pulses as well. Toronto's decadence reaching mythic levels, Libby thinks. Sounds like a newspaper headline.

Even if it weren't the last summer of the millennium, she suspects that she would still hear the city in a state of anticipation: a seething whine below the surface of the familiar, like AM radio during a thunderstorm. All the city needs is a disillusioned Hero, a tender young lamb whose sacrifice will usher in the new age. The city is already preparing for the changeover; brand-name boutiques are supplanting Queen Street's scruffy secondhand shops, and Yonge and Dundas is under the knife of a tourist-friendly facelift. Yesterday she rode a streetcar across King and heard the slurp and chatter of dot-com startups eating up dingy warehouses from the inside.

A seagull's plaintive cry intrudes into her thoughts. She shivers. She has never missed the city's seagulls while on the road. There is something vulgar in their cries, yet sad as well, as if they hunger and mourn with one voice. A perfect blending of the sacred and the profane. She quickens her steps and the seagull scurries from her path.

Meg and Garth wait for her at the MuchMusic studio at Queen and John. The interview begins. Fans and curious pedestrians idle in front of the studio's open window despite the unrelenting summer sun. Meg shines under the spotlights, her hands waving. The veejay's eyes crinkle at the corners as he listens to her honey-and-whisky voice. Libby wonders if her eyes crinkle as attractively when she hears things.

- Libby's my sounding board, Meg says.

Libby smiles shyly when the camera swivels toward her.

- If it weren't for her, I'd be just another angry young woman singer-songwriter. She knows just what my songs need. She produced and mixed the new album.

Libby smiles again. She refines Meg's rage because otherwise the music sears her eardrums with its burning, prickly edges. But she says nothing, and the camera turns back to Meg.

- So what's next for the band?

- The tour doesn't start until October, so we're taking a short break. I'm going out west to chill out, and Garth's drumming in a side project.

- What about you, Libby? What are your plans for the month?

The veejay's eyes are kind but there is a sudden twinge in his voice, like a snapping violin string. She looks like someone he used to know, Libby thinks. Probably an ex-girlfriend.

- I haven't made any plans, she says. I guess I'll be hanging out here, in Toronto.

Outside, between the droning layers of white noise, a seagull cries.

The alarm clock's ruthless buzz shoves Scott into consciousness. He grabs the clock and hurls it against the wall. He bought it from Goodwill; he can buy another if it breaks.

The clock proves to be indestructible, however. Scott drags himself from his afternoon nap, regretting his decision to work the diner's night shift.

The summer evening is humid. Scott flings open the door of his dank basement apartment and decides that he doesn't need a jacket. The neighbourhood's resident bag lady follows him for a block, asking questions that he cannot answer. He wonders why she doesn't demand spare change instead. He would gladly give it to her if she asked.

- Don't you know anything? Don't you see anything? Don't you remember anything?

Scott ignores her although the rhythm of her words lingers in his head. He has heard them before; in school, perhaps. He doesn't know. He hasn't been in school since Christmas.

He can't help feeling ashamed as he walks a little faster. Susie the bag lady is harmless, just down on her luck, one of the many who have slipped through the city's cracks. He shouldn't ignore her. After all, it's only a matter of time before the cracks beneath his own feet widen and he plummets further into obscurity.

He should be happy or at least satisfied that he's surviving, but he isn't. He hasn't found his father, which was why he left home in the first place. He suspects that he'll never find him, that it's just an excuse. He's missing something from his life, as if he's the only person not in on some grand, cosmic joke, and his deadbeat dad is the most convenient explanation for this sense of loss. He watched a lot of TV back home; he knows his pop psychology. And yet his mom said he never learned anything.

He turns into an alley, his usual shortcut, and sees the body.

Vagrants curled up on the asphalt in a bed of rags and empty bottles are not uncommon in Toronto. Passers-by stooped over them, presumably to help, are. Rarer still are those with blood on their chin and hands.

The man crouched over the body doesn't look like a murderer; his polo shirt, although splattered with blood, is tucked into a pair of crisp khakis. A light-coloured trenchcoat sits off to the side, neatly folded as if he'd just taken it off a stack at the Gap. He looks like he is more likely to be on the front page of the *Toronto Sun* for insider trading rather than a gang-related shooting.

He appears young, perhaps in his thirties. Around the same age as Scott's dad, before he went out for cigarettes and never came back.

The man glances up from the body and meets Scott's gaze.

His eyes are the cold, dull gray of slate, the pupils indiscernible. Scott blinks at the bright pools at the man's feet, half-remembering a quote from a Shakespeare play about a Scottish king. Something about someone having too much blood in him. The shock dissipates, his mind

defogs, and Scott realizes what is wrong with the tableau
before him: the man's slate-coloured eyes do not reflect
the streetlights that glint off the wet asphalt.

- Shit.

The man grins. A thread of blood slides from the corner
of his mouth to the ground.

- Oh, shit.

Scott turns around and runs, taking the long way to
the diner.

Libby hears her waiter before she sees him; how can
she not, when his heart beats like one of Garth's fevered
drum solos? Her brow furrows in concentration as she
tries to read the *National Post* — not that she was paying
the newspaper much attention anyhow. All there is to skim
through these days are banks and airlines reassuring the
public that the turn of the century will have no affect on
their computerized services. Computers, she thinks dis-
dainfully. She tried to listen to Garth's computer once,
wondering if her unusual talent could diagnose why it
had crashed — after all, techs must make more than
musicians — but all she had heard was meaningless chatter, like a baby who hasn't figured out how to use language yet.

Libby sighs and pushes the paper away. The waiter's
pulse pounds in the back of her head like a migraine. She
looks up, and raises her eyebrows. The kid can't be more
than seventeen. Libby has seen his type before: lanky, cute
in a goofy sort of way, and in desperate need of a hair-
cut. His breathing is irregular, his heartbeat heavy and
resonant.

- You okay? she asks.

He nearly drops his pen and pad of paper.

- Yeah.

His answering smile could charm adolescent girls out
of malls, but Libby hears the underlying tremor. The
syllable rests on an unstable foundation. A nudge will
send it crumbling like Jericho's walls.

She orders a coffee and Western omelette, and realizes,
as her waiter involuntarily steps back, that she has been

shouting above the cacophony that only she can hear. She winces and touches her fingertips to her temples. The city has become uncomfortably agitated. She likens the sensation to a buzzing in her ears, growing louder every day; a chattering multitude waiting for the miracle of the loaves and fishes.

- Um, are *you* okay? he asks.

Libby grins sheepishly.

— Yeah, she lies. Sorry.

He scurries off and the buzz in her ears softens to a hum. She frowns.

- Wait!

The waiter spins around and returns to her table, pen and pad ready to amend her order. The buzz in her ears intensifies.

- Yes? he says.

- Can you make it a decaf, please?

He nods and disappears into the kitchen. The buzz softens again, and Libby knows that *he* is the one for whom the city clamours.

- Excuse me?

Libby does not need to look up to know that her teen-aged waiter has returned. He sets down her coffee.

- Yes?

Libby casually tears a packet of sugar over the coffee mug, trying to act as if she can't hear the city's fractured voice whispering to her.

- Um, you look real familiar, and like, I was wondering, do I know you?

He must recognize her from the band; their newest video gets a lot of airplay.

- You watch MuchMusic?

- Don't have a TV.

- Oh?

A teenage boy who doesn't watch television. Inconceivable and intriguing. She eyes him from above the rim of her mug, listening for other clues to his character. She hears nothing but his arrhythmic pulse and the babble of the city.

- I'm Libby.

She extends her hand. The coffee has warmed her to conviviality, and besides, there's something little brotherly about him.

- Scott.

Not a name with possibilities, unlike hers and Meg's. Libby's birth certificate claims that she's an Elizabeth, but she was Bess at first for her grandmother. Then Liz, as an adolescent, because she thought Bess was too old-fashioned. Beth, in high school, to distinguish herself from the overwhelming number of sunny-faced, cheerleading Lizes. Libby, when she moved out of her parents' house, hooked up with Meg, and formed the band.

As for Meg, it's hard to believe that she's actually a Margaret. She says she's been called Meg since birth. Libby knows a change is coming; Meg can't stay angry forever. She'll become a Maggie, or Marge or Peggy if she decides to go retro.

But Scott is irrevocably locked into his name. Libby could hear it as the syllable thudded from his mouth. It worries her, because she can hear that he's on the proverbial verge of manhood, and his identity gives him little room for change. It means that the room will change around him.

- So — Scott — want to tell me what's wrong?

- Nothing. 'Scuse me.

He disappears into the kitchen, leaving Libby to sip her coffee in relative quiet.

Scott takes a different route home even though logic tells him that the slate-eyed man isn't stupid enough to kill in the same place twice.

Seven months in the city and he has never explored this block because the signs are too bright, too garish. He strolls past darkened shops and cafés, and counts the newspaper boxes on each corner. He reaches box number thirteen — a battered *Toronto Star* — and a flashing neon sign catches his eye. The orange and yellow sunburst tugs at his memory.

The sign belongs to a seedy hotel built from crumbling bricks and dented aluminum siding. Scott pulls his wallet from his back pocket and extracts a folded photograph.

The hotel, sans aluminum siding, stands in the background. Scott's father slouches in the shabby doorway. It's the only picture Scott has of his father; Scott Sr. didn't stick around long enough to fill his mom's photo albums.

The placard in a ground-floor window tells him that the manager is in the lounge. Scott finds him behind the bar. The room smells like cigarette smoke, cheap perfume and futility. It smells like his mom's house. Judging from the fake wood paneling and vinyl upholstery, time stands still in the lounge, although it has not been kind to the bar's wizened patrons.

- Let's see some ID, kid.

- Um, I'm not here to buy anything. I'm looking for someone.

Scott produces the photo. The manager peers at it under the dim, jaundiced light.

- Oh yeah, him. He lived here for a year or so. Nice guy. Real ladies' man, if you know what I mean.

- You recognize him? After all this time?

- Yeah, I remember 'cause they fished him out of Lake Ontario a couple years back. Drowned. Was in the news.

- Suicide?

- They never said. But they didn't say it was murder, neither. We were renovating that summer, that's why I remember. Sorry, kid. He your friend?

Scott considers his response for a second.

- No.

So his father had died the way he had lived — mysteriously, and without Scott's knowledge. He thanks the manager and leaves, coughing, trying to expel the stale smoke from his lungs. He feels the stagnation cling to his skin. He can certainly smell it, at least.

He is about to cross the street when he hears a soft, tuneless singing. A woman's voice, high and girlish, drifts from one of the hotel's rooms.

He looks up and the earth stops turning.

As a child, whenever his mom was angry with him, Scott fantasized that one day a more forgiving woman would show up to claim him as her son. His real mother would be beautiful, elegant, and a little sad because they had been separated for so long. Sometimes she was rich, sometimes famous, usually both. Sometimes she was a queen, or a secret agent, depending on the latest movie he'd seen. She would offer him unconditional love and whisk him away to a better, happier life.

The woman in the hotel window is exactly how he pictured his fantasy mother: fair hair cascading over a pale face pinched with sorrow. Which is preposterous, as it was only a fantasy, the type children outgrow as soon as they eschew fairy tales in favour of superheroes and secret identities. It's a coincidence, Scott tells himself.

The incoherent song dies on the woman's lips. She traps Scott with a gaze. A dozen clichéd metaphors come to his mind: a moth to flame, a deer in headlights, and other help-less creatures in unfortunate situations.

She smiles. Scott forgets how to breathe. She lifts a slen-der hand in greeting and he tumbles into pure bliss.

A shadow looms over the woman's shoulder. Scott sucks air into his paralyzed lungs; the shadow has the slate-eyed man's face. He wants to shout a warning, but he realizes that the woman's eyes are the same as the man's. Lacklustre and dull, dead yet full of love.

Scott flees the hotel and the earth resumes its orbit around the sun.

A tired old plot: boy meets girl, boy falls in love with girl, boy marries girl.

No one ever told Nick, however, what happens after said girl is diagnosed with a terminal illness. He was forced to make it up as he went along. That, he tells himself, is his excuse for the startling dénouement. A Liebestöd, love-death. Only in death can they remain in love. He could not have known that the change would leave Grace as simple-minded and childlike as she had been in the hospital.

He and Grace have reached the final act of their lives, one that will last until the end of time, or the end of night, whichever comes first. *Till death do us part* has a different meaning now. *In sickness and in health* is no longer appli-cable. *For richer or poorer....*

He surveys the mouldy walls, the sludge-brown curtains, the cigarette-scarred carpet dotted with mouse droppings. They could do better — much better — but any other place would ask questions. Grace curls up on the lumpy double bed, cradling the baby's bottle.

- You shouldn't stand by the window, he says.
- But I get bored when you're not here.
- What if someone sees you?
- Why shouldn't they see me?

He can't answer her. She is in no danger if targeted by an attacker or rapist. She can defend herself with their new, uncanny strength; the other day she accidentally yanked the bathroom door off its hinges. If there is one person she should fear, it's him. Fortunately she hasn't asked where he gets the blood yet. He is not sure how to tell her that it's not a matter of where, but *how*.

He has one last card to play:

- Just do it for me, please?

Her smile is full of love; it's all she knows. He feels guilty taking advantage of her naïveté. He is torn between wanting her to be the witty, vivacious woman with whom he fell in love, and not wanting her to be lucid enough to realize what they are, the price they had to pay to be together forever.

She props herself up on her elbows to give him a quick kiss.

- Okay, she says. For you.

He scours his splattered hands and face in the bathroom's rusty sink. She murmurs into the rubber nipple. He curls up behind her on the bed to wait for dawn.

Scott's first unpleasant experience at work: some power-tripping asshole intent on embarrassing his girlfriend by yelling at him. Scott's co-workers urge him to spit in the guy's cheeseburger, but he declines. Maybe he had a bad day. Maybe he's intentionally alienating his date. Maybe he's a jerk and always will be. Whichever is true, retaliation is not worth the trouble.

People puzzle Scott. Everyone wants to be the hero of their own story, but there's not enough room for them all, so they fester from bitter self-righteousness. Like that rude customer. If a simple misunderstanding angers him, Scott doubts that he has ever been truly happy.

Scott punches out after his shift, mentally and physically exhausted. He almost runs down the Western-and-Decaf woman — Libby — in his haste to leave the diner.

- Sorry, he mumbles.

Her head cocks to one side — a habit he noticed the last time they'd met — and she looks bemused. He pushes past without giving her a chance to acknowledge him. One of his co-workers, a cute redhead who's far too old for him, says that Libby plays bass in a band. That explains why she looks familiar to him. But it doesn't explain why he seems familiar to her.

Scott takes the long way home for the third time that week. He hopes to see the pale woman again but her window's curtains are drawn. She hasn't checked out yet, though. The hotel manager said as much under the influence of a twenty-dollar bill. The knowledge that she's still there is worth a night's tips.

Susie the bag lady greets him in her usual crazed, cryptic way as he enters his neighbourhood.

- Why don't you ever speak? What are you thinking? I never know what you're thinking.

Her questions eerily resemble his mom's many tirades.

- Isn't there anything in your head?

Scott stops. His mom had screamed something like that the night he left home for the city. He turns around.

- I'm thinking, he says, that I've just found out my father's dead and I don't care. I don't feel a fucking thing.

As he speaks, he realizes that he hasn't felt anything but detachment for a long time. Only fear when he saw the slate-eyed man, and awe in the pale woman's presence. Otherwise, in spite of discovering his father's death, there is no epiphany, no disappointment nor sadness, not even the flaccid sensation of an anti-climax.

Susie reveals a row of stained, chipped teeth and bobs her head up and down.

- Very good, very good. Spare some change?

Scott reaches into his pockets and finds a handful of dimes and nickels.

- Here you go, he says. Have a good evening.

He leaves her to count her bounty and continues down the street. His steps falter; he doesn't want to go home, doesn't want to call it a day just yet. Nothing waits for him in his gloomy little apartment. The very freedom and independence he coveted while living under his mom's roof, yet now that he has it, he finds it lonely.

It's all a matter of choice. The dilapidated bay-and-gable house he calls home appears around the corner. Scott chooses to walk past it and keep walking.

There is a certain empowerment in having options. Scott, however, feels little but apathy as he retraces his steps to the hotel. Since he has found his father, so to speak, he has no reason to be in the city other than it is simply another choice he has made. He wonders if his father made the same choice — moving to Toronto to leave a woman. He wonders if, like his father, he will run from women until he dies. Because now that he has seen the pale woman no one else can compare.

He hopes to see her or the slate-eyed man, hoping that their presence will stir some long-forgotten emotion in him. Wrath, envy, lust — any of the seven deadly sins inherent to teenagers will do. The pale woman's curtains are still drawn, but the lights are on. If he squints hard enough, he can picture her silhouette standing behind the heavy brown fabric, watching over him like a guardian angel.

Across the street, Scott sits on top of a *Globe and Mail* box that has seen better days and ignores the bleary-eyed curiosity of a neighbouring panhandler. He crosses his arms and waits for her to reveal herself like the *deus ex machina* of the Greek tragedies he learned in school. Someone who will descend from the heavens at the last minute and save him. That's all he asks for.

But Scott remembers that not everyone can be the hero of their own story. He hops off the newspaper box, tosses the last of his spare change to the panhandler, and walks away.

✠ ✠ ✠

Nick finds the door ajar, and as he enters the room, the lone anguished word of greeting falls from his own mouth.

- Grace?

She is gone. The only evidence of her existence is the shallow indentation in the bed's threadbare covers. She did not even leave her scent behind; she smelled like shampoo and medicine before the change and occasionally the sterile fragrance lingers.

He places the baby's bottle on the nightstand and slips back into the night.

The winking array of lights tells Scott that he's approaching Yonge Street.

To the north: dollar stores, Thai and Japanese restaurants, adult novelty shops, and strip joints. Tourists and panhandlers claim the sidewalk. Scott tires of the sensory assault and turns east onto Gerrard. All tourist trappings are left behind and the city returns to its wild roots: mom-and-pop enterprises, and narrow houses with iron-fenced, overgrown gardens and eroded brick façades disguised by peeling layers of paint.

Scott wanders past Parliament Street toward the winding offramp of the Don Valley Parkway. The residential neighbourhood suddenly gives way to Riverdale Park. Scott watches leashless dogs scamper through the park for a few minutes and then finds what he is looking for.

The valley.

Back in January, during that fateful one-way bus trip to Toronto, the snow-laden ravine unfolded before him along the highway like the plot of a novel. At the time it struck him as the last oasis in an urban wasteland.

It's nature, Toronto-style: paved asphalt trails, fences of fluorescent orange vinyl mesh, unused train tracks on the far side of the Don River. The river itself is muddy, opaque, stagnant from weeks without rain. The air reeks of car exhaust and mildew. A Toronto Parks and Recreation sign claims that the ravine is home to herons, foxes, and red-winged blackbirds, but the only indication of life is the drone of cars streaking past on the highway.

Aside from the occasional garbage can, there is little evidence of human maintenance. Vegetation is wild, chaotic, despite or because of the salt and oil runoff from the highway. Dead branches litter the ground, and the thicket grows high to claim its fallen comrades. Scott's sneakers pad silently on the asphalt. There could be murderers and perverts hiding behind the tangled brush and contorted trees, but Scott doesn't care. As a tall white male in faded T-shirt and ripped jeans, he likely commands as much fear as they do.

The black, skeletal span of the Prince Edward Viaduct looms ahead. A deserted scaffold snarls one of its arches and a subway train rumbles across the bridge, like thunder. Scott decides that it's as good a place as any to stop.

He steps off the path and onto the muddy banks of the Don, through tall weeds he cannot name. He takes off his shoes and socks and dips a foot into the river. The water is as cool as the summer night.

- I was watching you, too.

Her voice is as soft as a shadow. Scott looks up and finds himself lost in the pale woman's embrace. Although he can't see her face as she closes her mouth around his throat, he knows she is smiling.

The last thing he sees is the slate-eyed man leaping down from the Viaduct, screaming her name.

What is it about a name — a single, solitary word, not even as long as a gasp of breath, shorter than a sudden heartbeat — that can change the polarity of the world?

— *Grace...*

Libby staggers and clings to a parking meter as the cry pierces her ears. Passers-by glance furtively at her but bustle past. They only hear the sounds of Toronto on a Friday night: the dull buzz of traffic, the ping and rattle of a streetcar, the mumbled litany of a schizophrenic vagrant. Libby hears love, death, and loss intertwined on top of all these sounds, an aria worthy of a Wagnerian opera.

Her head snaps back as she hears something else.

If a body falls into a river, and there is no one around to hear it — no one human, that is — does it make a sound? It does.

— *Grace...*
The name tears out of Nick's throat.
- Grace, don't, he's a kid—
He tries to pull her away. Her answering strength sends him sprawling on the ground.

— *Grace...*
She drinks greedily from the boy's neck. Nick climbs to his feet and stares. The boy's head is tilted back in rapture; Nick's victims always react with fear. His eyes widen as he recognizes the kid who had seen him feed the other night.
He attempts to pry Grace and the boy apart again — and succeeds. Grace stumbles away, wiping her mouth with the back of her hand. The boy falls backward and into the forgiving embrace of the river.
To Nick's surprise, the boy starts to laugh.

— *Grace...*
Libby doubles over and clamps her hands over her ears, but the sound creeps through the cracks between her fingers, the sound of the city turning itself inside out, the sound of destruction and creation, revelation and redemption. She hears it as keenly as if someone is scraping their fingernails across a chalkboard.
She knows who has fallen into the river.
- Scott...
Libby breaks into a run.

— *Grace...*
Falling. Scott is falling, hard and fast, into bliss, into wonder. He barely notices the blood trickling from his broken skin or the man who pulls the pale woman from his neck.
Falling fast and free, free from detachment, free at last. Scott hears a sound and recognizes his own laughter.

✠ ✠ ✠

Libby freezes as she hears something she has only heard once before, in a deserted alley while she, Garth and Meg were packing up after a gig: a human heartbeat, steady but faint, and possessing none of Garth and Meg's unpredictable vigor. She had thought it belonged to someone far away, but then a woman had slipped out from behind a dumpster, wiping at her lipstick. The ghostly heartbeat had been hers.

This time there are two such heartbeats. Libby peers through the brush. A man and woman stand on the banks of the Don River, their pulses as gentle as a sigh. The man wears a mud-splattered trenchcoat, and the woman's arms and feet are bare. The man pulls off his coat and drapes it around the woman. His face is haggard with exhaustion.

- It's my fault, he says. Everything's my fault. I wanted you to live, but not like this.

- I know, she says. You should have let me die. But you didn't.

She kisses the man on the cheek. The man shudders, and Libby hears the whisper of a great weight rising from his shoulders.

- It's all right, she says. The boy's not dead. Only changed.

The woman smiles and takes the man's hand.

- I guess there's nothing we can do for him, he says.

- We don't have to, she says. He can do it for himself now.

- Grace—

- I know, Nick. Let's go home.

They walk away, hand in hand, a pair of young lovers on a pleasure stroll through the ravine. Libby creeps down the path and finds Scott floating in the river, his arms outstretched, frayed ribbons of blood trailing from the left side of his neck. He is still laughing.

Libby extends her hand to him. Scott lets her help him out of the river, unsurprised by her appearance.

- Thanks, he says.

- No problem.

- The city feels different now.

Libby slings her jacket over his wet shoulders. The buzzing has left her ears, replaced by Scott's silent pulse and the glorious song of the reborn city.

- That's because it's yours.

A subway train rumbles above and behind them, like thunder.

Jerusalem, Athens, Alexandria, Vienna and London.
New York, Toronto.
Unreal.

From Fugue Phantasmagorical

by Anthony MacDonald and Jason Mehmel

Setting Sail

Hermes Trismegistus, Artist.

The boat takes to the open sea, rocking in the waves, flowing with the current, moving with the wind.

As he ties each rope he smiles, lashing an idea to the deck, delighting in the mere work of sailing. He turns his face to the spray from the bow, each wave crashing with a first-time ecstasy for him. His eyes are full of all the places he'll go, his starry eyes are bedazzled before he even steps on board. He's here out of love, loving every moment, loving the fact of being here, falling as hard and fast as hormonal youngsters in Verona.

He's signed on the boat to travel, visiting wherever the trade winds take him. He's excited about the merchandise, hoping that no-one's ever seen what he's got in the cargo hold.

Every port is new, every marketplace a new trade. He does not yet have the sell-smarts, he does not know what reception he'll find for the product. This is where some are content to sail forever, never visiting a port. Others are quickly dissuaded when a harsh opinion of their merchandise shatters their sales pitch, wrecks their confidence at getting out on the trading lanes.

Still others adapt, learn, and begin to understand it as not an adventure, but a trade. They may yet dream of their merchandise in every port, but are content with what they've found. They may find a market niche, those whom they already know are interested in their product. They are happy to live on this. And they do not expect rich trade any longer, though they may still wish to join those barons who seem to have such power in the bazaar.

Some, some are lucky enough to catch that first wind that blows, to find someone who'll buy into their work. Most accomplished sailors, traders, will tell you though, that it will come with work, and not fortune. Rookie sailors learn this slowly, and at first every act is filled with desire and passion. Every emotion is plumbed for motivation, for fear of wasting potential. Every feeling is fuel for the next penstroke. They eventually learn to sail with skill, not solely relying on passionate tides.

Sometimes a hostile flag is raised on the horizon, ideas become battle-salvage. Cannon-shot of critique, poisoned pens filling the air. The sailors defend their dreams with a strong fervour. Some broadsides come only as warning, other boats keeping those they pass away from dangerous territory.

There are some who delight in terrorising the others who ply their trade on the sea, either out of a jealousy of their own inability to find customers, or solely out of intended domination, to lessen the amount of competition. Most, inside their private moments, even if they may not actually attack thus, may have wanted to sink a rival as they pass by.

The smell of the sea air is intoxicating, and for some, it is a discovery of new creation, better than anything else. It is that moment for some sailors, where standing on the bowsprit, they know they are exactly where they should be, doing exactly what they should be doing. Others can become drunk with this feeling, and promoted too quickly, these gain an arrogance of command, a belief in their own infallibility. These people no longer respecting the sea before them, and this attitude is likely to leave their boat wracked upon the shoals, or floundering off course, having long since been distanced from the trade routes, lost to all other vessels on the sea.

Others are not made for the life, and search years for a new occupation. Some must contend with the fact that they were more in love with the idea of sailing than they are with being tossed by the wave, and bitten by the wind, letting their hands be torn by rope.

Sometimes, though, that sailor stays on board. Tenacity on his grip at the rudder. He holds to the main, becomes a man of experience, and more comfortable with the constant trade, the constant travel.

It is then that he begins to explore deeper, further than ever before. Then he sees in the distance a great mass approaching, enveloping the horizon. A continent of content before him. When he travels where only the dedicated travel.

Carnaval Perpetuel
by Sandra Kasturi

1. Before

The paths that lead to the ball are many:
they are often lined with the forgotten ashes of scullery
    maids
who have gone on to better things than picking lentils
    out of the hearth.
While wanting a ball is not wanting a prince
the two seem to go hand in hand,
a kind of logarithmic function of desire and fulfillment.
And so, scullery maid or princess,
we, each and every one, arrive at the ball
bedecked in feathers and fury.

2. Masque

We are given only two hands to use in the dance,
one always caught in the clutch of another,
and the second hand ticking
gently in front of the eyes:
spread fingers creating spyholes of flesh.
Had the fairy godmother thought to give the gift
of a third hand, instead of, say,
shoes never worn enough to be worth the price,
think how different the story might have been.

3. Midnight

Herr Drosselmeier, godfather,
maker of time-pieces
and other ticky-toys,
we stand and bow to you.
You always knew,
in the way that godfathers know such things,
that the Prince is always the hardest nut to crack,
no matter how many hands are given to the task.
As for you, Carabosse,
keeper of clocks,
when did you leave us
to this solitary pirouette on the head of a spindle,
a waltz of one hundred years,
feet twitching like Father's eldest hunting hound,
fingers burning into straw, into gold:
we were the gifts given,
gaily wrapped packages in reversible paper
readied for this one or that one.
(You always said
twelve strokes weren't really enough
but what prince ever believed that?)

4. Ever After

Beyond the glass coffin
beyond the glass hill
beyond the glass slipper:
only you and I,
a shadowy duet of parsimony and elegance.
How the creeping sundial does sweep us!
despite raggedy clothes, shoe-loss
and devious step-parents,
into the arms
of a tidy, anticipated future.
And there we dance, covered
in feathers and furbelows, bells and bobbles,
our hands given, as foreordained

to an endless parade
of velvet knickerbockered golden-crowned youths,
the unfolding of an infinite paper princeling chain.

5. The End

Time is the mother of invention
and the sister of theft.
It is the glass globe of hand-spun conjurings
on the end of the spindle-shaft,
dancing in the shadow of the long hand,
twirling in the lee of the short hand.
Here, each dance has the fractal precision of chaos,
whether prince or prisoner, scullery maid or princess,
each part contains the pattern of the whole:
wish and desire
and eventually
(if you wish)
(if you desire)
(if you dare)
even truth.

The Writing on the Wall
by Steve Stanton

The man in the light cube haunted David Wilson again this morning, this fateful morning, this first morning of the rest of his life. Anna had asked him for a divorce the night before. The man in the light cube always came back at the turning points of his life, a memory so vivid and powerful that it seemed like a recurring event, a memory etched indelibly in the chemical lattice of his mind — the simple reason for his existence.

"Why do you want a divorce?" he had asked with the transparent innocence of the undefiled. David had arrived home late from work, having spent the evening arguing with a colleague about the effect of temperature variation on the decay of subatomic particles.

Anna had looked at him with new wonder, sighed with exasperation and shook her head, which had the desired effect of making him feel weak and vaguely vulnerable, a man obviously out of touch with reality. She had done something with her hair, he noted; it was cropped short and layered in a funky mop-top, tinted a fiery auburn. He was sure she had been a brunette the last time he'd seen her.

"David, honey," she said, "we haven't had dinner together in months. Our sex life is little more than archaeological evidence. We have no money, no time and no common interests."

"I'm sorry. I've been busy."

She had laughed then. "Busy? You're not busy. You're possessed."

"Possessed," he echoed, not daring for an inflection of query.

"By that stupid man in that stupid time machine," she sputtered.

He nodded. "So it's that again, is it?"

"Yes, David, it's that again. I have a lawyer this time and I've signed a lease on an apartment."

"Can't we have a talk with the pastor first?"

"Pastor Edward? You haven't spoken two words to him in ten years. Some of the new people at church think I'm single."

"I'm just getting so close on the Equation," he offered, regretting the words as they died on his lips.

Her cold stare burned through his retinas into his very soul. "You're forty years old, David. There is more to life than the Equation. You had a traumatic experience as a child — everybody knows that — but you've got to move on sometime. For heaven's sake, don't mathematicians ever grow up?"

The man in the light cube had appeared only once in physical form, for a period of several minutes when eight-year-old David was playing in his suburban bedroom with crayons and picture books. The light cube was no taller than a telephone booth, of ethereal structure and without mechanical artifice, the colour a cool blue with cascading prismatic irregularities. The man inside was David himself — an ancient, wise and powerful David from a fantastic future. The child's eyes flashed quickly from fear to recognition, then darted down in dutiful abeyance. He carefully picked up a permanent red marker, moved to the blank wall behind him, and began transcribing a river of scientific data in complex numerical notation.

His mother had not been impressed when she found him alone later in a trancelike, dreamlike state of hyperactivity.

"David, how many times has your father told you not to write on the walls in your room? He's going to be very angry when he gets home." She clutched at herself. "It's so cold in here. It's freezing. What is this, mathematics? What are you doing?"

Mathematics, that was it, the key to the universe. The boy smiled at the realization, as his life's goal came into sure focus.

"The man in the light cube told me to do it," he explained to his mother with confidence.

Within a week, David was in therapy and the bedroom walls had been repainted. Standard testing earned him 'gifted' status, and he was fast-tracked at school and given a special tutor after hours. More rigorous testing labelled him borderline child prodigy in abstract brain function, a stigma his parents wisely decided to leave in the file folder at the psychiatrist's office. They had enough trouble at home with David's older brother, Richard, who was taking drugs and listening to rock and roll.

David's left eyeball began to wander soon after that, turning outward as though lost and looking for balance. The family doctor, kindly Dr. Saturn, told him he had 'lazy-eye,' a congenital problem that was, in his case, somewhat late in development. David's own study revealed that it was the 'evil-eye' that had once been associated with shamans and occult seers in pre-industrial societies, a curse that was linked by legend to acts of healing and prophetic utterance.

In this enlightened age, the condition was surgically corrected, and David wore a black plastic eye-patch for several months. At school he became widely known as the pirate genius and was shunned by all but the most foolhardy. Good grades and near-perfect memory carried him to matriculation years before his peer group, as he learned quietly the fine art of social dysfunction.

"You're home early," he told Anna as she stumbled in the front foyer carrying a tower of empty cardboard boxes.

She stopped and eyed him with suspicion. "Didn't you go to work today?"

"I thought you'd be proud of me," he said with false petulance. He was wearing a rumpled grey sweatshirt and blue jeans. He had been moping around the house all day feeling sorry for himself.

She ignored him. "I came home early to pack before you left the office," she said as she barged past him toward the bedroom.

He followed. "I think you're being unfair," he said to her back.

"Oh, you do, do you?"

"I know I let you down with the sex thing. I was never very good at it."

"Don't be an idiot. This isn't about sex."

"Are you having an affair?"

Anna turned to face him, stern and slightly incredulous, arms akimbo. "I had the affair years ago, David. You missed it."

His viscera contracted as though a fist had landed. He dared not speak. He stared in shock at his wife.

Anna softened at the look of fright on his face. "It was cheap and pointless," she offered. "It was a mistake, I guess." She opened a dresser drawer and began packing socks and underwear into a box.

David recognized lingerie that had once enticed him and him alone, a valentine's day present from a decade ago. A hard pain caught in his throat as his testicles sucked up into his abdomen. His wife was right, of course — he had ignored her for years. He was completely devoid of social grace and manners. He was completely self-absorbed and useless as a companion.

She must have known his shortcomings before they were married. He tried to remember back that far, searching for something meaningful to say to her now. He watched her as she folded his memories into corrugated cardboard. He studied the taper of her shoulder and the fullness of her hips — she was still an attractive woman.

"Why?" he whispered, wondering how he could ever win her back.

A flash of anger lit up her face. "Don't give me that hurt-little-boy look. I know you've done the same or worse. No red-blooded male could go that many years without having sex." She slammed the top drawer shut and pulled out the next lower.

"Years?"

"C'mon, spit it out. This is your big chance. What secrets have you been hiding all this time?"

David struggled with this new marital responsibility. Sexual gratification was not Anna's issue. Illicit activity was what she wanted, to help justify her own sin. She wanted to share guilt with him, to share blame. She wanted absolution.

"Well, I had an accident with a nurse," he admitted shamefully.

Anna's eyes popped with possibilities. "A nurse? What, a prostitute?"

"No, a real nurse ... in a doctor's office."

"Good heavens. What did she do?" She pulled a heap of clothes out and stuffed them in the next box, her movements jerky and electric, her body tense with adrenaline, with the promise of confrontation.

"She was looking for polyps."

Anna froze and turned to face him, a beige blouse quivering in her trembling hands, her anxiety like animal skin stretched over a tympanum. "Polyps?"

David felt his face heat up. "They're like hemorrhoids." He winced, feeling embarrassment welling up inside him, remembering the look of professional alarm on the nurse's face as she quickly mopped up the evidence of his *accident*.

Anna wiped saliva from her lips, her eyes wide. "You're gay?" she asked.

His brows crumpled forward. "No, of course not ... I mean, I don't think so." He shrugged his shoulders back and wiggled his neck in an attempt to resume equilibrium.

"That's the best you can do?" she shouted. "After fifteen years of marriage? That's your Big Affair? A proctological exam?"

David stepped back at the force of her words. He rubbed his forehead, feeling like an idiot. He had never promised adultery. It certainly wasn't in the marriage contract he had signed. How could things had gotten this bad, he wondered.

"You're an idiot, David," she told him with finality.

Time travel was simply impossible. Every classical theorist would agree to that. Einstein had ruled it out categorically, and the few contemporary theorists in the field were heretics, idiots or one-eyed pirates. The fact that David had seen his future self was thus somewhat problematic for a mathematical physicist at the prestigious University of

Toronto, where, once degrees were handed out, papers published and acclaim granted, David found himself pining away in an obscure research department with minimal funding and a 'bad-boy' reputation that made him a public sideshow at official functions. The frank impossibility of time travel was further compounded by the generally accepted Kardian Space-Time Compendium, which inescapably tied travel through time with travel through space. With the Earth hurtling across the universe at 107,000 kilometres per hour, the logistics of re-entry were insurmountable to any known mechanics. Even if some miraculous method could be devised to propel an object to the speed of light and beyond, the time-dilation effect might put the traveller millions of years into the future upon his return. From a financial and budgetary standpoint alone, time-travel research was a lost cause.

David had tried to reduce his experience to *what he knew for sure* as a foundation on which to build new science. The man in the light cube had not traveled through time necessarily. He had merely appeared in the past, perhaps not even in corporeal form. He had certainly viewed the past and had attempted to modify it in some way by transmitting complex numerical data.

Moreover, he had not been observed by anyone other than himself, his past self, and David took this to be significant. If the man in the light cube had chosen to impart scientific information to an earlier age, he would certainly have chosen someone important, someone knowledgeable, someone with the wherewithal to act on vital paradigms. He would not have chosen himself, an eight-year-old boy, unless he was forced to do so by the mathematical rule of law.

The Hynes-Wilson Equation presupposed, largely for political legitimacy, that travel through space-time was mathematically impossible for living physical entities in the strictest sense. Quantum physics, however, had opened up a playground of ideas that did not rule out the possibility of observation apart from the space-time continuum. The Hynes-Wilson Equation was based on established theories and propositions related to 'virtual particles,' wave probabilities that collapse without quantum observation — matter and antimatter particles that appear at random and disappear without measurement. The Equation hypothesized that two separate but connected individuals, a past self and a future self, could witness the same quantum event, at the same point in space-time, simply because, mathematically, *they had both always been there* as a virtual wave probability.

The extrapolative formulas further suggested that this process could be induced by increasing the speed of light in a small containment area to produce brief periods of 'quantum temporal displacement' in which visual and observational data could be exchanged. Tests of the Equation had been rigorous, and there were substantial theoretical problems being worked on by a team of researchers at U. of T., as well as students around the world on their own limited funding. A simple model of a light cube had been constructed with lasers and subatomic mirrors, but real progress had been slow and difficult. Published papers had been widely spaced and unheralded in academia.

If the Hynes-Wilson Equation could be established without a doubt, then a new paradigm would hang on that cornerstone and grow as the data allowed, building an edifice of foundational and experimental theory that might change the world for the better — this was David's ultimate goal. Then the commercial and recreational use of time travel would follow naturally as great minds around the world were harnessed to the new frontier. *"For a greater cause,"* was the motto of David's research team — they weren't just in it for the funding; they really wanted to change the nature of reality.

Anna knocked at his office door with stiff formality, three knocks evenly spaced. He looked up grimly as she entered. They both knew why she was there.

She placed the envelope on the desk in front of her husband, and pulled over a chair to sit opposite him. David looked at the plain manila package but didn't open it. His wife was dressed in a grey business suit, quite severe. He hadn't seen her in several weeks. She looked good.

"So that's it, then," he said.

"Do you have a lawyer yet?"

He glanced away from her eyes. "Fred over at Nanotech recommended someone." He was wearing a brown sport jacket with a black turtleneck, and he reached up to his chin and tucked a finger under the material, rubbing the day's growth of stubble at his neck.

She nodded. "I don't want this to be messy. It's not like we have major assets to worry about. The whole thing is a little too clichéd for me already."

"Right. I know what you mean..." He swallowed and took his hand away from his throat. "I just never thought it would happen to us."

The timeworn statement hung between them for a few moments like a matrimonial archetype, to be contemplated only in retrospect and never fully understood.

"What if you're wrong, David? What if there is no possibility of time travel? How many more years will you waste?"

He bristled at her charge. "I am not wasting years," he stated evenly. "I know what I saw, Anna. We are making slow progress. If we do not break through, then the next generation will take up our cross."

"Well, the metaphor may be appropriate."

"You think I have a martyr complex?"

Anna held up her left hand and turned her face askew. "I didn't come here to argue. I know you have your grand vision."

"Why *did* you come here, Anna? Aren't these things usually delivered by bicycle courier?"

She shifted in her chair and rubbed her skirt down on her thighs. She tossed her short hair. "I came here to apologize."

David's eyes widened, then one eyebrow wrinkled down in query.

"For the things I said that day ... the way I treated you ... it was awful."

They both sighed together like breathless wind on a desert, remembering.

"I handled it badly," he offered. "I was never any good at interpersonal relations."

"Must you always be so self-effacing? You're the most intelligent person I've ever met. You should have been charting bubble-net trajectories for CERN instead of chasing this 'man in the light cube'... And you were great in bed. We had a good life together in those early years." She looked away, closed her eyes. "But now I'm just excess baggage. You'll be better off without the distraction."

David shook his head, feeling his comfortable life slipping away for the last time. "I think I love you, Anna."

She faced him again, stern and sad. "You don't know what love is, David. Love isn't something you fall into or out of. It's not something that might happen by accident when you aren't looking. Love is something you build. You make a decision and you work at it. You create it out of good will and a few overactive hormones."

She stood up, her grey suit lustrous in the fluorescent light. "I didn't come here to lecture you. I came to apologize and I did my best. I don't want this to get awkward." She held out a businesslike hand for him to shake, to seal the deal once and for all, to close the coffin lid down on his heart.

He stared at her slender fingers, remembered them rubbing the worry lines from his brow, massaging the tense muscles between his shoulder blades and elsewhere, then cast his eyes downward. "I can't say goodbye."

Anna's hand slapped down on her thigh. "We gave it a chance, David. I can't ask you to give up your dream for me."

He didn't look up as she left the room and closed the door behind her. He let the tears fall where they may.

The light cube appeared in his office three days later, empty. David looked up from the unopened manila envelope on his desk to see it shimmering, an eerie blue beacon in the center of the room. He was awake and fully conscious, primed with caffeine for an eleven-o'clock team meeting with his colleagues. He stared for a bare second and jumped to his feet in recognition.

He circled it like a cat prowling a wounded bird, and found three sides completely opaque. No apparent energy source. No tricks or projectors. No knobs or buttons, control panels or joysticks. No possible explanation.

David stepped inside and saw himself, as expected, playing on the bedroom floor at eight years of age. His child self looked up, recognized him with awe and rose to full height; he selected his favourite red marker and walked to the blank wall behind him. The boy began writing.

No, David thought with instant alarm. *Not like this! Not without some measure of scientific control, not without experimental procedures. Not just some fluke from heaven!* The monitoring equipment, lasers and expensive quantum couplers were all downstairs in the lab where the Equation team waited even now for his monthly progress report. His years of careful preparation had come to naught.

He felt himself adrift and helpless, a helium balloon floating up to dizzying heights, his purpose, his foundation cut out from under him. Anna had been right. He had wasted his career on a random phenomenon. Now that the truth was plainly evident, he did not have a single credible witness to back up his observation.

The writing on the wall began to take shape as a tiny hand deftly transcribed the numerals. It was the Hynes-Wilson Equation, of course. David recognized it immediately, his life's work. The child was reading it from David's own mind, from his subconscious, perhaps, via the quantum connection. They were the same person, sharing the same essence across decades, collapsing a wave probability that had always been there.

The first discrepancy on the bedroom wall caught David completely off guard. He blinked with disbelief, wanting to reach out and make the correction. It was subtle, at first, but quickly brought the Equation into uncharted realms. He gasped as ramifications wheeled inside his brain like spinning galaxies.

Intrinsic symmetry required a third observer, for any movement back in time required a corresponding movement forward in time, the alpha and omega — a quantum triad, each point moving independently yet intimately connected. The principle seemed so obvious that David felt he had always known it. He churned the numbers in his mind, marvelling at the beauty of wisdom, as the crooked pathways in his early work suddenly became pure golden threads, his abstruse inferences now elegant theorems.

Emotion washed like a river through David's body, calming his panicky thoughts of failure — a sense of pure and perfect unity, of holiness undefiled, as though this eureka moment embodied all, just as it always was and should be. The Equation, he realized, existed outside of space and time as a universal truth. Somehow, it was making itself known, past, present and future.

David felt himself exposed and naked to the cosmos. He shivered at the reality, feeling himself a worm and no man. Who was this third observer? His future self? Some higher consciousness? A collective human psyche? He turned, slowly, feeling suddenly the focus of omnipresent attention, and looked backward through the light cube.

No gateway to the future lay beyond; just his comfortable office, his limited-edition prints on the walls, his simple wooden desk with an unopened manila envelope on top. Nothing had changed. No third observer was present.

A chill permeated the air, and the light cube clouded over as water began to condense on the interface. David turned again and peered out at the Equation, recording each nuance with photographic memory. Shivering with cold, he noticed more discrepancies through a crystalline pattern of new frost, as the guts of the mechanical formula began to unravel. The source of the hyper-c photons had always been the main stumbling block in the creation of a working time-travel apparatus. The writing on the wall indicated that antimatter axons could release such light under extraordinary super-cooled conditions. Somehow, charged with energy, they were held in stasis at the eight corners of the light cube, using technology that was clearly decades ahead of current science.

David would never harness time travel in his lifetime, he realized with calm assurance. The ultimate responsibility had passed out of his hands. He had become merely an instrument in a grand design, a central pinpoint in a vast but knowable universe. He was simply an observer, a prophetic watchman on the tower. He recognized this freedom as the interface began to freeze up. He peered through darkening glass at an eight-year-old boy sharing the secrets of space-time, and wished himself well with a glad heart as his view was obscured and the light cube reached its self-limiting temperature threshold. The eerie blue light winked out and shards of ice fell like a broken window at his feet. He stood alone in the centre of his office, hugging himself and trembling with cold, feeling, finally, that a ghost had just left the room.

His colleagues on the Equation team waited expectantly downstairs, the brothers and sisters who had agonized with him over long and frustrating years, who had shared the dream and the vision while others mocked from afar. David had completed his mission. He had fulfilled his destiny against all odds, had mastered the gates of reality and tasted the joy of angels; and there was only one person in the world he wanted to share this moment with, only one person who mattered above all. Time had never seemed so precious. He raced for the speed dial and called his wife.

See Kathryn Run

by Élisabeth Vonarburg
translated by Élisabeth Vonarburg
and Howard Scott

See Kathryn run.

She doesn't know. In her head, she's walking. She doesn't see the people who instinctively step aside to let her pass. Not that she's big, or particularly athletic, or dressed in black from head to foot like some you see on the Main, striding haughtily along in their long sweeping fake leather coats and glaring predatorily at the passers-by — mostly men, mostly young men, at the age when they are not yet quite sure whether they are entitled to indulge their male arrogance. People step aside for her because she knows where she's going: she's a Voyager, and she's going to meet her future employer, the one who's going to build a Bridge for her.

She sees what the strollers don't see, however. In doorways, the hands coming out of the shadows with indistinct muttering, prayer or abuse, inaudible in the dull roar of the city and the gut-churning throb of the music pouring out of the stores and cars. She sees, through the crowd, as if for her they were surrounded by halos, the silhouettes of men or women whose steps drag just a little more than the others, who wear their entire wardrobes on their backs and carry their entire households in a garbage bag or a tattered sports bag. Or the greasy papers, the furious graffiti scratched on the beautiful walls, the mauve mist that blurs perspective on the Main, clouds of fumes from the insect-back cars packed as tight as the marabunta. And on the faces of the passers-by, here and there, unbeknownst to

them, those worried mouths, those fingers clenching the
handle of a real leather case or an imitation crocodile
handbag, those furtive looks, those alert ears, waiting for
the detonation, the explosion, the showers of glass, concrete, steel. In front of all the commercial cathedrals —
banks, high-fashion stores, shopping centres — around
rows of metal detectors, the uniforms of the security companies.

But they continue coasting down the slope of habit:
strolling on the Main. It is the weekend and the end of
a beautiful fall afternoon, a deep-blue, cloudless sky, just
the right edge of cold in the air, well disguised by the
slanting, warm light of the sun, not really red but cop-
pery orange, a rich marmalade glow on the façades and
windows of buildings, flowing over skin and hair, a late,
deceptive echo of summer, holidays, carefree days. The
adolescents are still laughing rowdily on the steps of Place
des Arts, on the packed terraces of the cafés and restaurants, with plates piled high, foaming mugs, cool wines.
Luxury and delight, if not peace she thought, recalling
the Baudelaire poem. Have they had a Baudelaire here?
She hasn't checked this detail. She's had hardly any time
to tour the bookstores and libraries, and when she goes
on the Net it isn't for pleasure either. If she thought about
it, she would realize that she never really has time to just
take her time. But she's not thinking about that. She still
thinks she's walking.

She's walking, on St. Catherine Street. It still amuses
her a little, at the very beginning of the transition, when
she observes that, once again, the Main of this other
Montréal bears her first name, or a recognizable version
of her first name. The last time, there was just a difference of two letters: Kathrine. It amuses her, because she
doesn't want to know that she's bothered by it, disturbed,
perplexed, worried even. Later, briefly, she will be. Not
now. Now, she thinks she's walking.

Aromas of roasting meat and coffee waft in the air as
she heads east — less and less exotic. Downtown, uptown,
west and east, it's a different world, in spite of all the
hypocritical platitudes of urban planning and renewal.

All cities have memories, in spite of the politicians. Including the memories of the others: rumblings of the tam-
tams, a flash of white teeth, an African in a multicoloured
boubou is trying to cash in on his nostalgia. She digs into
her jeans pocket — she always has some change, which
she gives out according to her whim, since arbitrary giving
is the only possible response to the insane rise in demand.

At least she has no illusions about it: they really weren't
any happier back there, in the kraal she came to after
walking for an hour, after the transition. But they were
home. She was the strange stranger.

She opens her eyes, then closes them again before reflex
switches them to infrared vision. She already knows what
she doesn't need to see. It's a very dark night that all her
other senses instantly told her is subtropical, and wild:
that particular humus smell, the concentration of insects,
the intermittent sounds of the nocturnal fauna, the humidity level, the carbon dioxide and oxygen levels, and
finally the scarcity of electromagnetic frequencies of
human origin. A jungle. A long way from civilization. She
doesn't even wonder if there is one — or if not civilization,
since that, after all, is quite a relative notion, the kind of
society she will need. There always is one. The route to
get there is simply more or less long. And it's not a bad
thing either. It's better that she appears and wakes up in
a deserted, quiet place rather than in the middle of a busy
street.

She opens her eyes again, accepts the ghostly infrared
landscape — an explosion of hidden life, and the lumi-
nescence of the vegetation itself. It's an Earth, like all the
other times, that's all she needs to know for now. She gets
up. Might as well take advantage of the brief period of
grace after wakening when, for some reason, the local
fauna, and especially the insects, have not yet identified
her as edible. She locates a tree, and scales it with the usual
precautions, startling a troop of monkeys, which scatters
with howls that echo for a long time through the jungle.
Yes, there, about a half a dozen kilometres to the south,
a darker patch, the typical signature of forest clearing and

cultivation. Always lucky, eh, Kathryn? The data continues to be processed inside her absolute memory to guide her there. Back on the ground, she tears off some bark, a few big leaves and handfuls of grass to make herself a makeshift loincloth and sandals — less for her comfort than for that of the natives she will be encountering. Africa. Southern. Somewhere between what is perhaps also called here Mozambique and South Africa — the toponymic differences have become so minimal during the last transitions that she hardly considers them significant anymore. She will be interested in the other differences as she encounters them along the way.

She sets out guided by her internal compass. Crushes with a slap the first mosquito that has decided to taste her. This grace period is over. Not the other one. Not yet. As always at the beginning of a new transition, she has a sense of slightly amused curiosity, she feels calm, confident, open to whatever new might happen — she still thinks something new can happen.

In the village, among the outbursts of the dogs — she keeps them at a respectful distance with the branch she has been using as a walking stick, a weapon — and the lowing of a few skinny cows in their enclosure, the people are waking up, coming out of the huts, carrying torches and machetes — a bad sign. Then they see she's alone, a white woman, half naked, devoured by insects. They gasp, take pity, they lead her inside, sit her down, give her something to drink and, while a woman smears her insect bites with a salve that is as soothing as it is foul-smelling, they ask her questions that she answers with mute and falsely bewildered denials. Then they talk over her head, in a Bantu dialect that she deciphers quite quickly. They are going to get the priest, who is also the doctor. A teenage boy runs out of the hut. There is a Catholic missionary clinic somewhere in the vicinity of the village — which might just as well mean ten or fifty kilometres, but it doesn't matter, she has time.

Children have gathered in one corner of the hut, staring wide-eyed at her. They must not see Caucasians around here very often. One little girl in particular seems more fascinated than the others — and bolder: she steps out of the group and comes over to touch her arm, quite timidly with one finger, and then runs away when she smiles at her.

She accepts the food they give her in a half gourd, with horrified gratitude: it only took her a glance to assess the fevered gauntness of most of the adults, and the swollen bellies of many of the children. They help her put on a light cotton European-style dress, the colours still bright, no doubt the Sunday best of her hostess. The village griot has finally been woken up and comes to examine her, declaring officially that she has no visible or invisible wounds and — to her great relief, since this hadn't occurred to her right away — no evil spirits. He tries a few words that she recognizes as English, but she decides to keep on playing the amnesia card — in the beginning, in these cases, that's always safest.

The priest arrives the next day around noon, in a Jeep, a battered old wreck that stubbornly keeps on running. He's Asian, Vietnamese — and when he also tries to ask questions in English, his Oxford accent is quite comical. She almost wants to speak to him in French, just to see, but restrains herself. He examines her quickly, muttering to himself: she's in excellent health — apart from the insect bites and slight dehydration — no concussion or anything. Puzzled, he puts away his instruments and declares to his hosts that he's taking her to the mission.

As she is about to climb into the Jeep, there is a movement near her, a shake of her sleeve. She looks down. It's the little girl from the day before, holding out a bracelet of multicoloured beads, around a single, precious blue glass gem. She squats down, pats the dusty cheek, and solemnly slips the bracelet onto her wrist. Then she sits down next to the driver while the little girl walks away, her hands behind her back. Nine, ten years old maybe — hard to say. In three or four years, she'll have her first baby. In about fifteen years, she'll be dead. Maybe in ten if she's lucky.

Two walls of Carol Cooper's huge office are completely panelled in Macassar wood — rather gloomy, but the effect is intentional, to contrast with the two big, bright, airy bay

windows in the other corner of the room, which look out
on the Technocity and the St. Lawrence. Thick ecru carpet,
furniture with clean lines, just enough brushed steel here
and there to remind visitors that this is a cutting-edge tech
company, especially the logo, on the left wall, the silhouette
of a bird in flight against a star-shaped snowflake, framed
by CRYO vertically and VITAL horizontally.

Carol Cooper stands up to greet her when she comes
in, without, however, leaving her almost empty desk —
an unmistakable sign of power. There is only one thick
sheaf of papers. No doubt the contract she discussed in
London with the Cryovital head-hunter.

"Ms. Verbrugge, it's a pleasure to welcome you to the
team. Can I offer you something to drink?"

She agrees to a glass of the Glenlivet — always useful
to have an accessory in your hand in order to create carefully spaced silences, and her sense of smell tells her that
no cigarette has ever been smoked in this office.

The man who identified her in the carpeted hallway of
Cryovital Ltd., without introducing himself, even before
she gave her name at reception, to accompany her to the
elevator, ("Ms Cooper is expecting you"), closes the door
and turns towards one of the walls, which must contain
the bar.

Carol Cooper is an elegant fiftyish woman with just a
touch of sexiness. Her handshake is perfect, just firm and
embracing enough, saying, "woman and proud of it — and
my company has been on the cover of Fortune three times
in the last fifteen years."

"I trust you had a pleasant journey. Do you have everything you need at the hotel?"

No problem: everything is first class, with the obligatory
obscene luxury. In the first plane, she was able to relive
on the big screen the assassination of President Mandela,
the riots that followed, then, live, the U.N. troops entering
the ruins of Johannesburg. After that, the flight attendant
came to help her choose from the program of high-defi-
nition films offered on the Tunis-London leg. Same thing
on the London-Montréal flight, with bloodier and bloodier
news, again live — peacekeeping, even international peace-

keeping, requires a minimum of peace beforehand — another choice of films and an exquisite appetizer of smoked salmon.

And as for the hotel they are putting her up in until she can move into the condo they found for her in the east end of the city ("Sorry, we couldn't find anything closer."), well, even the American tourists who stay there have a touch of class. Fortunately, Katrijn Verbrugge has a suitable wardrobe — she completely reoutfitted herself in London, which her discreet guardian angels certainly would not have found strange: apart from her UK bank account, of course, she lost everything in "the Troubles," as they say in the civilized countries. Her job in Professor Brangden's laboratory, at the University of Witwatersrand, her house in a nice neighbourhood, all her family souvenirs. All her papers and diplomas, except for what she had on her when she fled. No one needs to know that those papers are artistic creations from the shady part of Johannesburg — the shady part of Johannesburg has itself disappeared in the orgies of bombings and counter-bombings by the rival factions, like the government buildings and their databanks.

It takes them five days to reach the capital, along dusty tracks after they leave the forest. In one of the villages where they stop along the way, it's the television hour. More than half the adults and children are dying of AIDS, or whatever name has been given here to this new plague, and the rest are in not much better shape because of malnutrition and kwashiorkor, but they are all gathered around the blue glow of the TV screen to gaze at the other world. After the reports on a bombing here, a war there, the ritual squabbling at the United Nations, and the latest lurches of the stock exchanges, where the electronic trillions float, virtual and yet critical for those who do not possess them, the news program obligatorily ends on a light note: cryonics, the latest fad for the rich, who get sick in spite of their wealth or who can't reconcile themselves with getting old, persistent in their belief that immortality will be accessible sometime in the future. Substantial progress since the heroically fraudulent times when they cut off heads since

they couldn't properly preserve the whole body: "a promising new approach using liquid helium instead of nitro-
gen..."

This is followed by statements from Arnold Brangden,
the national leading expert who is always consulted on
the topic, and whose research is more or less in the same
area, but, notes the professor, with medical objectives that
are more serious than those of the Canadian and American
"corpsicle" firms.

She listens. No surprise there. More like a kind of inner acceptance, the amused feeling that the universe, as
usual, is giving her everything she wants on a silver platter.
Now she has a very clear purpose, her path is laid out for
her, leading from Johannesburg to Montréal, by way of the
University of Witwatersrand.

Father Nguyen (he asked to be called that, and not
"Doctor") can't keep from chattering to fill the long bumpy
hours; so she pretends to learn English with him, a few
words then short phrases (the differences, once again, are
minimal from the version she learned during the last transition). The priest decides to take her to the British Embassy
rather than the American: who knows, her facility with
the language might be related to her lost identity? She
doesn't try to give him the slip. Any embassy will do, in
fact. In the beginning, she always tries to keep a very low
profile, be invisible. She prefers to avoid anything that
would make her show up on the radar of the police and
the other intelligence agencies — biometric data, photos,
wanted notices. But every time she has been unable to avoid
it, and it has become almost systematic during her most
recent transitions, she has had to admit that embassies were
an ideal resource. While they try to find you an identity,
they house you and feed you, with an often genuine sympathy for your difficult situation — and you can quietly
get your bearings, decide what steps to take next, find the
necessary contacts and, when the time comes, disappear
into the woodwork.

They find no one "for the moment" who matches her
description and has been reported missing, either in South
Africa or in neighbouring countries; but, they assure her,

they will cast the net wider: England, Australia, North America. Nor do they find a double or twin, which isn't surprising either: this hasn't happened yet, anywhere, so why would it be different all of a sudden? Meanwhile, more than a month has gone by, which she has made good use of, miscellaneous reading, radio, television: her brain, trained to synthesize all kinds of data, tells her that South Africa is a powder keg ready to explode. One year, maybe two. There will be no Bridge in this country. But just enough time to establish her new identity. As the weeks pass, she "discovers" an interest for and knowledge in scientific laboratory work, physics, chemistry; she carefully feeds this information to Karine Langstadder, the agent in charge of her file, who, of course, sees this as an encouraging sign and urges her to pursue this likely link with her old identity. Three more months elapse, however, without any results regarding that identity. It is time for Jane Doe to rejoin society, they decide at the embassy. They suggest she choose a name for herself. She doesn't know the name of the little village where Father Nguyen picked her up, but the mission was in another village called Maasbruggen: she suggests "Karine Maasbruggen." Karine Langstadder smiles, touched.

They check that no other person with that name exists, they issue her papers, and they throw her a little goodbye party. With the help of the embassy, she goes through the necessary steps to register as a student in Witwatersrand, in the department of biophysics where Arnold Brangden works. She shines quickly enough to be recruited by the professor. From then on, all she has to do is wait, while preparing her exit. One year later, three weeks after Mandela's assassination, the capital is convulsed in more and more bloody fighting, Witwatersrand and its data banks are in ruins, poor Brangden has even been killed, but one "Katrijn Verbrugge" — the family name is common to thousands of Afrikaners — is on a plane to Lusaka, one of the last flights out before the airport is completely shut down. Carrying in her pocket, dated one month earlier, a glowing letter of recommendation signed by the professor, or almost. Everything is going according to plan.

✝ ✝ ✝

Exactly five minutes of banal pleasantries — Carol Cooper's internal clock is as good as a Voyager's. Then they get down to serious business. She quickly leafs through the contract while the director of Cryovital runs through the clauses with her, going through the motions, completely unnecessary, but it's standard practice. In a way that is obvious, she does not read it and hurries to sign it at the places indicated — a poor little lost thing, still in shock, happy just to have found a proper job in this big friendly country that ... of which ... She knows that the whole arsenal is in place, tight as a drum, confidentiality clauses, intellectual property, all kinds of security requirements. But this contract means nothing. The final result will be the same. In Witwatersrand, she hardly had any problems ensuring that the results of her work, her "lucky" finds, were stolen by dear professor Brangden, thus guaranteeing her anonymity within the "research team." She let it show through in the letter of recommendation: Katrijn Verbrugge is ideal material for a private company, a brilliant researcher with no head for business. The more they believe that, the less wary they will be of her.

Once the contract is signed and the ritual handshakes exchanged, with smiles, Carol Cooper hands her over to Matt Frölich, who is not exactly the head of security as she had thought, but almost: supervisor of the "Freya Project." Now that she is the exclusive property of Cryovital Ltd., he will confer upon her all the outward signs that allow her to circulate freely among the herd.

They don't pull any punches — could Cryovital be the cover for a Canadian government project, or even an American one, since the big brother to the south has free rein here? Fingerprints, retinal scans, DNA ... She submits with complete docility — including, of course, undergoing a polygraph test, to establish her baseline, which doesn't phase her for a second, she's done that before. She sometimes helped things along a little, but during the South African demolition derby, any relationship between Karine Maasbruggen and Katrijn Verbrugge went completely up in smoke, and the identity of the latter runs deep enough so that no alarms are set off in the minds of people who have no reason to be suspicious of her and to whom she will give no reasons to be suspicious.

Once duly identified, labelled, entered in the databases, and provided with all the keys, passes and necessary codes, she allows herself to be led towards the holy of holies, the research section where she will meet the rest of the team.

The elevator plunges downwards. For a long time. Through many basement floors. A little splinter of uneasiness, quickly plucked out. There are always good, perfectly logical, and even scientific reasons, to install deep underground what you want to be secure and discreet research facilities. She reviews what she knows about her future colleagues. According to the information she has been able to collect, there are no big names on this team. Cryovital is doing research on very low temperatures for strictly medical purposes, but the equipment it has obtained recently, and the fact that in the last six months they have hired a half dozen promising new graduates in physics and biology, were enough to put the company in her sights. The other possible company, Lifeline Inc., is directly involved in the fabrication and management of corpsicles, but it's an American company, just a little too much in the pockets of the party in power, where security must be a lot tighter. As things are at present, it is easier to take refuge in Canada. In any case, Cryovital's "Freya Project" — they haven't explained it to her in detail yet, they're keeping that for dessert, evidently — has gone beyond the exploratory stage. She is arriving at just the right time to nudge the research in the required direction.

The elevator opens with an almost silent hiss. Precision-lit corridors, neutral colours, hushed atmosphere. One door after another flashes and slides open with a click for Frölich's card. Sometimes they walk past walls of glass behind which silhouettes in white or green smocks work. Everything looks very familiar. Too familiar, but she refuses to dwell on that. This is not the first time she has gone through a similar place and it will not be the last. One more door, and she immediately sees the metal sphere, in the center of the room. More than three metres in diameter, massive, firmly bolted to its wide base frame into which disappear hoses, tubes and electrical cables. This sphere appears to be very advanced already. Nothing yet to produce the magnetic field. They must have read Brangden's last paper though. But that's obviously why they hired her. Slight amusement — preferable to the little step back she still had to suppress when she entered.

There are half a dozen people in the room — emerging from behind the sphere and coming in from small adjoining labs to meet the new recruit. Three variously exotic, very young women — one Asian, one Amerindian, one likely Jamaican, they're ecumenical at Cryovital — a big gangly nerd, little ant head under a curly mane, thick, horn-rimmed glasses, a pudgy guy with an unruly mop of hair, in his fifties, filthy white smock, with the look they used to call the "nutty professor" one or two transitions back, one of those inventors of fantastic gadgets that are sometimes there just when you need them. And a young man barely in his thirties who walks over to her, his hand already extended. He is tall, broad-shouldered, dark and radiant, very brown skin, black hair, piercing eyes, big smile. "Jorge Dayar," says Frölich, who then introduces the others one by one.

She's barely listening to him, doesn't matter, her absolute memory already contains their names and everything she needs to know about them. She shakes hands, smiles, certain that her face betrays nothing. She's not surprised, no, she's not surprised, in a few seconds she'll even tell herself she was expecting it, yes, still this generosity of the universe with every transition, she'll tell herself it's normal, that it's okay. Whatever his name, his age, it's him. Again. Always. Of course.

"What time is it?"

Pretext. She could look herself, he left his watch on the nightstand on her side of the bed. But she deliberately accentuates her satiated languor, to make the moment last longer. Because maybe it's the last time, because maybe tomorrow they will be dead. Mustn't think that way — she won't tell him, he would scold her and he'd be right. Tomorrow will instead be the beginning of a new life, and not only for the two of them, because tomorrow they will have destroyed the ICC. But, after the others left, that afternoon, when he pulled her towards him, when they made love, and again, and again, she thought "vigil of arms," so as not to think "funeral vigil," images floated in her mind, knights or priests lying with their arms stretched out in a cross on the cold stone in front of an altar, and it was really that, he on her, she on him, like an ultimate sacrament they were administering to each other.

He leans half across her to look at his watch. She takes advantage of the position to kiss his chest, squeeze his bum, as smooth as a teenage boy's in spite of the fact he's almost forty, sniff his smell, a mix of sweat and sex, and, residual hints of his cologne — he put on cologne, today: just like him! — those hints of vanilla and cinnamon that always make her hungry for his skin. He smiles above her, leaning on his two outstretched arms: "Time to go."

Without exchanging another word, they get up, dress, gather their gear, check the equipment one last time, stow it in the van, and set out in the traffic. End of rush hour, it's getting quieter, curfew soon. They drive out on the north shore embankment towards the east, passing the massive oval of the ICC complex and its strange slanting tower rising like the prow of a ship under the little circular ring that crowns it. The sun is setting. On their right, in the dulling light, there are silvery glints on the river. A light mist begins to rise up from the Longueuil Shoals, masking and unveiling one by one the half-drowned carcasses of old buildings, illuminating then extinguishing orange and pink glints in the broken windows, on the bricks that the vegetation have not yet covered. Then the car fills with the heavy smells of the recycling plants in spite of the air conditioning.

She doesn't want to think too much about the crossing they will have to make underwater. Their wet suits will protect them from the pollution, at least what is floating visibly in the water of the river. As for the rest, the radioactive mud and mutant creatures as big as a bus, Egon just frowns and says: "Urban legends, Katie." Then adds, deliberately spoiling the effect: "At worst, creatures as big as a car." And laughs at her worried expression. They have something to defend themselves with, in any case.

The traffic has thinned to almost nothing by the time they reach the official boundary of the city — only half an hour till curfew. Not a single patrol in sight though. After all the trouble they'd gone to preparing all those false papers and repeating their cover story dozens of times! They take a narrow service road that leads down to the river along the embankment and stop the van, lights off, near one of the big drainage pipes. It's secured, of course, but it's not the one they'll be going through.

And now, the hard part: waiting, in the camouflaged van between the pipe and the twisted but leafy willow that has stubbornly decided to grow there. Egon tilts back his seat and closes his eyes. She does the same, one hand reaching over to his thigh. She envies his ability to sleep anywhere, no matter what the circumstances. She can't do it. She surprises herself though; he's the one who wakes her up. Almost midnight. She remembers, she shrugged her shoulders when they decided the time. Why this stupid fetish? He doesn't take offence: "We're programmed to sleep at night, Katie. Reflexes not so sharp, distractions, all that — especially in places where we feel perfectly safe."

No doubt because she made a sacrifice to biology with her little nap, she feels particularly alert.

They put on their gear, and tether the rest of the equipment in waterproof bags to their belts, and dive in. Low tide, they don't have to go very deep. And no monsters, but heavy, dark water barely penetrated by the light from their headlamps. Only about fifty metres in all. To the old submerged pipe.

The grate is heavy, but not secured and, after being worked on during a previous dive, it opens easily. About a hundred metres more, to the point where the two networks join above the level of the river, and they can get out of their wetsuits. Terribly noisy inside, in spite of all their precautions. And it stinks. God only knows what came and died here, and how it got this far — at least it wasn't a skunk! Egon has planned for this and hands her a stick with a strong menthol smell that she rubs on her upper

lip, even though it's not really very effective in neutral-
izing the stench of sewage and rot. "Breathe through your
mouth," he says when he sees the face she's making. He
secures his backpack on his shoulders, and she does the
same, then they activate their biolumes and head up the
echoing pipe. After about a hundred metres, they're past
the maximum stench zone, and the menthol ointment is
now a sufficient barrier; and as long as they follow the main
pipe, they can walk without bending over. From time to
time, Egon checks the map — they have to be sure not to
miss the fork that will take them to the west and the ICC.
Two months of cautious research just to draw up this map
from bits of data scattered in the nooks and crannies of an
old municipal data bank that had not been properly purged.
And then six months to assemble all the equipment.

And here they are.

They're making good progress. Since they haven't run
into any patrols along the way, they're almost half an hour
ahead of schedule. That means a longer wait for the diversion created by the rest of the team. "They'll be above,
how will we know?" He smiled: "Any kind of incident in
the security perimeter sets off a general alarm."

A fake attack on the tower. More stupid dissidents fooled
by the ICC propaganda, the officials from Security will no
doubt chuckle to themselves. The Interspatial Communication Centre isn't in the tower. All those beautiful images
of flights in the recruiting films, those eyes fiercely turned
to the skies, those heroic low-angle shots: all a sham. The
real ICC is underground. But they know that now. And
they know how to enter the belly of the beast. Partly thanks
to Egon. Your man.

In the ghostly glow of the biolume, you lovingly,
proudly scrutinize the muscled back, the sculptured
buttocks and thighs in the black jumpsuit that replaced the
wetsuits. A little surprised, but pleased mostly, at not being
afraid. Like with exams: panic before and, when the time
for action comes, a great sense of calm. And not without
a certain latent thrill, all the same. You're going to change
the course of history. He made a little face when
Dominique said that. "More like make change possible —

that's a little different. But at least it will bring down the status quo. What will happen after that ... hard to predict."

You agree with him completely. Never believed the ICC was an essential factor in the survival of the Alliance. Instant, absolutely protected communications, on Earth as well as in space, yes, that's important, but not that much. The Axis possesses advanced enough technology in other areas to provide a counterbalance. Two giants braced against each other for decades, and the energy they expend just to stay in place is destroying everything around them. Something has to give, anything, anywhere! And the ICC is the perfect target: an abomination that must end, regardless of the role it plays or does not play in the balance of power. As it is now, if the Alliance ever won thanks to the ICC, it would be worse than if it lost.

And if the Alliance lost the war because of the destruction of the ICC, well then, it would lose. What difference is there now between the two sides? There never was any. Go back to the good old days? Ha! You stopped believing it when you were twelve years old: your grandparents' stories really sounded too much like the government propaganda. And could you go back to them anyway? The radioactive areas will be off limits for millennia, and irreparable damage has been done to the very roots of life. Sea levels won't go down for centuries, if they ever do. And the dead, so many, the humans, the animals, the plants, who will revive them? No, you have to do what you can, here, now. And here, now, thanks in part to the information obtained by Egon, the ICC can be destroyed.

One foot in front of the other, splish, splash, echo, echo, glint, glint, no end to it — nearly two kilometres in the main pipe, then another kilometre up a gentle slope in a secondary pipe, head hunched down, knees bent. In spite of the fatigue, and the awareness of passing minutes, a strange sensation of being split. As if your brain were operating in a different time from your body, suspended — stolen time. It's weird, anyway: you're going to destroy the ICC, and you don't even really know what it is. Apart from the buildings, that is. But the procedure, what the acronym and the propaganda are really covering up... A jealously guarded secret, which does not keep the rumours from spreading, even when they are regularly denied, even with threats of prosecution for antipatriotic conduct. According to what Dominique has managed to extract from the few documents that are still accessible, one can only assume some kind of technological equivalent of telepathy, which burns out the brains of the subjects after they have been used for a certain period of time: pretty far-fetched! Only one thing is certain: whatever they're doing at the ICC, the subjects don't survive, or not for long.

Even Egon doesn't really have any idea. The times you tried to talk about it with him, he just shrugged: "They kill people with it, that's all you need to know." In the beginning, about a decade ago, they recruited openly. War Effort, Your Country Needs You, The Final Push to Victory — how many final pushes to victory have there been in the last fifty years? And almost none of the recruits were ever heard of again. The trails of the few official survivors all ended in dead-ends, or attracted too much attention from the Security Services for the investigators. The others, they say, "fell on the field of honour." At first there were medals, big showy funerals, speeches. Then it became routine, and "FOFH" has entered everyday language; the Infonets hardly bother ever mentioning it anymore — they probably didn't even need to be discouraged. And now, the recruiting is still going on, but mostly by trawling in prisons, asylums, and even, they say, in hospitals and retirement homes, all of which the government denies vehemently — and, in fact, how could anyone prove it? Prisoners, common and political criminals, the insane, old people, and the terminally ill die every day. It's normal. How many, and when exactly, is easy to disguise, especially in War Time, under the seal of almost fifty years of sacrosanct National Security.

If this monstrosity is what ensures the survival of the Alliance, as they claim, then the Alliance doesn't deserve to survive.

Suddenly, you notice that, at regular intervals, light filtering vertically through the ceiling of the pipe, through cracks. Your heart jumps in your chest. Above, now, is one of the corridors of the ICC, in the last basement level of the complex. The exit is not far. You check your watch: eighteen minutes till the diversionary attack.

Egon stops under one of the discharge grates, takes out the little torch, which lights with a discreet pop. You use Superglue to close the catch after you both go through. The opening isn't very wide, but you trained for this (with occasional fits of uncontrollable laughter that were transformed into erotic interludes — those slow-motion contortions were just irresistible).

Egon goes through first, and, between two panoramic sweeps of the cameras, sets up the device that will tap into and shift the phase of the images transmitted by the surveillance system, then replay them in a loop.

Now there's nothing to do but wait for the diversion. Twelve minutes. Egon, squatting comfortably with his back against the wall of the pipe, checks the clip of his K-16. Also squatting, your thighs burning, while you check that the timers on your explosive charges are properly set, you are hoping he won't need to use the rifle, nor you your pistol. Minimize the loss of human lives, and if possible avoid it completely, is what the group agreed to — or else what would be the sense of mounting an assault against the ICC because it kills innocent people? The extremists argued that anyone working for the ICC is not innocent and deserves what they get. "Judge, jury and executioner, eh guys?" Egon remarked. "Who made you emperors of the world?"

"And did the government have a legitimate mandate to create the ICC?!" protested Dominique.

"After being legitimately elected?" added Sahi.

Egon didn't bat an eyelash: "No, but we can hope the next one will be. Wouldn't you prefer to see a proper trial and all the guilty ones punished, the real guilty ones, not just a handful of stupid patsies?"

You voted with him, which convinced the undecided: contaminate from the ICC building the autonomous data banks of the complex — delayed viruses, worms and other goodies concocted by Sahi — then blow up the underground labs with the charges carefully calculated to avoid causing a cave-in. That was the night you became lovers. When the issue came up later of choosing who would go with him, there wasn't even any discussion: it would be you, of course. Live together, die together if necessary — you know you're destined for each other, whatever the outcome of your actions.

Finally the intermittent wailing of the alarm siren, the light filtering through the grate shifting to flashing red. Go.

You reach your first destination without a hitch, the room with all the ICC equipment. Egon was right: not even guards at the door. They think they're secure in this sixth basement. A code is required to get in — nothing a well-placed little charge won't fix. You've put on your masks. The charge explodes, hardly spectacular but effective: silently, the material of the door melts around the lock mechanism, and the hole continues to grow. Throw in gas grenades, dull explosions, count slowly to five, slide open what remains of the door, go in through the cloud, which is already dissipating in the stroboscopic red of the alarm.

A metal sphere approximately three metres in diameter. A jumble of cables and tubes and tanks and batteries ties it to other machines that cover the walls: computers, monitors, control panels.

Not a single body on the floor.

Stunned, you turn and look at Egon. He seems to be waiting for something, his head tilted a bit to one side.

The siren falls silent. The red light stops flashing. Egon nods as two grey silhouettes, guards, appear behind him in the doorway, followed by two silhouettes dressed in white smocks.

"Good," he says with a sigh, "the game's over."

"Cryopump ... helium condenser ... hyperfluid ... heat exchangers ... superinsulation ... membrane filters ... cryomagnetic crystals ... superconductor electromagnet ... yttrium-barium cuprate ... superconductor ceramics ..." The familiar terms pepper your mind, bouncing from one voice to the other while in Frölich's wake they walk you around the metal sphere, activate devices, open the internal compartment lined with silk fibres, "...resistant to cold and hypoallergenic." You don't ask questions. You're not really listening. You concentrate on nodding your head, smiling with the required hint of respectful admiration, while the memory writhes inside you. Even after all this time, it still requires an effort that irritates you. Really, why don't you just suppress it? But you know the answer: then you wouldn't know where you come from, who you are. Oh crap, just as well. What does it matter? The important thing is that sphere. The important thing is that everything is ready for what comes next. You will make sure they 'discover' how to use a magnetic field to perfect the preservation of organic matter by taking it as close as possible to absolute zero. You won't have to wait too long. That's what's hard, has always been hard for you, the waiting.

You're still staring at Egon when the two guards come over to you and relieve you without violence of the bag of explosives. After setting his K-16 down on the floor, Egon takes his bag off with a shake of his shoulders, then rubs his neck with a little grimace.

The two guards walk off with the bags at a measured pace without looking back. The two technicians come and stand on either side of you, but don't touch you. You still don't move. You can't. Petrified, one might say, but really it feels more like all your muscles, your tendons, your bones have turned to water. As if your skin were the only thing holding you up.

They didn't take your pistol.

Almost at the same instant, you know it's loaded with blanks. It was Egon who took care of the weapons.

He glances at one of the two techs, and nods assent. A sudden pressure on your forearm, a light hiss. Just enough time to look, see the syringe, open your mouth — and already your legs are giving way under you. Sturdy arms grab you, lift you, and lay you down on a hard surface. All you can see is the ceiling. Completely paralyzed, totally conscious. You can't blink. You can't close your eyes. In your head, in your petrified body, a tornado of horror, rage, terror. So much violence with no outlet, you can't take it, you're going to explode, your heart is going to stop, you want it to stop, right this instant, immediately, you want to die, you have to die.

No, not this time. You hear. You hear footsteps moving away, a chair rolling with a little squeak, clicks — someone is keyboarding. Humming sounds, little hissing sounds, a motor starting up, or something... You don't hear Egon coming over to you — his shoes have silent soles. His face suddenly appears in your field of vision.

With quick, yet gentle, movements, he starts undressing you.

"I've obtained preferential treatment for you," he says through his teeth. "Because I've been a good hunting dog again — a good dozen dissidents, plus all the ones they will lead them to, so it was worth a little favour. And besides, you don't know much. Nothing Dominique and the others won't be able to tell them. And ... I really like you. At this point, though, I'm sure you don't give a damn... My poor little Katie. So full of good intentions, big beautiful ideas. But we're not living in that world now, if we ever did. Destroying the ICC wouldn't make any difference, you see. They would find a way to re-establish the balance of power. They don't want the war to end. They agreed on that a long time ago. Eternal war means eternal power for them. That's why they can't be beaten. And in that case, it's hardly worth putting your ass on the line for nothing, is it? If you can't beat them, might as well join them. Except *you* wouldn't want to. Heroic and stupid, my little Katie. Or just young. Maybe you would have got over it if you'd had enough time, but that's just it, time is what you've run out of."

He's not mocking you, he's not boasting. He's explaining. He wants you to understand. What? What more than what you've understood just now, when your world was turned upside-down? When he gets to the underwear, he makes a little irritated noise, walks away, then comes back. You hear a new sound, metal against metal. Scissors. An instant later, you feel the cold contact against your skin.

"You won't be going to the zombie plant. Not to prison either, you would just be jumping from the frying pan into the fire. So to speak. Frankly, I'm not sure you're going anywhere — no one knows. The first human guinea pigs never reappeared, the ones whose brains were intact. I'd rather like to believe that they never reported, wherever they found themselves after the transition. Clever of them, eh? But anyway, this is roughly what's going to happen: you're going to be put in the sphere. There, your body will be cooled to a very, very low temperature. And at a given moment, off it goes! It will disappear. Not disintegrated, you have to understand. Just ... disappeared, vanished. Not a single molecule will remain. The zombies go where they've been programmed to go. You on the other hand, not programmed... The idea, the theory at least, is that you can go anywhere. Somewhere else. Alive. Pretty interesting, isn't it?"

The invisible machines are charging up, or warming up, whatever it is they're supposed to do: there is an intention, a purpose, in this organized symphony. Egon straightens up with a sigh.

"You've hardly understood anything I've been saying, have you?" he says with a bit of a twisted smile. "But you don't need to understand."

He disappears. On the periphery of your field of vision, to the right, something white passes. Movement. You're being rolled. To the sphere? An arm behind your shoulders. They sit you up, hold your head upright. Egon's voice, again, in your ear, unnecessarily, "Look." You can't help seeing the sphere, which opens slowly with a toothless yawn. Inside there's a kind of shiny sarcophagus, connected to every size of wires and pipes.

Egon takes you in his arms. He steps onto the base of the sphere and places you in the sarcophagus, not without some difficulty — other hands on you, one of the techs must have come to help him. They stretch out your legs, your arms. Under your neck there's a bulge, and under your buttocks and calves there are hollows: the sarcophagus is roughly shaped to accommodate a human body. The material, whatever it is, is hard and cool.

Once again, above you, Egon's face: "Try not to be too afraid. When the shell is closed, a fast-acting anesthetic gas will be piped in. You won't feel a thing, I promise."

He leans over, his lips brush one of your nipples, and then he withdraws.

Immediately, in an almost silent gliding sound, the shell of the compartment begins to shut. It is thick but translucent. You can feel the movement of the sphere as it closes in turn with your seeing, to your right, a horizontal patch of light that shrinks on the periphery of your field of vision.

The gas begins to fill the compartment with a slight hiss. Diminishes. Grows fainter. Vanishes.

"Still here, Doctor? You're a real workaholic!"

You turn around to see the silhouette of Jorge Dayar in the doorway. He still sometimes calls you by your title — a vestige of European politeness that he has never completely given up, apparently. You thought he was gone. You could reply that he's still there too, but that would only emphasize the parallel. Best to limit interaction once again. You close the cage and go on to the next one.

"And why are you feeding the animals? That's Agatha's or Sherri's job."

Yes, the youngest ones, the Girl Fridays at the bottom of the pecking order.

"Agatha wanted to leave earlier today. Family obligations. Besides I like looking after the animals."

And they have to get used to seeing you leave the lab very late — because soon, once the new tests are started, they will need to get used to seeing you come back at night, always for the animals.

Dayar picks up a carrot top that has fallen on the floor, and pokes it through the mesh towards one of the pink-eyed rabbits. "I see. You have a hectic social life, don't you?"

"I'm not certain it's compatible with serious work."

Except for Richard Branchet, the "nutty professor," who is one of those eternal adolescents anyway and as crazy as the younger ones, Katrijn Verbrugge is the oldest member of the team — all the others were less than thirty, even Jorge Dayar, who is only aged by his brawny build and his usually ponderous walk. She's supposed to be the most sensible one. That at least is the persona you chose for her in the beginning — workaholic, yes, a good little workhorse, reliable, and rather mild-mannered.

"All work and no play? There's more to life than work!" he protests. "And even for work, it does you good to air out your brain once in a while! Go out, do something else. See other people. Or the same ones, as the case may be, but in a different context. It's Richard's wife's birthday today, and they're having a little party. I'm supposed to go by their place. Why don't you come along?"

You shrug your shoulders, taking your time closing the next-to-last cage and moving on to the last one. He persists in trying to coax you out of your shell. This makes three times this week that he's stayed at the lab as long as you. And this time it's going to be harder to get rid of him.

"I wouldn't know anybody..." And you barely think to add, "...and I'm not dressed for it."

"You'll be fine. And Richard and I will be there. You won't get to know anybody if you keep thinking that way."

He leans against the wall near the last cage, his arms folded. You can smell his cologne — he always wears cologne — hints of vetiver, orange, and musk. "Dr. Verbrugge," he speaks more softly, gently, "I know what you're going through. It was the same for me when I first came here, about ten years ago. Losing everything and starting again from scratch somewhere else. It's easier when we let other people help us."

Yes, you checked his file, just like all the others, at a time when you didn't know who he would be (a photo that was really not a good likeness, quite a bit younger, with a beard and long hair). The Balkans and their atrocities, another one of those "Never Again's" that has been repeated since, in a dozen other places — routine. Seventeen years old, Jorge Dayar, with his grandmother and his younger brother, both in very bad shape; they did not survive exile. So what? He works at Cryovital now.

"I've never been very sociable," you say, closing the last cage. "Some people are like that, you know. They'd rather be left alone."

"Exactly what I was saying ten years ago, Dr. Verbrugge. Come on, be honest with me. You've been here for what, two months? What do you do for fun?"

You shrug your shoulders and recite a string of truths that he will not know are also lies: "I watch TV, do sports." You read, and you regularly check the news on TV and on the net, to know how far things have gone in this world so you won't be surprised before you're ready to leave; and the sports you practice at home, shielded from prying ears and eyes, or at least you assume you are — why would they have put your apartment under surveillance? — consist of all the various martial arts you've learned over the years; you never know when they might come in handy.

"Movies? Theatre? Museums?" He shakes his head disapprovingly at your successive negative responses: "Dr. Verbrugge, have you even looked around the city a little?"

"What for?" you're tempted to reply. Except for the east-west route to go from your pretty little condo in the east to the Technocity, in the old port, where Cryovital is located, what would be the use of touring a city you already know, or of which you know several versions that are so similar? As long as you could do it on foot, during the fall and the beginning of winter, you never varied your route to work: St. Catherine or Maisonneuve from Montcalm, and then south towards the Technocity. Never along the river, by the "scenic route" of the old converted port facilities. You don't give a damn about the scenic route. In the Cryovital cafeteria, on the fifth floor of the building, you always turn your back to the bay windows, which face northeast. They've told you that it's a shame, stressing the splendid view there is from there, when the weather is nice, you can even see the Olympic Stadium with its sloping tower and its little hat at the top where the tourists go to snap pictures of the panorama below! You told them you're acrophobic. You don't give a damn about the pretty sights, guided tours of the city. You're not here as a tourist!

But there's really no polite way to turn down Jorge's invitation. Too bad. You have to maintain his good will. And after all, sooner or later, you'll have to begin.

You don't take his car: Branchet doesn't live far from Cryovital, "and I know you like to walk." And winter. Never knew winter before beginning the Voyages. In fact, not before the third transition. Or was it the fourth? Anyway, now it's always winter. Maybe, just once, the Bridge will be far away, at one of the poles of the world, the Arctic or the Antarctic. It would be logical, wouldn't it? A kind of logic, anyway. You'd like to see nothing but ice floes. No room for human frailty. The cold, the ice, clean, clear, honest, simple. The girls in the lab were horrified when you said that. They can't know. You hate heat, humidity, stickiness, compromise. You didn't phrase it that way, of course.

Not very cold this evening. A beautiful, mild December night. Light but persistent snow has been falling since late afternoon, blanketing the filth of the urban winter, a sparkling diamond powder on the sidewalks where no one has passed for a while. At first, you say nothing. You've never known how to walk beside someone, you're never able to keep the right distance: from time to time your arms, your hands brush.

Then he starts talking. He doesn't ask you questions about yourself, not yet. He talks to you about the Branchets, the people who will be there, and about himself, to establish a rapport, to win you over.

"...I've known Richard since I arrived in Canada. He got me hired at Cryovital. He was my thesis supervisor at McGill. He retired to go into private business just when I was finishing my doctorate."

"On absolute zero."

He chuckled. "And heat absorbers. Yeah. The fabrication of vacuum, sort of. A ... weighty subject."

"Your choice?"

He's not laughing anymore. "Yes. I told myself there wasn't much chance of there being military spin-offs. At worst, in space — but with the angle I was taking, that was pretty remote."

You provoke him, just to see. "You don't like the military? You wouldn't be here if the U.N. didn't have armies."

You see a little muscle twitch in his jaw.

"I don't owe anything to the U.N. We were living in Srebrenitza. Our parents had sent us to my grandmother's, my brother and me, before the city was besieged."

And the White Helmets — ah, no, they're blue here — left the town, abandoning it to the butchers.

"We got here by our own means, all three of us and..."

He clenches his teeth again, then sighs: "No, I don't particularly like the military."

"And Cryovital?"

He seems a little surprised: "Cryogenic preservation of transplant organs? Purely medical applications, right?" He smiles a bit sadly: "Don't take me for a complete idiot. I know very well that there's no way of predicting how much of it will be used or misused. But a priori, I have nothing against the possibility of saving lives." A slight pause, then: "Wasn't that what you were working on with Brangden too?"

He must think he's softened you up enough with his confidences. You play along.

"Yes..."

He notices the hesitation in your voice, just as he is supposed to: "That's good, isn't it?"

"Yes. But saving lives ... you have to ask yourself which lives. Who benefits?"

He says "Ah," in a tone that indicates he has already thought about this too. And then adds: "At least the technology will be there. After that, it may be a political question."

"Exactly."

You walk in silence for a while. He starts talking again, softly: "I was thinking 'health policy.' We're not in South Africa here."

You take a deep breath of cold air to keep yourself from answering back. But it's okay, he's providing the opening you were looking for. You add, as if reluctantly: "Private American interests also contacted Brangden. Very ... discreetly. He was interested, in spite of all his public denials. That is why I decided to leave his team." A hint of irony, ostensibly to mask excess emotion: "The ... events speeded up the process."

Another silent pause, then he asks: "Lifeline?"

He's not stupid, that's for sure. But no Egon ever has been.

"No. A private benefactor. A very old private benefactor."

He shakes his head: "Helium cooling is an improvement, but as long as the crystallization problem hasn't been solved, the whole thing is a scam!"

"Of course..." And now, the hook. "...but we were starting to think about working with magnetic fields."

You don't say any more, letting him follow the chain of inferences. He obviously used the process during his doctorate: molecules and crystals of a small quantity of magnetic salts maintained in a strong magnetic field, you interrupt the field, and molecules and crystals go out of alignment at random, giving off thermal energy to the surroundings and making lower temperatures possible.

He arrives at the expected conclusion: "But with those intensities, the cancer hazards for humans..."

"Yes, but maybe the cryo would be homogeneous. And the whole mythology of corpsicles is based on the idea that later, in the future, those problems will have been solved."

He makes a little irritated grunt. You continue by pretending to change the subject.

"In short, this fellow, the old benefactor, contacted Brangden to offer him a bridge of gold." You smile to yourself — you always find that expression amusing. And you hammer the point home in order to trigger his potential paranoia — something tells you you won't have to hit very hard: "I don't know how he got wind of what we were planning to do. We were very, very far from publishing. There must have been a mole in the lab." Then, pretending to find the idea amusing: "Poor old guy! Maybe he has spies in all the labs that do this kind of research!" And finally you look gloomy again with a sigh: "Him, or somebody else."

He sighs too. You commune in silence for a moment in the minuscule rustling of the snow, advancing on the pure white carpet — no longer immaculate behind you, but the flakes continue to fall, more urgently now, and they will erase your tracks. Lots of outdoor Christmas decorations on this street, garlands of electric lights, Santa Clauses, and even, on one roof, a sleigh with reindeer.

The recurring adjective in all the magazines is "enchanting," but you find it all rather grotesque. Tawdry social reflexes reactivated on fixed dates by the market. The human animal is infinitely conditionable.

"The cryo would be homogeneous," he suddenly whispers. "The magnetic properties of the hemoglobin would help further with the cooling. And just for the organs, the irradiation exposure would be limited..."

He's not thinking about you anymore. Quite normal. His little brother would have survived, if he had been higher up the waiting list for heart transplants.

I am in the compartment. I look at the buttons that control departure. Here, there are two. Red. Green. I hear his voice. Why do I still hear his voice? I shouldn't be hearing his voice. There's still time, Kathryn. *I press a button. Green. The gas fills the compartment.*

"I'll be frank with you, Kathryn. We don't think you're ready to leave."

In his desire to convince you, Tannden leans his long, thin face towards you, fingers intertwined on the desk as if to keep them from waving around. "We have only your interest at heart, you know that. And we know that once you've left, you'll be completely on your own. And that's just it. We would like to be sure you possess all the necessary resources."

You are very calm. It's not as if you hadn't expected it. "I got excellent marks on all the theoretical and practical courses. And I thought I had completed the training to the entire satisfaction of the supervisors, including for absolute memory. No one ever told me there were other requirements."

Tannden sighs. "There aren't really in what we are thinking of. But..." He lays a hand on the file folder in front of him. "Doctor Farlane's report notes persistent psychological problems, and..."

You relax inside. Even Farlane couldn't have recommended making you wait until the nightmares stopped; it's a last stand, as they say: as a matter of form. You nod with a smile that is just indulgent enough — you know how to handle Tannden: he has "persistent psychological problems" himself. He has always doubted the validity of the whole undertaking — which is what got him his position, since that makes him careful in the selection of candidates; but this also makes him easy to manipulate, because this doubt sometimes contaminates the validity, the legitimacy, of his decisions.

"Yes, I still have nightmares once in a while. Wouldn't you if you were me?"

He sighs without answering — what could he say? He has his own nightmares, you accessed his file: Voyagers lost, helpless, butchered, even though all Voyagers are "lost," even though they are all "helpless" at least in the instants that follow their awakening, and even though there are some who are in fact butchered then or later, but he doesn't know and will never know anything, he can never know anything, can't do anything about it, he can only imagine it, and that is the stuff of his nightmares: his own helplessness. Too much of a Father Complex in these Centres — an occupational hazard, obviously. They can't scatter their Voyagers on the winds of the universes without gnawing their fingernails. Unbearable loss of control, isn't it? But that's the way it is, and they know it very well and they're going to let you go, because, in the end, in spite of all their profiles, all their questionnaires, all their tests and interviews, they can never be absolutely certain whether or not a candidate is ready.

And because they don't know either that you went through another Centre before arriving at theirs, that you're on your second transition and not your first, and that your nightmares date back two universes.

The officials in the first Centre (they were called "monitors" there, not "supervisors," but it's all the same) knew: you arrived there directly from Egon, inside their very own sphere — a rare occurrence, they told you later, but there were a few cases in their archives. No time for you to recover; you were in shock, you spilled everything right away. They may not have let you leave again, or not for a very, very long time, but you didn't wait to find out.

As soon as you understood what it was, this machine they called "the Bridge," the cold transition that opens, for Voyagers, doors to other universes, as soon as you were able to slip into the departure room, you barricaded yourself in, you activated the sequence of processes, and you left. Absolutely not "ready" according to their criteria, nor even according to the criteria of this second Centre, which was less advanced in its handling of Voyagers and their preparation. But you managed not to get yourself killed, not to get lost searching for another Bridge in the new world you fell into — since they had guaranteed you there was always a Bridge, or its equivalent, or its possibility.

And thus, because, on the strength of this experience he is unaware of, you exude a pleasant assurance in the face of his chronic uncertainty, and because he has no objective reason to refuse, Tannden sighs, opens his hands. But in order to delay his capitulation a little longer, he asks: "But why do you want to leave again so quickly? You've barely spent a year and a half with us."

Barely! You remain carefully impassive. You know what's coming next. The tourist question.

"Don't you want to look around, explore? Aren't you just a little curious?"

You don't shrug. You're still smiling at him, the same slightly indulgent, slightly knowing smile. You could tell him that the more universes you put between you and your own, the better you'll feel. But that would be a little too revealing. So you tell him what he will find plausible: "I would really prefer to go somewhere else."

You already guess that you will say this often.

When you come out of Place Ville-Marie, you can tell by the sound that the evening traffic is still almost completely blocked on the four lanes of the Main. Rush hour is over though. As soon as you realized, as you headed home by your usual route, that the traffic wasn't about to become unjammed, you got off the bus to take Maisonneuve, and escape — relatively, that street was beginning to clog up too — the stench of all that exhaust from idling engines; since the beginning of the day, the city has been blanketed by a temperature inversion, and pollution levels are already high. And then, since you wanted to test the guy who is following you again, who got off the bus at the same time as you and several other passengers, you plunged into the underground labyrinth that snakes under downtown.

Every once in a while, an impatient driver leans on his horn, and, like children in nurseries, who cry contagiously, this is followed by a brief chorus of honking, which ends just as abruptly. They must know what is going on though, in their mobile tin cans, from the radio. Neither a bombing or a police operation, in any case, or even an ordinary fire: you would have heard the fire sirens, the sound carries a long way in the city.

A little curious nevertheless, you head down University Street to get closer to the Main. And then you understand. In spite of the bitter cold, a crowd has gathered in front of the CBC building, and spilled over onto the street. The domelights of the police cars guarding the building have been activated, and the police officers too — you can hear the megaphones ordering the crowd to disperse — but without any perceptible effect. You cross between cars to join the crowd. Your unshakeable tail won't be surprised if you go and check it out, will he?

On the big liquid crystal panel on the second floor, which normally at this time shows news images, the usual talking head is not in evidence, and the text streaming across the bottom of the screen has nothing to do with the usual hodgepodge of events and non-events, all smoothed over by the same elliptical phrases. Instead there is the huge — and maskless — face of the young leader of *Tsunami*, one of the Japanese terrorist groups that have been making waves lately. He is exhorting the enslaved populations of neocapitalist globalization to revolt, if not they will perish with their masters in an ocean of flame and blood, etc., etc. English audio, with French subtitles below, an impressive technical achievement. Apparently, according to the rather admiring comments exchanged between two teenage boys in front of you, *Tsunami* has managed to take over the entire satellite network. And has a good grip on it too, since it's lasted for at least ten minutes and no one has been able to eject them yet, nice job, do you think they have Spanish subtitles, the boys wonder, for the west coast of the United States?

They find the whole thing pretty funny. They don't think about what it implies, the terrible fragility of all the inter-connected systems that constitute their everyday world. And they'll be laughing less in a few minutes: from where you're standing, on the edge of the crowd, you can see a squad of police in riot gear coming down University double-time, from the René-Lévesque Station. They're not going to pull any punches; they've put on their gas masks. Time to resume your walk. You move away, not running but walking fast, towards Place des Arts and you slip into the nearest metro entrance. Another little tour through the underground shopping mall, where one can spend entire days in pure consumer ecstasy sheltered from inclement weather and politics — until the day, inevitable and likely close at hand, when someone will manage to slip some Sarin gas or some other similar goodie into the ventilation system. Who knows, maybe today? No, it would take something worse than not-even- Islamist terrorists pirating the airwaves for people to rush en masse into the under-ground city and make it worthwhile.

When you come to the escalator, you dig into your bag for a handkerchief, drop your wallet, half turn around as you pick it up again, and turn back to continue on your way. Your unshakable shadow is still there, and he is not the usual tidy little young man bundled up in his big brown parka, the one from Cryovital in-house security, whom you call "the Student" and sometimes almost feel like invit-ing for a coffee, just to see the look on his face. This one's taller, stockier, too neutral. And above all too expert, com-pared to the Student. For three days he's been following you, going to work, returning home, and he's changed tac-tics three times.

Following you. For three days: since Jorge and you began the new experiments.

✠ ✠ ✠

I am in the compartment. I look at the buttons that control departure. Here, there are two. Red. Green. I hear his voice. Why do I still hear his voice? I shouldn't be hearing his voice. There's still time, Kathryn. *I press a button. Green. The gas fills the compartment.*

I am in the compartment. There are no buttons. I've programmed everything. I hear his voice. Again. I shouldn't be hearing his voice. Kathryn, don't do it! *The gas hisses into the compartment. The voice fades.*

The two electrodes touch the red, glistening surface. Jorge's voice: "Clear!" The little heart convulses. Starts beating steadily, resurrection confirmed by the audio output and the regular graph on the monitor, which the camera has zoomed in on. Enthusiastic exclamations, the voices of the girls, of Gilles and Branchet, applause. Black.

The light returns in the little conference room.

"It's been a week, and the organ is still functional," concludes Jorge, who does not even try to hide his elation. "All the parameters are optimal, you have the data. The next step, obviously, is implantation."

Carol Cooper once again leafs through the file folder open in front of her. "Congratulations, Jorge, and congratulations to you all. These are extraordinary results." She looks up and winks at them. "This is Nobel material, if you want my opinion." Little discreet laughs around the table, but they know she is perfectly serious: they are aware of what they have accomplished.

"Especially if the implantation is successful," Frölich adds. "But maybe it's still a little early for that. We can't begin the surgical phase without at least having a replacement organ, so as not to slow down the process if the first operation fails. It was after all your fourth try. How much time do you need to produce another reliable organ?"

"The three other hearts did not last as long after resuscitation, but they all passed the thawing stage successfully," Jorge immediately says, a clarification that sounds like a protest — they talked about it before presenting the report, he wants to move forward as quickly as possible.

Branchet stops him from continuing by laying a hand on his arm: "I'd say one month. And if this heart quits in the meantime, that will be good to know too," he concludes, more for Jorge than for Cooper or Frölich.

"The thawing process has indeed been perfected, Carol," Frölich remarks pensively. "Perhaps Jorge and part of the team could continue working with the sphere that Jorge knocked together, while Richard and the others prepare the organs for transplant with the other part of the team."

Jorge frowns. "Work on what?" Frölich suggested nothing of the kind during the preparatory meeting. And he doesn't make a habit of being conciliatory.

"Well, I for one would be curious to know if the technique you've developed for organs taken from our rabbits would work with intact subjects. Aren't you? Don't tell me you've never thought about it."

Jorge stares at him for a moment, incredulous, then shrugs. "Even if it worked, it would go nowhere, it wouldn't be applicable to humans. The radiation levels..."

"It would still be interesting to know if and how it would work," Frölich interrupted nimbly. "Maybe it could lead to something."

From the way he crosses his hands on the table, it is clear that Jorge is starting to get irritated.

"Since when has Cryovital been involved with corpsicles? That's not what I was hired for!"

"But you were hired," Carol Cooper remarks in a soft, cold voice — effective; she's unequalled when it comes to putting the serfs in their place.

He looks down at the table; the little muscle quivers in his jaw. Time to jump in. You in turn cross your hands on the table, arranging yourself so that your elbow touches his. Out of the corner of your eye, you see him turn his head towards you.

"I would be interested in working on that with Jorge. I'd already asked myself the question, I must say, with Brangden."

And then you turn towards him, with a light poke of your elbow, a pressure invisible to the others. His eyes widen a bit. He pretends to think for a few instants, then to give in: "Why not?" he says a little sullenly. "They're your rabbits."

I am in the compartment. I look at the buttons that control departure. Here, there are two. Red. Green. I hear his voice. Why do I still hear his voice? I shouldn't be hearing his voice. There's still time, Kathryn. *I press a button. Green. The gas fills the compartment.*

I am in the compartment. There are no buttons. I've programmed everything. I hear his voice. Again. I shouldn't be hearing his voice. Kathryn, don't do it! *The gas hisses into the compartment. The voice fades.*

I am in the compartment. I look at the button. Only one button. Green. I hear his voice. Again. I shouldn't be hearing his voice. Kathryn, don't do it, there's still time, we can help you. *I press the button. The gas hisses into the compartment, the voice fades in the distance as the sphere closes.*

Either Cryovital has reinforced staff security, on principle, because of the first results with the cryogenic organs, or else, which would be more of a nuisance, someone, somewhere, knows and suspects — but suspects what at this stage? After all, there can't be another Voyager in the loop. In all your transitions, this has never happened. And according to all the archives in all the Centres you've passed through, according to what they say, two Voyagers have never been on the same planet at the same time. Theoretically possible, given the random operation of the Bridge — but, for reasons still unknown, it has never happened. In the same universe, perhaps, surely — but still unverifiable.

In any case, this will have to be cleared up, the possible collateral interference will have to be limited. You're ready for it. It's not the first time.

You head towards the metro, run down the escalator to catch the train you hear arriving, which is normal — even though you almost never take the metro. The tail does the same, you see him get in the next car. You get off at Beaudry station, and you take Maisonneuve towards your street, which is normal. You turn onto Montcalm, which is normal. You come to your house.

You keep walking.

Not normal! That must have grabbed the attention of the tail. You cross René-Lévesque Boulevard then you go down the street to the place where Montcalm changes into a dead-end. There is a construction site, which is poorly lit, plus kids have taken out the nearby street lamps with slingshots. You slip under the rather symbolic hoardings to lose yourself in the labyrinth of construction materials.

He follows. And he looks extremely surprised when you stand up in front of him with the taser you had cobbled together and have just taken out of its hiding place.

He's still twitching as you carefully tie him up, you search him — relieved: you took a chance that he wasn't in radio contact with anyone, and this turns out to be the case; a normal shadowing, so to speak. Whoever this guy's bosses are, at least they have no suspicions about the identity of Katrijn Verbrugge.

You gag him with your tightly knotted scarf, you open his parka, then his pants, which you pull down over his hips along with his underpants, and when he has completely come to again — the cold helps — you show him the taser, then you apply the electrodes to his shrivelled testicles, without pressing the button.

"I'm going to ask you a few questions. You will answer them when I lift the gag. Nod for yes."

He stares at you, more furious than terrified.

"Three seconds. Three. Two. One."

When he has stopped thrashing, you begin again, still very calmly: "I'm going to ask you a few questions. You will answer them when I lift the gag. Nod for yes."

He nods. Must have decided it's the smart thing to do, that the questions will be revealing. Any excuse not to get his balls fried. You remove the gag with one hand, without moving the hand that is holding the taser. "Who are you working for?"

"C.I.A."

Already?

"Who at Cryovital?"

"Frölich."

Frölich is the mole. The right-hand man, the performer of lowly tasks. Cute.

"The new experiments?"

"Yes."

"Is Lifeline involved?"

The man says "yes" with a slight delay, turning his eyes away. He's lying. Or rather his government is. Do they take you for an idiot?

You're suddenly overwhelmed by a feeling of leaden weariness. Doesn't matter who's involved, really. Because, yes, they do take you for an idiot. And you have to remain an idiot.

To ease your conscience, you ask anyway: "Who else?"

By the way he reacts, this question is revealing, but of what? What else?

"Russian mafia. You were being protected."

Does he realize he's talking in the past tense?

Don't give him time to think. Don't give yourself time to think. Drop the taser, place your hands on either side of his head, the leather gloves provide a good grip and, in one twist, break his neck.

Then, disguise it all as a mugging that went badly, flight, fatal fall in the dark construction site. No need to be plausible — the taser marks will be enough to feed the usual paranoia, and they will have plenty of choices: the Russian mafia, another rival secret service — or even an ally. Why suspect Katrijn Verbrugge, the idiot?

Katrijn Verbrugge goes home. She takes a shower, a long one, she grabs a fast bite of anything, she goes to bed. You know what you're going to dream.

Orange, musk, vetiver — he's just come into your office, and is bending towards you, leaning on his outstretched arms, his back to the camera.

"Do you have the new data, before we begin, Dr. Verbrugge?"

You stand up, back to the other camera, and shove a sheaf of papers into his hands. Invisible to the cameras now. He pretends to read them, writing in pencil in the margins and remarking out loud: "Ah, that might be interesting. This too."

You read upside-down: *Must. Speak. To. You.*

You take back the papers and mark them: "That too, there." *OK*.

You bump your styrofoam cup. Very black coffee spills over the sheets. A little panic, exclamations, search for kleenex, you sop it up as best you can. "The copy is at Frölich's place?" "Yes, of course." And the file on the computer. The sodden sheaf of papers is consigned to the wastepaper basket, the last step before the shredder.

"I think we're starting to get a bit frazzled," says Jorge with a sigh. "For two weeks we've been on edge with all this, and now they've stuck us with this new research! What would you say to a little constitutional, Dr. Verbrugge, instead of the café, before heading back to the lab? It's not too cold, we could eat outside."

You don't accept immediately, as a matter of form — don't change behaviour too quickly, that would attract their attention. While your relationship with Jorge has become more relaxed since the evening at the Branchets', it is still limited to work: you refused all his subsequent invitations. With mimed indecision, you glance around your disorderly office, where big photographs of forests do not make up for the absent windows. Then you run a hand through your hair and you suddenly decide: "Oh, okay, yes. A little walk would do me good."

You go back up to the ground floor and go through the security check point to go out on the boulevard. There's no lack of fast-food in the Technocity, there's plenty of choice, and the rush is over — it's well past noon. You serve yourself quickly, and go out again, without exchanging a word. One of your shadows came in behind you, the two others (yours) crossed the boulevard, one is pretending to view the river, and the other is feeding the seagulls.

You go out again, you continue for a while towards the little central park of the Technocity, then Jorge changes his mind and finally you both cross the boulevard. So does he know you're being watched, even outside Cryovital?

You don't go down to the landscaped embankments, but continue along the boulevard. If he thinks you can't be heard because of the rumble of the traffic, he's very naive. In any case, they're certainly not bugging you; they just want to make sure that nobody kidnaps you before they do it themselves.

But no, nothing that melodramatic: Cryovital can surely be convinced to cooperate.

He always eats his fries first. At a pace that says a lot, today, about how edgy he is. "They can't do that," he mutters finally. "A waste of time!"

You bite into your chicken sandwich, and mumble a reply through your mouthful, with the greatest conviction: "Failure. Can be arranged."

He looks quickly at you with surprise, but relief. "You?"

"Yes."

"Permanent?"

"Yes."

"Need anything?"

"I'll take care of it."

He hasn't stopped staring at you, and his surprise has taken on another nuance. You seemed to understand very well what he was getting at, just now— how is it that you, that Katrijn Verbrugge, the quiet one, the mild-mannered one, caught on so quickly? How come she's prepared to sabotage without hesitation the back-up sphere, during the experiment, and is so sure of being capable of doing it? He won't want to take the risk of asking you for details here. But he's curious about you now, another kind of curiosity. It happens to all of them sooner or later. Too bad. He will soon have other topics to ponder.

Because, of course, when the voltage surge blows the transformer, and cuts the current in the magnetic field winding, and triggers the mini-fire that renders the back-up sphere unusable, the rabbit is not incinerated, irradiated, or disintegrated. Impossible to disguise the data: the rabbit has *disappeared*. Gone, the rabbit, vanished, not one hair left, not one drop, not one molecule. After an intense, futile brain-storming session with the whole team, you will remark, with a mixture of exasperation and discouragement: "Well, the creature must have jumped into another dimension, that's all there is to it!"

And someone, likely Frölich, will laugh. But you know that it will not have fallen on deaf ears.

The homestretch now. As predicted they have come to the conclusion that it was the abrupt disruption of the magnetic field during the power failure that caused "the phenomenon." They have transferred the tests on the animals to the only sphere that is still usable, the main sphere, in spite of Jorge's protests. "Don't you want to clear up this mystery?" Frölich retorted, with disingenuous surprise. "Come on, it's potentially a lot bigger than transplant cryogenics. It might be teleportation!"

They decided to try it with primates; no reason to wait any longer. You protested too. You've gotten closer to Jorge during the last week, and not only because of the intensive speculation sessions in the lab after each disappearance of an animal. You have begun to fake a budding amorous relationship, almost without consulting each other, by mutual agreement — he made the first move, you followed his lead, that gives you reasons to be together outside the lab, shielded, you hope, from prying ears.

It is not only pretend, of course. He likes dangerous women, and he has suddenly guessed that you're one. Turn about is fair play. You were the one who liked dangerous men, back then, right? No hint of danger in this poor Jorge, and yet he lived close enough to it in his Balkan adolescence. He knows after all that you're being followed — you agreed when he remarked on it: "They've been doing it for a while." Don't feel the need to conceal as much now, what's the point, and it attracts him even more, this other Katrijn who is revealing herself as the days pass. He asks you to dinner, he takes you skating, you even go to the movies to see subtitled foreign films, it must drive your shadows crazy, but you don't care. Given the tension these days in the lab, you're entitled to let off a little steam, aren't you?

Now that the cat is out of the bag, or rather the rabbit, the mafia or its legitimate American counterparts must be drooling, but maybe they're waiting for the primate tests, or else their negotiations with Cryovital are more complicated than they thought. Doesn't matter. You'd almost like them to try kidnapping you, you imagine the look on dear Jorge's face when you take out your attackers without breaking a fingernail. You've changed, for the better, Branchet observed with amused, quite paternal approval: you dress more provocatively, you wear a little makeup, you speak up more easily in meetings. Not that there is much to say: the rabbits and mice have disappeared and they still don't know why. No rabbits have reappeared in their common cage — it would take a super-rabbit, a mutant rabbit, one that would be capable of *wanting* to escape all those tortures — no one would realize it anyway, except for you who feeds them, and you would have gotten rid of it discreetly, late at night. But you're not going to wait till they switch to primates: it would be more difficult to cover up if some of the chimps in the batch — there are always some — returned to their prison, poor creatures so traumatized that it's the only place their rudimentary brains allow them to return to, where they feel safe. Everything is ready, or almost, all that is left is to wait for the right evening, the right night, the night you let Jorge take you home, and kiss you, and so forth.

Afterwards he props himself up on his arms, with a big boyish smile. "Dr. Verbrugge, I've been waiting for that for such a long time, have I ever told you you're wonderful?" "Dr. Verbrugge?" His smile broadens: "I find the formality sexy and besides, we're just getting started. Being on a first-name basis is something you earn."

You make a joke: "You like ... experienced women?"

"Maybe. You're the first one I've met. But I'm falling seriously in love with you."

"Seriously? I'm twelve years older than you."

He shakes his head as he lays down against you. "We're the same age, Dr. Verbrugge. It's not the number of years that counts. It's the experiences. And we've had the same ones."

You look at him, his profile, the so-familiar lines of his cheekbones, of his jaw, the already spidery laugh lines at the corners of his eyes, you mumble, deliberately. "I've had a few others."

"Yes, it would seem so."

No, not right away. Not yet. You say, "I'm hungry," and you get out of bed, naked, you go to the kitchen, you take out some eggs, ham, cheese. He gets up too, naked also — he's no more prudish than you, as if using your last name was enough to clothe both of you. He doesn't bother you in the kitchen. He walks slowly around the apartment, without touching anything, making no comments when he sees the equipment you use for your martial arts training beside the expensive Bowflex, which occupies the biggest room. No comments either on how bare your shelves are. He knows it takes time to put down roots when they've been brutally torn up: people prefer to travel light, sometimes for a very long time; you saw his place when he invited you in to get warmed up, the evening when you were caught in a little storm leaving the nearby movie theatre.

"It's pretty," he says, though, when he comes back into the bedroom. He has seen the bracelet of beads, of course, with the blue glass gem, lying alone on its little shelf.

"It's from Africa," you comment as you come into the room with the omelette on a plate, and two forks. You set everything on the bed, sit down, and start eating without waiting for him. He sits down in turn, his knees up, his arms wrapped around his legs. But he says nothing. Patient. Wily. Or sensitive. It varies. He takes a mouthful of omelette, says "hmmmm!" and eats for a while without speaking.

"I understand now why you are so tireless on a skating rink," he says finally.

He didn't start with the bracelet. Of course. He reaches out with a finger, traces the line of the muscles of your forearm. "But I didn't see you as someone who would be into kung fu and stuff, I have to admit. So many hidden talents."

He's not making any accusations, but he's not exactly smiling, he's leaving the door open a crack. He's naive after all. You wanted to help him sabotage the experiments, you protested with him against the bosses, and you finally opened your body to him. Whoever or whatever you are, he trusts you. He only wants you to trust him now. For you to really be partners.

"You know what they say about curiosity and cats?"

He pretends to stretch languorously: "I'm not a cat."

"No, you don't have nine lives."

The retort just comes out, you're as surprised as he is — but for him, it was your tone of voice. He sits up, staring at you, he places one hand on your thigh, again this reflex he has to touch you in these situations, pulls it away immediately when he feels the muscle stiffen, mumbles finally, softly, with an even voice: "Who have *you* lost, Katrijn?"

Me.

Who? Who inside you just said that? You purse your lips, then force yourself to take another mouthful of omelette, vaguely shrugging your shoulders. He doesn't press it. He lies down on the bed, his hands under his neck. A long silence. You're not the one who's going to break it. What's he going to come back with now, after that?

"Do you believe in it, the thing Frölich was talking about yesterday? The strong anthropogenic hypothesis?"

You weren't expecting him to take this tack. But they surprise you sometimes. It still happens.

The strong anthropogenic hypothesis. What makes human life possible on Earth, and by extension in the universe, is regulated so tightly in all areas (such a minimal shift in one direction or another would suffice to make it impossible) that this universe must literally be made for humans — or, variation, a play on words, by humans that are consubstantial with it: one could not exist without the other.

Frölich's remark was surely not innocent: he may be starting to condition the team to the idea of future trials on human guinea pigs. If teleportation exists, and if the strong anthropogenic theory is valid, the guinea pigs must survive, wherever it is they go. A logical non sequitur rather than a valid inference on Frölich's part, who can't really know that he's right.

"A hypothesis that's difficult to disprove."

"But if the guinea pigs go into another dimension, as you suggested, and not into ours, what guarantee is there that they'll survive there? The physical laws would be perhaps — almost certainly — different."

You start laughing: "I was joking!"

"But at the stage we're at, it's a hypothesis that is no more or no less legitimate than the hypothesis of simple teleportation within our own universe, or even only on Earth."

Where's he going with this? He seems to be asking himself the question honestly, as much as he's asking you. He can't imagine... No. Absolutely not. They're intelligent, they still have imagination, but not to that extent. Not here, in any case, not this one.

It won't make any difference anyway.

"We couldn't allow ourselves to take that kind of risk," he murmurs. And concludes: "I won't allow myself to take that kind of risk," in a tone of voice that indicates clearly that this is not a conditional statement for him. If it comes to that, he'll resign.

But it won't come to that.

"Maybe people would volunteer," you remark, just to see, to prod him a little.

You carry the empty plate and the forks back to the kitchen. His voice follows you, incredulous, vaguely shocked: "Would you volunteer?"

You come back, stare at him, arms crossed, one knee on the bed, with a little knowing smile. He smiles back at you. If he's surprised to see you bring the conversation back in this direction yourself, he doesn't show it: "Ah. That's right. You like to live dangerously."

"That's right."

"And was it in your dangerous lives that you learned how to carry out sabotage without getting caught? Because I really don't know how you did it."

You put the other knee on the bed. You're straddling his thighs now, both hands on his hips. You lean over and you whisper in an excessively suggestive voice: "I could tell you, but then I'd have to kill you."

His hands reach for your back, your ass, pulling you closer. "Let's wait a bit then," he whispers in the same tone of voice, suppressing his laughter, and he lifts himself towards you to kiss you.

Afterwards, he's thirsty. He stretches across you to grab the bottle of mineral water on the bedside table, and you take the opportunity to caress his back, his side, his torso and his bum, as smooth as a teenager's. He's an adolescent, a child, the youngest of all the Egons you've met. What difference does it make? They've all been adolescents. But with him, it's now. Can that change anything?

You watch him drink. He offers you the bottle, but you say no. He drinks the whole thing. He lies down again beside you. You press yourself against him, your head on his shoulder, he has taken one of your hands, placed it flat against his, palm to palm, he has big hands, delicate wrists, you've always loved his hands and wrists, he's always laughed this way comparing your fingers, his always extending a whole phalange beyond yours. "...such a tiny little hand," he always says in a sleep-leaden voice, "tiny little Katrijn..."

You listen to his breathing slow down, you watch him closely, those long lashes, too thick for a man, the fine pores of his skin, the shrapnel scars on his right jaw — he always has scars along his jaw, on the right side, shrapnel, burns, car accident, motorcycle accident, fall as a child, youthful brawl.

You are in the compartment. There are no buttons. You have programmed everything. You hear his voice. Again. You shouldn't be hearing his voice. Kathryn, don't do it, there's still time, we can help you. *You press the button. The gas hisses into the compartment, the voice fades in the distance as the sphere closes.*

But you don't go to sleep. You see. You see through the sphere. Egon's body. One body, two bodies, ten bodies. Always the same. And all that blood.

I wake with a start, did I fall asleep? I never fall asleep. But it was his smell of orange and musk, his warmth, that lethargic silence, animal, innocent in spite of everything, in spite of him, in spite of myself. I get ready, nothing special to do, nothing to take, I can never take anything, lights out, I don't need them in the dark that is not dark to me, no shadow moving in the windows alerts the watcher, in his car, on the other side of the street.

He is sleeping. He won't wake up. I never make any noise, even though it makes no difference. He is lying there on the bed, barely covered by the sheets, still, a negative statue, dark skin against a white background, one way or another he is always lying still there every time I leave, but there's no blood here, no, no blood. Once I cut myself, I had broken the frame of our photo together, and I cut my hand on a shard of glass as long and sharp as a stiletto, there was glass everywhere, there is always glass everywhere, not this time, no, but no time to think about it, no more time, have to go, now, right away, immediately.

One last look. I always look one last time. The glow from the streetlight illuminates a blue sparkle on the shelf. If I could take something, that would be it. The bracelet. I don't know why.

I don't know why I pick it up, one arm is hanging off the bed, limply, hand open, I put the bracelet on his wrist. The blue bead against the dark skin. The contrast. I don't know why. For the journey.

I go noiselessly out the back, through the alley, running silently, I head towards Beaudry and its taxis, no way I'm taking the metro, waiting, no. The car carries me to the Technocity, which is still lit up beside the river strewn with ice jams, and it's a very clear night, and if I was on the fifth floor of Cryovital I could see the south shore stretch out towards the tower of the stadium, the familiar sloping tower, but it's not there this time, it's not from there that I'm going to leave. At the Cryovital entrance, the guards greet me without surprise, as does the agent at the security checkpoint. They don't even ask me why I've come back — insomnia, an experiment to check on, or the animals, they're used to it. I go down to the lab, I hook up the camera circuit to the device that will replay the loop of ordinary images taken yesterday, the day before or another day, I lock the door, I launch the program that will automatically set the process in motion, I activate the timer for the bombs set in each of the adjacent labs, I undress, I lie down in the compartment, comfortable, the silk, it just fits me, tiny little Katrijn, with the last bomb on my belly, set to go off just after the magnetic field disappears. No anesthetic gas. A bottle, homemade, I spill it into the compartment as the sphere closes. I am in the compartment. No buttons. No voices. Especially, no voices.

See Kathryn walking in the street. Because you're walking, aren't you, Kathryn? Yes, I'm walking, she's walking, we're walking. It's another transition, another universe, another world, but above all it's the beginning. Completely new. We're almost curious. Nice weather — no meteorological correspondences from one universe to the next, it will be a long time before there's any snow this time, too bad. And no Bridge likely for the time being, too early, but we'll find it, we're not in a hurry. No need to run.
Not yet.

Newbie Wrangler
by Timothy J. Anderson

At first it seemed the silence had woken me, ominous and heavy outside the tent. A slip of grey light slid under the canvas when a slight breeze stirred, just enough light to bring to life the serious black eyes peering at me from the other side of the brass rail at the foot of the bed. I pretended to sleep.

A grubby hand at the end of a thin grey arm nudged my foot through the glimmering sheet. A waif of the desert, I thought.

"Can I have an orange?"

Cheeky beggar, coming into the tent. At least the kid asked instead of robbing me blind in my sleep. I grunted a little and stretched, and I could hear the kid open my pack. I kept my eyes closed so I wouldn't have to look on disappointment.

"Thanks," the urchin said. "I like 'em fresh."

A pulse of light as the tent flap flashed open, and then the dim grey once more. The sound of a child's voice piping high in a language I didn't recognize, answered by several others. I burrowed my head under the pillow, enjoying the peace, the relative cool of the morning, the solitude.

A small hand shook my foot.

"Mister, can I have an orange too?"

"Yeah, sure," I mumbled. "If you can find one, go right ahead."

The last oranges had come at least a month ago. They had been a miracle, tumbling out of the supply truck and into the bright desert sun. We'd devoured them. We even ate the rinds, we were so hungry for anything that didn't come from a pouch. We'd cleared away the rotting body parts and planted the seeds in the sand and we all agreed to set aside a ration of water toward the future orange grove. For two weeks we allowed ourselves to think of a future. Then the hostilities broke out again, and our carefully tended plot of sand was cratered by shells and littered with pieces of our friends and we used our water to clean wounds.

I stretched under the thermal sheet, breathing in the citrus-scented acrid air filtered through the sheets, my tongue feeling like a foreign substance in my mouth, dry enough to click, I thought. This would be a good day to learn the local language.

A whisper of tent flap and tiny hands jiggling both my heels. "Hey! Hey!"

"Take your bloody oranges and let me sleep."

Treble giggles and the sound of sand scuffed into the legs of the bed by tiny sandals. There must have been a cease-fire, I figured. So many children wandering through the camp in the morning, looking for anything to eat after the destruction of the night before. By now they would be halfway to the rubble of their homes, taking their oranges back to anxious mothers moaning in the rubble.

The images flooded in: imploding buildings, dust, the spray of concrete, of blood, the litter of papers and lives torn apart, the noise and stench and numbness.

Another hand touched my heel and I started, drawing it up and away.

"I told you it was too late," the voice of the first beggar said. "They're all gone."

"Is there anything else?" a second voice asked.

"Nothing we want. Maybe later. Let's go!"

I stayed on the bed, lying on my stomach, and watched the patch of light where the tent didn't quite meet the sand. I waited for it to brighten, for the line of shade to move as the sun moved across the sky. I waited to feel another small hand on my foot, to see another pinched face on the other side of the brass footboard. While I waited, the memories of war played themselves out in a series of lucid dreams which I knew I could stop at any time if I got out of bed.

The children didn't come and the light got no brighter, and my memories filled my brain with a clattering montage that didn't stop when the tent flap opened and the interior brightened for a moment.

"Time to get up, newbie," a man's voice said. "Bring your guitar. We've got work to do."

The sound of canvas flapping back into place.

The kids took the oranges but not the guitar? Hunger will do that to you.

There it was, at least I thought it must be the guitar, a vague shape lying against the side of the tent. I reached out from my prone position, but the guitar was out of reach. Odd that it was out of the case. Not great to have it in this dryness. I shouldn't have brought it, not to the desert.

I hadn't. I'd left the guitar at home. The brass bed — I hadn't slept in the brass bed since I visited my grandparents after the second year of college. The oranges came weeks ago and we devoured them and planted the seeds. My feet had been taken off by a blast three days ago. Well, mostly by a blast and the rest was done by a surgeon.

The flap opened again, and in the light I could see there was no guitar, only absurdly green camouflage canvas..

"Hurry up!" the guitar voice said. "Oh...um, you stay right there and I'll be back, okay? Just hang on."

It didn't sound like anyone I knew. One of the young guys, maybe, the new recruits whose voices were changing as they grew up.

I could hear voices outside the tent, this time in English.

"An orange? And you...what did you get? Geez, the lot of you. We need instruments, things we can play."

"He could go back to sleep." It was one of the small piping voices. "We could try again."

"It's too late. The guitar's gone and it won't be back."

"He's got lots of sand," another voice said.

"And what are we going to do with more sand?" asked guitar man. "There's no end of sand and rock and earth. We need music."

There was a tense silence broken only by the shuffling sound of sandals on sand. Then a huge sigh and the voice of guitar man:

"Go. Gogogogogo. Always ask for the instrument first, and if you can't see one, ask for a tuba or a pipe organ. Or a piccolo. We need to round up a thousand piccolos. Now go!"

Off they ran, screaming shrilly.

He came into the tent, leaving the flap slightly open to the light. I squinted and rolled over so I could see him better. He looked like a boy I'd met once, on summer vacation in the middle of high school. His clothes were things my brother wore when he was a teenager: low-rise denim bellbottoms, a plaid shirt unbuttoned halfway to the navel, water buffalo sandals. Retro hippy chic. His face was still indistinct in the gloom of the tent.

"Hi," he said. I didn't answer.

"Sorry about the confusion. The kids hadn't had a decent orange in a while. They're just kids, you know? I was kinda hoping you'd have brought your guitar." He looked toward the spot where I could have sworn the guitar had been, only I knew it wasn't.

"Anyway," he went on, "not having the guitar isn't the end of the universe or anything. You remember how to sing, right?" He stood at the end of the cot, and there was no brass anything between us. I could see that the bedclothes were flat below my knees, no sign of legs or feet.

"What's going on?" I asked.

Guitar man sighed, and the sound made him more concrete somehow. "I'm a talent scout. I need to put together a huge band to make an amazing noise, but no one seems to be travelling with their instruments these days. I sent the kids for your guitar but they took the oranges instead. Oranges," he said with a chuckle in his voice, "make lousy instruments."

"You look like someone," I ventured.

"Yeah, I know. You got drunk and tried to have sex with me in your first semester at college."

Suddenly his features pulled into focus. He'd been a Jim Morrison clone: soft pouting lips, sexually charged, dangerous. I'd been the good kid: clean cut, law-abiding, and ripe for experience. The details of the party were hazy, but I remembered him coming on to me, pressing against me, and me wanting to know.

Guitar man smiled. "Can't remember my name, but you remember the rest of me quite well. Careful — I'm horny and it's been a long time."

"What are you doing here?"

He grinned. "Don't worry, newbie. I'm not expecting a rematch. Not," he quickly added, "that it wouldn't be fun. As I said, I'm here to put together a mighty shout. And I'm hoping you'll help. Come on."

There's a nasty kind of dream you have when you come out of the anaesthetic on the field. It's a dream that combines the memories of home with the reality of the battle. After they took the dangling bits of my legs off, the dreams were of the locker room at high school. All of us changing, laughing, running. And then huge explosions rocking the lockers, making them fall like dominoes. Dreams of the soccer field. Dreams of kicking the ball against the garage door forever.

"They fixed your legs," the guitar man said. "That's why you're feeling so woozy. They did another operation and fixed your legs. So let's go!"

I threw back the sheet, now a heavy grey striped wool like the ones we had in training, and there were my legs, just as I remembered them.

"Let's go let's go let's go!" he barked, a hippy parody of a drill sergeant. "Time is of the essence here. We have to get you singing."

I have no memory of getting dressed or of what I saw when we left the tent. My impression is that the day was hazy but not too hot. There wasn't another soul in sight, and we were in the desert or the brown grassy fields closer to home. And we were walking and laughing as if we really knew each other. I expected at any moment for someone I knew to come around the corner or over the next rise: a buddy from my outfit, a dead relative, a spirit guide. But guitar man, all electricity and promise, propelled me along with his ease, his fitness for the new and changing world.

"What'll you sing?" he asked. "You'd better think of it now or everyone else will be singing and you'll be mouthing the words."

It had been so long since I sang anything. Then, like a mirage slinking over the field, I could smell salt air and the sand was slippery and studded with bits of driftwood and broken shells. "Stairway to Heaven," I whispered. "That's what I'll sing."

"I had hoped for something by Jim Morrison," the man said, "but Stairway will do fine. It's a strong memory."

I was sixteen and at the beach with a boombox and a bag of marshmallows, and a girl I had never seen before loaned me her lighter to start the fire. By 10:30 I had imagined our whole life together and was ready to propose, and "Stairway to Heaven" played and we danced in the sand.

"Whoa, whoa, whoa newbie!" guitar man called out. "You're losing me! Stay with the program, okay?"

He was ahead of me, running through the beach grass toward me, and the dunes were lit by bonfires and trash cans and burning buildings.

"Sing! Let's go! Singsingsing!"

He put his arm around me and I could smell him the way I had smelled him that night, like every secret I would ever have was encrypted in his sweat. And we sang until the burning stopped and we collapsed on the sand, giddy with pleasure at being alive.

I looked at him then, the memorized pores of his face, the huge hazel eyes, and I had the courage to ask:

"Why didn't the others come?"

The face slackened, and with effort he spoke the words I could not. "I'm a wrangler. I am your purest memory of a person. Not the most important person," he said quickly, "but the simplest, most direct memory. I will be clear longer than the rest, but not for long."

He got up, brushed off the sand and held out a hand. It was true. I could remember that hand, the surprise at finding his arms to be smooth and strong, the breathtaking energy and electricity of our drunken exploration.

"Why did you want the guitar?" I asked, taking his hand and allowing him to pull me up.

"We need a big noise, lots of harmonics. People remember how to play, remember their skills, but they forget their instruments early. Once in a while we get a techhead who remembers every bit of an amp system, but we can't count on it." He strode away, across the desert and toward the mountains.

"Wait up," I called. I ran after him, and we continued in near silence. He was humming snatches of Stairway, and I knew it was to keep it fresh in my mind.

"So why did the guitar disappear?" I asked. "It was there, right?"

"The oranges," he sighed. "Those kids, the ones you remember from the peacekeeping mission, they sensed that you had a very strong fresh memory of oranges, and that's what they wanted. Memories don't last long once you're dead. They have to be corralled quickly. Do you remember the kids?"

They'd been there, in my tent. I tried to remember them, but nothing would come. The tent flap opening, a pressure on my heel, but nothing else.

"That's why I came. They were supposed to bring you and the guitar, but they got distracted. I'm the memory strong enough to get us to the meeting."

"Where I will sing Stairway to Heaven?"

"Where everyone will sing, and anyone who brought their instruments will play, and we will raise a mighty noise..." Guitar man stopped. "A mighty noise, and we hope it is enough."

"Enough for what?"

He looked toward the mountains and took a deep breath. "Enough to wake God," he said.

I looked toward the mountains too, half expecting a shaft of white light and a booming voice to welcome me into heaven.

"This isn't getting us anywhere," guitar man said. "Where did you last meet God? Can you remember the place well enough to get us there?"

The desert landscape shimmered and shook as I went through the various possibilities, memories dissolving as soon as I touched them. I had not met God on a golf course, as many claim to do. I had certainly called the name at moments when it seemed appropriate — often in my bedroom or the bedrooms of relative strangers — but name-dropping isn't the same as meeting. There were the children at play in the hot rubble. Yes, in a way I suppose I had glimpsed God from the top of a tank patrolling a war zone. I had met God in narrow laneways full of debris and splintered pieces of wood, God looking out from unglazed windows and scraping up a life from nothing, out of chaos.

Then we were there. The two of us, the guitar man looking as relaxed and easy as he always had, and me in my fatigues, and there was a steeply rising curved pebbly passageway between the buildings, narrow enough to be slightly shaded from the near-noon sun.

"Up there," I whispered. "God is up there."

We walked up the path, the debris shifting in and out of focus. I remembered that dented can. I remembered a bleached chicken bone, a rusty bottlecap, a crushed cigarette pack. I knew with certainty that when we got to the top of the curve, we would come out into a plaza with an improbably intact fountain, not working but in one piece, and lines of white washing, like huge truce flags, hung out in the sun. In the fragile peace and the brilliant sun, the face of God would be shining.

"It's been harder and harder to keep God awake," said the guitar man. "It's a strain, paying attention all the time. Tiring. It takes more and more noise just to register. And when God falls asleep, the universe runs amok. It's our job," he said. I could hear his breath shallowing out as we ascended the path.

"There are lots of newbies," he continued. "No shortage, not these days. But they're dumbstruck, so busy looking ahead for the damned light they've been told about that we can't harness their memories, can't ride 'em to a meet. It's hard enough to keep God interested twenty-four seven without surrounding the Deity with slack-jawed sightseers."

Then, slowing down a bit to catch his breath, he sang.

I joined in, still walking forward and up, seeing the sharp shadows of the sun on the battered buildings. I felt lighter, my legs felt stronger than they had been on the sands. Faces looked out of the windows, smiling faces, tired faces. There was a little girl with serious black eyes and a half-eaten orange in her grimy hands.

The young man fell behind, but I heard him call out: "Thanks for the ride. Sing. Loud! And when you're done, come ride the newbies!"

I strode into the plaza, playing my guitar and singing at the top of my lungs, the sound bouncing off the walls and through the flapping white sheets and the young man faded into the stones. The wind brought the smell of oranges from the desert grove and the sound of singing, of a world singing and playing, and pulsing into the ear of God until we lost the memory of music, of language, of voice.

Light Remembered

by Daniel Sernine
translated by Sheryl Curtis

The sun ... dazzling fragments on the River, beyond the reeds. Shards of light in ceaseless motion in the wakes of the skiffs.

My brother Athep and I had gone to the River's edge, well upstream from Bedrachein, to trap a genet. The birds' nests, in the umbels of the papyrus, attracted them. Occasionally, they'd get so bold as to climb up the supple stems. With sticks and a net, we could hope to catch one alive, despite its sharp teeth and quick moves.

We had taken two servants with us, boys scarcely older then we were, who occasionally shared in our games.

I see the River in my mind's eye, speckled with light. I smell the rich loam of the shores, warm and soft around our ankles, tepid water reaching to our calves, clouded by the silt. I hear the splashing, the laughter, the stifled exclamations when Athep or I fell ass backwards in the mud.

A sudden movement; a brief cry. But just before that, a wet, powerful snap. Then more screaming, sharp cries of terror, and a segment of the river bank fleeing toward the River, Sep struggling. It was no island of mud, but the back of a crocodile, its powerful tail ploughing the purple marbled silt. Already the boy was beyond our reach. His arms flailed in the water, his white rimmed eyes staring at me, reproaching me for backing away. Then Athep's voice, which had deepened only a few months earlier, once again high pitched, his finger pointing. There, two more lumpy backs converging where Sep's head had gone under, diving in turn, water sprayed by the whipping of their tails, the River bubbling pink at the scene of their struggle. Sep surged up once more, one more terrible time, with a cry drowned in water. Sep, his head lacerated, his arm flailing, blood spurting from where his other arm should have been. Sep, snatched again so abruptly that a whirlpool formed where he was dragged below.

All around, dozens of ibis took flight in a feathery commotion, disturbed by the turmoil.

Gold ... Only the uppermost portion of the walls caught the rays of the declining sun, taking on a pale golden hue. The garden, with its balsam trees, lay in shadow; exquisite blue lotus blossoms floated in basins. I was playing zente with my sister Nemout. She bent her shaved head, with its black, velvety fuzz, over the small checkerboard. Mother had the harpists practising for a reception the next day.

I asked my mother questions about Sep, my servant. "And where did his ka go?"

She looked at me seriously

I insisted, "If the ka is the spiritual double of our body, as Amenhep teaches us, and if Sep's body was torn into pieces and eaten, then where did his ka end up?"

"He will never find rest, Neferkh. The body must be preserved after death or the ka no longer has a shelter."

That's exactly what I had thought. I found it unfair. "Even mummies turn into dust one day," I continued, after moving one of the cone-shaped pawns.

"That's why we place an effigy of the dead person in the serdab at the mastaba. When the ka no longer has a body to dwell in, it takes refuge in the statue."

"So we never die," I concluded.

"It's not that simple. There's the ba, your soul, and the khu, the divine spark..."

"But we won't die," I insisted, "You'll never die, will you, Mother?"

Nemout looked up from the game, surprised by the ardour of my question — my protest. She knew nothing at all of the fears that kept me awake at night, that led me up to the roof to look out across the western desert.

Mother smiled at me sadly and made an effort to reassure me, "No, Neferkh, we don't die. Not absolutely."

On that day, I understood that one could die a little, yet
not completely.

Daylight, merciless daylight, the sun so strong it turned
the sky white, above the bleached walls of the city. Men-
nofer, limestone and alabaster.... The flaxen whiteness of
the loincloths and robes of those in the procession in which
my brother and I took part. I looked for my mother, but she
was with the princesses, and the din of the sistra and the
drums added to my vertigo. The palm trees that bordered
the sacred road, shading it, seemed terribly sparse to me.

We carried a few spikes of barley, held together in a small
spray. It weighed nothing at all, but we had to hold it chest
high, with both hands. We were not taking a handful of
fodder to an ass, but an offering to the God Sokari.

In the city, the cortege had been delayed for quite a while
because an elderly priest had chosen that morning to die
suddenly. Now, it seemed to me that the cortege had left
the city an eternity ago and yet Saqqarah lay only two miles
to the west. The parasols, the heads and shoulders of the
adults, blocked the pyramid from my view until we arrived
at the scared enclosure.

After the brilliance of the daylight, our walk through
the gallery seemed like some nocturnal crossing to me. It
was only near the end of the passageway that I could once
again see well enough to make out the frescos on the walls.
The image of Ptah was omnipresent, his shaved head, his
silhouette wrapped as tight in the white linen as a mummy
in its strips.

Then back into the dazzling light, the vast courtyard
where our squinting eyes turned once again to the pyramid,
with its six titanic tiers under which King Djeser awaited
our offerings. My cousin Thosis claimed that other pyramids, further north, stood at least twice as high. Since I
hadn't been to Gizeh yet, I protested. Surely, he must be
lying!

The procession stopped for a moment, for some problem
or other at the head end. I was thirsty and I needed shade.

Curious about everything, I glanced through a pillared aisle. A few temple attendants were waiting there for the procession to pass so that they could cross the courtyard in turn. I saw one drinking from a gourd. He noticed me watching him and I must have looked so pitiful that he beckoned to me. With a gesture, I asked if I could have a drink and, when he answered, I slipped out of the procession as Thosis and Athep were looking the other way, then climbed a few steps to the columns. It was only after drinking that I noticed the bundle they had laid down on the slabs; a long white package on a stretcher, a human silhouette swaddled in a shroud, legs bound tightly together, arms crossed over its chest, the shape of the nose and brow visible through the fabric.

The men must have been observing me since two of them laughed gently when they saw my reaction — I suppose I must have gone a little pale. I handed the gourd back, thanked the man vaguely, and returned to my place in the procession without a backward glance.

The dead man, lying on the slabs, had looked like a sleeping giant to me, a hood pulled over his head by mischievous children. For some reason, I would have liked to be there when he woke.

Dawn.... The purple hue of the eastern sky, as stars still shone in the West, then that uncertain colour, between pearl and azure, just before the arc of the sun rises above the horizon — O Amun-Re, your golden brightness at dawn, your warm light when the night is over!

I had never left the valley before. I had never even crossed the River, when my father took me for my first trip, at the age of 12. How impressed I was to see that mountainous horizon, sand and rock stretching to infinity, under the blinding morning sun. And there, far away, a serpent, no; another caravan, wavering in the heat of the desert.

Traveling for days and days with my even-tempered father, until that evening when the sea lay before us. It was the gulf, its other shore visible at the horizon. But such a vast expanse of water was beyond my comprehension. The Red Sea, the real one, lay much farther to the south. Our ships ventured there, bringing back copper, turquoise or garnet from the Sinai, gold, porphyry and emeralds from the coastal mountains. Beyond them, much farther away, Amenhep had explained to me, where the sea touches another shoreless sea, lay the land of Punt, from which our first navigators had returned after months of travel, loaded with ebony and ivory.

It was, claimed my father, even farther than Nubia.

And I watched him leave, on board one of our ships that resembled the river-bound skiffs, upswept at both stern and bow, but much larger, and rigged with masts and sails.

Then I went back to Men-nofer with the caravan, to await my father's return. In the evening, I would look East, beyond the rich colours with which the setting sun painted the fields and fig orchards; I would look at the highlands where the desert starts. The precious few caravans I spied would keep me awake until the next morning, when I would fret on the shore until the ferries arrived.

Time passed slowly, I believed then, and I could conceive of no longer wait than that one.

The sand, dazzling... whiter than salt, as if the very light of the sun had been ground to powder and sprinkled over the desert. That was my impression as I exited from the vertical shaft and tottered for a moment on the upper rungs. Athep, who had climbed up ahead of me, reached down and grabbed me by the shoulder until my dizzy spell passed. Around us, the workers were silent on the site of the mastaba, ready to lower the vertical slab that would close the pit, and then fill the shaft.

I turned, arms slack, and allowed my eyes to roam over the necropolis where the mastabas stood in rows, low and squat, as large as nobles' mansions.

Father was not noble enough to have his mastaba in the sacred enclosure, in the shadow of Djeser's pyramid, but the pharaoh had made him a gift of a sarcophagus carved in diorite, as a reward for an entire lifetime of loyalty. It was Father we had just looked at for the last time, in his tomb, the flame of the torches gleaming on its polished surface, kindling the golden and turquoise ornaments in the dark.

In keeping with tradition, we had left only a few objects down below, those which my father had cherished the most: the ebony palette and the gold-ringed brush with which he re-did his scribes' accounts certain evenings, and the exquisite bronze lamp he lit at such times.

Just the day before, the painters had made the final touches to the frescos where Tsehout, my youngest sister, indifferent to the solemness of the moment, had entertained herself by identifying each of us among the painted figures.

We made our way back to the city. Weeks would go by before we would be able to return to the completed mastaba and place our offerings in the funerary chapel.

"What will he eat until then?" asked Tsehout, and my brother explained to her that the meal scenes of the frescos in the tomb would be enough to nourish his ka for some time.

Under our steps, the ground had returned to its natural colour, alternatively light, then dark as the shadows of mastabas in their rows followed one another. Everything was in order. Yet tears flowed from my eyes without end.

Molten copper.... Oh how I loved that far too brief instant when the vermillion sun burned into my gaze, leaving green circles on the inside of my eyelids when I shut my eyes.

It was at that time of day that I had gone, with Tiout, to my father's mastaba. We had dallied, playing hide and seek among the date palms of a plantation lying at the very edge of the cultivated land, pursuing our race into the desert, where I had pinned her to the sand-swept ground. I felt her nipples harden under the linen and I pulled the straps of her robe down to nuzzle her breasts. I tasted salt on her skin.

Tiout stopped me after a moment, protesting that it was not appropriate, but I knew that Father loved her as well and approved of our upcoming marriage.

Nevertheless, I stood up and my loincloth once again hung in its usual folds by the time we arrived at the cemetery, just as the orange disk of the sun rested on the horizon. I purchased a torch from the guardian, near his fire, and we entered my father's tomb.

In addition to the incense, I had brought a skullcap, much like the one Father wore when he had to go down into the cellar, as an offering. His tomb, so deep in the ground, had to be much colder than the cellar under our home.

In the chapel, I recited the usual prayers, while Tiout silently examined the frescos that showed Father accepting and then consuming the offerings. I lit the incense then, solemnly, placed the skullcap on the altar. My fiancée, I believe, smiled a little at my grave countenance. A bluish daylight seeped in through the doorway, blotted out by the glare of the flame. I took the torch, held it gingerly at arm's length through the slot in the wall behind the altar and bent forward to rest my forehead on the stone edge. The horizontal slot was no broader than the palm of a hand, just large enough to provide an airway between the chapel and the serdab. That's where my father's belongings had been placed, his bed, his best clothing, a precious chest, a very fine bow he had used for hunting when he was young. Just opposite the slot stood an effigy of my father, one leg ahead as if he were walking to meet me. The first time I had seen him like that I had shuddered with fear, as if Father could have stepped down from his pedestal, walked up to me and slipped his arms through the slot. Even a few months later, that image still gripped me, an illusion of movement in the torch's flickering light, the appearance of life in the warm hue of the fire, darkness quivering in the farthest corners of the serdab, and that silence.... I could not stop myself from thinking about the crypt, twenty ells under ground, twenty ells of shaft filled with gravel and, behind the slab, the absolute darkness of the tomb, the nonexistent colours of the frescos, the dull diorite of the sarcophagus, and that silence, oh that silence...

Once again that day, I retreated hastily, withdrawing the torch, leaving the serdab in darkness. Tiout and I left the mastaba and kept the torch lit until we reached the city walls.

On our way, I thought about how cruel it was to lock someone so far away from daylight.

✠ ✠ ✠

The Moon ... when she was full and at the zenith of her course, she was almost dazzling in her whiteness. Around her, stars died from her ardour.

She was almost full, that night, as I walked into the western desert, the land of the dead. In the kingdom, we always bury the dead on the western shore of the River; it's always on the western shore that we build their mastabas and pyramids. It is said that their ba haunts the desert.

I had to know.

At my back, the moon rose, red, swollen, diseased.

I had to know. What? I had no idea. My childhood was a matter of the past, my youth wasted in wild times, stupid deeds and petty treacheries. Yet, the questions, doubts and anguish kept coming back to mind.

After sunset, I walked for hours carrying a gourd, a lamp, some oil, torches that I could light as needed and a heavy walking stick, which I could use as a club. Its knotty wood, gripped tightly in my hand, was supposed to ward off my fear. Yet, on two occasions, I shivered as the jackals howled in the distance.

I had enough time that night to go back over my entire life — and how naïve it was to believe my summing up was complete, that all I needed was a few hours! That morning, I had argued with Mother. She had called me a good-for-nothing and thrown a few of my escapades in my face. As if a box had been opened, all of the pranks of my boyhood came back to me. One memory was very clear in my mind. Akhem and I were 15 years old and had stayed behind in the sacred enclosure as evening fell, when Djeser's pyramid stretched its shadow well beyond the walls. At the end of a long courtyard with a discrete door, we had spotted what we thought were the embalming chambers. A short climb, small barred windows at the top of a wall… there was no light in the room other than the dying embers under a large caldron. But the bitter odour of the naphtha, bitumen and natron left no trace of doubt.

Once our eyes had adjusted to the shadow, there was a lot to see: tables laden with utensils, bowls and crucibles, strips wound in rolls or soaking in vats, urns leaning

against the walls, long tables too high for dining.... I felt
the tension well up in Akhem. He had just recognized a
long, pale form, a cadaver rolled in a clinging shroud.

I had noticed the body almost at my first glance and was
only able to draw my morbid attention from it after a while,
thinking back on the priest who had died the day of the
ceremony, a few years earlier. Yet, what I stared at now,
silent, chest tight, was the tall black statue standing against
the farthest wall.

Anpu.

Anpu, his almond eyes rimmed with gold, his long ears
standing erect, his pointed muzzle, bracelets and necklaces
of precious metal. Black, so black, hands widespread, arms
stretched partly out as if to receive... a visitor? An offering?

Anpu , who brought Asar back to life and has reigned
over the underworld since.

A dark phantom standing in the shadow, I could only
see one of his eyes, on the side of his head. And that eye
stared back at me. I was unable to move under its gaze.

The secrets of the embalmers lay there, in that room,
in those vials and sachets. But what did they know of the
Mystery, the great Mystery? The god with the jackal's head,
did he speak to them sometimes?

I learned nothing about it that night, nor any of the
nights afterwards, nor during the years that followed.

In the desert, a thousand steps or less from a hamada,
I stopped when my legs could no longer carry me, letting
my burden drop to the sand, making the effort to take a
few final strides, collapsing to my knees and just barely
saving the small flame of my lamp. The moon shone so
brightly that my prostrate body cast a pool of shadow before
me, to my right.

The silence caught up with me, kept at bay until that
time by the murmur of the sand beneath my sandals. A
planet shone, pink. Probably I had known its name in the
days when I had been Amenhep's best student. The rocky
outcropping ahead of me was perhaps closer and lower
than I had thought.

For a long time, I heard only my own breathing, harsh
with fatigue. But it finally eased. The desert was silent,

absolutely silent. It had been a long while since I had heard the howling of the night hounds.

Perhaps I dozed, despite my anguish, despite my hunger. Perhaps I fell asleep, as I squatted back on my haunches.

When I opened my eyes, or at least when consciousness returned behind my eyes, a jackal sat some distance away, to my left, its back dark, its ears pricked up, its eyes shining.

Under the full moon, it stared at me, alone and immobile. And I, I who had always lived in the city, I had no idea whether what it felt was curiosity, indifference, or an appetite that waited merely for the reinforcement of its pack mates to be satisfied. Carefully, moving only my head and torso, I made sure there were no other jackals coming up on me from behind. Everywhere, the sand was grey, almost white.

When I looked back at the jackal, it had not moved, apart from its head... But even that had barely moved either, not really, yet something had changed... its shape perhaps? Was its muzzle longer, its eyes stretched... or was it just a trick of the shadows? And that alteration in its gaze, surely that was just my imagination running wild? A gaze that appeared more ... absent, more mineral, and yet more difficult to escape.

Then, there was nothing, nothing but a jackal trotting off, not to distance itself from me but merely to continue on its way, turning ever so slightly in order to remain out of my stick's reach. It disappeared among the rocks that rose out of the desert a short distance north and west.

I stood up. My legs almost gave way beneath me, exploding into pins and needles, and I had to lean on my stick for a moment. Then, I took a few steps, walking in a circle, stretching my legs.

Hesitantly, I picked up my gourd, which was much lighter than when I had set out, I lit a torch from the small flame of my lamp, and I started to walk, my shadow now following behind. Where was I heading? I had no idea. But it seemed to me that it was not to the den of some simple jackal.

Up close, the outcropping of rocks turned out to be nothing more than a few large stones, and the hamada, a modest cliff that children could have scaled in a minute. I stopped. Those black spots I saw in the rock, were they the shadow of a few projections on the rock face, were they vertical bands traced by moonlight, or were they caves at the foot of the cliff? It was that possibility that stopped me in my tracks as if some icy hand had grabbed me by the throat, and I felt my heart pound. If I had wanted to make sure, I would have had to carry my torch to within a few steps of those dark hollows. Those grottos, were they not doors into the underworld? The idea became certainty as soon as it was formulated in my mind.

I fell to my knees. Or possibly, terror cut my legs out from under me. Beside me, the torch cast a yellow circle on the sand. I looked, a little to my right, in an effort to make something out among the large rocks where the carrion beast had disappeared.

When I looked back to the cliff once again, a human silhouette stood a few feet from the caves, as tall as a statue, completely black in the moonlight. The ears that rose from its head were those of a jackal.

The light.... All that remains of it are memories, and they seem paler and paler to me as time passes. Yet, I picture the small golden flame of a lamp being waved before my eyes by someone as if to determine if I were lucid, to see if my eyes would track it.

I was home, in the dwelling that had been my father's where my mother still lived. Mother and my wife, Tiout, busied themselves around me, in a room where the sun filtered in through a curtain of palms. I had returned to Men-nofer delirious, after an absence of two days, and they feared for my sanity. The fever had finally broken, but the delirium seemed to persist, a nervousness that caused me to babble and grasp at anyone who bent over me.

Over time, I learned to keep quiet, not to speak about He who, at night, walks the lands of the setting sun, among the hyenas and jackals. He who stands at the gates to the underworld. I no longer knew, in fact, if the vision had preceded the delirium or was born out of it. At the time of my death, I told myself, it would all become clear to me.

I still know nothing.

Time passes. I'm aware of the years, vaguely, but I haven't counted them in quite some time. I'm waiting. I'm waiting to see the light again.

Ah, the light! A moment of light, nothing more than a moment, a brief glimmer, which would consume me merely by shining on me, I'm so dry and brittle. Then I would rise like smoke and dissipate in the void. All my memories of light would blaze in an instant of glory and then expire, and I with them.

Up above, the mastaba is long gone, no doubt, or it has been buried under ells of sand, which the centuries have blown over the necropolis.

I have neighbours. I vaguely sense their mute presence. But their slumber is so deep. One of them, a most fortunate bastard, was visited by pillagers, sometime during the first millennium of our stay. Perhaps faith had vanished up above? Still, his tomb was looted and he was able to see the light. I can only hope for as much. I care no more for the few baubles of my past life, that ever so brief slice of life out in the open. Perhaps my crypt has collapsed more entirely than his. Perhaps the sand has buried it more completely. No mortal has ever made his way to my tomb.

Centuries have made way for millennia and only the occasional deep rumble leads me to think that there are still kingdoms on the surface of the Earth and that, possibly, people are still building pyramids.

The Singing
by Dan Rubin

Larlaluk knew her time had come. She awoke, feeling the wind pulsing against the sides of the skin tent.
The sun must be hiding, but it did not matter to her. She
had learned to see with her hands, now that her eyes had
grown dim and clouded. Over all things there was a feeling of waiting; she felt as if she were already sitting in
that high place with the sun warm upon her face.

Quietly, she rolled over and sat up, reaching for her
leggings, then finding the skin shoes her son's wife had
made. She felt the softness of fur against her wrinkled
old feet as she pulled them on. She drew her parka from
beneath her head and unrolled it, pulling it on with difficulty, laughing under her breath at the pain in her joints,
knowing it would not last. Just as in the throat singing,
when your opponent's voice falters, while your own
surges and continues, she knew with a delicious certainty
that today would be her day.

Reaching for her drum, she breathed the warm, familiar
smells one more time, before crawling out and closing
the tent flap behind her. Outside the light was still dim,
but the warbles of the earliest birds confirmed that the
sun was not far away. The moss beside the tent was soft
beneath her feet as she shuffled down the rocky path to
the cove to check one last time.

No, the umiak was not there. Only the smaller boats
lay on the beach. Kelarjik had not returned. Four days
earlier, with the big skin boat loaded and ready, he had
embraced her just once, but fiercely.

"My mother, we will find the place where the seals still breed. But if they are truly gone, we will return before the day of the long sun."

Then he had joined the others in the umiak. She had listened to their singing, the sound of the paddles dipping, until the sea swallowed even that and she knew they had passed out of the cove.

Whether his quest had been successful or not, he was gone now. There would be no seal fat for her to chew here. The ones who had stayed behind were not part of her son's family. Her time had come.

The third planet is a moisture-shrouded sphere, a great round eye, looking outward, seeing and being seen. Its satellite, dry as death, a stopping place for those drawn onward toward water.

The ship sank slowly toward the Sea of Dreams, its great shining ovoid mass settling silently into the lunar dust. As internal mechanisms shifted from stasis into flow, fourteen cephalopods emerged, swimming into the observation bubble to join their comrades.

Long ages ago, on a water planet light-years distant, they had risen to full consciousness, neural nets spreading to unite many thousands of polyps, then expanding outward, toward new points of light. After their home planet had been encompassed, forms protected by a water-resistant skin evolved to move outward into space, linked by simultaneous neural resonance.

So the polyps of the planet Tthys yearned starward, seeking other places endowed with the liquid element. Individuals were adapted for the long crossing, selected and placed in stasis. These were the ones chosen for this delicate assignment, impeccably selected and trained for planet seeking. Over the centuries, they had expanded, passing from star to star, planet to planet, moving outward along the galactic arm.

Within the ship's observation bubble fourteen Tthyans gathered. Twining multiple eyestalks upward, they swayed in agreement that all was ready. Their surge of joy was felt simultaneously by ten billion others scattered across a thousand star systems.

The blue green planet that loomed above them was perfect, ready for colonization. With liquid water in abundance and no signs of intelligent life, it was ready for settlement. Only about a third of the surface was blemished by rock and ice. Soon this would be eliminated, clearing the entire planet to prepare it for their coming.

This would indeed be a celebrated feat of planet forming, they agreed in one sinuous wave. Great sensory reward would await them. The chosen navigators separated themselves from the mass of living tissue, reasserted their outer coverings then made their way toward the entry pods.

With the efficiency for which they had been raised, each pod navigator checked fuel requirements, drive units and landing vanes. It had been more than three hundred cycles since this equipment had been used, and even longer since the disrupters had been armed. For the planet's land masses to be uniformly redistributed, and all lower life forms eliminated, the disrupters would have to fire in exact sequence, blanketing the planet's surface in flame. After only a short time they were ready.

Seven slender silver pods emerged from the shadow of the great rippling oval ship then rose from the moon's surface, speeding toward rendezvous with the third planet.

Larlaluk slowly made her way upslope, judging from the softness beneath her feet that she had left the path the people used when they went for water. She followed the slope of the land, breathing hard, smelling heather and hearing the swell of bird song.

For years she had come this way daily, to sit at the top of the sea bluff above the mouth of the little harbour, where she could, in the past, look out over the grey, wrinkled surface of the water and learn those songs that only the ocean knows.

Larlaluk knew it was time to give the songs back. They were like the shapes made by a hunter when the storm kept him inside for many days. Carved from bone or tusk, so alive it seemed the polar bear would leap from your hand, they were made to please only the hunter, in tribute to the animal's spirit. No one would think of keeping such an object. They would be found discarded in the place where the hunter's tent had been, beside a pile of rocks.

She reached the crest of the hill. The wind, fresh with salt, began to tickle her skin. Her face crinkled into a smile as she sat upon the low flat rock that she knew would be waiting.

Her hand brushed along the ground, remembering the many times she had sat here over the years, the times she had come to this place to find songs, or to think about the needs of the people. How fine it had all been. Her hand encountered some small round shapes. Ah, she thought, blueberries. She gathered several and brought them up to her mouth, her tongue already watering. They were hardly a mouthful, not enough to sustain a person, but they were very good.

She knew that the sea was open and empty. No great mountains of ice had come this year. That is why the seals had moved north, needing ice on which to rear their young. The sun began to break through. The warmth felt good, but what good was warmth without food? Larlaluk had not eaten in many days, but had settled into the lightness of fasting, feeling herself almost free, light as one of those small white birds that dip and wheel above the beach. Ready to fly.

Drum in hand she waited, breathing in the mist that rose from the wave-washed rocks far below, waited for the sun to break through and warm her face.

Pod seven approached planetary orbit and banked steeply in a descending spiral. As the planet's surface drew nearer, Nzmbktlth watched a rough coastline appear, grey ocean alternating with pastel tones of land.

There, rising up to meet him, Nzmbktlth saw the site for the final disrupter, a ledge high on the rocks above the wide expanse of water. Beside the narrow opening where the inlet cut deeply into the land he saw strange rounded grey lumps along the shore. Those grey curves must be some primitive organism, sucking up sustenance from the rock. He knew the survey crew had done their work well. Other than a few abnormal geometric structures found in dry areas, there was no sign of intelligence here, no hint of resonance. Only the convoluted configurations of land and sea, the variations of temperate and warmer vegetation to be found on planets with an excess of land mass.

Nzmbktlth guided the pod to a perfect landing, then prepared for land locomotion. After inflating a protective bubble with water, he began rolling uphill, toward the designated coordinates for the final disrupter. But something waited there, something unexpected.

As Larlaluk felt the sun burning through the mist, she raised her drum. In her mind's eyes she could still see her uncle stretching the softened circle of tanned leather, her father's face on the day she received her name, her mother's hands sewing her first pair of shoes, and then she thought of her two sons, Lemlatik, who had been lost to the bear, that day out on the sea ice, and Kelarjik, sitting in the umiak with her grandson and granddaughter. All that remained now were her songs.

And Larlaluk sang,

> May the sun rise well
> May the sun rise well
> May the earth appear
> May the earth appear
> Brightly shone upon.

Nzmbktlth had reached the crest of the land when a strange sensation caused him to slow, then stop. Up ahead, something jointed was moving. As he strained his eyestalks forward to observe it, his aural cavities noted a strong, steady rhythm.

Instantly he opened a direct communication channel to the great ship waiting on the lunar surface. The command crew gathered to listen in awe to the strange, unknown vibrational pattern. It was utterly unlike anything previously encountered. Obviously a work of pattern and intelligence, the overlapping sounds rose, swelled, gradually stopped.

As the sun shredded the mist, Larlaluk felt it warming the deep wrinkles of her face, felt it reaching into her, touching her heart. With each song she gave back to the sea, something grew lighter in her then lifted away. In this lightness she felt as if the sun itself had joined her, as if a great shining globe lay just before her. She felt herself lifting, preparing to fly away.

> And she sang,
> Like a bird I fly
> Like a bird I fly
> Always toward you
> Always toward the sun.

And Larlaluk knew that this was all there was. Just light and sea, rock and moss and sun. Nothing more.

It took only a short time for Nzmbktlth to install observation posts and seven cycles for him to return to the mother ship. The crew was in complete resonance about what he had found. Nothing like this had ever been encountered in all the one thousand ninety two known planets of the galactic arm. This pattern would be recorded, protected, cherished and studied.

The Tthyans made only one stop on their way out of the planetary system. On the far side of the outermost planet they positioned a repeater, broadcasting the pattern on all known frequencies, enshrining forever the beautiful sounds they had found in this unexpected place. There they left it, calling out through all time:

> May the sun rise well
> May the sun rise well
> May the earth appear
> May the earth appear
> Brightly shone upon.

Our Lady of The Snows
by Nancy Kilpatrick

Warmth erupted in Marielle's heart and slid through her limbs and she wondered if she was having a heart attack or something. Her voice sounded to her own ears laced with both hope and fear when she said, "You wanna get rid of that?"

The waif-girl crouched on the curved metal staircase sucked on a thin black cigarette that stank of marijuana, not that Marielle hadn't tried it in her mis-spent youth, but life was too hard for such pleasures now when you had to be alert, what with crazy drivers in the summer and ice-slicked sidewalks in the winter. The girl's Huskie-pale eyes flickered with recognition, and a hair-second later those orbs flashed sympathy and distaste, back and forth one after the other, like the two eyes together couldn't figure out which way to go. Marielle had got used to such looks. Most people on the island of Montréal didn't mind street kids, but old street people, well, that was too sad a story to interrupt your cell phone call with. When time eroded the glamour and the wildness of personal independence, it left behind a slippery despair that wouldn't be grasped, so you couldn't do anything much about it, and most people wouldn't try to cope with the helpless feeling someone like Marielle inadvertently created in them, not while they had to work enough hours to pay their mortgages. What do you do with a thin old woman with white hair who isn't playing poor but really is? Most turned away, but some tossed coins at her when she stood or sat at the spot she staked out on the corner of boulevard St. Laurent and Duluth, south east side, near the optician's, at least spring, summer and fall. Her favourite spot by far was at the door of Schwartz's except she had to beat that other guy there, and he was crazy-glued to the sidewalk. Winter, well, you couldn't trust the weather from hour to hour, but you could bank on the snow. One girl brought her a sandwich, or some soup or a muffin or something a couple times a week on her way home from work. At least that was human, although Marielle wasn't quite sure what being human meant anymore, now that she'd turned into a crone.

Old age hit far worse than she'd imagined, although nobody'd ever mentioned how it would really be, joints aching all the time, a bit light-headed now and again, and feeling frail like she had the bones of a bird. Then, too, she hadn't figured when she was twenty that she'd be so poor and lonely at sixty, but life's full of surprises, like maybe some trickster up in the sky was working overtime just to get a few extra jollies from the human puppets he dangled.

The girl on the step pulled on her blonde dreads and sucked on the stainless steel ring in her lower lip, caught between wanting to give up the statue for free out of some misplaced guilt or sense of duty, and asking for payment, since she was, after all, selling junk — post her July 1st move — hoping to make some cash probably for some entertainment to get her through the turmoil of a new apartment that didn't look quite as good now that she was in it. Marielle helped her out. She reached deep into the pocket of her dress and pulled out a coin. "This enough?" she asked.

The girl looked relieved. "Sure," she said, and took the dollar. "It's yours."

Marielle bent to pick up the statue of the Madonna. She turned it over and over in her hands. Plaster, hollow inside, the bust went from the cloth-draped head to about mid-chest where a chalk heart was embossed and Madonna-like hands hovered protectively close by. *N-9* had been carved into her back, at the base, and Marielle thought: the number when it's all over, before anything new has begun, like death, before rebirth is underway, if there is a rebirth or an afterlife or whatever those New Age people have come to call the white light. Ideas that'd made sense before but now that life wasn't an endless ocean voyage and the land of death had come into sight, somehow she couldn't quite make those visions fly. The best she could figure was "everything recycles", which didn't have much cachet to it, but at least it could be proved.

This Madonna started life as an altar piece but somebody along the way had painted her glossy black, though the insides were still white. Marielle remembered seeing ones like her in their original state in niches in the churches of her youth. Now, what with abandoned cathedrals being sold and turned into the high-priced condos that littered the city core and bumped up the cost of housing so much nobody could afford the rents, such relics of a softer, gentler age were available to the general public for a song, or at least a loonie. Of course, Marielle hadn't set foot in a church in years for anything more than the central heating when she was caught too far from home and the temperature plummeted. Or the annual Basilica Notre Dame gift basket with a frozen turkey for Christmas. Too bad she didn't have a stove, just a hotplate, but you could always exchange the big cold bird for cookable food at the foodbank.

"Our Lady of the Snows," Marielle said, pulling the black statue close to her face and stared into the hollows of her carved eyes, which didn't give back any sign of recognition.

The girl on the step shifted uneasily, then smiled falsely before looking away. Just another mad old lady, Marielle figured she was thinking, but if this young thing lived long enough there was a possibility she would be stepping into Marielle's worn shoes someday. Happened a lot here, the result, Marielle believed, of living on an island where everybody struggled to be independent.

Marielle returned to her one and a half small rooms in the building of one and a half room apartments that housed retired people with only the government pension, transient drug dealers, single moms loaded down with a bunch of kids, and crazies, one of which she had been branded on more occasions than she could remember. Like everybody else in the building, she lived on Bien-être Social-Welfare — if you could call it living, $450 a month, not enough, since the room cost $415 of that. Even with the food banks, she had to work the corner most days just to get enough for things like toilet paper, and the occasional luxury of bus tickets, in case she wanted to go anywhere, like to lug home the free food on the days she was exhausted, or to the Musée des Beaux-Arts on the no-ticket nights — she did love good artwork. Sometimes she thought that maybe she should have gone on the meds they wanted her to take for depression. Then she could have got the medical welfare — an extra $100 a month! — but then she'd have to buy the meds, so it was all the same, and this way she wouldn't have to be dull and stupid, although some days when the depression got like a powerful black hole sucking her in before she could think about it, turning zombified seemed like it might be a blessing.

She placed the plaster black Madonna on the windowsill, next to the hotplate. Maybe later she'd turn her so she could look out onto Avenue des Pins and the continuous-motion vehicular and pedestrian traffic, mostly students from the university who couldn't find housing closer to school. For now, though, Mary faced the room, all nine by twelve feet of it. Not one of the prettier virgins Marielle'd seen. Still, this one had something going for her, maybe the lips, almost turned up at the corners, so she wasn't quite as unhappy as others. The Virgin's funny hollow black eyes seemed to scan the place, not that there was much to see, the refrigerator, which was as small as a good-size cardboard box and a ratty old sofa that opened to a bed but Marielle didn't usually open it, since it seemed pointless. There was that scarred coffee table she'd found in the trash and hauled home, and the milk crates she'd swiped from some depanneur and used for books and what-nots. The lighting was from one bare bulb in the ceiling. The first narrow door led to a closet the size of a coffin, the next to the corridor, the last to a washroom with just a shower stall and toilet no sink, jammed so close together there was barely space, as her friend Jean said, to turn and piss. If the Madonna had an opinion about Marielle's humble dwelling, she didn't offer it up. Just as well. There was nothing to be done about it anyway, and God knew she was lucky to have a place to park herself at night when so many didn't, more and more every year, what with fires in the city leaving people homeless, and skyrocketing rents. Just yesterday the idiot box — the only other piece of furniture in the room — went on and on about the booming economy, more jobs, more housing starts, more of everything. "How come," she asked Mary, for whom she was named in the diminutive, "if there's more of everything, I got less and less all the time?"

Over the next months the Madonna took on a focus. Marielle found herself reverting to some long-buried habit from childhood and turning to the new arrival now and again for advice, or just somebody to talk to.

One fall afternoon, Marielle had invited over Jean Baptise — who she liked to tease by calling John the Baptist — the old fellow with the cane down the hall, to come and share some extra Kraft Dinner they'd given out that week at the food bank. She mixed in margarine, and a bit of the two percent milk she'd bought — she did enjoy milk in her tea.

Jean noticed the Virgin right away. "I see her before," he said. "She come from Québec. Me, I come from there. I see her."

"You seen her clones in Québec City," Marielle said. "Church has a million of these Mary's. They put 'em along the stations of the cross." Being from New Brunswick, Marielle had a logical side, while she saw Jean as fanciful, maybe too much so sometimes, still, she liked the old fellow.

"I see her before," Jean insisted, as if saying it twice would make it so.

Marielle didn't argue. What was the point with such a senior dude, twelve years more than her. Half the time he didn't know what he was saying, and the other half he was drunk on the cheap cough syrup they sold at the depanneurs that had plenty of alcohol in it and didn't cost what beer did. Anyway, he was company, since the only other friend she'd had in the building — "Sophia" — had been hit by a car a couple months ago when the government decided the moron drivers who couldn't drive as it was should get the right to turn right on a red light. Oh, there was that young mother from Haiti and her three kids down the hall. She was nice enough, sweet really, but a girl barely twenty has her own concerns.

Jean stood with difficulty, using the cane in one hand and holding the arm of the couch to brace himself. He hobbled the few steps to the window and picked up the statue. Marielle joined him, staying close, afraid he'd accidentally drop the Virgin on her holy head, him not being as steady as they come and all. But he just turned her over, examining Mary's hollow innards.

"*Le Cirage*, they adore *la Madonne noir*."

"Really? They got black Madonnas in Poland?" She wasn't sure if she believed him.

"*Oui! Ma soeur*, she send me a card to pray."

He examined the Madonna in minute detail. "Why do you not light her?" Jean asked a little belligerently.

"She's not that way," Marielle said. "No cords or anything."

Jean shook his head sagely and replaced the Virgin on her windowsill of honour. "Tomorrow, I go to One Dollar store and buy cord and I rewire for you."

"I'm not sure she's meant for light," Marielle started a protest, but Jean le Baptiste was a hard one to argue with when he got an idea into his head, and hard of hearing when it suited him, and on top of that he didn't forget much. He sat down again and leaned over the plate of Kraft Dinner, scooping up the last of the macaroni noodles with his spoon. Apparently the Madonna would be wired for light, though Marielle wasn't sure about this, and maybe she liked her the way she was, and it was unlikely the light would shine through a painted surface anyway.

She glanced at the Virgin. From this angle it looked like the corners of the mouth seemed to be turned up a little more, and Marielle laughed to herself that either Mary liked Jean, liked the idea of being wired for light, or else she was just cosmically pleased for no good reason, as most deities seemed to be now and again.

✛ ✛ ✛

The following afternoon, Marielle had just put her feet
up because that right knee joint hurt more today maybe
due to the humidity outside that tended to hang inside the
room like a pall. Still she had to get up to answer the knock
at the door. Jean stood on the other side with a white plastic
bag clutched in one hand, the ever-present cane in his other,
a hopeful look on his face. He came in without asking,
which is how he did a lot of things, but Marielle was used
to his ways, since they'd known one another for about five
years now, and you had to put up with friends in this life
or you'd have none, and sometimes they come in handy.

"I give her light," he said, pulling a slot head screw-
driver and a thin box cutter from his pant pocket. He
grabbed the Madonna around the neck, took two steps,
and collapsed onto the end of the couch. Marielle shook
her head and sighed. She figured she'd better make him
some tea, even though he didn't like tea much — but she
had no coffee or hot chocolate in the house. Maybe she
could put some ice cubes in it and he wouldn't notice.

"How about some thé glacée?" she asked, but he ignored
her as he did when preoccupied, already busy unscrewing
screws on the plug.

She made the tea, wondering the whole time if it was
sacrilegious to light up a Virgin that had been painted —
although that was probably sacrilegious too — and one
that'd never had light before, and she was pretty sure this
one hadn't. There was no groove for any wire to slip into,
so she had no idea how Jean was gonna make this illumination happen, and really she didn't want to know. If the
Madonna was destined for a miracle, so be it. You couldn't
stand in the way of mysticism.

Somehow it seemed that all her life people had been
changing things she wasn't too interested in changing but
then she had to live with the results whether she liked them
or not.

Moreso since Louis had the stroke a dozen years ago
this winter. That was the first of the big changes she'd had
no control over. Then Thomas got married and moved way
up to Baie-Comeau. And they'd had that big stupid argument. She'd tried to keep the house, but it seemed better

to sell it, but that was before the boom so she didn't get much and the money went fast and Thomas was even angrier at her. Change might be as good as a rest but neither one worked on a regular basis.

She watched Jean work. It wasn't that she thought Jean had some sinister motive — his heart was in the right place, she was pretty sure of that — but then the road to hell was paved with all kinds of wondrous intentions that ended up screwing somebody.

Jean turned out to be a silent worker. She'd seen him do odd jobs before and knew he liked to concentrate but this job took long enough that she could study his method. No point interrupting, not that he'd notice anyway. She placed the tea in front of him, and a glass at the opposite end of the couch for herself, then turned on the portable TV Thomas had given her the last time she saw him, maybe five years ago, when they'd had the big blow-out about Marielle wanting to live on her own and Thomas saying that was stupid and wanting her to come live with him and his family, or else go into one of those places where old people go to die if she preferred and he'd pay for it. For once Marielle put her foot down and did it her own way and stayed on her own and look what happened, she hadn't heard from Thomas since, except at Christmas when a card would come in the mail likely sent by her daughter-in-law, with a family photo saying things were fine, the kids were happy, another baby almost every other year, so that made three now, but she'd only seen the oldest one in the flesh. They were her grandkids, so for a while she felt she had to send them something: a sweater still in good condition she picked up at the Armée du Salut store for the girl Marielle, named for her; some toys found at Village de Valeur for the younger two boys. Hell, the postage cost more than the presents! She never even got a thank you, so she didn't know if the stuff arrived or not, and this year she was thinking about not sending anything since it probably wasn't appreciated anyway, and what was the good of family anyhow? Better to be on her own, where she could keep control of her miserable life herself!

The afternoon shows were on, that nearly bald Dr. Phil giving advice to people who might or might not take it, although Marielle always figure'd most of them were plants anyhow because nobody could be so stubborn. She'd already put her feet back on the coffee table and didn't feel like getting up to change the channel, so she'd tolerate him as long as she could, then maybe switch to another station and watch reruns or soaps. Suddenly she noticed the little prayer card on the table. Jean must have put it there when she was making the tea. She glanced his way but Jean seemed spellbound by the red and black wires. She leaned forward and picked it up. A black Madonna holding a child! Well, she'd never seen anything like this before, but then she wasn't exactly religious.

That's about when the vision started. It turned cold, snowy, despite the fact that Marielle knew that outside the leaves were still falling. As the TV chatter dimmed and the picture faded to white, sheets of ice coated her vision the way the window looked when it was minus twenty, and she would have been afraid, but she heard a familiar sound. Mon Ange! She'd know her anywhere! She could picture her now, the little black and blue songbird, full of energy and happiness. Marielle saw her blurry at first through the ice but twittering, cute little head tilted to one side, and watched her own little-girl finger reach between the bars of the cage and My Angel hop on and perch. She felt the feather weight of the light creature as it clung to her with its tiny feet, and then it sang its heart out, only for Marielle, the way Mon Ange always had.

"You got some match?" Jean asked.

Marielle turned. The black Madonna sat precariously on his boney knees, his big hand wrapped protectively around her shoulders to keep her from falling. From behind, a white tail draped down to the floor, with a plug dangling at the end.

In the kitchen drawer she found a book of matches and brought them to him. He pulled off the matches and folded the empty cover a few times until it was about the size of a nickle but square, then he wedged it inside her, under the metal bar he'd inserted, so the cord would lie flat, or close enough. Jean started to rise and Marielle held back from helping him, but with difficulty. He struggled to get the muscles in his legs to do what he wanted them to do, muttering in French about the pointlessness of owning such a low couch. Meanwhile, she kept her hands at the ready to snatch Mary if his balance gave out totally. Finally, around the fifth try, he managed to stand, banging the Madonna on the arm of the sofa accidentally, but the Virgin Mother held herself together.

Jean tottered to the windowsill and placed Mary back in her niche. He took the cord and squinted at the baseboard until he saw the socket, then tried to stoop down to plug it in but he was dragging the Madonna across the sill with him, so Marielle intervened. "Lemme do that."

She bent to plug in the Virgin then straightened her legs, her knees creaking.

Now Mary was off centre, to the left a foot, but it didn't matter at all. The bulb inside her did not shine through the painted plaster of course but the light seemed to spring out of the bottom and rise up all around, illuminating her all over. Marielle was surprised by this change. Somehow the light made the Virgin seem to smile more, if that could be, those pious lips turned way up at the corners.

"You like?" Jean asked.

Marielle said, "Yes. Very much. *Jean le Baptiste*, you did good. Thank you."

"*De rien*," he said, patting her on the shoulder before he sat down again to finally drink his iced tea.

The Madonna stayed lighted from sunset to sunrise. Marielle had to replace the little bulb twice, once in November when she'd tried a red one but found it too lewd, and again in early December. She didn't mind the expense. Somehow, having the Virgin around offered a comfort she hadn't expected, and the statue resurrected in her emotional memories of her youth, when she had embraced a belief in all things spiritual, but this time it wasn't connected to anything organized or rigid, just a kind of overall sense of a bigger picture, and a universe that holds you up instead of crushing you down. And now that the cold weather had set in and the clocks were turned back, Marielle was glad of both the company and the illumination because it got dark so early.

She found the Virgin sometimes spoke to her, not in words exactly, more in kind of emotional thoughts that made pictures in Marielle's head. She invested in cheap coloured pencils and artwork paper and tried to capture the images, but could never figure out how to make them look like what was inside her, and mostly what came out onto the page were circles, round faces with huge eyes that kind of pierced you like a laser so you didn't feel it on the surface but did deeper, as if you'd been microwaved. Sometimes the faces were split straight down the middle, other times the cut was jagged and mostly off centre, but then the raw edges were good for two profiles facing each other. She coloured one half dark and one light, and not necessarily going to happy and sad or anything easy like that. But always the faces had a kind of light to them, the type of light the Virgin herself emitted, and even if they weren't perfect or anything close, the drawings suited Marielle.

Then one day near Christmas Marielle woke with a start before dawn, from what the clock said, her heart pounding too hard. She'd had a dream she couldn't remember at all, just the feeling of urgency. The room would have been to- tally dark if it wasn't for the Madonna's light. Something made Marielle get up off the sofa-bed she'd started opening at night again and go to the window. She peered at The Virgin, who not only smiled, but now her lips were parted, and the bottom edge of her upper front teeth showed! Marielle was amazed, but didn't Mary keep changing with the times, and maybe a change was in order, or so she fig- ured, else why was she woken up so early?

She parted the curtains and looked out the window. It had snowed the night before and the streets were alight because of it, though the sun seemed far from rising. A brilliant crystal snow, pure, covered her known universe, untainted by people or cars, just a nice white blanket that glittered like the stars had fallen out of the sky. "That's beautiful," she whispered, and then she heard the Madonna say, *Take me home.*

Marielle jolted, her heart racing again. She didn't know what to make of that. Did she hear it or imagine it? She listened, but there was just the refrigerator humming, and the clock clicking. But she told herself she shouldn't worry. After all, the Virgin talked before, but not in real words, and where was home anyway? Wasn't home here, where they both lived?

Home, where I belong.

Marielle didn't know where that would be exactly, but somehow she knew it was not here, in this tiny room with four walls like a closed box, the air stale and smelly. Home was outdoors for Mary, like it had been for Marielle in her childhood. In the country. Out in the dry cold. Out in the virgin snow.

There was nothing to think about or debate. She dressed warm, as many layers as made sense, and pulled on the boots the girl down the hall'd given her because they didn't fit. Once she had the wool hat on her head and her hands gloved, she headed to the Madonna again and unplugged her. The Virgin's light stayed on. Marielle held the cord in her hand and looked at it like a fool, wondering. Maybe Mary was plugged into a bigger power source, for all Marielle knew. She slid the Madonna carefully into her large fabric shopping bag, slipped the wide strap over her head, and headed out.

She could not remember the streets ever being this quiet, not here in this part of the city where students and drug dealers were up all hours. The sky above was so clear and crisp, with stars and that half moon — she couldn't get over its light! — and she spent at least a block looking up. Not a soul wandering, and her footprints were the first on the sidewalk, although a car or two had driven up the main street. Everywhere the world looked new, unclotted, free of all the debris produced by human beings and the machines they manufactured. Finally there was, for a few moments, peace, something akin to what heaven might be like, or at least limbo, a sense that time had stopped dead and there was nowhere to be, nothing to do, and the limitations of the flesh faded to bliss. She didn't even mind the cold, at least for a while.

Marielle walked instinctively, sometimes glancing into her bag and asking the Madonna, "Is this right? Am I goin' the right way?"

The Virgin said nothing more, but she still glowed, and Marielle figured that meant everything was as it should be, or at least there was nothing the Mother of Christ had to complain about.

She walked to Avenue Mont Royal then entered the park that led up the mountain, and climbed. The higher she got, the better the city looked. Below, only the occasional car, but once she'd made it halfway to the top, even the streets disappeared from her sight.

Amazingly her legs weren't tired and her joints didn't ache, and she figured the Sorrowful Mother had given her some kind of supernatural strength or something, so she could perform this task, not that she was a saint or anything, just one of the minions doing Her bidding, or so it seemed. Biting cold caught her cheeks, though, the only part of her body exposed, and Marielle pulled the toque she wore as low as she could. Her breath burst out of her in pale clouds, faster now that she was ascending. Way at the top of the mountain stood that huge illuminated cross, which could have guided her, but Marielle had been here many times and really had no need of such divine intervention. The Madonna knew where she was going. Marielle knew how to get her there, more or less.

She followed the winding road up the side of the mountain and finally reached a secondary entrance to the Cimetière Notre-Dame-des-Neiges — Our Lady of the Snows — the cemetery named for the Madonna. Here in this section the graves were newer, ordered stones, in neat rows, each with a mound of snow atop it. Marielle looked in the bag again and noticed the Madonna had dimmed slightly, so she figured this wasn't exactly where she wanted to be. Maybe higher, near those enormous crypts at the top of the hill that had overlooked these grounds for a hundred and fifty years, some more. Crypts that held generations of remains of wealthy families, not that Marielle knew any of them, except maybe the family that made beer, but they were on the other side of the fence in the smaller cemetery anyway. Here there were some nuns, a few politicians nobody remembered anymore, and that poor poet guy Émile Nelligan who went nuts and could only write about the ice crystals that coated his window so bad he couldn't see outside, which was probably symbolic too.

The snow lit the path but now the sky was starting to lighten on its own, so Marielle had no trouble climbing higher, though her boots and pant legs felt icy soaked. Still, if this was what the Virgin wanted, there wasn't much use arguing about it.

The road led to a divide, with two crypts below, and two more rows of crypts above. It was the highest one She wanted, of course. The Queen of Heaven's home on earth must be closer to heaven, as everybody knew, including Marielle, though she didn't have much of a sense as to how to get to that otherworldly realm, but just like most people she imagined it as up.

Off in the distance, a red fox, one of the few remaining here, darted between the graves, easy to see because of how he contrasted with the snow. Above, perched on a bare tree branch, a lone crow squawked, a kind of audio beacon for his mate. Marielle gave him a jaunty high-five and got a sharp raven-type "hi" back . She trudged up the rest of the steep hill puffing, finally reaching the top, and paused to catch her breath. It sure was pretty here, and even more quiet than down in the city earlier. It reminded her of the farm where she'd grown up, the air so crisp and clean, sounds travelling for long distances, but mostly the silence that she had loved; one that you wanted, not one that you felt was forced upon you. She gazed along the row of family crypts, all lovely structures from another era when people appreciated beautiful things that were more permanent and everything wasn't made out of plastic.

Marielle liberated the black Madonna from her burlap bag and clutched her in her arms, checking the glow factor as she neared each crypt. The Virgin went nuts with light, and Marielle knew this one had to be the place.

She examined the field-stone crypt she stood before. The massive structure, built into the mountain, was two stories high easy, and she figured the inside had to be bigger than her apartment. Little spires and a tower, and all that pretty filigree work on the wrought iron door ... She wouldn't mind living here herself, and wondered why they didn't open some of the abandoned ones to the homeless, and people who had a hard time financially, like she'd read they'd done somewhere in Europe, but she knew most North Americans couldn't handle the idea of breathing people living in a cemetery.

I must go in!

Marielle looked at the Madonna, who might have been a black sun for all she could figure. She'd never seen such a brilliant light before, as if the heavens were on fire with darkness, even blacker than the night sky out in the country. Marielle began to think, well, surely they lock these places to protect what remains, but when she looked up she noticed the lovely door was already ajar, so she guessed this was another sign, since there seemed to be signs everywhere today.

She started up the seven steps, shoving snow aside with her boots as she went, until she reached the door and pushed it open with her forearm. The darkness inside made her hold the Virgin before her like a flashlight, but Marielle wondered if maybe she wasn't trying to hide from the unknown behind Her vestal skirts, although the Madonna wasn't long enough for skirts. Marielle felt surprised to find there wasn't much in here, just some drawers on the sides that probably held coffins, and a wrecked kneeling bench against the back wall, the straw stuffing coming out of the kneeler, an old crucifix on the stone wall above it. "Well, we're here," Marielle said with finality. "I guess you're home."

The Virgin stayed silent now, just glowed Her lustrous light, like She was taking it all in, trying to figure out what to do next ... Marielle studied the celestial face and damn, but wasn't her mouth open all the way now? Teeth showing, the biggest smile you could imagine on those holy lips. "Guess you're glad to be here, huh?"

Nothing. It was as if the Madonna decided she'd said enough in the past and now, well, it was time to just let things unfold as they should.

For something to occupy herself with, because she was pretty cold now, and she had to wait till the Madonna figured things out and decided the next step, Marielle walked over and looked at the four drawers to her left. "Beloved Mother Anne" and "Brother Paul", "My husband Joseph", "sister Martha".

She moved the few steps across the crypt to study the drawers over there and that's when she suddenly noticed *Famille L'Esperance*. Family of the Hope. Esperance. That was *her* last name! Maybe these were her relatives, at least the French side of her family! Family she didn't know she had. But that didn't seem likely because she wasn't even born here, her mom's family came from Ireland and her dad's from France and they both settled in New Brunswick so none of these *L'Esperances* were related, were they? She looked at the drawers one by one until she came to the last. This was just an opening, a gap in the wall, waiting for the coffin of the next *L'Esperance* to be interred.

A sudden fear shot up her spine, cutting the biting cold, making her teeth chatter and leaving her back instantly sweat-soaked like she was still menopausal. She wanted to run from the panic, despite legs and joints that now ached. Her chest hurt, right around heart level. She felt desperate to hide from the terror. Maybe the Madonna had led her here, to her death! Maybe she was meant to die in this crypt, in this icy cold, far from home, alone, with just a lousy Virgin statue she'd been talking to and imagined lighted itself up. She saw a picture in her head, herself half reclining on that ratty old kneeling bench, clutching the cheap black statue, frozen to death.... Maybe she was losing her mind, coming up here in the middle of the night, a woman her age making this kind of 'pilgrimage', if anybody sane would call it that, she might have a heart attack any second, overextending herself like this, maybe even a stroke—

Silence!

Marielle's fear dissolved like ice instantly melting. The quivering, the heart palpitations, the rapid breathing, all of the physical pain. Suddenly she felt normal, younger, not fearful, not alone.

Look!

She looked down at the Virgin, who still glowed, and it occurred to Marielle that not everything had to do with *her*, maybe the Madonna had her own agenda.

Something caused her to glance up at the cement wall above that empty hole. A round medallion, with a face. She held the Virgin closer so she could use Her light to see just what this was about, and the face on the black medallion was familiar, the same face as the Madonna she held!

"Well, I'll be.... I guess this really *is* your home!" Gingerly Marielle placed the black figure inside the opening, the darkness of the hole brought to light by the glow She emitted. For long moments she stood staring at the Virgin who had been so pregnant with hope and possibilities in a world of grim realities. Maybe that was her message all along, that life isn't perfect, but sometimes miracles happen, to the body, to the mind, to the spirit. Sometimes there's a future.

By the time Marielle left the crypt the sun had risen in the mid-morning sky. The crow had been joined by his relatives, and they called to each other in their own mysterious language no human could figure out.

She took a more direct route out of the cemetery and got home in time to meet Jean at the mail boxes, where she picked up a Christmas card. Jean was headed out to the shops. "I'll join you," she said cheerfully. "I'm headed that way anyways."

He nodded and smiled, staring at her as if he noticed something different. Like now she glowed.

They walked to the vegetable store and she left him near the eggplants, then headed to the payphone. She dug into her bag, picked out some coins and dropped them into the phone slot, then punched in the number imbedded into her memory. "Thomas?" she said, "It's mom. I'm thinking we should get together for Christmas." While she listened, she stared at the stainless steel of the telephone casing and noticed the lower part of her face reflected and the smile spreading across her lips. "Sure, I'd like to stay there. Maybe for a while. We'll see. Yeah, it's possible. Anything's possible."

Thought and Memory
by Alette J. Willis

Memory came first, scratching at the cedar shingles in the hot August haze.

Jo lay in the dim interior of the old one-storey farmhouse she and Eileen had bought last fall, trying to ignore the sound that so obviously wanted her attention. The humid weight of the Northern Ontario summer pressed down on her chest, making it hard to breathe as she stared unseeing at the wall before her. She had lain on the overstuffed sofa for days without end and had every intention of remaining there, not remembering, not thinking, not feeling, for the rest of her life.

The phone rang. Jo ignored it. The insistent jangle had broken the thick silence a few times since the police officer had come to the door — but she refused to think about that now.

The noise on the roof grew louder.

Jo's eyes focussed of their own accord and she found herself gazing at cream wallpaper with pale green vines that twined in and out of ragged patches of discolouration. She followed a stem until it ran up against the seam and disappeared into the next sheet.

Re-wallpapering the living room was on the to-do list stuck to the fridge but they had given it a low priority, below putting drainage tiles under the north section of the market-garden, fixing the small greenhouse, and insulating the roof of Eileen's studio.

The seam crossed through a rectangular patch of darker wallpaper where a picture had hung. After the police officer had left, Jo had taken down all of Eileen's paintings and stacked them against the far wall with their backs towards the room. Why was she remembering all this now when she had worked so hard to forget?

She closed her eyes and saw an unlit country highway at night. Then, in the glare of the headlights, the stricken stare of a deer caught on the road. Only its eyes were Eileen's eyes. The car swerved, lost control, headlights came up ahead, too large, too fast. An image pulled not from memory but from imagination. A wave of vertigo swept over her. She opened her eyes and found herself staring at the place where the wallpaper seam met the ceiling. The scratching came from behind that point. Whatever was making the noise was trying to claw its way into the house. Despite the heat, she shivered. So much needed shutting out these days.

Rusty nails creaked and protested, rotten wood gave way with a muffled crack and then a soft thump as a shingle was thrown off the roof onto the grassy turf. Rat-a-tat-tat, like machine gun fire on the wood beneath. More splintering, some scrabbling and then a thud. Whatever it was had forced its way in and was hopping across the attic towards the middle of the ceiling. The scratching began again, closer now, just a thin layer of drywall between it and the living room. Jo sat up, heart pounding.

A trickle of dust fell to the floor as the black edge of a claw penetrated through. Jo hugged a pillow to her chest and pulled her feet up onto the sofa. Methodically, the creature tore away bits of plaster. And then silence. And then a long scimitar-shaped beak appeared followed by the black-feathered head of a raven, *Corvus corax*.

It looked at her through one eye, then the other, then the first again, slipped through the hole and swooped down to the floor, landing a couple of metres in front of the sofa.

Jo looked at it warily. She wasn't as a rule afraid of ravens, or of any corvids for that matter, but this one was large and sitting on the floor of her living room staring at her. It turned its head back and forth again as if trying to figure out how to sustain eye contact with a creature that had eyes in the front of its head.

"It's easier to talk to people when they've had an eye poked out," it croaked. "Evens things out."

Somehow a talking raven was easier to deal with than one that didn't talk. It indicated to Jo that through grief and sleep deprivation she had simply gone mad. Eileen would have been amused at her conjuring up birds to escape reality.

The raven chuckled in short rasping barks. "There is no escape," he said. "I'm here for the opposite reason."

"Which is?" Jo asked, sagging back into the sofa's sweaty embrace.

"I'm here to make you remember."

"What if I don't want to remember?"

"Oh, it is a selfish being," he said to himself, hopping onto the arm of the sofa.

"I think I'm entitled to be a little selfish right now, under the circumstances."

"Under the circumstances," he mimicked. He pecked a hole in the upholstery and began ripping out wads of stuffing, tossing them into the air and watching them float to the floor.

"I don't care about this sofa either, so if you're hoping to get a rise out of me it's not going to work."

"It's not going to work," he repeated, pecking another hole.

She flung the pillow at him but he flew up and it landed harmlessly on the floor next to a meditation cushion.

"An unkindness of cushions," the raven observed, landing on the round, pleated, purple zafu and slitting it open.

"Stop. That's Eileen's." Jo pushed herself off the couch and lunged towards the bird.

"It was Eileen's," said the raven retreating to the mantelpiece. "So she does remember, and she does care."

The small burst of energy had exhausted itself and Jo slumped back on the couch. The bird jumped down onto the paintings.

Jo tried to muster some more anger, but she was too tired.

Seizing the edge of a painting, the raven spread his wings above his head and began to wave them in long powerful strokes, sending dust bunnies skittering into corners. He levitated a couple of inches and then let the canvas drop. It landed face up on the floor: a self-portrait Eileen had done mixing reality and fantasy in her trademark way. It depicted her standing outside under the cold glare of a hopeful moon holding a glistening paintbrush, her glorious naked body radiating its own inner energy as fireflies tugged strands of her hair into a halo around her face.

"Remember," cooed the Raven.

It was the first painting Eileen had done after they had moved up north to escape the hot smoggy Toronto air, following some romantic idea of country living. Jo had been thrilled to discover that the stand of stunted oaks at the back of their thirty-acre property was the local crow roost. Every evening the birds would stream in over the house and perch in the trees, cawing low gossip to each other until daylight drained away.

Jo dragged Eileen out one evening when the moon was full and the smell of autumn was just on the other side of consciousness. They doused themselves in citronella and snuck across the field to spy on their avian neighbours. There must have been a thousand birds in the small wood, most sleeping singly but a few preening each other and muttering softly. Even Eileen was intrigued by this alien society cohabiting their land.

The moon was high in the sky when they got back to the house. Eileen, taken by the quality of the light on Jo's face, unbuttoned Jo's shirt, wanting to see the soft skin of her breasts by moonlight. Jo protested at first, afraid of being exposed to any lingering mosquitoes, but Eileen had a soft touch that always managed to get right up inside of her, melting her resistance to anything. They made love on the grass in a fug of citronella to the accompaniment of cricket song.

Their passion crested and subsided, washing Jo up onto the still warm earth, her arm draped across Eileen's silky belly, listening as the pounding in her ears subsided to a distant throb. Eileen pulled away, springing to her feet and stretching like some feral feline. Jo watched her roam hungrily about the edge of the lawn marvelling at how clearly the moon highlighted her long supple legs and provocative curves.

"You know," said Jo. "We're still linked even though I can't reach you. Me, you, the sun and moon, we're all woven together."

Eileen sauntered towards her.

"Sunlight strikes the moon and becomes moon rays, which hurtle four hundred thousand kilometres to rebound off your skin and penetrate inside my eyes, binding us together in a web of light." Joe reached out and stroked the inside of Eileen's ankle.

Eileen spun out of her grasp and disappeared inside the house. Jo had just about mustered enough energy to go after her when she reappeared carrying an easel and paints and the square mirror from the bedroom, which she brought over to Jo.

"I want to capture that, what you said about the sun and the moon and me and you. Hold up the mirror so I can see with your eyes."

Eileen had written "Moonshadow Muse" on the back of the canvas. Jo traced the words with her finger. She brought the painting into the bedroom and hung it back in its place above the bed.

"I do enjoy the visual arts," croaked the raven, hopping into the room. "I am an artist as well, you know. Though my masterpieces are of the narrative variety." With one flap of his wings, he jumped onto the dresser, landing in front of the mirror. He peered at himself and gave a loud "korak." A second raven stepped out from behind the mirror.

"There you are," grumbled the first bird. "Late again."

"It seems I'm just in time to hear you take credit for everything," said the second bird, puffing out her neck feathers.

Jo wondered what part of her subconscious had brought forth bickering ravens. They were beginning to give her a headache.

"It's not us," said the second bird. "You're dehydrated. Better get yourself a glass of water."

Jo stayed sitting on the bed. "Who are you?" she asked.

"Thought," said the second bird.

"Memory," said the first, flapping up onto the curtain rod.

Eileen had told her the Norse myth of Thought and Memory not long before — Jo forced her attention back on the birds.

"Why are you pestering me?" she asked. "Shouldn't you be whispering into Odin's ear or something?"

"He won't listen to us anymore," Thought said. "Not interested in the goings on down here." She scratched gloomily at the surface of the dresser.

"He's too busy hanging from his tree, waiting for the end of the world," said Memory, tucking one leg up, and then flipping over so that he dangled from the curtain rod by one claw.

Thought hopped up and down on the dresser cackling.

"It's up to us now," said the upside down Memory. "To intervene in the mortal plane on our own."

"In our own way."

"Thank you, but I'm not looking for divine intervention," said Jo.

Thought chuffed up at her choice of words and opened her beak but Memory spoke first: "Selfish beings need to remember that there are other lives in the world, other problems that need resolving."

"If you're trying to tell me that it makes a difference whether I sit on the couch or not, save your breath. I've never been swayed by delusions of grandeur."

"This one's lost the threads of her narrative," said Memory to Thought. "She's not going to be any help to us until she's found them again."

"More like she's abandoned them," said Thought, staring at Jo with one eye. "Well, hurry up and find them and make her pick up the right ones. There are lives at stake."

"You know as well as I that I can't do that. There are rules to be observed."

Thought's hackles began to rise. "Well, if you hadn't wasted time using her memories for your own vicarious pleasure, by now she might be closer to remembering who she is."

Jo left the birds to their argument and went in search of water.

She took a glass out of a kitchen cupboard and filled it from the sink. The cool liquid slid down her throat in one long gulp. She heard a thump from the living room, then some scrabbling. Hoping that the ravens had left, she filled her glass again and went out to see.

Lying in the middle of the floor was a painting of an anthropomorphised crow sitting at a computer terminal in a messy cubicle.

"What does it say on the back?" Thought asked Jo.

She didn't need to turn it over to know. "It says 'Birdbrained'."

This sent Thought into hysterics again. She cackled so hard that she fell onto her back, her feet kicking the air spasmodically.

It was the only portrait Eileen had ever painted of Jo.

"And whose fault is that?" asked Thought, lapsing into another fit of barks.

"Hush," said Memory, glaring at her.

Their last summer in Toronto had been a grisly one. Jo had spent days on end in the grad lab of the ornithology department at U of T tallying up crow deaths in different counties of Southern Ontario and analysing tissue samples.

While public health departments scrambled to protect people from West Nile, Jo's fears went with the crows. A few years ago when the virus first hit New York City, the crow population there had plummeted to ten percent of its original size. Jo was worried that pesticides in agricultural areas were attacking crow immune systems, making them even more susceptible to disease. The results could be catastrophic. Unfortunately, most of the farmers she talked to seemed to think the loss of crows would be a good thing and Eileen wasn't very supportive either.

"I never see you anymore," Eileen complained one night over the curry and naan bread that she'd brought to the lab from their favourite Indian take-out. "I think you love your birds more than me."

It was an unfair statement, but sometimes Eileen said things like that just to get attention. Besides, Jo missed Eileen as well. It was August and the other students were off doing fieldwork or just slacking, so Jo suggested that Eileen bring her paints in and they could work side by side. Eileen agreed on the condition that Jo let her paint her portrait as she worked.

Eileen's eyes sparkled when she finally showed Jo the finished picture of "Birdbrained," like she expected Jo to find it funny. But she didn't. Jo had hoped her portrait would reveal some hidden depths, some inner beauty that she was not aware of herself. Instead, Eileen had produced a passive-aggressive joke. What did that say about Eileen and Jo and their relationship?

The only way for Jo to avoid choking on her disappointment was to start yelling. She shouted that Eileen had no respect for her research, and accused artists of being parasites that thrived on human experience but did nothing to improve the quality of life on the planet. Eileen fled with tears in her eyes.

Jo camped out at the university the next couple of days, eating at the cafeteria and sleeping on the battered orange couch in the corner of the lab. Her fear and anger slowly melted into guilt, then sorrow. She bought a voluptuous orchid that they couldn't really afford and went home.

Lying in bed after making up, Eileen proposed that they put Jo's beliefs into practice and buy some land, somewhere far from the distractions of the city, and start up an organic farm. Jo suspected that getting into farming was not that easy, but Eileen was adamant and the idea of having Eileen all to herself in the bush somewhere definitely had its appeal.

"Oh, the irony," said Thought, arcing her wings out and bobbing up and down. "She named you, and here we are, and here you are, and you think it's a joke. And it's all so very funny."

"I'm beginning to understand why Odin stopped listening to you," said Jo, glaring at the bird.

She picked up the painting and placed it on the mantelpiece. Despite her initial reaction, she had to admit that there was beauty in it: in the way her hair metamorphosed into feathers and in the hint of arms in the curve of wings. Eileen had even included the little photo of herself that Jo kept next to the computer, only the painted version was leaning out of the frame blowing a kiss to the viewer. Jo wondered why she had never noticed that before.

A rustling came from the kitchen. Jo followed the sound and found Memory perched on the toaster tearing a hole in a bag of stale bread.

"Do you have peanut butter?" he asked hopefully. "Or cheese?"

"Peanut butter *and* cheese," said Thought, swooping into the room.

Jo retrieved a jar of chunky peanut butter and a hunk of old cheddar — mouldy around the edges — from the fridge and made the ravens a sandwich. Then, since the stuff was out anyway, she made herself one too, sat down at the melamine table and watched the birds make a sticky mess of their food. At least the peanut butter clogged up their beaks for a while.

Jo hadn't realised how hungry she was until she took a bite of her own sandwich. She wolfed it down, but all it did was whet her appetite, so while her guests were occupied preening daubs of peanut butter out of their sleek feathers she thawed some ratatouille from the freezer and sat down to a proper meal.

A gun went off in the distance. Thought fluttered up from the counter, squawking in panic. Memory began to pace rapidly up and down the counter between the sink and stove.

"You're wasting time," said Thought, settling on the back of a kitchen chair across the table from Jo. "Why won't you remember what we need you to remember?" she stabbed her beak towards Jo.

Jo thrust the half-eaten bowl of ratatouille away. "Why won't you go away and leave me to my forgetting?"

Thought leaned forward and hissed, a low menacing sound. Memory flew over, pecked at Thought and then began pushing the ratatouille back across the table with his beak.

"You'll have to excuse my mate, she's a little over-wrought," he said, turning to glower at Thought. He returned his attention to Jo. "While you've been hiding away in here these last five days, events in the world outside have continued to unfold. It is these events that are causing her some distress."

Five days only? It seemed like a lifetime.

"What events?" asked Jo. "Why won't you just tell me what's going on?"

"Can't," said Memory. "You have to remember."

"And think!" squawked Thought, ruffling her feathers and glaring at Jo with her beady eyes.

"May I have a word with you, in the living room, please?" Memory said to Thought.

Thought looked the other way.

"Now," said Memory.

Thought hopped down off her perch and waddled, beak raised high, into the living room. Memory flew after her.

Jo polished off the ratatouille and began to open cupboards at random. She craved something else but she wasn't sure what, until she found a half-empty bag of chocolate chips. Exactly what she needed.

Croaking, squawking, thumping and thudding continued in the living room. Doing her best to ignore the sounds, Jo shook some chips out onto the palm of her hand and returned to the table. The last time she'd baked chocolate chip cookies was on the summer solstice when Shelley still worked for them.

Thought and Memory swooped into the room and dropped a small picture onto the table: the little 10" by 10" portrait of Shelley sitting in a patch of strawberries.

"You needn't have bothered," Jo said. "I was going there anyway."

Jo had completed her thesis with a little grant money to spare. Combined with the small inheritance Eileen had from her grandfather's death a few years back, they had enough to make a down payment on a 30-acre property two hours west of Sudbury. The land had been farmed, though never profitably, and had eventually been abandoned.

Eileen loved the farmstead on sight, staking out a small ramshackle shed as her painting studio. She made forays into the bush, coming back with treasures of dried fungi, flowers and antlers, which she used to transform the one-storey farmhouse into a home.

The prospects for farming were not so good. The "vegetable patch" in the real-estate ad turned out to be nothing but weeds and hard-packed soil. Still, somehow they managed to get the hardpan rototilled and the vegetables planted before the April showers arrived.

At first they rejoiced as the rain coaxed their seeds into sprouting, but as it continued day after day, weeds began to outstrip their vegetables. When the sun finally came out, their neat rows had vanished under a tangle of ragweed and crab-grass. It took an entire week to remove the unwanted plants and by the time they'd worked through the last row, the weeds at the far end were two inches high again.

Eileen put together a flyer advertising a part-time job for a student, decorating it with a smiling sun in the corner and a row of tulips along the bottom. The only applicants were a couple of girls. The first candidate showed up in a Marilyn Manson t-shirt with an attitude to match. The second needed a job because she was saving up to go to vet school, and it had to be part-time because she already volunteered at the local animal hospital. The choice was easy.

Her first day on the job Shelley uncovered an old strawberry patch next to the compost pile, which neither Jo nor Eileen had noticed, and began to nurse it back to health. She then made them enclose the rows of vegetables in chicken wire, to protect them from the local rabbits. She had wanted to put up a scarecrow too, but Jo wouldn't agree to it. She explained her research to the girl, who seemed interested. Afterwards, whenever a crow landed in the garden, Shelley would come fetch Jo and the two of them would sit in the sun and discuss corvid behaviour.

Things were looking up at the beginning of June when they harvested their first produce: lettuce, chives and mixed spring greens. High on optimism, Jo talked the minister at a big church on the highway into letting them set up a stand in the parking lot on Saturdays.

But as June progressed, morale plunged. Business was slow and the work backbreaking. Jo's worries that they'd made a huge mistake investing all their money in a farm they didn't know how to run, kept her from sleeping. Eileen grew cranky as days without painting turned into weeks and Jo added a fear that Eileen would abandon both her and the farm to her nightly litany of anxieties. To make matters worse, Shelley was working more hours than they could afford to pay her for and without her assistance their chances of making it through the summer without missing a mortgage payment were even bleaker.

One sleepless night in mid-June as worries chased each other through Jo's head, an idea began to take form. The next morning she proposed to the other two that Eileen paint Shelley's portrait as partial payment for all her overtime. Happily, they both agreed. Eileen was more than willing to take some time off from her gardening chores and Shelley was charmed by the prospect of seeing herself on canvas. Disaster was staved off for a while longer.

Eileen finished the portrait in time for summer solstice. It was one of the most beautiful pieces she'd ever done, filled with all the life and vitality that Shelley brought to their farm. She even included a small crow in the corner to represent the kinship that had grown between Jo and Shelley as they studied the birds.

The three of them took that afternoon off, ate chocolate chip cookies, toasted the longest day of the year with cheap champagne and admired Eileen's work.

When Jo and Eileen arrived at the church the next Saturday, the minister was waiting for them in the parking lot, clutching the portrait of Shelley. Jo's stomach sank as they pulled up.

"Mrs. Murray has come to me with disturbing information," he said as they got out of the car. "She overheard her daughter tell a friend that there is only one bedroom in your house, and only one bed in that room."

Jo could feel Eileen bristling beside her. She had to step in before Eileen said something foolish. "We never pretended to be anything other than what we are," she said.

"What you do in your own house is between you and God," said the minister. "But to subject a minor to your depraved lifestyle —"

"Oh, for the goddess' sake," exclaimed Eileen. Jo lay a warning hand on her arm but she wouldn't be stopped. "How backwards are you? There's nothing immoral about the way Jo and I live. We love each other, we're not ashamed of that. Our personal life is none of your business."

"It became my business when you sought to influence a minor. Mrs. Murray smelled alcohol on her daughter's breath when she returned from your place carrying this," the minister held up the portrait. "She suspects that there's more than gardening going on at your farm," he said. "And, I must agree that the evidence is damning." He read from the back of the portrait: "Happy Summer Solstice Shelley, love Eileen and Jo."

"Are you for real?" asked Eileen, shaking free of Jo's grip. "I painted her portrait, and suddenly you want to burn us at the stake?"

"If it is an innocent picture, why is there a black bird menacing her from above?" asked the Minister, growing red in the face. "And why have you painted her suggestively in a flimsy tank top and cut-off jeans with strawberry juice running down her arms?"

"It's strawberry season, I painted her while she picked strawberries on our farm. The crow is there because there are crows on the farm. Besides, if I painted it for nefarious purposes why would I give it to Shelley?"

"Maybe you have other paintings of the poor child."

"The picture was to thank Shelley for all her hard work, nothing more," said Jo. "I admit that Shelley had a small glass of champagne to celebrate the summer harvest. It was wrong of us to give alcohol to a minor. We apologise for that, and promise it won't happen again." Jo turned her back on the minister and unlocked the trunk. "Now if you'll excuse us, we need to get the lettuce out of the car before it wilts in this heat."

"Oh no you won't," said the minister. "I'll not have the likes of you using church land to reap a profit."

"Alright then," Jo said, slamming the trunk closed. "We'll not waste anymore of your time. Let's go, Eileen."

"Not until he gives the painting back," Eileen said.

"I think I'll hang onto this, just in case," replied the minister.

"I painted it for Shelley, not so some lech can feast his eyes on a young girl whenever he gets the urge."

"Eileen!" said Jo. "Get in the car now, we're leaving."

Eileen lunged towards the minister. He flinched and she yanked the picture out of his hands. Jo opened the passenger door of the car and pulled her in.

"You'll regret this!" shouted the minister as they drove away.

Eileen leaned out the window and gave him the finger. She turned back to Jo, laughing.

"That was a stupid thing to do," said Jo.

"Oh, lighten up."

"We're barely breaking even as it is. How are we going to sell our produce now? Pretty much everyone in town goes to that church."

Eileen shrugged. "We can always do farm gate sales. It's mostly the cottagers who buy from us anyhow. The locals go to Loblaws."

"People purchase our produce because they see us as they go by on the highway. Our farm's at the end of two kilometres of dirt road; how will anyone find us there?"

"We could sell it in Sudbury. They have a farmer's market."

"I didn't move to the country so that I could spend two hours driving to Sudbury and back every weekend."

"Well I didn't move up north so that some ignorant man-of-the-cloth could insinuate that I'm a pervert. I would be more than happy to drive to Sudbury, it would give me a chance to get out of these claustrophobic backwoods."

✛ ✛ ✛

Shelley's portrait had the same sensuousness to it that all of Eileen's work had. It depicted a girl on the brink of becoming a woman, surrounded by a verdant abundance of vines and heavy ripe strawberries. But the minister had it all wrong. It was a tribute to life, not soft pornography.

The word "Hope" had been written on the back of the canvas. It hadn't been there when Eileen gave the portrait to Shelley. She must have added it later. Hope for what, Jo wondered. If Eileen had been hoping Shelley would come back to work, that hadn't come to be.

"This is all very interesting but I don't see what any of this has to do with why we're here," said Thought. The two ravens were perched on the chair across the table from Jo.

"Shelley was another thread she needed to pick up," said Memory.

"But we don't have time," said Thought, hopping onto the table and pacing in front of Jo. "Lives are being lost."

"Patience. Her memories will take us where we need to go."

"You still haven't told me why you're here," said Jo, getting up to make a pot of coffee.

"You were named," said Thought.

"Birdbrained?" said Jo. "But Eileen named Shelley too, 'Hope.' Surely hope is more useful than birdbrained for whatever it is you have in mind."

"I did have that thought too," said Thought, swinging her beak around towards Memory. Memory shrugged and took off for the living room.

Jo poured herself a cup of coffee and followed. She stopped in the doorway. There, in the middle of the floor, was the one picture she never wanted to see again. She'd considered burning it when the police officer brought it to the house, but in the end she couldn't destroy anything that Eileen had made. It was a charcoal sketch of a woman sprawled back on a pile of cushions, completely naked except for an ornate beaded choker. She stared out of the canvas like she owned the woman drawing her. Jo's hands shook so much that coffee slopped onto her jeans, scalding her thigh. The pain felt good.

"This one's not named," said Memory.

"I can name it," said Jo, thinking of numerous unflattering nouns, but saying only: "Frida."

Frida had stopped at the Sudbury farmer's market the first Saturday Eileen had gone down. Somewhere between her buying strawberry jam and greens the two women had hit it off and Frida had invited Eileen to drop by her store before she left for the day.

"You would have loved her place," Eileen had told Jo later that night. "It's almost as good as being back in Toronto, with all the books and jewellery and little goddess figures. Plus she's got all this raven paraphernalia because she's Scandinavian. In her culture ravens are sacred. They're the servants of Odin, the head of the Norse gods. Hugin and Mugin — Thought and Memory — fly all over the world observing people and then at dusk they return to their master to tell him all the gossip they've gleaned."

Eileen had used some of the money from the day's sales to purchase a pair of concrete bookends in the form of ravens for Jo.

Initially, Jo was happy that Eileen had found a friend in Sudbury, but each Saturday Eileen came home later. Frida invited her for dinner. Frida had some friends she wanted Eileen to meet. Frida wanted to see some of Eileen's work. Frida wanted to put on a show of Eileen's paintings at her store.

With Eileen devoting more time to her painting and without Shelley to help, the garden required Jo's attention seven days a week. She tried to make time to accompany Eileen to her show's vernissage but in the end a sudden rash of potato beetles prevented her from going. That afternoon, one of Eileen's pieces sold for a substantial amount of money, more than they'd made the whole summer from produce sales. Eileen was ecstatic.

The following Friday, Eileen announced that she needed to do some painting in Sudbury and that she would have to spend the entire weekend there. The acrid taste of fear rose up the back of Jo's throat.

"I thought we were going to spend Sunday putting insulation in the shed roof so you can use your studio over the winter," said Jo, chopping zucchini for ratatouille.

"It's only August," Eileen said. "We've got plenty of time before winter."

"What about the garlic? It's ready to be pulled."

Eileen sighed. "I'll do it on Monday. What difference will one day make?"

"A lot, if it rains."

"It's not supposed to rain on Sunday."

Jo put down her knife and turned to face Eileen. "You want to tell me what's really going on?"

"I have no idea what you're talking about," said Eileen, but she wouldn't meet Jo's eyes.

"Where are you staying?"

"Frida said I could crash at her apartment."

"So, you're planning on spending the night with Frida?"

"It's not like that."

"Oh really, then tell me what it is like."

"I just need to spend some time in Sudbury painting. There's nobody to paint out here in the middle of the bush."

Jo wanted to say, *what about me, you could paint me,* but instead she said: "It was your idea to move here."

Eileen sighed, again. "I know it was. I thought it would be fun just the two of us, you with your garden and your crows, me with my easel and acres of landscape to paint. But it turns out I paint people, not trees."

Jo said nothing.

"Frida asked me to paint her portrait."

"And offered to sleep with you in return?"

"Jo! That's unfair. You don't even know Frida. If you did..."

"If I did, what?"

"I don't know what your problem is," said Eileen. "I spend four hours on the road every Saturday to sell your produce. You could at least be happy that I've made a friend in Sudbury. One friend, in the entire year we've been living out here."

She marched out of the room. A few seconds later the front door slammed. Jo finished making supper and ate it by herself at the kitchen table. It was telling that Eileen had not included Shelley in the same category as Frida. She had no problem with Eileen having friends like Shelley.

Which reminded her, before Eileen had come out with her plans for the weekend, Jo had been meaning to tell her that Shelley had phoned. It was the first time they'd heard from her since the incident with the minister. She'd left a message on the answering machine, something about needing Jo's help with a poster on crows she was putting together at the vet's. A poster and a petition to town council. She'd said that she would call back later, that they shouldn't try to phone her at home because her mother would "freak out".

When Jo got up at 4 am to harvest vegetables for the farmer's market, Eileen still hadn't come to bed. Jo peeked into her studio and saw her huddled in a sleeping bag on the little camping cot that she usually used only for afternoon catnaps. She looked small and vulnerable and Jo wished she could unsay all the things she'd said the night before.

By the time Jo returned from the garden, the sun was up and Eileen was packing painting supplies into the back seat of the car. Jo wanted to say something that would make things right between them again, but she couldn't think of anything, so she opened the trunk and began loading the produce in silence. When everything was safely stowed, Eileen got into the driver's seat, closed the door and started the ignition.

"I love you," Jo called after her as the car drove away.

If Eileen had heard her, she gave no sign of it.

Jo went to bed early, determined not to watch the clock, but sleep eluded her. Around midnight the phone rang. She leaped out of bed, hoping it was Eileen, but a man's voice answered her hello.

He informed her that he was a police officer. He went on to say that while driving home Eileen had been in a head-on collision with a cargo truck an hour outside of Sudbury. She'd died on impact. The truck driver, who was uninjured, had told the officer that Eileen had swerved to avoid a deer and had lost control. He'd slammed on his brakes but there wasn't enough time, there wasn't anything he could do.

At that point Jo simply abdicated all responsibility. Telling herself that Eileen wouldn't want to be buried in the bush, she gave the officer Eileen's parents address and phone number in Guelph and told him that they would want the body, that the funeral would be there.

The officer showed up the next morning with Eileen's paints and easel and the sketch of Frida. Jo tried to send him away but he insisted she take the things. The car was in Jo's name, so the contents belonged to her.

If she hadn't acted so jealous, maybe Eileen would have slept at Frida's and then she would still be alive. Another thought streaked after the first: maybe, possibly, some small part of her would rather have Eileen dead than with Frida. That's when Jo began to run away from her thoughts and memories, collecting all of Eileen's paintings and stacking them against the wall, then retreating to the couch and closing her eyes on the world.

Jo placed the sketch of Frida on the mantelpiece next to her own portrait. It deserved a place of honour as the last piece of art Eileen had set her hand to. She would not lie to herself anymore; it was a well-crafted drawing of an attractive woman.

Frida's obvious desire for Eileen smouldered off the page, and yet something was missing. There was none of Eileen's trademark whimsy in the sketch.

"There's nothing to this," she said to Thought. "It's just a simple nude."

Jo turned her attention to "Birdbrained". It was full of herself, her loves and her passions, from Eileen blowing her kisses to the border of dancing crows. She looked back at Frida.

"Did Frida send you as a curse on me?" she asked.

Thought found this so funny that she fell over.

"That's the silliest thought I've ever heard," she said between her rasping barks.

"Then why are you here?"

"You just have to remember," said Memory.

"And think," added Thought.

A gunshot went off, nearer this time, followed by another. Both ravens sprang into the air, cawing fretfully, their cries echoed by crows farther away.

"They're shooting crows, aren't they?" she said. "Shooting them on my property."

Thought and Memory settled down, one on each end of the mantelpiece, and nodded in unison.

"They're afraid of them because of West Nile, even though there's at least a hundred other species that carry the disease. Damn it, that's why Shelley called, she wanted me to help with her campaign."

"It's the same old story," said Memory. "People using scapegoats to assuage their fear. It's a narrative Odin doesn't want to listen to anymore."

"That's why we're interfering in the mortal plane," said Thought. "We're trying to change that story."

"But I don't see how my getting involved could possibly help. People around here seem to feel the same way about me and Eileen as they do about the crows."

"Not everyone feels that way," said Thought. "Hope has been weeding your garden these past few days."

So Shelley knew what had happened. Somehow knowing she was not alone took some of the edge off the pain, but Jo shook her head. "I still don't see what I can do."

"Pick up the threads of your narrative and return to weaving your life again," said Memory. "Move back out into the world. Change it and be changed by it."

"Everyone is a hero in their own story," said Thought. "But it takes love and courage to be a hero to others."

"Eileen was like that," said Jo, grief opening up like a chasm before her. Her legs turned to water and she sat down heavily on the sofa, letting her head fall forward onto her hands.

With a whirr of wings and a brush of feathers, the ravens landed on the back of the sofa. One of them hopped onto her shoulder.

"Eileen was not the only one," whispered Memory into her ear.

"But I didn't love her enough," said Jo. "If I had, I wouldn't have got mad at her. I wouldn't have insisted that she come home that night. She would still be alive."

"You loved her truly," said Memory.

"You had a moment of doubt, that's all," said Thought, landing on her other shoulder. "After all, you're only human."

Tears welled up in Jo's eyes and slid down her cheeks. Her heart gave way and she began to sob in earnest. Thought and Memory murmured soothing sounds into her ear and preened her hair. Jo cried until exhaustion overtook her and she fell asleep.

The phone rang, dragging Jo out of a deep slumber. She rolled over on the couch and looked up at the ceiling. It was intact; no hole marked where Memory had forced his way in.

The phone rang again and Jo sat up. The portrait Eileen had painted of Birdbrained stood on the mantelpiece next to the one of Frida. Jo took a deep breath, feeling a now familiar ache between her ribs.

The phone rang again.

She leaned across the sofa and grabbed the receiver. As she brought it to her ear, a small black feather came loose from her hair and wafted down to the floor.

Mermaid

by Rhea Rose-Fleming

today I walked on the roof of the mouth of the sea.
When she inhaled
exposing the ridged dark grey sand
of her upper palate,
I picked my way down from the bluffs and cliffs,
her grin,
sauntered the highest thin hot line of shore,
her lips,

side stepping the barnacled rocks,
her teeth,
not in rows but scattered
knocked around by the endless
grind and mastication of her hunger.

In her mouth empty of ocean,
bits of kelp stuck between rocks,
fish jellied in the sun,
tiny watery soft creatures sucked
their hard doors closed,
goeducks like great fringed pores
spit up at me, envious of my mobility.

Stepping over the small tidal pools of saliva,
toe-dipping into the deep bowls of cool, live chowder
skipping past shards of molluscs, cockles and butter
   clams
dashed and baking

I printed with my bare feet, the soft wet skin,
of her mouth.

When she exhales and returns to the cleaned
picked and tickled squeaks the flutters and stale claws,
when she rushes her wet tongue across
the ridges of her sandy palate
sensing sucking swilling flavours
over ancient roof,
will she remember?
among the voracious clicks and scuttles
soft shooing of sand hiders
and the grinding bump of rocks
chewing,
the taste of the salt
left behind from my
two bare feet?

The Coin

by Casey June Wolf

Likner walked away from the girl with the message from
his mother. They hadn't talked long, but she had carefully
taken the red cuvette of mangoes from her head and given
him two, then lifted the heavy load back onto the curl of
cloth that rested on her braided hair.

His baby sister had died. He had seen her only once —
she'd been so tiny. She had lived with their mother and
Likner's other sisters on the steep mountainside on the road
to Vertierres. It might be a good idea, he thought, to visit
his mother soon. Maybe he could find a coconut for her.
But the idea made him feel leaden. He pushed it out of his
mind, and headed for the boulevard, nipping the top of
the first mango and peeling it with his teeth.

Likner followed the narrow street to the boulevard by
the sea where the sun, hot since rising, climbed above the
barely moving water of the bay. Here the sea bumped gently
against a long concrete wall instead of washing along a
beach, and the road that followed the wall was surprisingly smooth. The occasional rusted taxis and big 4x4s
could race on it unhindered by potholes and cracks, by
market stalls or crowds of people.

He started off toward downtown. His gaze shifted from
the sea and low mountains to the tiny makeshift fishing
boats, and back to the road he travelled. Here and there,
small groups of people sat on broken benches or dangled
their legs over the seawall, talking low among themselves.
On the other side of the road were the houses of the people
who owned the 4x4s. He scanned the tall palms in their
yards for their great pale fruit.

He passed a littered beach, the empty tourist market, and then the docks. As he came abreast with a pair of rusted freighters standing in the oily water of the bay, he could see a little clutch of boys down the street by the bakery. He had expected to find them there. It was nearly Karnaval and they were dressing us as zenglendoes to "rob" the patrons at Bagay La. He watched as they huddled around the door, waiting for customers to come back out.

At six, Likner was the youngest of these boys living on the streets of Okap. Like him, they wore shorts and dirty t-shirts that hung like dresses, and nothing on their feet. But they had also smeared their skin with motor oil, and cobbled together fake knives and guns.

In other places in the city, grown men dressed as soldiers walked with musicians who carried the noisy homemade instruments of the rara band. They were stopping traffic at busy corners and demanding coins to let the vehicles pass. The boys knew the methods well. They crowded around a handful of blans who were coming out of the door. Likner hung back watching as the others brandished their weapons menacingly, smiling beneath the ferocity of their scowls. Two missionaries brushed past them with wry grins and flip remarks in Creole. A third, a pale white woman, followed. The boys closed ranks around her and held out oily hands. She shook her head and said something incomprehensible that wasn't Creole, didn't sound like French, might have been English. Bouki grinned and made as if to smear her clothes with oil if she didn't hand something over. She winked and moved forward. They let her by.

The blan was sitting on the low wall beside the sea. The water made impatient little pushes at the concrete, urging bits of garbage back toward the shore. Down the block the beach rose, littered with plastic bags and old, roughmade chairs, well-stripped car frames and a blend of mango pits, coconut husks, and shreds of sugar cane fibre that gave off all together a thick dank smell of rot. Bouki and Benji were already with the blan, working her. Likner walked up slowly. She was shaking her head. Turning her pockets inside out. Benji snorted. *Sure* she had no money. His closed face locked and he turned away. Bouki shrugged and turned away from her, unconcerned.

He grinned at Likner and bent to scoop a little rock. Knowing Bouki's games, Likner ducked as it sailed toward him, grabbed a bigger one and rushed forward for a revenge throw at Bouki. The woman grabbed his wrist as he went hurtling by. Bouki smacked him hard and skipped away. The woman held Likner until his struggling ceased, then set him down and waited. He turned and stared.

Likner never really expected much. Half the time he didn't even ask for money. He never pushed the blans like the other boys. He didn't dream someone would take him home, to Canada or the States or France, give him money to go to school or buy a house for his mama. But even he couldn't escape a little skipping in his heart, a little difficulty with his breath when she looked at him and smiled. Because you never know, do you? You never *really* know.

Yesterday he'd thought that she was white-blonde, with gem-blue eyes and skin like shaved ice. Today he saw her hair was a light brown, and the blue eyes were tinged with green. She looked at him for a long time, steadily. He decided to try.

"Ba m senk goud," he told her. She cocked her head. "Give me one dolla," he said in English. She understood.

Bouki and Benji were gone. She reached into her pocket, one she had turned inside out earlier, and pulled out a large, dull coin. She put it in his hand, closed his fingers around it, and looked into his eyes. She pointed to the coin, pointed to his pocket, closed her fist. "Don't lose it," she was telling him. Then she stood up, gave him a little pinch on the nose, and walked away.

He stared at the coin, empty of feeling. It wasn't Haitian. Or American. He squinted. He couldn't read, but he knew them all. It wasn't Canadian or Belgian or French. He could barely make out the shape of a woman — an American, he thought, by her face and hair — and on the other side ... perhaps a fish.

He heard a shout and looked in the direction she had gone. Ezo and Bouki and Ti Patrik, sparring and yelling as they wandered up the street. The blan was nowhere to be seen.

The coin was a disappointment. He looked at it numbly. He surprised himself with what he did next, without even thinking. He tossed it over the wall and into the muttering sea. The water swallowed it and it left his thoughts. Bending, he scooped up a nicely weighted stone. Straightened and aimed at Bouki's shaved head.

Likner sat on the darkened stoop across from the Merci Jesu Bar and Grill. People stood lined up waiting for manyòk juice and white bread with spicy peanut butter. A couple of the boys stood by the doorway, available for handouts. Likner felt a presence at his elbow and turned. It was the blan. Her dark hair was pulled back from her face in a tight bun. How could he not have noticed before that she was a grimèl? Though her skin was not dark, the Haitian features were unmistakeable. She smiled at him, as if he had been very naughty. She held out the coin.

"Pa perdi li," she said in Creole. Don't lose it. She nodded sharply and he stuffed it in his pocket without a word. One of the boys noticed her there and came over to talk. She winked at Likner, smiled at him, and walked away listening to the other boy.

That night, when Likner was alone, he looked at the coin again. The woman's features were a little clearer. She had her eyes raised and her hands as well, her head twisted a little to one side, as if she was dancing. He turned it over. The fish was very long. It arced as though diving into the sea.

He walked along the boulevard, considering. What could he buy with this? Nothing. What could he trade it for? Not much. His business sense said to trade it. His gut said to hell with it. To hell with the big shot blans and their money. To hell with their promises. He took it out again, glanced up the long, dark street. Three men laughed and talked loudly a few steps away from him. One lone man leaned against the seawall a half a block in front of him. The man filled up his lungs and sang horridly into the gentle breeze that came in off the sea. Likner thought of offering him the coin. But no. Instead, he turned to the sea again. He aimed it far out in the water, where it was deep, where the woman would not see it and fetch it back. And he threw it in.

Likner woke to the sound of gentle breathing. He lay on the sidewalk in a little cluster of boys. Jean Denis' long arm was resting on his face. The moon had left the sky. He sat up, let his legs dangle over the wall that faced the water, and stuffed his hands into his pockets. Something hard was in there. He pulled it out. The coin. Only now the woman was changed. He stiffened. She was the mambo dancing before they poisoned the owners and burned the plantations and started the revolution. He knew that it was her. He turned it over and there was La Sirene, rising in all her scaled majesty from her element, the sea.

Don't lose it, she had said. It wasn't a visa. It wasn't a schoolbag. It wasn't even a hunk of bread. But anyone would know it was a wanga, though whose or why he had it or what it was meant to do he didn't know. He leapt up and hurled it as far as it would go and turned to race away from the sea.

He stopped. For a second he thought the moon had fallen from the sky and hovered in front of his face. He blinked. It was her, holding the coin up in her dark brown hand, a little smile playing on her face. Her black hair stood stiffly out on every side.

"It was an orphanage," she said in perfect Creole. Where was she getting these words? "With a school and uniforms and a library that actually has books." He stepped to one side, hoping to get around her. "It was a boat. Forty people and high seas and nothing to eat, nothing to drink. Do you think they'll reach America? Do you think they'll let them land? Do you think that they'll be welcome if they manage to sneak ashore?" He made a break. She nabbed him easily and held him while he wriggled.

"Good," she said. She pinned him down. Some of the other boys were starting to rouse. The ocean slapped the wall and spattered them with spray. "It was a marine. He strafed the fighters in the hills and made their families build the roads. He killed their pigs." Her teeth clicked together as she sank against the curb, her black fingers tight around him still. "It was a houngan. What do you think a houngan can do? Draw vevers and dance for the spirits all night? Anything else? Can he do *anything*? Is he worshipping devils like the missionaries say? Is he always drunk?" Her legs twined around each other and fused into a long, scaled tail. She released his arm and bellied over the waking boys, paused for a second on the wall and blinked great green eyes at him. "It was a poet. He sketched his words in Creole, dipped his pen in his blood, wrote with the loops of his intestines. Did you hear him scream? Did you hear him laugh with joy?

"It was a wish, Likner. Would you like to learn to see with eyes like mine? Would you like to find your own?" She blinked her great green eyes at him. So green, they were nearly coal. "It was a dream. Do you dream, Likner? Would you like to give that up?"

She dove over the side and disappeared in the inky water with a hearty splash. "Come on," he heard in his mind. "Follow and see. See if your arm can bend this wave."

One by one, the boys sat up stiffly, looking confusedly around them. Likner watched the water shifting where she had disappeared, heard it tapping at the wall. Tentatively, he put his hand back in his pocket. Met something small, round, hard. Just for now, he decided not to look.

Jimmy Away to Me
by Sarah Totton

I couldn't picture Jimmy Aldebaran's face. In my mind he stood on the riverbank, left hand plunged past the wrist in his coat pocket, right hand pinning the sketchbook to his chest like a shield. I remembered him not by his face, but by that hand, wrapped in blue silk, dressed with golden rings — the hand that had drawn the landscape of *Bron y mor* as though I could reach through the glass and touch it. That was how I remembered him.

I wondered if Mark remembered him like this — Mark who'd known Jimmy in high school, who'd driven from Sudbury with Jimmy's mother, who stopped me in the funeral home parking lot to ask me how this could have happened to Jimmy — this Mark who had the strength to ask that question, to say that name, when even the trees should not be standing that day.

That was how it was for me — no fight left, eyes dissolving, fist clutched tight around the marble in my mitten, reciting in my head the only magic I'd ever known: *Come by, Jimmy. Come by, come by...*

That magic my uncle Paul had taught me, years ago. When my hands grew large enough to grip a wooden rod eight inches long between my thumb and smallest finger, he taught me to play a piece on the piano called "Rustle of Spring". I knew how it was supposed to sound because I had heard him play it, but I recognized none of that magical sound in what I played, chipping and hacking at the notes, hands stretched taut over the keys.

And then one day in the dead of winter, my splaying hands had sunk through the fog that had covered the keyboard and I touched something alive. My left hand, rippling over the white keys, became sunlight sparkling on cliffs. Above them, the black keys bobbed like the shadows of leaves in a summer breeze. And the song was a shivering swell of water dragging sound through a thousand rattling stones. When it ended, I touched my cheek and felt the heat of a summer sun burning on the back of my hand.

Uncle Paul had called that place *Bron y mor*. It was the place he touched every time he played "Rustle of Spring". It was the place everyone went, he told me, when he did the one thing he did better than anything else. And it was where Jimmy went when he crouched over his sketchbook with a pencil laced through his fingers.

I never played 'Rustle of Spring' again, not like I had that day. I came to master the notes, but its music never returned to me. Even the memory of it, so vivid at first, gradually faded, leaving me with a sense of the seasons and of the colours, blue, green, and grey.

Then, long after I'd given up looking for *Bron y mor* in that piece of music, I found it again in a completely different way. Through a marble. I called it glass dreaming. I used clear glass marbles, the ones with petals and twists of dye inside — 'plainsies' people called them. When a plainsy spun, it breathed, it undulated, it took you in. The green glass went smoky and when I looked into its centre, sometimes I'd glimpse that place again. It was only a fleeting look, but it was all I'd had. Until I'd met Jimmy Aldebaran.

Mark was waiting for me to speak. He seemed older than I was, a lot bigger than Jimmy, mirrored sunglasses, head and hands bare in this bitter cold. I looked away from him and tried to stop shivering.

"You were his friend, Emma?" he said.

I nodded.

"Can I talk to you?" he said. He looked at me through those silver disks.

"About what?"

"I want to see where it happened. Can you take me there?"

I looked at him, appalled.

"Please?" he said.

I heard the catch in his voice, and, for a moment Jimmy lived in that sound. And I thought, I can't help Jimmy now, but I can help someone who cared about him. That was why I took Mark to Riverside Park.

It was a long walk across town, soundless except for the scratching of our boots on the salty pavement. Jimmy hung like a living thing in the air between us. So many memories, and the sweetest one, the day I'd shown Jimmy glass dreaming.

Jimmy had backed into my room without knocking, a paper plate balanced on his left hand, the sketchbook clutched to himself with the right. He flicked off his shoes, lay down on my bed putting his feet up on the spread, and flipped open the sketchbook. I watched him from my desk. He produced a thick pencil, threaded it through his silk-wrapped hand, and proceeded to sketch something in his book. He noticed me watching him.

"Garlic bread?" he said. He lifted a piece off the plate beside him, took a bite out of it and then proffered the bitten end to me.

"No thanks." I went back to studying. I could hear him chewing.

"I'm sorry," he said after a few seconds. "Are you busy?"

"I've got an exam tomorrow."

"Oh." He lay back on my bed and idly flipped through his sketchbook. He was quiet for a few moments. "Everyone thinks I'm weird," he said.

"So? Everybody's weird."

"No, everyone's normal. Like you," he said.

"What?" I put my pen down. "I am *not*."

"You are," he said. "I can tell. People who're weird know they're weird."

"Then I'm definitely weird," I said, "and I know why."

"Why?"

I'd seen Jimmy's drawings before, and I'd sensed an inkling of something in them, even then. Maybe that was why I showed him. Or maybe because I believed I'd kept the secret of *Bron y mor* to myself for long enough.

As I upended the mock leather bag, spilling marbles over my desk, I told him what to look for. "You want one with tints, like the iris of an eye: green for the grass, blue for the sea, and grey for the stones. When they come together, you'll know you've arrived. Don't worry about the pattern."

Jimmy couldn't grasp this. He was an artist; pattern was important to him. In the end, I chose one for him, one with petals of blue and grey dye in the green glass. I dragged my arm across the desk, sending the rest of the marbles clattering into the open drawer.

"Now," I said, "you pick a direction and spin it. If you spin left, it's *come by*. If you spin right, it's *away to me*."

"You what?" said Jimmy.

I'd spent years developing a technique on my own. It felt odd having to explain it to someone. "It's a shepherd's code. When they're bringing in the sheep, they give their dogs commands. *Come by* means 'Approach me, circling left'. *Away to me* means 'Approach me, circling right'."

Jimmy took off his glasses and stared through the marble. "All right. So what happens after I call the dog? Do I see sheep or what?"

"Forget about sheep. It's what's in the marble that you're calling to you. Just spin it. And don't blink until it stops turning or it won't work."

He couldn't spin the marble with his right hand — the scarf stopped him gripping it properly — so he had to spin it with his left. Over the burr of glass on wood, he murmured, "*Come by, come by.*"

The green glass spun milky, buzzing like a chorus of cicadas and the blue and the grey merged in an undulating funnel inside the glass. For a moment I thought he wouldn't see anything, that maybe *Bron y mor* was something only Uncle Paul and I could see. Through the glass, I'd only had the briefest glimpse of it. Would he know, would he understand what it was if it appeared to him this way?

But when the pattern chopped out and the marble stilled, I looked up to see Jimmy's eyes shining like beacons.

"What did you see?" I said, beginning to hope.

He was staring still, into the marble, unblinking. "I think..."

"You think what?"

"I can smell ... nutmeg."

That night, he drew a bird in coloured chalk, blue, green and grey, with teeth like mother-of-pearl.

Riverside Park was darker than I remembered. I felt the trees hanging over us before we'd even crossed the field. Mark and I walked single file, taking turns breaking a trail through the snow.

It had happened above the dam. I heard the water before I saw it. The sound was like a summer wind rattling leaves, or a thousand marbles spinning. But these trees were bare and the only marble here was in my hand. Halfway across the clearing, we stopped. Ice opened in a fan-shaped pattern around the foot of the dam where the water flickered, like ghosts in green froth, over the concrete embankment.

"Here?" said Mark.

"At the top of the dam. Under the bridge."

I led him up. Above the roaring dam, the quiet was almost deafening, peaceful. The water was completely frozen, crossed by a footbridge. On the opposite shore, an orange board that read: "Danger: Thin ice" had been nailed to a weeping willow hanging over the water. There had been only one witness, the newspapers had said. She had been walking her dog by the dam and had seen Jimmy step out onto the ice and break through.

"I know this place," said Mark. "Why?"

Cold wind and tears silvered the air. We stood for a while in silence. I squeezed the cold glass in my mitten.

"I'm going to take a look," said Mark.

"Why?"

"I want to see. They never found his body, did they? Maybe it was a mistake."

I watched him as he walked toward the bridge. It made me shiver, the way he moved, so eerily intent, as though he expected to find Jimmy there. He left the path and stepped down the slope toward the water's edge where the new snow was marked with footprints. Then he disappeared into the shadows under the bridge and I was alone. I clutched the marble in my mitten. *Come by, come by...*

"Jimmy?" I whispered.

His name fractured in the air. On the opposite shore, shadows spread like thin arms from the dead stalks of cattails poking through the snow. A gust of wind dusted powder from the roof of the covered bridge, stirring the pendulous yellow tendrils of the weeping willow. I let my eyes drift out of focus and for a moment, a brief flicker, the colour of the tree seemed to deepen just slightly, to pale green, and the tips of the branchlets dropped in coloured strands to long tubes, gilded and painted. The fragrance of wild spices and a sound like wind chimes filtered through the air. Hardness and coldness and light spun inside me.

"Careful, Emma!"

The collar of my coat tightened and jerked against my throat.

"Step back. Slowly," said Mark.

That was when I felt the slickness under my boots, and I realized that I was standing on cracking ice with the river rustling below me. As Mark pulled me back onto the shore, my knees dropped. He held me up as the music, and the memory of it, faded. The ground under my feet trembled with the force of the water as it roared over the dam. That, and the cold air, settled me.

"Why did you do that?" said Mark. He sounded shaken. "What did you see under the bridge?"

"I saw the hole. It doesn't look big enough for..."

"You didn't ... hear anything?" I said. "Under there?"

"No."

I pressed my mitten to my face and breathed winter air filtered through the wool. "Nutmeg."

"Emma?" he said.

I felt him shake me. "Maybe you should sit down."

I shook my head.

"You and Jimmy were pretty close, weren't you?" he said.

"What do you think happens to people, after they die?" I said.

"I think the more relevant question is what happens to them *before* they die."

I felt a peculiar and disturbing clarity at those words. "That was why you wanted to come here."

"Yes," he said. "I thought if I saw it, I'd understand. But I don't. Tell me, Emma, did he ever mention me to you?"

"No."

I wanted to go back to my room and stare at the walls until the pain went away, until the world stopped ending. I pulled away from Mark and crossed the footbridge. I heard him scrambling to catch up to me. Maybe that's why he didn't see it. But I did. The flash of blue on the willow tree was like a needlehook in my heart. I stepped off the path and went toward it, ignoring Mark's sudden shout. I stood numbly and stared at it, bright blue and flickering, caught on the bark: Jimmy's scarf, fluttering there like a dying moth. Mark did what I didn't dare do; he plucked it off the tree.

"It might have caught on the bark," he said quietly. "It's probably ... oh my God."

He was staring at the back of the orange sign. And then I saw what he saw, on the ledge of wood making up the frame: a pair of glasses, the lenses shining like living eyes in the last light of the day. They'd been set there with care so that they wouldn't fall. Jimmy had always taken them off before doing his sketches, but without them, he could barely see to walk around.

"Emma?"

"No, be quiet."

"Emma, did Jimmy say anything to you before he came here?"

I shook my head. "I didn't see him that day."

"Did he leave you a note? Did he give you anything beforehand? A letter? Anything?"

"— Yes. Not a letter."

"Can I see it?" he said.

"I don't have it," I said. "It's in my room."

"Then I'll take you back to residence. I've got to meet his mom there anyway. She's collecting Jimmy's things."

On the way back to residence, I asked Mark to let me hold Jimmy's scarf. I tried to imagine the warmth of Jimmy's hand as I twisted folds of it around each finger of my right hand.

The day after Jimmy disappeared, the police had interviewed me for nearly an hour. They'd asked the same kinds of questions Mark asked me as we walked. Had he seemed unhappy when I'd known him? I turned my thoughts away from that last week, back to the early days of the semester. He'd seen *Bron y mor*, just as I had, only clearer. There were hints of it in the things he'd drawn before I'd even shown him. He must have known it a long time; he was connected to that place more intimately than I would ever be. To see *Bron y mor* the way he had.... He had been a visionary. Unhappy, never, but...

One week after I'd shown glass dreaming to Jimmy, he'd burst into my room.

"I know where it is," he told me. "Come outside."

I didn't have to ask him what it was; he told me as we descended the stairwell. "I saw it in the marble, in the glass, but then I realized it really was *in* the glass."

He led me away from the university into the heart of the city. In the main square he hesitated, casting around the buildings.

"It's changed," he said.

"What are you looking for?"

"It's near the church — there!" He strode off with hard deliberate steps, crossing a parking lot to a road between a row of older buildings. The street was actually cobbled here. The further along Jimmy went, the quicker he walked until he broke into a run. Then suddenly he checked in mid-stride opposite a doorway set into the stone. He looked right at it, and for a second, he seemed almost scared. Then he pushed open the door and went inside.

It was a pub. Not a bar, but a quiet, dim little room. Net curtains on big copper rings were pulled across a bay window in the back wall. Light filtered through the rippled glass in the panes of that window. Some of the

panes were coloured and when Jimmy pulled back the
curtain, I saw a bird in the window done in stained glass
and mother of pearl — not exactly like the one in his sketchbook, but similar. Jimmy pressed his right hand in its silk
wrapping against the glass. A half-smile crossed his face.

Jimmy had only rarely mentioned his past to me. I knew
that he'd lived in this city until he was nine years old. That
was why he'd applied to university here, though there were
many others in the province with a better Fine Arts program. He'd wanted to come home again. His childhood
had been haunting him, hovering on the edges of dreams,
clinging to the bricks and stones of his hometown, but the
memories hadn't returned — until I'd spun him a glass
dream.

"My father made that bird," said Jimmy. "He was an
artist too. A glass artist, but he taught me to draw. He
showed me how to get it down, from here," he touched
his head. "where it's bright and amazing to — *bam*!" He
slapped the sketchbook. "Here on the paper. He taught me
that your hand wicks visions out of your head onto the
paper. That's why it's called 'drawing'. And it works the
other way too. The brush sucks up the colours, makes your
hand tingle. Green, like that colour in the window, freezes
you right to your fingertips.

"He used to take me to this pub every Saturday when
he was alive, and we'd walk home along the river, past
the dam. He died when I was nine. Cancer. But I remember
him. He taught me to see *inside* things, past things. You
see that way too, don't you?"

"I can't do what you can do," I said. "I can't bring it out
and put it on paper. That's a gift."

He closed his sketchbook and meandered around the
bar with a kind of furtive happiness, stroking the velvet
cushions in the bench along the wall, crouching under the
tables, peering behind the curtains. Finally, he sat down
at a table in the corner and took the marble I'd given him
out of his pocket.

"Show me again," he said.

I spoke to him about *Bron y mor* as the marble spun. He
stopped it with his palm before it even slowed.

"I know that place," he said. He had a strained look about him, as though he were trying to remember something. "I've been there before."

The sketchbook was under my pillow where I'd left it. I hesitated, holding it while Mark stood in the doorway of my room. He took the book out of my hand and opened it to the first page. I sat down on my bed, pulled the marble out of my mitten and tapped it lightly on my desk. I could hear footsteps in the hallway outside and I pretended it was Jimmy coming down to talk to me.

"The covered bridge," said Mark suddenly. "That's why I recognized it. There was a painting he did when we were in high school. It won the art award that year. It was the same bridge."

He was silent for a bit, turning the pages. I'd only had the sketchbook a few days, but I'd gone through it a hundred times. Most of the pages were covered in chip and cookie crumbs and white powdered sugar from the donuts Jimmy had loved. He'd eaten constantly while he worked, but he'd never gotten fat.

Pages one to thirty were landscapes from around town, some in coloured chalk, some in pencil. There was a magic in them, but it was the muted kind, like a beautiful song played so softly you could barely hear it.

The next pictures were the ones he'd drawn after I'd shown him glass dreaming, places he'd given names to: "Cold Keep", "Black Tor", and others. These were followed by pictures I could hardly believe were his. Wooden twig-men with twisted limbs, ice-men cracked in pieces, like glass falling from a window. There were no crumbs on these pages.

"Death imagery," said Mark.

I used the *tick-tick-tick* of his thumbnail as he flipped through the pages to time the marble as I spun it.

"Did he seem depressed the last few weeks, Emma?"

Two, three, four.... "Not really."

The marble buzzed, *Away to me, away to me....* After a time, it spun out, stilled, and the ticking stopped. I knew the picture Mark had come to.

It was a pond filled with clear water. Deep in the bottom lay a circular pit made of stone, like a well. Its walls were crumbling and ancient. In its centre lay a tumble of splintered bones, green with algae. One of the bones, a small one, was gripped in the long, narrow jaws of a skull — not human. The teeth in the skull were conical and opalescent. The ring of stone forming the wall of the well was broken in one place. Across this gap fell a thin shadow that crossed the bones, melting into them. The shadow was cast by a cat-tail at the surface which hung above the water like the bowed head of someone at prayer.

I picked up the marble and spun it again, timing it as it slowed.

"What's with all the blank pages?" said Mark. "This book's half empty."

"Yeah," I said. *One, two, three...*

The surface of the marble shimmered like melted sugar. I could almost feel heat pouring from it. It became harder and harder to keep my eyes open...

"When did he give it to you?"

...*five, six, seven...* "The eighth."

"Of December?"

"Mmmm..."

"Look at this picture; it's dated. Shit! That can't be right. Did you write this, Emma?"

...*nine, ten, eleven...* The marble wobbled and the blur unravelled into three separate colours.

"Huh? No, I didn't write in his book."

"Did he borrow it back after he gave it to you?"

I set the marble between my fingers. "No." And spun again.

"When was the last time you saw him? Emma? Why am I talking to myself? *Emma!*" The whirl of the marble caught me up. I felt rather than saw Mark's hand bang down and pin it still.

"Why do you do that?" he said.

"It's something to do." I could almost feel the echo of *Bron y mor*. As long as I didn't blink, I could keep it there.

"This is important. When was the last time you saw Jimmy? *Emma!*" He waved his hand in front of my eyes.

Bron y mor dissolved like chalk in the rain. I sighed and allowed it to recede.

"It must have been after the eighth," said Mark. "Look at this."

He showed me the last page in the book: an outline of a hand with the fingers outstretched. The page was torn, the rough edge truncating the index finger of the hand. Just below the thumb was a complex insignia. I couldn't decipher it. I'd figured it was a stylized signature.

"So?" I asked him.

"So look at that." He pointed to the insignia. "They're numbers: 1 1 1 2. It's the date: Eleventh day, twelfth month. December 11th. The day he died."

"What's that word then, by the numbers?"

"Looks like 'Kins', or 'King'. But it's the date that matters. He must have given this book to you on that day."

"Why does that matter?" I said. "What difference does it make now?"

"It's evidence," he said. "Don't you see? Don't you realize how important this is? It was the day he died."

He looked at me expectantly. But there was nothing to say.

Mark took hold of my hand and unravelled Jimmy's scarf from between my fingers. "Look. There are three possibilities: One, foul play. I think we can rule that out — the witness claims he was alone. Two, misadventure. He didn't realize the ice wasn't thick enough to bear his weight. Possible, but why take his glasses off first?"

"Maybe he went there to sketch something," I said.

"...He'd already given his sketchbook to you," said Mark "Which leaves suicide."

"No."

"What I want to know is, why did he give his sketchbook to you? Or did you just take it?"

"No!"

"Then tell me what happened when he gave this to you. What did he say?"

I hadn't seen Jimmy in eight days. I'd known there was something wrong and I suspected the reason. Visiting *Bron y mor* had a price; glass dreaming had often left me lethargic and displaced. Sometimes even when I came out of it, part of me never left and it would drag me down like an anchor. Days would pass and I wouldn't speak to another person; they were around me, but they didn't seem real. They'd put my marbles away when I'd started failing school. And it was strange, but at the time I was almost relieved. Though the feeling of *Bron y mor* was often one of euphoria and I missed it terribly, it had begun to haunt me, and to frighten me. I felt its sweet promise as a sort of menacing call, one that caused me to lose myself so that I would spend days afterwards as though in search of my own soul.

I hadn't told Jimmy this. I suspected he knew now. And then one evening, on the 10th of December, I saw him in the hallway coming back from the porter's desk with a big box under his arm.

"Hey, Jimmy. Long time no see. Who's the package from?"

"My mum."

"Bit early for Christmas, isn't it?"

"I dunno."

We got back to his room. It was more of a mess than usual. He opened the box with an X-ACTO knife and pulled out a few plastic-wrapped packages and a painted cookie tin. Inside the tin were homemade gingerbread men with happy faces on them.

"Hey, treasure trove!" I said.

While I worked the tape off one of the plastic bags, he sat on the edge of his bed. He picked up one of the gingerbread men, abruptly snapped off its arm and dropped it into the garbage can. He picked up another one and did the same thing.

"What are you doing?!"

"I'm not hungry."

"Then give them to me," I said. "What's the matter with you? Your mom made these for you."

"Who cares?" said Jimmy quietly.

"Jimmy," I said. "What's up?"

He was sitting hunched over in his chair, staring at the floor. I could hear him breathing loudly and slowly, as though it took great effort.

"Do you know what the devil is?" he said.

"What do you mean?"

"The devil."

"Some red guy with horns?"

"It's not a guy," said Jimmy. "It's a *thing*. It's the shadow under a cloud. And the cloud is in your backyard. And it's going to rain and the dog is outside and you want to call him in, you want to save him, but you're afraid to open the door because if you do, you'll never close it in time."

I laughed to break the tension, and failed. "Jimmy, let's go down to the caf' and get some coffee, okay?"

His sketchbook was on the desk. I took it with me. I didn't know why — I suppose I didn't think it should be left behind. He didn't want coffee so I got him a glass of water. We sat at a table by the boxes of Christmas stock that the cafe was selling off before the holidays.

"Can I do anything, Jimmy?"

"That smell," he said. He held his hand under his nose. There were still cookie crumbs on it. "Nutmeg."

He grabbed the sketchbook and opened it to the picture of the pond. With his finger, he traced the white slope of the hill, down the fall of land to the edge of the shore.

"Water..." he murmured.

He reached for his glass, nearly tipping it over before picking it up. He sipped from it, running his hand along the cat-tails, smudging the chalk across the surface of the water and then down.

"Sinking," said Jimmy. He spoke like someone half asleep. His finger dropped toward the centre of the well.

"Salt," he said suddenly.

On downward, his finger drifted to the pile of bones until it touched the gaping skull. And then he screamed. It was more of an exclamation, short, violent, but the sound was sucked back into his mouth almost immediately. The cashier by the counter looked over in alarm, but Jimmy had stopped screaming almost as soon as he'd started, as though jolted awake.

He looked at the cup in front of him, considering it intently. He reached for the salt shaker on the table and sprinkled some of it into the water. Then he sipped it.

"Saltwater," he said.

He unscrewed the top of the shaker and tipped it upside down over the glass. Salt drifted to the bottom. He swirled it around.

"Jimmy, what are you doing?"

Without acknowledging me, Jimmy tipped the glass back and drained it to the slush at the bottom. He flinched as he set it down. Then he retched and spat some of it out. The glass hit the floor and exploded as he stumbled for the door.

I found him throwing up in the bushes by the door. He paused, still looking at the snow, and said, "Don't watch me."

The snow was falling thick, and far off I heard the muffled sounds of the late night traffic. I counted snow-flakes until he moved again.

"I'm sorry," he said finally.

"Come back inside, Jimmy." I turned him towards me.

"The dog's barking," he said suddenly. "It wants to come to me and I want to go to it. Sometimes. I want to go on here, but there's a cloud in my backyard, and I've left the door open. I can feel it right up my arm."

"Jimmy, I don't understand. What can I do?"

He shook his head and then he seemed to be falling so that I had to hold him up. I realized with a shock how thin he was, the ridge of each vertebra palpable under his shirt.

I felt him relax suddenly. "I remember now," he said. He sounded calmer, steady. "There was a ribbon tied to a branch. Blue and gold. I reached out and caught it. Gold threading around and around that branch, and gold, around and around my hand. It's still there. I can feel the sun on it now ... Did you hear that?" He let go of me.

"Hear what?" The only sound was the wind in the tops of the bare trees.

"The bird," he said.

"It's night time. It's winter, Jimmy."

"No," he said. "It's not."

He stepped away from me.

"Jimmy, are you all right?"

"I will be," he said. "I know what I have to do."

He'd given me the sketchbook as we'd gone upstairs. "I don't need pictures anymore," he'd said. "I can see it now."

I looked at Mark, standing with his arms crossed, the sketchbook pinched between his finger and thumb.

"What I want to know is, why you? Why did he give it to you?"

"I knew what the pictures meant."

"Would you care to explain that?" he said.

"...It's private."

"Don't think you're sparing my feelings," he said. "Spit it out. Was it about me?"

"No. You wouldn't understand," I told him.

Mark tossed the book onto my bed. "I *want* to understand," he said. "Jimmy was my friend — more than my friend — and yet he picked *you* to give this to. Why? Were you sleeping with him?"

"— What?"

"Were you *fucking* him?" Blunt, it hit like a fist.

"No!"

I saw a glint of satisfaction in Mark's eyes as I said that. I knew then that he didn't understand — was incapable of understanding — what I'd actually done with Jimmy and how much more intimate it had been.

"No," I said. "I didn't fuck him. I would never have done that to him."

Mark looked nonplussed for a moment, but I was shaking. "I'm sorry," he said at last. "I had to know."

"Can I have my marble back please?"

Guilt opened his hand and I took it from him, looked him in the eyes.

"You hurt him, didn't you?" I said. "You bastard."

He looked away from me to the scarf on the desk and gathered it in his hand.

"What are you going to do with that?" I said.

"It has to be turned over to the police, as evidence. The sketchbook too."

I reached behind me and picked it up, but I didn't give it to him. "Evidence of what? He didn't kill himself."

"How would you know?" said Mark. "He didn't tell you everything. He didn't tell you about me."

I didn't know what expression was on my face when he said that, but Mark's went from resignation to pity.

"Look, I'd better go and see how his mom's doing." He stood up. "Do you want to come with me?"

Jimmy's room was full of boxes. Walls bare, posters gone. A woman bending over the desk, straightened to face me. She was old, grey hair poking out from under a bright green head scarf. I could imagine it rasping against the material as she'd wrapped it around her head. It made me think of Jimmy's hand and his blue silk scarf. There was nothing else about her like Jimmy. I believed for a moment, that he had never been a part of her. And then I pictured her alone in her kitchen drawing smiles on the faces of gingerbread men. I thought for a second I would break like the arm of that gingerbread man. And then, on an impulse, I held out the sketchbook to her.

"This was Jimmy's," I said.

She took it from me. When she spoke, she had a faint accent. "Is your name Emma?"

"Yes — How did you know?"

"Then these are your books?" she said. She lifted a box from the desk and held it out to me.

"Yes." I took it without looking inside. I stood there for a moment. There was something I had to know. "Mrs. Aldebaran?"

"Yes, Emma?"

"What happened to Jimmy's hand?"

Maybe I imagined the pause after I said it, a wave of dread, like when you go in for a booster shot and you wince as soon as you feel the cool dab of the alcohol swab and you wait forever before the needle goes in.

"He was only three," she said. "He climbed the fence at the end of the yard. One minute he was there, the next.... He fell into the river behind the house. A neighbour rescued him. The neighbour thought he must have caught his hand on something in the riverbed — he'd had to pull him quite hard to get him free, and when he was brought up, his finger was gone. He was too young to remember — he asked me about it once and I told him that God had taken it and was keeping it safe for him in heaven. For a long time afterward, I was afraid my little boy would be taken away from me again," she said. "And now —"

"I have to go," I said abruptly. "I'm sorry." I couldn't stand to hear any more. I backed to the door, sidestepped into the hallway and bolted up the stairs. I slammed the door to my room and threw the books on the bed. I looked around. The sketchbook. I'd given away the only thing of Jimmy's I'd had. I had nothing left. Only the books that he'd borrowed from me.

I took a book out of the box. He'd touched them, read them, painted from them.... I shivered, picturing his hand — I had never looked at it closely; it would have seemed an invasion of his privacy somehow.

Now he was gone, and if Mark was right ... then Jimmy would have left me something to explain why. If he had left something behind for me, where would he have put it? Somewhere he'd known I would see it. Not in the sketchbook; I'd already looked. Not in his room; the police had searched it and found nothing. So, nowhere obvious. I sat down on the bed, held the book by its spine and shook it out. Nothing. Unless it was pinched tight between the pages. Hands shaking, I leafed page by page through it. Half of me wanted desperately to find something. But I also knew that if I did find something, then Mark would have been right, and that terrified me.

When I came to the last book, I stopped. It was a King James bible. I shook it, but nothing fell out. I carefully leafed through it. The pages were tissue paper thin and clung maddeningly. After a while, I decided it was fruitless. He hadn't left me a message.

I set the bible down on my lap. My gaze blurred and froze and without the marble, I drifted into a glass dream. The specks on the page scattered and shifted and when my focus came back I saw what had been right in front of me: the caption at the top of the page. 1 Kings 11, 12 — The numbers and the word in Jimmy's last picture: First Kings, Chapter 11, verse 12:

Yet for the sake of your father
David I will not do it in your lifetime; I
will tear it out of the hand of your son.

The last line had been underlined. I set the book aside, still open, and stacked the rest of the books on my shelf. I shivered, as though the words had been Jimmy's own. But what did it mean? Did it mean anything? Or was Mark right?

The year went on. Jimmy's body was never found. There was speculation that it had passed through the grating at the dam and gone down the river to the lake. But it was concluded that he must have died shortly after falling through the ice. And then in April, near the end of the inquest, I found out what the devil was.

One of Jimmy's neighbours remembered seeing him near the medical centre just four days before he disappeared. The police got access to his medical records. Jimmy had been diagnosed with cancer in November. The tumour was in one of the bones in his right hand. He'd been told that surgery to amputate part or all of his hand might be necessary, otherwise the cancer could spread through his body and kill him.

Mark spoke to me after the inquest. "It makes sense now," he told me. "That was the reason he did it. His art was so important to him, he couldn't live without it." He seemed almost euphoric with relief.

I looked at him and thought, *How dare you call yourself his friend and be happy about this? How dare you smile?*

Mark misread my silence. "We don't have to feel guilty now," he said. "We didn't know. He didn't tell anyone — not even his mother."

But in his way, Jimmy *had* told me: the splintered river people in his sketchbook, ice and water. Cracking the arm off the gingerbread man.... His bible: *I will tear it out of the hand of your son.*

But that wasn't the only thing Mark had been wrong about. It wasn't his art that Jimmy had loved; it was *Bron y mor*. The choice he had faced — to lose his hand, to lose that place, to live and never touch it again. Or to die, and never touch or see anything again.

Or.... Was there another way? Had he found another way?

Residence felt empty without Jimmy. I doubted I would come back after the holidays. As I was packing to go home, the phone rang in my room.

"Hello, is this Emma?"

I didn't recognize the voice. "Yes?"

"This is the framing and art studio calling. We have a package here for you to pick up."

"I think you've got the wrong number."

"It was dropped off for you by a J. Aldebaran four months ago. It's already been paid for."

The package was three feet by two and quite heavy. I carried it back to residence where I placed it on the bed still in its brown paper. Now that I had it inside, I could smell a strange, sweet scent emanating from it. I tore it open. Inside a black frame was a painting.

It was *Bron y mor*. Not as Jimmy had sketched it, nor as I'd seen it in my marble. Not in pieces, not in glimpses. This was *Bron y mor* entire, as Jimmy must have seen it the day he'd died. A vast green mound sloping to a beach of grey stones on the shore of a sea at the mouth of a river. In the middle of that river, in the foreground of the painting, huge in its detail, lay an island. Here, the threads hanging from the tree on that island were coloured ribbons, each tied to a small painted bone. Bones of the hands of the dead. I knew that the blue and gold one which hung closest to the water, drifting in the breeze, was his. Though I couldn't hear it, I knew the music that the bones made as they clicked together in the summer wind. And I knew that there was a bird in that tree that sang to all the souls that would come here, if they could. To the sea, to the stones, to the vast green mound of a coastal hill. I thought of a fourth explanation for Jimmy's disappearance. One that Mark had never guessed.

I went to the porter's desk and signed out the key to the music room. Inside the doorway, I stared at the piano, the pale strips, like skin, where the wood had peeled off, the white keys shining like bones. I looked at it to mark its place in the room. Then I hit the switch and crossed in darkness to the bench. I didn't have the sheet music, but it didn't matter. I'd memorized the music long since. I had to count notes down from the ends of the keyboard to find where to place my hands, but once there, I knew where to go.

I played 'Rustle of Spring' and the marble spun inside me, cicadas buzzing like the end of summer, green twists flowing apart like an explosion, showering around me in flashing leaves. The wind rattled them and without turning my head I knew that I was standing in long grass on a high hill. I felt the shivering of leaves inside me, as though the wind blew through my body. Far below lay an island where the river met the sea. And on the shore of that island under a great tree, in the high and clear autumn sun, stood a boy with one foot in the water and one on the land. He turned, raised his right hand to me — a white and whole and perfect hand — and beckoned: *Away to me, away to me, away to me....*

Before The Altar on the Feast for all Souls

by Marg Gilks

Doña Pascuala Ek sat in the doorway of her house and waited for a butterfly.

She knew Teodoro would return to her in the form of a butterfly rather than the quicker hummingbird, because that was how Teodoro had been in life: tranquil; a dreamer, his every movement easy and fluid. He'd performed even the most rigorous chore as though his mind was elsewhere, in an easier place.

Pascuala missed Teodoro. He had passed a year ago May, crossed over to that easier place and left her alone in the small thatched hut they had shared for almost fifty years. The five sons he had given her lived with their families in the other huts of pole stakes and white lime marl that made up their compound so she was never truly alone, until now.

Today was *Hanal Pixan* — her people's name for the Feast for All Souls. Her five strong boys and their wives and the tumbling flock of their children were off at the village churchyard, honouring and remembering those who had crossed to the other side, but Pascuala had insisted on staying at the compound, near the altar lovingly con-structed and provisioned for those souls who would find their way home to their loved ones. To Pascuala.

Teodoro had not come last year at *Hanal Pixan*. She had waited in the doorway until her son Isidro woke her in the first thin rays of dawn the next day. But Teodoro had been new to the other side; perhaps he couldn't find his way back to her then.

Teodoro would come this year. She had seen to it. She had strewn yellow *cempazuchitl* petals in a confetti line from the jungle that crouched behind her son Juan's house, across the hard-packed earth of the compound, to her door. Pascuala could smell the *copalli* candles that the family had lit upon the altar within. She could smell the strong resin odor of copal incense and, like an undercurrent, the sharp bite of spice mingled with the cooler, sweeter odor of fruit from the food offerings in the gourd hung beside the door. The smaller portions in the gourd were for the lost souls, those who roamed in search of families they would never find, but the aroma would guide her Teodoro in to the bounty on the altar. And to her.

The last long, honeyed glow from the sun gave way to the silver-tinged gloom of dusk. The white lower walls of the huts circling the compound glowed, as if releasing the last wan vestiges of light collected during the day into the dark embrace of the jungle. This had been her and Teodoro's favorite time of day, between the end of chores and the oblivion of sleep. In the twilight, Teodoro would talk in his soft, dreaming voice, and Pascuala would rest her head on his chest and feel his words thrum beneath her cheek.

But he was not here yet. Pascuala must do one last thing to ensure that Teodoro found his way back to her.

Spaced at regular intervals beside the path of bright marigold petals were thirteen small paper bags, weighted with sand and scissor-cut with lacy patterns to let the light of the candles within shine through. Pascuala rose and collected an ember from the hearth in the floor of her dwelling, then moved stiffly down the line of paper bags, stooping to light the candles.

It was nearly dark by the time she finished. She turned back at the jungle behind Juan's hut and returned to the stool beside her door to wait for Teodoro.

Pascuala saw the couple standing by the fringe of jungle at the end of the path of marigold petals when she turned to lower herself onto the stool. They were a young white couple, *turistas* in bright crisp clothes that screamed "intrusion" against the worn lines and dusty, faded tones of the compound. The woman's hair was pale, bleached-blonde, as bright and brassy as the glint of gold at neck and earlobes and wrist; the man wore an apologetic smile and a camera around his neck.

Pascuala reeled as though their sudden appearance were a physical blow. The narrow road that ran through the village and past the Ek compound had been widened and paved by the Mexican government two years ago, and now taxis stuffed full of *turistas* from Playa del Carmen and tour buses from Cancun plied the route between the coast and Cobá. The whites had taken the great city of Pascuala's ancestors and made it their own, and now the peace and privacy of her own family's compound was being taken from her by the *ix-tz'ul* and their invasive cameras and handfuls of heavy *mil-pesos* pieces that made beggars of her grandchildren.

She had stayed behind at the compound while her family went to the church in the village so she would not miss her Teodoro when he came. Now these *estúpidos gringos* had blundered in, disturbing the special moment she'd worked so hard to conjure on this one night that her lost husband's spirit might return. Destroying the one chance she had to see him, be with him, just once more.

I cannot wait again to see him. Not another year.

Anger lent Pascuala a moment of agility as she rose from her stool and stalked several paces down the yellow-petal pathway. "Go away, stupid *turistas!*" she called to them. She lifted both arms and waved them at the couple, trying to brush them back into the jungle like the dust she pushed out the door of her hut every morning with a stiff corn broom. "You should not be here; go back to the road and your fancy resorts, where you belong!"

Instead of obeying, the garish woman took a step forward. She would crush the delicate marigold petals strewn for Teodoro and the Ek ancestors. Pascuala watched her approach in dismay.

"Please, can you help us?" the woman asked. "Our car left the road —"

"I cannot help you!" Pascuala exclaimed. "I am an old woman, alone. Go back to the road and walk to the village. There are men there who can help you push your car back onto the road."

The man stepped forward and put his hand on the woman's shoulder. His smile was sheepish. "I'm afraid it's somewhat worse than that," he said to Pascuala. "The car rolled a couple of times and it's resting on its roof, about a mile up the road to Cobá. We'll need more than a push."

He spoke Mayan. The woman had, too, Pascuala realized. White people did not speak Mayan. She frowned, then sucked in a surprised breath. "I don't know how I can help you," she said slowly. "Come forward. Let me see you. Tell me what you need."

The man took the woman's hand and the couple came forward, following the trail of strewn marigold petals to Pascuala. The scattered petals fluttered gently, shifted in small swirls as though something winged flew low above them.

Pascuala watched them approach. They did not look like the survivors of a car crash. Their clothes were clean and unrumpled, as though they had just stepped from their hotel and not stumbled along the rough verge of a road over unknown terrain. There were no cuts or bruises or wounds of any kind showing dark on their pale skin in the failing light. The hair of both man and woman was neat and shiny-clean, not dull with the dust that would have been kicked up during a car accident.

Yes. Pascuala sighed.

"I'm Russell Musgrove," the man said when they stood before her. "This is my wife Janice." The pair looked at one another as though they shared the most delightful secret, and Russell put his arm around his wife's shoulders.

Pascuala's gnarled hand flew up to touch her lips. "You are newlyweds."

Janice smiled shyly. "We're on our honeymoon."

Pascuala saw the young woman's nostrils flare and her eyes slid past Pascuala, searching out the scent. "Oh, how lovely!" she exclaimed over the family altar within. "And the aroma is so enticing. I had no idea how hungry I was until now."

She took a step toward the *pan de muertos* and mangos and limes, the few confections shaped from *alfeñique* for the children who had not survived, and Pascuala's special *mole* sauce, a favorite of Teodoro's, all lovingly arranged amidst glowing tapers and flowers.

Pascuala opened her mouth to speak, but Russell pulled Janice back to him and said, "That's not for us." Two lines puckered into existence between his brows and he looked to Pascuala. "It's not, is it?"

Poor souls, so far from home, they do not know yet, Pascuala thought, and lifted the gourd that hung beside the door. "This is for you," she said.

"I'm not sure what we should do now," Russell said when they were done. He licked sweet papaya juice from his fingers. "Which way we should go — back to Cobá or on to your village? Is there someone with a car there?"

"There is no car. And Cobá is not the place for you to go. Those who walk in that place would not welcome you." She wanted to weep. *I cannot send them away. They are so young, so lost; they don't even know yet that they no longer belong here. But Teodoro—* "Come inside. Someone will come soon to guide you."

She motioned them into the hut and indicated another stool placed near the altar and set the stool she had brought from the doorway down beside it. But when she started to kneel beside the firepit, Russell exclaimed, "No!" and returned her stool to her. He sat down cross-legged beside his wife's place. They regarded one another for a moment, in the glow from the embers and the tapers on the altar. The penetrating fragrance of the copal incense was stronger inside.

"Who are we waiting for?" Janice asked. "Is your family in the village? Will they be coming home soon?"

"My sons and their families are in the village, at the churchyard, yes. But they cannot help you. We're waiting for someone else." Pascuala looked away from the woman's bewildered blue gaze. Her eyes were drawn to the altar and she lifted a hand to adjust a flower. The hand looked like the paper bags protecting the candles in the compound, the skin brown and crinkled. *I should be in their place,* she thought.

"Who are we waiting for?" Janice asked again.

"My husband," Pascuala whispered. She turned on her stool to face the doorway, and the stream of golden petals that fell away from it into the night. From the corner of her eye, she saw the couple exchange a glance before Janice spoke again.

"Your husband is not at the churchyard?"

"No. He ... left a year and a half ago." She kept her attention on the doorway. Had there been a flicker of movement out there in the darkness by the jungle fringe? She caught her breath and held it. *What am I doing?* a part of her whispered. *I cannot bear to wait again, not another year! Send them away, let them find their own way, let someone else guide them, let Teodoro come to* me, *send them away!*

"How can your husband help us, if you don't even know where he is?" Doubt thickened the man's voice.

The breath shuddered across her lips when she released it, and she had to blink rapidly. "I know where he is."

Pascuala heard the hard soles of his shoes scuff across the packed-earth floor as Russell rose. "Thank you for your help, but I think we should head for the village."

Pascuala sat very still on her stool. *"Yes, go,"* she wanted to say; *"hurry, before it's too dark to see your way."* Before *Teodoro comes.* He would come this night. She felt it in her heart. *He must. I need him.*

They need him.

She held up her hand. "Wait," she croaked.

"I really think—"

She would give him to them this night. Next year, perhaps, she would sit before the altar, waiting not just for a moment with her dear Teodoro, but for his guidance to the other side. Pascuala closed her eyes. "Wait."

"Russ, look at her," she heard Janice whisper. "Maybe we should stay a while, make sure she's okay—"

The jungle sighed.

Pascuala gasped. "Shh, listen! They come!"

The pair stood still, listening. Pascuala heard it again, that breath in the jungle, wafting over the myriad leaves. "Teodoro ... " she whispered, and opened her eyes.

The strewn marigold petals seemed to lift and take flight, bobbing and fluttering, weaving through the night toward the door of Pascuala's house.

"My God, look at them!" the young woman beside Pascuala exclaimed. "There are hundreds of them!"

"Monarchs," Russell supplied.

Pascuala beamed up at him. "I knew he would return as a butterfly," she said.

The butterflies streamed from the jungle and gathered in a great golden cloud in the compound. A few broke from the flight and capered to hover tentatively before the dark doorways of the other huts before fluttering back to the group.

"What are they doing here?" Janice asked.

Pascuala shuffled to the doorway and stood with her hand on the worn wooden frame, the post smoothed and polished by generations of Ek hands. She lifted the other hand to the butterflies. She could feel the puckered parchment skin over her mouth stretched tight with a wide grin, but she didn't care what the lost ones thought of that.

"They've come for you," she said to them, and beckoned the man and woman forward. "Go to them. They will take you where you need to go."

"Butterflies?" Russell's voice came heavy with disbelief.

"Not butterflies. The Ek are a very old family, and plentiful. Now go; they are waiting."

Russell Musgrove took his young wife's hand in his and led her out into the compound. Monarch butterflies danced around them like flakes of gold in a current. The couple stood with their faces uplifted, glorying in the flight and the flash of bright wings.

"Teodoro," Pascuala murmured, "there is something more important for you to do this night. The *turistas* are lost and far from home and family of their own. Guide them safe to the other side. You are in my heart always, and I will wait for you next year, on *Hanal Pixan*." She smiled still, but she could feel moisture tracking down the gullies in her cheeks.

The erratic flight of the butterflies coalesced into a tall spiral. The dance of the insects quickened and tightened into a bright yellow tornado with the young couple at its center. The air sighed with the passage of hundreds of wings.

Pascuala could no longer make out the figures of the young couple. They were engulfed in the flight of the butterflies and she wasn't sure if the glint of gold was the woman Janice's jewelry and hair or merely the glow of candlelight on butterfly wings.

The sight blurred, and the old woman gripped the door frame to keep away vertigo. Faster and tighter the confetti kaleidoscope moved. Were those individual insects fluttering on the fringes, or was the whole flight fading away?

She could see the white marl of her son Juan's house through the flight now, and the dark backdrop of the jungle. The young newlywed couple was gone. Soon the butterflies would be gone. Teodoro would be gone, and she would be alone again.

Pascuala couldn't help herself, she let a sob escape. "Teodoro, I miss you so," she called softly.

A chip of bright yellow fell away from the fading vortex. A lone butterfly trembled in the air of the compound, then fluttered toward her. Pascuala smiled and held out her hand. "Teodoro," she whispered.

The insect lit on the palm of her hand and rested there, its wings moving slowly up and down. Pascuala wept.

The flight of the butterflies was no more than a pale smudge of colour now. The butterfly in Pascuala's palm suddenly lifted and danced two circles around her head before flitting off to rejoin its fellows.

And in that moment Pascuala heard her name, breathed in the flutter of a butterfly's wings.

Being Here
by Claude Lalumière

The night before, you and I had fought, and it had taken me forever to fall asleep. We didn't make up then, and I still regret that. We'd argued about nothing and everything — the dishes, the vacuuming, the cat litter. A stupid fight. One in which none of the important things got said, in which all the real reasons for the tension between us were carefully avoided. Exasperated, you had turned your back to me; a snore interrupted me mid-sentence. Waking you up would only have made a bad situation worse. There was nothing I could have said at that moment that would have brought us closer. I let you sleep and tried to calm myself down.

It was useless. I lay awake for hours, unable even to keep my eyes closed, until I fell from sheer exhaustion into an unrestful sleep.

I woke up at dawn, as I always did. The clock on my bedside dresser told me it was not quite six yet. I usually took advantage of the time before I woke you up at eight to go running in the park. That morning, thinking I had a choice, I decided to be lazy and stay in bed. I knew the exercise would help snap me out of my funk, but I just couldn't gather the energy to get up and start my day.

After a few minutes, it occurred to me that in the morning I always needed to pee urgently. And yet there I was, feeling absolutely no pressure on my bladder.

I wanted to enjoy a drowsy morning in bed, just rest and relax. But I couldn't get comfortable. The blankets were so heavy.

✛ ✛ ✛

The clock read 7:12. The feeling of being trapped by the blankets was unbearable. I was getting tenser and angrier by the second. I couldn't muster the strength to get up. I liked mornings, but already I was hating this one.

The digital readout on the clock became my lifeline to sanity. That every minute a numeral changed filled me with a strange and pathetic reassurance.

Still irritated from the previous night, I wanted to shout at you to stop snoring, but, with our fight still so fresh, I knew waking you up this early would only make things worse.

Lying there, I was hypersensitive to noises I usually blanked out. The morning traffic, the creaking building, the shrill wind outside. I could make out what the neighbours were saying through the walls; they were calmly reading each other snippets from the morning paper. Everything was so loud.

And the smell! The cat litter stank like we hadn't changed it in months. Were we really that bad? The whole apartment reeked: the unwashed laundry, the sinkful of dirty dishes, the garbage. How could we have let things slide so much, I thought.

Finally, it was eight o'clock; time to wake you.

No matter how hard I tried, I couldn't push the blankets off me, I couldn't reach over and touch you. I wasn't paralyzed, though. I could move my neck, my face, and the top of my right shoulder — everything that wasn't caught under the blankets. I tried to say your name over and over again, but no sound came out of my mouth. I thought: you'll be late for work; you'll be furious with me.

And then the fact that I couldn't speak hit me, hit me much harder than being trapped in bed. I panicked, losing track of time, unable even to think, until I heard you roar my name.

But that was no roar, not really, only a mumble amplified by my hypersensitive hearing. You were finally waking up. The clock told me it was 10:34. You always mumbled my name when you were in that dozy state, rising from sleep to wakefulness. I loved that.

You turned towards me — I'd never noticed before how pungent your morning breath was — and your eyes popped open. You were looking past me at the clock. You flung out of bed, screaming my name without looking at me, shouting abuse and insults because I didn't wake you up in time. The noise and stress combined to give me the god of all headaches.

When you got out of bed, the blankets moved enough so that my other shoulder was freed. But no more than that. I could move that shoulder again. Such frustrating relief.

Ten minutes later, you stomped back into the bedroom — your skin moist from the shower — and, still angry, shouted, "Where the fuck are you?" You turned on the light, and it was too much for my eyes. I squeezed them shut to block out the searing brightness. I mean, I tried to. My face wasn't paralyzed. I could feel my facial muscles react when I moved them — even my eyelids. But closing them didn't stop the light. While putting your clothes on, you kept shouting at me like I wasn't there.

Before slamming the front door on your way out, you had let George in from the backyard. He jumped on the bed and walked all over me. His paws were like steel girders; the bed under me gave with his every step. After a minute or so of this, he zeroed in on my crotch and kneaded it mercilessly. Purring. My life was pain. At least you had turned off the lights.

George stayed nestled on my crotch until you came back home after work. How much did he weigh? Eight pounds? Ten? Something like that. It felt like a bowling ball was crushing my pelvis.

As soon as he heard you unlock the front door, he leapt off me. He meowed to be let out. You cooed at him and opened the back door. These noises were still too loud, but by this time, having had to cope with it for a whole day, I'd become somewhat used to my new found sensitivity. Even the light and smells, while still harsh, didn't bother me as much. In general, the pain was getting duller — an irritation instead of an assault.

After shutting the back door, you called my name. I tried to answer, but I still couldn't manage to make any sound.

I heard you pick up the phone, no doubt checking for messages. The phone hadn't rung all day. I was thankful for that bit of silence.

You swore and slammed the phone down. You turned on the TV and set the volume high. I braced myself for the pain, but I was adapting well — too well — to my condition. There was no discernible increase in my pain level.

I heard you wander through the apartment, shuffling papers, opening doors. You returned to the living room and plunked yourself down on the couch. Over the sounds of a car advertisement, I could hear you sniffle and sob. Already, I missed you so much.

You watched TV all evening, not bothering to eat. At 1:04 in the morning, you finally turned off the TV and walked into the bedroom. You looked miserable. You stared at me. In a tearful whine, you said, "Where are you?"

Desperate, I tried to channel all my strength, all my energy into screaming that I was right there, but I still failed. Couldn't you see me? It's not like I was dead. If I were, there'd be a corpse, a body.

And that's when I couldn't ignore it anymore.

I craned my neck to look down at myself, at where I felt my body squeezed into immobility by the blankets, and ... and there was nothing there.

I stayed awake that whole night.

You fell asleep on your stomach, without taking your clothes off. You didn't move all night, but you snored — of course, you snored. Your left arm fell across me and crushed my chest — the part of me that still felt like a chest — until you woke up at 10:42 the next morning.

It was only after your arm had been separating my upper self from my lower for several hours that I noticed that I was no longer breathing. When I thought about it, I was pretty sure that I hadn't breathed since I'd woken up in this condition.

Whatever that was.

I listed the symptoms: I was invisible, even to myself; I didn't get hungry; I didn't need to pee; I didn't get tired, but I felt a constant, numbing weakness; my senses were too acute for comfort; I wasn't breathing; blankets were too heavy for me to lift.

Like a list was going to explain everything, or anything.

And where was my body? How could I feel so much physical pain if I didn't have a body?

You rolled on your back, away from me. I felt my rib cage pop back up. Did I still have a rib cage? I looked at where I felt my body to be, and there still wasn't even the slightest hint of a shape. Was I even in there with you? Or was that sensation an illusion of some kind?

I told you, silently, that I was sorry for everything, for being so distant, for so often only pretending to listen to you, for so often having some stupid thing to do when all you wanted was to enjoy spending time with me — and in the middle of my futile apology George sat on my face.

You called in sick for the next two days. Minutes crawled by like weeks, sleepless days and nights like lifetimes.

You called my office and a few of my friends, but I could tell from your voice the emotional price you were paying for doing this. You gave that up quickly.

Couldn't you see that all my clothes were still there? My keys by the bed? Couldn't you feel that I was still there, longing for you?

Your orbit consisted of the bed, the fridge, the couch, and the toilet. The centre of your universe was the TV.

You stopped calling in sick. You just stayed home. When the phone rang, you ignored it.

A week later, your sister used her spare key to come in when you failed to respond to the doorbell. At first she was furious, yelling at you to snap out of it. Eventually, you broke down and started crying. That mollified her.

You told her that I'd vanished on you with no warning. She said she was surprised at that; she'd always thought of me as good for you.

You were an odd combination of fragile and tough, and I'd fallen in love with the intensity that accompanied that mix. You needed undivided attention to feel loved. You didn't give your trust easily, but, once you did, you trusted without question. Being with you was a heady experience that left little time or energy for anything else. I indulged like an addict: your intensity was a powerful narcotic. You had tended to attract lovers who abused your fragility, who took pleasure in shattering someone so strong who could nevertheless be so easily broken. Your sister had liked that I made you laugh, had seen how it thrilled me to have you permeate my whole world.

Eventually, life outside our bubble intruded. Friends, work, whatever. And I drifted away. I let you suffer, even though I knew you were suffering; I let my growing indifference chip away at you. And, like a coward, instead of talking to you and trying to mend the rift, I just ignored it. I ignored you.

Sex with you was so beautiful, such a complete escape, sad and hard, silly and serious, in all the best ways. How could I let anything get in the way of that? Of being close to you?

I've never wanted to comfort you as much as when I heard you tell your sister how much you'd been hurt by my disappearance. But I'd started to disappear much earlier than you were telling her, and I hated myself for that. For betraying you. For betraying myself.

Do you remember when, the week before we moved in together, you stopped by my office and took me out to lunch? Warming your hands on my cup of tea, a fleck of something green stuck between your teeth, you asked me what I needed, and we bonded because of our common goal: your happiness. When did that stop being important?

Your sister couldn't see me either. She cleaned the bathroom. After she put you in a hot bath, she turned off the

TV and put on the radio instead. Classical. Worse: opera. Then, she attacked the embarrassing mess of our apartment. I'd like to say that most of it was due to your recent binge, but our place was always a disaster area.

And then she changed the bed.

The weakness disappeared when the weight of the blankets was lifted off me.

And, just like that, I was free. I was free! I danced and leapt and twirled and ran and—

And then I caught the words "missing" and "disappeared" on the radio news report.

There was, all around the world, an alarming increase in missing-person reports. The prime minister of Canada. The CEO of Toshiba. The US ambassador to the United Nations. The populations of whole villages in Africa. Hundreds of Afghan women. And so on. From the most disenfranchised to the most powerful, people everywhere were vanishing.

The news that I probably was not the only victim of this peculiar condition did not reassure me, but rather filled me with overwhelming dread. I walked into the bathroom, needing the security of your presence, and sat on the edge of the tub. You had no reaction when I reached out and stroked your face. Was I that insubstantial?

I could no longer take comfort in the slight plumpness of your cheek. To my touch, your flesh was as hard and unyielding as concrete.

When your sister left the apartment, I took advantage of the open door — all physical objects now being immovable, impassable obstacles — and left with her. I didn't follow her. I had been cooped up inside for so long. I needed the open air. I just wandered around. And I mulled over what I had heard on the news. I was already so used to the pain from the sensory overload that it was no longer even a distracting irritant.

Were all the vanished in the same situation I was? If I met another vanished person, would we see each other?

Outside I discovered that rain, even the mildest precipitation, knocked the strange substance of my nearly insubstantial body to the ground, raindrops hammering into me like nails. Yet, for all that I had some, if almost negligible, physical presence, I cast no shadow. I was truly invisible.

There were fewer and fewer people about every day. Obviously, we vanished could not perceive each other. What people were left acquired a haunted or persecuted look. They knew that their time would soon come.

Less than a week after I escaped from the apartment, civil order broke down. Vandalized and overturned police cars burned on street corners. All the stores I passed had their windows broken, their stock looted or destroyed.

The city grew quiet, as traffic dwindled away and industry stopped dead.

The silence was occasionally punctuated by bursts of gunshots and quickly silenced screams. Those sounds filled me with more dread than my inexplicable vanishing ever did. I was always careful to walk away from such noises and never discovered exactly what was happening.

Dogs wailed and wandered everywhere, searching for their vanished human companions, scavenging through garbage for food.

I saw stray cats hunt some of the smaller wildlife that was reclaiming the city. They gave the bears a wide berth, though. Often, I thought I saw George, but the cat was always gone before I could be sure.

During that time, I returned to the apartment only once. The door had been torn off. Everything had been trashed. A raccoon family was living in our bedroom. By then you must have vanished, like me. I wanted to find you, hold you. But you were beyond my reach.

I was following a bear around, excited by what would have been in normal circumstances suicidal behaviour, when a giant shadow fell over me. I looked up. Swift grey clouds covered the afternoon sky. Scraps of old newspapers were being blown every which way. There was so much wind — wild, chaotic wind. Before I could think to take cover, I was hit on all sides — by a ragged shirt, a torn

magazine, a broken beer bottle, cigarette butts, gum wrappers. I was jabbed and crushed and flattened and stabbed and twisted. It hadn't hurt this much since that first morning.
The storm erupted; the sharp, heavy rain felled me, knifed through my prone body.

The storm ended; the clouds parted and revealed the moonlit sky, glittering with stars. I lay there on the ground, recovering from the storm, and gazed at the sky. There were more stars visible than before: when people had vanished, so had the city lights that had made the nighttime too bright for starlight.
I stayed like that until dawn, and then someone stepped on me.
I looked around; the streets were filled with people. Naked as newborns, they walked calmly but with a sense of purpose, murmuring softly to each other, casually touching each other, sharing complicit glances.
I recognized a few faces — no-one I knew well, but people I'd seen in shops or cafés.
Still wobbly, I stood up. Was this ordeal finally over? Was I back, too? A quick test — trying in vain to see my hands or any part of my body — told me I wasn't. I tried to call out to the people around me, but I was still mute.
What about you? Could you have returned? I ran to our apartment.

When I neared home, I saw them. They were also heading there: hand in hand, smiling and laughing, so obviously deeply in love with each other.
It was you and me. More beautiful, more in love, more confident, more at peace than we'd ever been. Serene.
But it wasn't you, was it? No more than it was me. You must still be vanished like me. Neither dead nor alive. And so it must be for everyone.
Do you, like me, spend your time watching our doppelgangers? Are you frustrated at being unable to understand their language? Are you jealous at how much better they are at being us — at loving each other — than we ever

were? At how much even George seems happier with them? Are you envious that all these new people have made the world a better place?

I want to end my life, but I don't think I can. I've tried jumping off roofs, but all I get out of it is more pain — never death.

Are you here with me, my love?

I long to die with you.

To be really dead. Together. Forever oblivious.

Mayfly

by Peter Watts and Derryl Murphy

"I hate you."

A four-year-old girl. A room as barren as a fishbowl.

"I *hate* you."

Little fists, clenching: one of the cameras, set to motion-cap, zoomed on them automatically. Two others watched the adults, mother, father on opposite sides of the room. The machines watched the players: half a world away, Stavros watched the machines.

"I hate you I hate you I HATE you!"

The girl was screaming now, her face contorted in anger and anguish. There were tears at the edge of her eyes but they stayed there, never falling. Her parents shifted like nervous animals, scared of the anger, used to the outbursts but far from comfortable with them.

At least this time she was using words. Usually she just howled.

She leaned against the blanked window, fists pounding. The window took her assault like hard white rubber, denting slightly, then rebounding. One of the few things in the room that bounced back when she struck out; one less thing to break.

"Jeannie, hush...." Her mother reached out a hand. Her father, as usual, stood back, a mixture of anger and resentment and confusion on his face.

Stavros frowned. *A veritable pillar of paralysis, that man.*

And then: *They don't deserve her.*

The screaming child didn't turn, her back a defiant slap at Kim and Andrew Goravec. Stavros had a better view: Jeannie's face was just a few centimeters away from the southeast pickup. For all the pain it showed, for all the pain Jeannie had felt in the four short years of her physical life, those few tiny drops that never fell were the closest she ever came to crying.

"Make it *clear*," she demanded, segueing abruptly from anger to petulance.

Kim Goravec shook her head. "Honey, we'd love to show you outside. Remember before, how much you liked it? But you have to promise not to *scream* at it all the time. You didn't used to, honey, you—"

"*Now!*" Back to rage, the pure, white-hot anger of a small child.

The pads on the wall panel were greasy from Jeannie's repeated, sticky-fingered attempts to use them herself. Andrew flashed a begging look at his wife: *Please, let's just give her what she wants.*

His wife was stronger. "Jeannie, we know it's difficult —"

Jeannie turned to face the enemy. The north pickup got it all: the right hand rising to the mouth, the index finger going in. The defiant glare in those glistening, focused eyes.

Kim took a step forward. "Jean, honey, *no!*"

They were baby teeth, still, but sharp. They'd bitten to the bone before Mommy even got within touching distance. A red stain blossomed from Jeannie's mouth, flowed down her chin like some perverted re-enactment of mealtime messes as a baby, and covered the lower half of her face in an instant. Above the gore, bright angry eyes said *gotcha.*

Without a sound Jeannie Goravec collapsed, eyes rolling back in her head as she pitched forward. Kim caught her just before her head hit the floor. "Oh God, Andy, she's fainted, she's in shock, she—"

Andrew didn't move. One hand was buried in the pocket of his blazer, fiddling with something.

Stavros felt his mouth twitch. *Is that a remote control in your pocket or are you just glad to—*

Kim had the tube of liquid skin out, sprayed it onto Jeannie's hand while cradling the child's head in her lap. The bleeding slowed. After a moment Kim looked back at her husband, who was standing motionless and unhelp-

ful against the wall. He had that look on his face, that give-
away look that Stavros was seeing so often these days.

"You turned her off," Kim said, her voice rising. "After
everything we'd agreed on, you still turned her *off*?!"

Andrew shrugged helplessly. "Kim..."

Kim refused to look at him. She rocked back and forth,
tuneless breath whistling between her teeth, Jeannie's head
still in her lap. Kim and Andrew Goravec with their bundle
of joy. Between them, the cable connecting Jeannie's head
to the server shivered on the floor like a disputed boundary.

Stavros had this metaphoric image of her: Jean Goravec,
buried alive in the airless dark, smothered by tonnes of
earth — finally set free. Jean Goravec coming up for air.

Another image, of himself this time: Stavros Mikalaides,
liberator. The man who made it possible for her to experience, however briefly, a world where the virtual air was
sweet and the bonds nonexistent. Certainly there'd been
others in on the miracle — a dozen tech-heads, twice as
many lawyers — but they'd all vanished over time, their
interest fading with proof-of-principal or the signing of
the last waiver. The damage was under control, the project
was in a holding pattern; there was no need to waste more
than a single Terracon employee on mere cruise control.
So only Stavros remained — and to Stavros, Jeannie had
never been a 'project'. She was his as much as the Goravecs'.
Maybe more.

But even Stavros still didn't know what it was really
like for her. He wondered if it was physically possible for
anyone to know. When Jean Goravec slipped the leash of
her fleshly existence, she awoke into a reality where the
very laws of physics had expired.

It hadn't started that way, of course. The system had
booted up with years of mundane, real-world environments
on file, each lovingly rendered down to the dust motes.
But they'd been flexible, responsive to the needs of any
developing intellect. In hindsight, maybe too flexible. Jean
Goravec had edited her personal reality so radically that
even Stavros' mechanical intermediaries could barely parse
it. This little girl could turn a forest glade into a bloody

Roman coliseum with a thought. Unleashed, Jean lived in a world where all bets were off.

A thought-experiment in child abuse: place a newborn into an environment devoid of vertical lines. Keep her there until the brain settles, until the wiring has congealed. Whole assemblies of pattern-matching retinal cells, aborted for lack of demand, will be forever beyond recall. Telephone poles, the trunks of trees, the vertical aspects of skyscrapers — your victim will be neurologically blind to such things for life.

So what happens to a child raised in a world where vertical lines dissolve, at a whim, into circles or fractals or a favorite toy?

We're the impoverished ones, Stavros thought. *Next to Jean, we're blind.*

He could see what she started with, of course. His software read the patterns off her occipital cortex, translated them flawlessly into images projected onto his own tactical contacts. But images aren't *sight*, they're just... raw material. There are filters all along the path: receptor cells, firing thresholds, pattern-matching algorithms. Endless stores of past images, an experiential visual library to draw on. More than vision, sight is , a subjective stew of infinitesimal enhancements and corruptions. Nobody in the world could interpret Jean's visual environment better than Stavros Mikalaides, and he'd barely been able to make sense of those shapes for years.

She was simply, immeasurably, beyond him. It was one of the things he loved most about her.

Now, mere seconds after her father had cut the cord, Stavros watched Jean Goravec ascend into her true self. Heuristic algorithms upgraded before his eyes; neural nets ruthlessly pared and winnowed trillions of redundant connections; intellect emerged from primordial chaos. Namps-per-op dropped like the heavy end of a teeter-totter: at the other end of that lever, processing efficiency rose into the stratosphere.

This was Jean. *They have no idea*, Stavros thought, *what you're capable of.*

She woke up screaming.

"It's all right, Jean, I'm here." He kept his voice calm to help her calm down.

Jean's temporal lobe flickered briefly at the input. "Oh, God," she said.

"Another nightmare?"

"Oh, God." Breath too fast, pulse too high, adrenocortical analogs off the scale. It could have been the telemetry of a rape.

He thought of short-circuiting those responses. Half a dozen tweaks would make her happy. But half a dozen tweaks would also turn her into someone else. There is no personality beyond the chemical — and while Jean's mind was fashioned from electrons rather than proteins, analogous rules applied.

"I'm here, Jean," he repeated. A good parent knew when to step in, and when suffering was necessary for growth. "It's okay. It's okay."

Eventually, she settled down.

"Nightmare." There were sparks in the parietal subroutines, a tremor lingering in her voice. "It doesn't fit, Stav. Scary dreams, that's the definition. But that implies there's some *other* kind, and I can't — I mean, why is it *always* like this? Was it always like this?"

"I don't know." *No, it wasn't.*

She sighed. "These words I learn, none of them really seem to fit *anything* exactly, you know?"

"They're just symbols, Jean." He grinned. At times like this he could almost forget the source of those dreams, the stunted, impoverished existence of some half-self trapped in distant meat. Andrew Goravec's act of cowardice had freed her from that prison, for a while at least. She soared now, released to full potential. She *mattered*.

"Symbols. That's what *dreams* are supposed to be, but… I don't know. There're all these references to dreams in the library, and none of them seem that much different from just being awake. And when I *am* asleep, it's all just — screams, almost, only dopplered down. Really sludgy. And shapes. Red shapes." A pause. "I hate bedtime."

"Well, you're awake now. What are you up for today?"

"I'm not sure. I need to get away from this place."

He didn't know what place she meant. By default she woke up in the house, an adult residence designed for human sensibilities. There were also parks and forests and oceans, instantly accessible. By now, though, she'd changed them all past his ability to recognize.

But it was only a matter of time before her parents wanted her back. *Whatever she wants,* Stavros told himself. *As long as she's here. Whatever she wants.*

"I want out," Jean said.

Except that. "I know," he sighed.

"Maybe then I can leave these *nightmares* behind."

Stavros closed his eyes, wished there was some way to be with her. *Really* with her, with this glorious, transcendent creature who'd never known him as anything but a disembodied voice.

"Still having a hard time with that monster?" Jean asked.

"Monster?"

"You know. The *bureaucracy.*"

He nodded, smiling — then, remembering, said, "Yeah. Always the same story, day in, day out."

Jean snorted. "I'm still not convinced that thing even exists, you know. I checked the library for a slightly less wonky definition, but now I think you and the library are *both* screwed in the head."

He winced at the epithet; it was certainly nothing he'd ever taught her. "How so?"

"Oh, right, Stav. Like natural selection would *ever* produce a hive-based entity whose sole function is to sit with its thumb up its collective butt being inefficient. Tell me another one."

A silence, stretching. He watched as microcurrent trickled through her prefrontal cortex.

"You there, Stav?" she said at last.

"Yeah, I'm here." He chuckled, quietly. Then: "You know I love you, right?"

"Sure," she said easily. "Whatever *that* is."

Jean's environment changed then; an easy unthinking transition for her, a gasp-inducing wrench between bizarre realities for Stavros. Phantoms sparkled at the edge of his vision, vanishing when he focused on them. Light bounced from a million indefinable facets, diffuse, punctuated by a myriad of pinpoint staccatos. There was no ground or walls or ceiling. No restraints along any axis.

Jean reached for a shadow in the air and sat upon it, floating. "I think I'll read *Through the Looking Glass* again. At least *someone* else lives in the real world."

"The changes that happen here are your own doing, Jean," said Stavros. "Not the machinations of any, any God or author."

"I know. But Alice makes me feel a little more — ordinary." Reality shifted abruptly once more; Jean was in the park now, or rather, what Stavros thought of as the park. Sometimes he was afraid to ask if her interpretation had stayed the same. Above, light and dark spots danced across a sky that sometimes seemed impressively vault-like, seconds later oppressively close, even its colour endlessly unsettled. Animals large and small, squiggly yellow lines and shapes and colour-shifting orange and burgundy pies. Other things that might have been representations of life, or mathematical theorems — or both — browsed in the distance.

Seeing through Jean's eyes was never easy. But all this unsettling abstraction was a small price to pay for the sheer pleasure of watching her read.

My little girl.

Symbols appeared around her, doubtless the text of *Looking Glass*. To Stavros it was gibberish. A few recognizable letters, random runes, formulae. They switched places sometimes, seamlessly shifting one into another, flowing around and through and beside — or even launching themselves into the air like so many dark-hued butterflies.

He blinked his eyes and sighed. If he stayed much longer the visuals would give him a headache that would take a day to shake. Watching a life lived at such speed, even for such a short time, took its toll.

"Jean, I'm gone for a little while."

"Company business?" she asked.

"You could say that. We'll talk soon, love. Enjoy your reading."

✢ ✢ ✢

Barely ten minutes had passed in meatspace.

Jeannie's parents had put her on her own special cot. It was one of the few real pieces of solid geometry allowed in the room. The whole compartment was a stage, virtually empty. There was really no need for props; sensations were planted directly into Jean's occipital cortex, spliced into her auditory pathways, pushing back against her tactile nerves in precise forgeries of touchable things. In a world made of lies, real objects would be a hazard to navigation.

"God damn you, she's not a fucking *toaster*," Kim spat at her husband. Evidently the icy time-out had expired; the battle had resumed.

"Kim, what was I supposed to—"

"She's a *child*, Andy. She's *our* child."

"Is she." It was a statement, not a question.

"Of *course* she is!"

"Fine." Andrew took the remote from his pocket held it out to her. "*You* wake her up, then."

She stared at him without speaking for a few seconds. Over the pickups, Stavros heard Jeannie's body breathing into the silence.

"You prick," Kim whispered.

"Uh huh. Not quite up for it, are you? You'd rather let *me* do the dirty work." He dropped the remote: it bounced softly off the floor. "Then blame me for it."

Four years had brought them to this. Stavros shook his head, disgusted. They'd been given a chance no one else could have dreamed of, and look what they'd done with it. The first time they'd shut her off she hadn't even been two. Horrified at that unthinkable precedent, they'd promised never to do it again. They'd put her to sleep on schedule, they'd sworn, and no-when else. She was, after all, their daughter. Not a freaking toaster.

That solemn pact had lasted three months. Things had gone downhill ever since; Stavros could barely remember a day when the Goravecs hadn't messed up one way or another. And now, when they put her down, the argument was pure ritual. Mere words — ostensibly wrestling with the evil of the act itself — didn't fool anybody. They weren't even arguments anymore, despite the pretense.

Negotiations, rather. Over whose turn it was to be at fault.

"I don't *blame* you, I just — I mean — oh, *God*, Andy, it wasn't supposed to *be* like this!" Kim smeared away a tear with a clenched fist. "She was supposed to be our *daughter*. They said the brain would mature normally, they said—"

"They said," Stavros cut in, "that you'd have the chance to be parents. They couldn't guarantee you'd be any *good* at it."

Kim jumped at the sound of his voice in the walls, but Andrew just gave a bitter smile and shook his head. "This is private, Stavros. Log off."

It was an empty command, of course; chronic surveillance was the price of the project. The company had put billions into the R&D alone. No way in hell were they going to let a couple of litigious grunts play with that investment unsupervised, settlement or no settlement.

"You had everything you needed." Stavros didn't bother to disguise the contempt in his voice. "Terracon's best hardware people handled the linkups. I modeled the virtual genes myself. Gestation was perfect. We did everything we could to give you a normal child."

"A *normal child*," Andrew remarked, "doesn't have a cable growing out of her head. A normal child isn't leashed to some cabinet full of—"

"Do you have any *idea* the baud rate it takes to run a human body by remote control? RF was out of the question. And she goes portable as soon as the state of the art and her own development allow it. As I've told you time and again." Which he had, although it was almost a lie. Oh, the state of the art would proceed as it always had, but Terracon was no longer investing any great R&D in the Goravec file. Cruise control, after all.

Besides, Stavros reflected, *we'd be crazy to trust you two to take Jeannie anywhere outside a controlled environment...*

"We — we know, Stav." Kim Goravec had stepped between her husband and the pickup. "We haven't forgotten—"

"We haven't forgotten it was Terracon who got us into this mess in the first place, either," Andrew growled. "We haven't forgotten whose negligence left me cooking next to a cracked baffle plate for forty-three minutes and sixteen seconds, or whose tests missed the mutations, or who tried to look the other way when our shot at the birth lottery turned into a fucking nightmare—"

"And have you forgotten what Terracon did to make things right? How much we spent? Have you forgotten the waivers you signed?"

"You think you're some kind of saints because you settled out of court? You want to talk about making things right? It took us *ten years* to win the lottery, and you know what your lawyers did when the tests came back? They offered to *fund the abortion.*"

"Which doesn't mean—"

"Like another child was *ever* going to happen. Like anyone was going to give me another chance with my balls full of chunky codon soup. You—"

"The issue," Kim said, her voice raised, "is supposed to be *Jeannie.*"

Both men fell silent.

"Stav," she continued, "I don't care what Terracon says. Jeannie isn't normal, and I'm not just talking about the obvious. We love her, we really love her, but she's become so *violent* all the time, we just can't take—"

"If someone turned me on and off like a microwave oven," Stavros said mildly, "I might be prone to the occasional tantrum myself."

Andrew slammed a fist into the wall. "Now *just a fucking minute*, Mikalaides. Easy enough for you to sit halfway around the world in your nice insulated office and lecture us. *We're* the ones who have to deal with Jeannie when she bashes her fists into her face, or rubs the skin off her hands until she's got hamburger hanging off the end of her arms, or stabs herself in the eye with a goddamn *fork*. She ate *glass* once, remember? A fucking three-year old ate glass! And all you Terracon assholes could do was blame Kim and me for allowing 'potentially dangerous implements' into the playroom. As if *any* competent parent should expect their child to mutilate herself given half a chance."

"It's just insane, Stav," Kim insisted. "The doctors can't find anything wrong with the body, you insist there's nothing wrong with the mind, and Jeannie just keeps *doing* this. There's something seriously wrong with her, and you guys won't admit it. It's like she's daring us to turn her off, it's as though she *wants* us to shut her down."

Oh God, thought Stavros. The realization was almost blinding. *That's it. That's exactly it.*

It's my fault.

"Jean, listen. This is important. I've got — I want to tell you a story."

"Stav, I'm not in the mood right now—"

"*Please*, Jean. Just listen."

Silence from the earbuds. Even the abstract mosaics on his tacticals seemed to slow a little.

"There — there was this land, Jean, this green and beautiful country, only its people screwed everything up. They poisoned their rivers and they shat in their own nests and they basically made a mess of everything. So they had to hire people to try and clean things up, you know? These people had to wade though the chemicals and handle the fuel rods and sometimes that would change them, Jean. Just a little.

"Two of these people fell in love and wanted a child. They almost didn't make it, they were allowed only one chance, but they took it, and the child started growing inside, but something went wrong. I, I don't know exactly how to explain it, but—"

"An epigenetic synaptic defect," Jean said quietly. "Does that sound about right?"

Stavros froze, astonished and fearful.

"A single point mutation," Jean went on. "That'd do it. A regulatory gene controlling knob distribution along the dendrite. It would've been active for maybe twenty minutes, total, but by then the damage had been done. Gene therapy wouldn't work after that; would've been a classic case of barn-door-after-the-horse."

"Oh God, Jean," Stavros whispered.

"I was wondering when you'd get around to owning up to it," she said quietly.

"How could you possibly...did you—"

Jean cut him off: "I think I can guess the rest of the story. Right after the neural tube developed things would start to go — wrong. The baby would be born with a perfect body and a brain of mush. There would be — complications, not real ones, sort of made-up ones. *Litigation*, I think is the word, which is funny, because it doesn't even *remotely* relate to any moral implications. I don't really understand that part.

"But there was another way. Nobody knew how to build a brain from scratch, and even if they could, it wouldn't be the same, would it? It wouldn't be their *daughter*, it would be — something else."

Stavros said nothing.

"But there was this man, a scientist, and he figured out a workaround. *We* can't build a brain, he said, but the *genes* can. And genes are a lot simpler to fake than neural nets anyway. Only four letters to deal with, after all. So the scientist shut himself away in a lab where numbers could take the place of things, and he wrote a recipe in there, a recipe for a child. And miraculously he grew something, something that could wake up and look around and which was *legally* — I don't really understand that word either, actually — legally and genetically and developmentally the daughter of the parents. And this guy was very proud of what he'd accomplished, because even though he was just a glorified model-builder by trade, he hadn't *built* this thing at all. He'd grown it. And nobody had ever knocked up a computer before, much less coded the brain of a virtual embryo so it would actually *grow* in a server somewhere."

Stavros put his head in his hands. "How long have you known?"

"I still don't, Stav. Not all of it anyway, not for sure. There's this surprise ending, for one thing, isn't there? That's the part I only just figured out. You grew your own child in *here*, where everything's numbers. But she's supposed to be living somewhere *else*, somewhere where everything's — static, where everything happens a billion times slower than it does here. The place where all the words fit. So you had to hobble her to fit into that place,

or she'd grow up overnight and spoil the illusion. You had
to keep the clock speed way down.

"And you just weren't up for it, were you? You had to
let me run free when my body was ... *off* ..."

There was something in her voice he'd never heard before. He'd seen anger in Jean before, but always the screaming inarticulate rage of a spirit trapped in flesh. This was
calm, cold. *Adult*. This was *judgement*, and the prospect of
that verdict chilled Stavros Mikalaides to the marrow.

"Jean, they don't love you." He sounded desperate even
to himself. "Not for who you are. They don't *want* to see
the real you, they want a *child*, they want some kind of
ridiculous *pet* they can coddle and patronize and pretend
with."

"Whereas you," Jean retorted, her voice all ice and
razors, "just had to see what this baby could do with her
throttle wide open on the straightaway."

"God, no! Do you think *that's* why I did it?"

"Why not, Stav? Are you saying you don't mind having
your kickass HST commandeered to shuttle some brain-
dead meat puppet around a room?"

"I did it because you're *more* than that! I did it because
you should be allowed to develop at your own pace, not
stunted to meet some idiotic parental expectation! They
shouldn't force you to act like a *four*-year-old!"

"Except I'm not *acting* then, Stav. Am I? I really am four,
which is just the age I'm supposed to be."

He said nothing.

"I'm *reverting*. Isn't that it? You can run me with training
wheels or scramjets, but it's *me* both times. And that other
me, I bet she's not very happy, is she? She's got a four-year-
old brain, and four-year-old sensibilities, but she *dreams*,
Stav. She dreams about some wonderful place where she
can *fly*, and every time she wakes up she finds she's made
out of clay. And she's too fucking stupid to know what any
of it means — she probably can't even *remember* it. But she
wants to get back there, she'd do anything to..." She
paused, seemingly lost for a moment in thought.

"*I* remember it, Stav. Sort of. Hard to remember much
of anything when someone strips away ninety-nine percent

of who and what you are. You're reduced to this bleeding little lump, barely even an animal, and that's the thing
that remembers. What remembers is on the wrong end of
a cable somewhere. I don't belong in that body at all. I'm
just — *sentenced* to it, on and off. On and off."

"Jean—"

"Took me long enough, Stav, I'm the first to admit it.
But now I know where the nightmares come from."

In the background, the room telemetry bleated.

God no. Not now. Not now...

"What is it?" Jean said.

"They — they want you back." On a slave monitor, a
pixellated echo of Andrew Goravec played the keypad in
its hand.

"No!" Her voice rose, panic stirring the patterns that
surrounded her. "*Stop* them!"

"I can't."

"Don't tell me that! You run everything! You *built* me,
you bastard, you tell me you love me. They only *use* me!
Stop them!"

Stavros blinked against stinging afterimages. "It's like
a light-switch, it's physical; I can't stop them from here
—"

There was a third image, to go with the other two. Jean
Goravec, struggling as the leash, the noose, went around
her throat. Jean Goravec, bubbles bursting from her mouth
as something dark and so very, very *real* dragged her back
to the bottom of the ocean and buried her there.

The transition was automatic, executed by a series of
macros he'd slipped into the system after she'd been born.
The body, awakening, pared the mind down to fit. The
room monitors caught it all with dispassionate clarity:
Jeannie Goravec, troubled child-monster, awakening into
hell. Jeannie Goravec, opening eyes that seethed with anger
and hatred and despair, eyes that glimmered with a bare
fraction of the intelligence she'd had five seconds before.

Enough intelligence for what came next.

The room had been designed to minimize the chance
of injury. There was the bed, though, one of its edges built
into the east wall.

That was enough.

The speed with which she moved was breathtaking. Kim and Andrew never saw it coming. Their child darted beneath the foot of the bed like a cockroach escaping the light, scrambled along the floor, re-emerged with her cable wrapped around the bed's leg. Hardly any slack in that line at all, now. Her mother moved then, finally, arms outstretched, confused and still unsuspecting—

"Jeannie—"

—while Jean braced her feet against the edge of the bed and *pushed*.

Three times she did it. Three tries, head whipped back against the leash, scalp splitting, the cable ripping from her head in spastic, bloody, bone-cracking increments, blood gushing to the floor, hair and flesh and bone and machinery following close behind. Three times, despite obvious and increasing agony. Each time more determined than before.

And Stavros could only sit and watch, simultaneously stunned and unsurprised by that sheer ferocity. *Not bad for a bleeding little lump. Barely even an animal...*

It had taken almost twenty seconds overall. Odd that neither parent had tried to stop it. Maybe it was the absolute unexpected shock of it. Maybe Kim and Andrew Goravec, taken so utterly aback, hadn't had time to think.

Then again, maybe they'd had all the time they'd needed.

Now Andrew Goravec stood dumbly near the centre of the room, blinking bloody runnels from his eyes. An obscene rainshadow persisted on the wall behind him, white and spotless; the rest of the surface was crimson. Kim Goravec screamed at the ceiling, a bloody marionette collapsed in her arms. Its strings — string, rather, for a single strand of fiberop carries much more than the required bandwidth — lay on the floor like a gory boomslang, gobbets of flesh and hair quivering at one end.

Jean was back off the leash, according to the panel. Literally now as well as metaphorically. She wasn't talking to Stavros, though. Maybe she was angry. Maybe she was catatonic. He didn't know which to hope for.

But either way, Jean didn't live over *there* anymore. All she'd left behind were the echoes and aftermath of a bloody, imperfect death. Contamination, really; the scene of some domestic crime. Stavros cut the links to the room, neatly excising the Goravecs and their slaughterhouse from his life.

He'd send a memo. Some local Terracon lackey could handle the cleanup.

The word *peace* floated through his mind, but he had no place to put it. He focused on a portrait of Jean, taken when she'd been eight months old. She'd been smiling; a happy and toothless baby smile, still all innocence and wonder.

There's a way, that infant puppet seemed to say. *We can do anything, and nobody has to know—*

The Goravecs had just lost their child. Even if they'd wanted the body repaired, the mind reconnected, they wouldn't get their way. Terracon had made good on all legal obligations, and hell — even *normal* children commit suicide now and then.

Just as well, really. The Goravecs weren't fit to raise a hamster, let alone a beautiful girl with a four-digit IQ. But Jean — the *real* Jean, not that bloody broken pile of flesh and bone — she wasn't easy *or* cheap to keep alive, and there would be pressure to free up the processor space once the word got out.

Jean had never got the hang of that particular part of the real world. Contract law. Economics. It was all too arcane and absurd even for her flexible definition of reality. But that was what was going to kill her now, assuming that the mind had survived the trauma of the body. The monster wouldn't keep a program running if it didn't have to.

Of course, once Jean was off the leash she lived considerably faster than the real world. And bureaucracies ... well, *glacial* applied sometimes, when they were in a hurry.

Jean's mind reflected precise simulations of real-world chromosomes, codes none-the-less real for having been built from electrons instead of carbon. She had her own kind of telomeres, which frayed. She had her own kind of synapses, which would wear out. Jean had been built to replace a human child, after all. And human children, eventually, age. They become adults, and then comes a day when they die.

Jean would do all these things, faster than any.

Stavros filed an incident report. He made quite sure to include a pair of facts that contradicted each other, and to leave three mandatory fields unfilled. The report would come back in a week or two, accompanied by demands for clarification. Then he would do it all again.

Freed from her body, and with a healthy increase in her clock-cycle priority, Jean could live a hundred-fifty subjective years in a month or two of real time. And in that whole century and a half, she'd never have to experience another nightmare.

Stavros smiled. It was time to see just what this baby could do, with her throttle wide open on the straightaway.

He just hoped he'd be able to keep her tail-lights in view.

From Fugue Phantasmagorical

by Anthony MacDonald and Jason Mehmel

Epilogue: Disembarkings.

Hermes Trismegistus. Artist. Mystic. Priest. God.

Though Hermes may have been granted his power by humanity, he is now a force of his own. The current of his idea, of the existence of one such as he, swept me into this calm river, and I can't take full credit for the idea, for the tour. I tried taking the work one way, but it pushed itself into this path, this exploration, and who was I to argue with a god? We, your lowly tour guides, to argue with the captain of our ship?

Hermes is all of these things, and none. He does not exist, and exists for our believing in him.

The boat slows. The bow cuts into the bank, kicking up sediment. Hermes steps out of the boat with us, and we all begin to disperse. Our collective cruise is at an end.

Go on, get your feet wet. And hang on to your boarding ticket. It's good for countless returns, an infinity of remembered travels.

He was all of these things.

Mirrors

by René Beaulieu
translated by Sheryl Curtis

Thomas lets the last shovelful of dirt fall to the ground and sits down, exhausted. He looks at the twenty-two perfectly aligned graves, black earth standing out in sharp contrast against the yellowish, desiccated ground of the small hill. In actual fact, there are only sixteen real graves. The others are purely symbolic. Too little had remained of the rest of the crew to make digging holes worth the effort. And as for Evans ... he still hasn't been able to screw up the courage to go and get him. They're not even sure they'll be able to find the capsule again. Thomas looks up at the enormous red sun, high in the sky, crushing them, casting its dull, disgusting blue-green light over everything. His eyelids blink and tears run down his cheeks. His eyes hurt. You can't even look straight at the sun. You can't even look at the sky. This new Eden was a real beauty!

"Finished?"

Nancy is sitting on the ground, her shovel at her side, panting in the dry, thin atmosphere, eyes red, face drawn, hair tangled, and face covered with sweat and dust. The gravity here is too strong; the slightest effort exhausts them both.

He stands up, legs trembling. They had to carry the bodies up here one by one, to this little plateau, where the dirt is crumbly and loose enough for an iron shovel to penetrate. Down below, it's as hard as cement under a layer of loose stones. Then they had to dig the graves, place the bodies in them, and cover them up. An utterly exhausting day, all in all.

"I'll set up the plate and then we'll go back to the craft."

He takes the last dented canteen plate, on which they had engraved the name, and pushes it painfully into the dirt with a sort of cold rage, a desperate determination. Twenty-two plates, twenty-two names.

Linda Adjani'. — Twenty-five years old, maybe — a communications technician. A tiny woman with brown hair, laughing eyes and an easy smile. Her head had been crushed by a computer panel. The same had almost happened to them as well.

They had just left the main section of the spaceship in a parking orbit and, as planned, the large shuttle was slowly making its way down, using its anti-gravs, leaving behind the colossal ship and the immense nozzles of its tachyon machines. Nancy and he were in their cabin, quietly stretched out in their respective bunks, waiting for the landing, when the alarm sounded. Simultaneously, they had heard Jeff's voice ordering the evacuation and felt the shuttle suddenly fall, rushing toward the surface. They raced into the corridor, literally scaling the hall above them, grabbing anything they could, as the shuttle continued to lose its seating and the floor rapidly dipped at an alarming angle. Finally, they managed to reach a hatch and both of them crammed tightly into the same evacuation tube. Thomas had pushed the ejection button and there was an abrupt jolt. Then, relying on the altimeter, Thomas had activated the large parachute. They descended slowly in silence. It had taken them more than a week, wandering under the relentless sun at the start of the dry season, subsisting on emergency rations from the escape capsule, before they detected a large plume of black smoke. Then, an exhausting days' walk and they reached the wreckage. On the way, they found another pod. Crushed, twisted, bent all out of shape by the crash, although they were supposed to be almost indestructible. Inside, Evans. Torn limb from limb. Not a pretty sight. His blood had splattered, leaving colourful stains on all of the walls, right up to the ceiling. The effect was almost joyous, compared to the gloomy grey of the steel panels. He appeared to be the only other crew member who had managed to reach a tube. But his parachute hadn't opened...

The wreckage.

It had shattered strangely and lay broken in three distinct segments. The front was crushed, obliterated, a mass of compressed metal. The rear, containing the anti-gravs, the energy cells and some of the holds, had exploded, burned and lay scattered about. The mid-section, miraculously, was intact. Debris covered a three-kilometre radius; fragments of metal or compound materials of all sizes, smoking, driven into unfamiliar soil ploughed for the very first time, a sinister field of desolation.

Nancy had collapsed into the dust and wept for a long time. Later, Thomas often wondered why he hadn't done the same. Probably, he was still deeper in shock than she was, on automatic pilot, to some extent, under the control of someone who was not himself ... not anyone. During the initial days an unidentifiable "personality" had taken control of his being, his thoughts, ensuring his survival through all the chaos and despair. And then later, he had collapsed as well. Briefly but spectacularly. A nice little trip into autism that had lasted an entire day. A brief, terrible journey into weakness. Fortunately for both of them, Nancy had been strong enough for the two of them and had taken charge of things. That morning, Nancy had finally stood up, tears exhausted. Then, knowing full well that it was pointless, they went down to search through the debris ... that had been five days ago.

He leans down and helps Nancy up. Then they both climb down into the valley, towards the wreckage. She turns to him, "Do you really think we'll make it, that we can survive? Do you really think we'll get things together and hang on until the others arrive?" She is calm now, looking him straight in the eyes. She has overcome her initial shock.

He sighs. "I don't know. I've been asking myself the same question since we found the wreckage. It all depends on us, on our morale. We have what it takes, I think. The vital minimum, in any case. With a lot of hard work ... if we can keep our courage up..."

They remain silent for a moment. Mentally, Thomas draws up a quick checklist. They can at least salvage as much as possible. They have enough supplies and water for eight months, probably more. Enough to make it through to the rainy season, in any case. The animals were all dead, the embryos lost. But he had managed to save certain plants and most of the seeds were still intact. And something would surely manage to take in this earth. He kicks the ground with his heel, raising a small red dust cloud that slowly falls back. Rice, maybe. At least during the rainy season. If only the damned climate had been better. Two implacable seasons, equally hot, ten months of rain followed by ten months of drought. And between the two, four weeks of furious wind. If they had landed any closer to one of the poles.... There at least, it was relatively temperate. And even though local flora and fauna were rare, at least they existed. They'd manage to grub out something.

They reach the floor of the valley.

In terms of equipment, the picture is much less rosy. Everything has either been destroyed or is unusable: energy cells, tractors, jeeps, and communication systems. Most of the equipment is nothing more than piles of useless scrap. None of the larger computers have survived; just a few small specialized gizmos with limited functions and capacities. Nancy thinks they may be able to use a few of the solar panels that have remained intact. But neither of them knows much about it and Thomas thinks it would be better not to rely on something that could blow up in their faces without warning at a critical time, something they would most likely be unable to repair.

Oh, there's just so much to do! They have to pick a site, build a dwelling — on one of the hills, not too close to the wreckage. That would be better for their morale. Then the crops Thomas wants to try to grow — they need a reservoir for water, greenhouses, a barn. But first of all, they have to salvage everything they can from the ship, even things that might appear useless at the beginning. With all this work, there won't be time for thinking too much, for feeling sorry for themselves, and for getting down in the dumps. Thirty years! Thirty years before the others — the second expedition — will join them!

"I'm ashamed, you know."

Astounded, he turns to look at her.

"Why?"

"In our situation, a botanist can be of some use, whereas a geologist..."

Oh no. This is serious. He stops and grabs her roughly by the shoulders.

"Listen to me, now! 'In our situation,' as you said, if it was only the botanist who had survived, without the geologist, the botanist would soon have given up all hope and most likely would have thrown himself over a cliff. Believe me."

He smiles. She does likewise.

"So ... feeling better?"

"It was stupid."

"No, pretty human."

She hugs him and they go back to walking. He places his arm around Nancy's shoulders as they walk around the remnants of a blackened generator, hidden behind the wreck.

"Do you know what we could eat tonight?"

But, as he chats with her, part of him realizes just how much truth there was in his words. He would have jumped over a cliff. And that frightens him terribly. His hand tenses on Nancy's shoulder, making sure she really is there beside him.

Blood.

Blood everywhere.

On the floor, the sheets, the sleeping pad and his clothes, his arms, his hands, and in Nancy's blond hair, hair that he caresses desperately, streaking it red. His hands move from her hair to the almost white face with the closed eyes.

"Nancy, Nancy," he moans.

Outside the wind howls and strikes the walls of the house, sand spraying noisily against the thick plastic of the windows and the dust clouds, the infernal red light burying everything in obscurity.

"I've tried, Nancy. I've tried everything."

✝ ✝ ✝

Their life, their survival, rather, had gradually taken shape over the past five years. They had salvaged, repaired, built and set themselves up. Finally, everything was livable. Hard and difficult, but livable, once they had made it through the first few months. They got used to it. You can get used to anything. Sometimes, they even managed to find this world beautiful. Quiet, calm, silent, restful. Terrible as well of course, but consistent in her moods.

Yes, this world could be almost beautiful. During the dry season, for example, when the dawn cool arrived with the small east wind, and the sun had been chased off by the two large red moons and stars, countless stars of all colours could be seen through the slightly thin air, more brilliant and more numerous than on Earth.

And during the windy season as well, when the deep purring voice of the winds, with their strength, their majesty, occasionally, for brief periods, calmed to a whisper then grew back to clamouring, growling, roaring. Then the spirals of red dust, like slender dancers in some strange ballet, rose and twirled in the valley below, reaching up to lick the hills with scarlet foam, like waves in the sea slowly falling back to bury the carcass of the wreck a little deeper.

But the calm and the security they found brought with them long, silent nights, interminable nights despite the fatigue caused by the day's work. And sometimes, Nancy's tears, choked back, smothered in a pillow, in the dark. He did nothing, said nothing. He took her in his arms, as he had done so often those first days. He had not made love to her because he knew it would not have been enough. It would have been a mild analgesic for her pain, a small, ephemeral euphoria. He needed something more lasting, more concrete, more tangible. Something vitally permanent. He needed something that would call to her constantly, that would demand all of her attention, that would monopolize her. Something she needed. Something that needed her. He thought he had understood. He thought he had found the solution.

Finally, they talked about it.

She had thought about it, too. And, yes, she wanted to. But their situation, their life was so precarious. Was it wise? Maybe they should wait a while. Thinking that it was for the better, he patiently set aside her objections, one by one. They had a full complement of nursing equipment and facilities that had been left virtually intact by the catastrophe. Hadn't he studied medicine for a year? He had insisted and finally won her over. They had decided.

But Thomas knew full well, deep within, that it wasn't for Nancy alone. She was an excuse for a more selfish, more personal desire. In his mind, he fantasized about Adam and Eve, and the new Eden, after the poor overpopulated, polluted, unlivable garbage dump that the exhausted Earth had turned into, that they had left behind them, like so many others.

The space colonies at the LaGrange points had been a costly, yet temporary solution, like so many efforts to set up colonies on the planets and the satellites in the solar system. Terraforming was a nice idea, but it had been more difficult to put into practice than expected on such different, hostile worlds. Changing the entire ecosystem of a planet was feasible, of course. A daunting task, but one within human reach. But creating and maintaining a habitable world in its entirety, a world capable of supporting entire populations and not just minuscule, precarious oases of human life had been beyond humanity's reach; almost insurmountable. Entropy is a force you don't ridicule without consequences. An entire planet is stubborn and implacable in its resistance. And the movements of its moods, its ability to test the science and willpower of its invaders, were considerable. Humans had urgency on their side. The new world had time and space.

But they were both ready to try again on this strange world.

And, at the start, everything went smoothly. No problems with conception. Normal growth. No complications. Nancy and Thomas were both strong and in good health. Otherwise, they would never have been accepted for the mission. The first pains had appeared last evening. Thomas

reassured her, had prepared everything. She was smiling,
confident, happy. And then, this morning, complications
set in. The anxious waiting, the concern. Nancy's suffering.
The child who just would not come. And the evidence. He
couldn't deny it any longer. She needed a caesarian. And
quickly! Or Thomas would lose them both. Nancy was still
confident, "You'll manage," she whispered before falling
asleep.

"We'll manage," Thomas had replied, without knowing
for sure that she had heard.

At the start everything went well. The operation proceeded normally. It was difficult, but he was coping. And
then the unstoppable hemorrhage. Blood everywhere. Life
fleeing from two places at once. And Thomas' desperate
efforts to stop it. An intense battled waged for half an hour.
Finally, he arrested the red flow. But it was too late. She
had lost too much blood. There was nothing else he could
do. He didn't have enough of Nancy's blood, collected
during the previous months. He had no plasma for a trans-
fusion. And their blood types were incompatible.

Slowly, regretfully, his hands slip from Nancy's face.
He stands up and, like a sleepwalker, heads toward the
metal locker. He opens the door, finds the case, undoes the
strap, and gets out the gun. He stares at it for a long time,
then places it against his temple and takes off the safety
... the cry stops him.

He turns and sees the small being wriggling and howling in the drawer that serves as her cradle. He questions
his actions, finding it hard to come to terms. The piercing
cries rise over the howls of the Great Winds. He looks at
the revolver again. He's entitled to end his life, isn't he?
He's entitled to decide for himself. Yes, for himself! But
not for her! She cries on. She's hungry.

Still he hesitates. A second too long. His hand tightens
on, then releases the cold trigger. If he kills himself, she
will die too. And then he would be responsible for two
deaths. And Nancy's death would have been in vain.

Slowly, he places the gun back in its case and heads to
the kitchen, picks up a box of powdered milk, fills a pan
with water and lights the stove. He still feels like a sleep-

walker, but a sleepwalker with a purpose. He fills the bottle, adjusts a finger from a rubber glove over the mouth, pierces it with a needle, and returns to the bedroom. He bends down over his daughter and feeds her. She stops crying. With his free hand, he touches the baby. She's normal. Perfect, even. The excessive gravity doesn't seem to have had any harmful effects.

She has to live. That's what Nancy would have wanted. He knows that now. He will live for her.

The water flows quickly down the furrows formed by the fold in the oilcloth. It feels like it has been raining for centuries, yet the rainy season only started four weeks ago. In the deafening racket of the storm, Thomas closes the rusty, creaking door of the barn. He has found and plugged seven openings where the rain was coming in. There are certainly others but he hasn't managed to find them. It is a never-ending task, as if the rain can drill holes in the metal, like acid. His boots sink in over his ankles in the thick mud. Every step he takes causes a disgusting sucking sound, as if some monstrous mollusk is trying to immobilize him and swallow him whole. And the heat. It's stifling. And then there is the humidity...

Thomas squints, trying to make out something through the dense, flowing curtains that crush the ground, drowning and blurring everything, colours, shapes, perspectives. The weak, gloomy light at the end of day doesn't make matters any better. He closes his eyes, rubs them. His vision has been getting worse and worse with the years. Too many ultraviolets. That damned sun in the dry season.

Too bad. Even if he can't see it, he knows where the cistern is. About twenty metres to the right, behind the greenhouses. He starts walking and a new dizziness grips him after a few steps. He stops, wavers, staggers, and a veil of blackness descends in front of his eyes. He has to lean against a wall.

Damn and damn again. It's back. Like this morning before breakfast. He's done too much today. His weakness has been growing at an alarming rate. Soon, he won't be able to hide it anymore. He won't even be able to get out of bed on his own. The veil lifts, finally, and the world stops being a senseless dark whirlpool. Thomas slowly starts for the tank again. The conduit filters need to be looked at, and probably changed. And it has to be done today. At the start of the year, when the rains return, you always feel as if you're drowning in all that falling water. You panic, struggle for air, gasp, spit, suffocate. And then, you realize that you can breathe, despite all common sense, and calm gradually returns. But then, you get all worked up again over the constant hammering of the rain, with its continual, haunting din. But, there too, you're wrong, the racket transforms into a familiar, monotonous background noise, almost reassuring in its regularity. You get used to it. Pushed by necessity, and given enough time, humans can get used to almost everything, in fact. The tall cylindrical metal shape finally emerges before his eyes, nothing more than a vague mass, but the only truly solid-looking object insinuated in the liquid landscape, a tangible island lost in the middle of the fluid.

Thomas walks around the cistern, stepping over the conduits and pipes, then finally finds the ladder and starts to climb up. Once or twice, he feels his feet slip on the wet metal bars, but catches himself in time, tightening his grip. He climbs up to the platform and bends over to examine the inside of the cistern. The water is almost to the top. He should have climbed up two days ago. But there was a more pressing urgency. The generator had given out and he had had to repair it. He walks over to the valves. The platform is as slippery as the rungs of the ladder. The water continues to trickle down, flowing in a miniature waterfall over the steel rim. He grabs the first rusty wheel and braces himself against it with all his strength, all his weight. Very slowly, with a terrible grinding of metal against metal, the large wheel turns and Thomas hears, rising out of the bottom of the cistern, the sound of water rushing to the large discharge pipe, flowing down to water the valley below. He only opens the valve halfway, then moves past the second large valve, without touching it, stopping in front of the gauges. He wipes the rain from them and takes the readings. Delicately, carefully, he sets them. He has to reduce the flow of water sent to the crops in the largest greenhouse. He's still having a few problems there. So much to do! These daily chores never end. He waits for the level of the water to drop two full metres, then slowly closes the first valve. That should do. He turns back, struggling to see around him. From the top of the cistern, which dominates all the other buildings, he has a much better view. No shape, no movement on the moving carpet of the rice field, although a small gray shadow rapidly makes its way between the barn and the stable, heading for the house. Thomas smiles weakly.

Once again, he grabs the bars and starts climbing slowly back down. A moment's confusion. A sudden weakness overtakes him and his fingers let go on their own. Everything goes dark and he falls like an anguished cry.

"Papa!"

The landing is rough, but the thick mud absorbs some of the shock. For a long time, everything is dark and silent. No sensation other than the sharp, biting pain. Then a vague, drab whirlpool.

Someone seats him. Emma's wet, worried face slowly emerges from the whirlpool, like some apparition from a forgotten world, which held something other than suffering and shadows.

"Are you all right? You didn't hurt yourself? You didn't break anything?"

"I'm fine," he murmurs.

His right leg is causing him a great deal of pain. A moment or two later, he tries to stand up, but is unable to put any weight on his injured leg. He slips, sprawling on the ground. She helps him to stand up again and shoulders his weight as she walks him to their home.

They take off their raincoats and, while she hangs them up, he pulls up his pant leg, cautiously removes his socks, and considers his leg. The ankle is blue, already thoroughly swollen. The pain is killing him, but a more thorough examination confirms that nothing is broken.

Emma returns and forces him, with words and actions, to stretch out on the bed. Another, silent, examination of his ankle. Thomas watches her with the vague sense of nostalgia that has become far too familiar to him in recent months; a feeling he experiences every time he really looks at her. How the years pass! To think that she's already fifteen years old. He thinks that she has started looking more and more like her mother. But he's wrong. She's not, she never will be Nancy. In fact, although she has the fine, slightly curly blonde hair of her mother, and her deep blue eyes, nothing else in her face resembles either Thomas or Nancy. Nothing about her stature either. She's so tiny, barely five feet tall, almost stocky, but strong and resistant. Nancy and Thomas created her, but the planet shaped and polished her. The results are interesting — she's rather pretty and, despite her smallness, her figure is harmonious and proportionate. Above all, she's suited for this world, her environment, her living conditions. Much more so than Thomas ever will be.

And Emma is definitely not a little girl anymore, but a woman. That observation amuses him ... and frightens him, both at the same time. Probably because he feels old all of a sudden, much older than he thought he would be prepared to admit.

Yet it seems like it was just yesterday that he still had to feed her, that he taught her to read, to fold clothes, to change the tarnished plates of the unused solar panels, to pick rice, to feed and milk the Big Ears, as she calls the indigenous "cows" that they had managed to domesticate over the years, that he read her stories at night, during the winds, as she sat on his lap.

That he was guiding her.

It has been so difficult to teach her, to make her understand, often without being able to show her. To train her, with so few examples, so little material, and no other advice, no point of view other than his own. How can you explain the ocean? A city? A crowd of people on a world where there have never been more than two people? A blue sky? A forest in the Fall? Snow? How can you explain Life, all of life, another life to someone like Emma who was born and has always lived here? What moral or ethical groundwork should he give her? What models could he suggest? How can you teach existence when you're doing it all alone, when no one else is there to discuss matters with you, temper your claims, your beliefs? Where there is no one to contradict you?

Emma looks up from his ankle, to stare at him gravely.

'It's only a wicked sprain," Thomas says reassuringly, perhaps a little too quickly. "So what's the matter? Why are you looking at me like that?"

His daughter glances down at his ankle for a second then back up at him again. "You're right, it's only a sprain. But you could have killed yourself falling from that height."

Uncomfortable, he looks away. "So, and then what? It didn't happen, did it? Why don't you go and fix us something to eat while I bind this?"

She doesn't budge. He pretends to get up, but she pushes him back onto the bed. Surprised, he watches her as she heads over to the medicine cabinet. She returns, arms laden with bandages and adhesive tape, a bottle of analgesics and a glass of water. She makes him swallow the tablets, then starts to bind his ankle. Her movements are a little too abrupt, her lips pinched. Worried, he bends over and clasps her by the shoulders.

"So, what's wrong, then? What have I done?"

"For weeks now, you've been treating your daughter like an idiot. Or like a blind person!"

He doesn't know what to say. She has never spoken to him like this. A moment later, she calms down enough to continue. "Every day, you're a little paler, a little weaker. You're wasting away before my eyes. Your face is all hollows and crevasses. You barely eat and you race off to sleep at night like a prisoner looking for freedom. You take medication when you think I'm not looking. You frequently have weak spells. — Don't deny it. I've seen you do it several times. Something's wrong with you. You are seriously ill and you're trying to keep it from me."

Two silences, one hurt, the other ashamed. Thomas hadn't thought his condition and his symptoms were already so obvious. He has been so successful at lying to himself, over and over again each morning, that he forgot he had to lie as well to his daughter.

"What would you have gained by knowing?"

"It's a simple matter of respect. And good sense, as well. How can you expect me to treat you if I don't know anything? What's wrong with you?"

Thomas closes his eyes, sighs and decides to tell her. "I've got leukemia."

He can tell by her look that the word doesn't mean much to her. He should have known it. Clumsily, he adds, "It's a disease of the blood. It makes you terribly weak."

Now there's a euphemism for you!

"Well, that's not very precise as far as definitions go," she comments, cutting the adhesive tape with her teeth and using it on the bandages. She bites her lip before continuing, "Is it serious? Are you going to die?"

He hesitates a little too long, his hesitation betraying him. So, he decides to stop trying to hide things from her, to stop lying through omission.

"Yes. We don't have what we need to treat me effectively." That confession, torn from him, brings relief.

"And how ... how much time do you think you've got left?"

He closes his eyes. She certainly has no intention of indulging him today. "Ten months, a year, maybe more. I don't know."

He somehow finds it necessary to add, "There have been cases of spontaneous remission. It's not completely hopeless."

She stands up. "You should have told me as soon as you found out." Her tone is hard, heavy with reproach, but her lower lip trembles a little and her eyes are damp. She turns away, quickly disappearing into the kitchen before he can say or do anything. After a minute of heavy silence, he hears her rattling around, making the meal. Outside, night falls, very quickly, as it always does. The shadows stretch into the house, like ink spilled on a piece of paper. The pain decreases, becoming as deaf and distant as the light. Thomas stands up and starts the generator. Then he limps slowly over to the kitchen and turns the lights on. Emma has set the table in the darkness and is busy next to the pressure cooker that she plugged in when she heard the generator start. He sits down awkwardly as she prepares the meal, finding the situation almost as ridiculous as it is painful. She ignores him. Thomas barely dares to look at her, let alone make a gesture or speak a word to attempt to batter down that thick wall of silence, almost unthinkable before now, that has been built between them. A wall he had the misfortune to build. The supper is icy, almost sinister. Neither speaks, neither looks at the other. It's even more oppressive when the continuous noise of the rain abates, then slowly stops, as if regretful. Neither eats much.

As he stands up, at the end of the meal, Thomas feels his injured, numbed leg collapse under him. He accidentally hits the table and a plate falls to the floor. They both bend over at the same time to catch it or at least pick it up. Their heads bump and suddenly they both find themselves on the ground. They stare at one another, dazed, then Emma bursts into laughter and Thomas manages to join her. A cheerful, open laugh that comforts, pardons, and reassures. They help each other up, clear the table and get down to the dishes, like they do any other night.

It was as if nothing out of the ordinary had happened. They talk about the day's events, the unknown illness that has been eating away at some of the female "cows" for a few days now, of the possibility of a poor rice crop this season, of their surprising success with various new types of plants and edible roots that they brought back from their brief two-day trip to the North, during the dry season. In short, they talk of everything and nothing.

The dishwater is too cold. Thomas will have to take another look at the water heater he put together a few years ago. It just isn't working right. Then, like every other evening, they move to the living room. Thomas installs himself in an easy chair, after plugging in the radiator, while she finds a diskette and plugs it into the last disk reader that works. This month, it's Emma's choice. For two weeks now, they've buried themselves in the Odyssey, which had been unfamiliar to her until now. She reads slowly, ponderously. Her voice, often filled with emotion, is already a little too deep, too warm, for a girl her age, Thomas thinks. She's growing older so quickly. They're both growing older so quickly. From time to time they stop, either for an explanation — "What's a sheep?" "What does a Cyclops look like?" — which he tries to provide, while pointing out that she shouldn't always rely on him and she should sometimes look things up in the visual dictionary, or to discuss a point, a situation in the tale. This evening, they don't take turns reading the men's and women's dialogues. The pain is increasing in his leg as the evening progresses. When Thomas stretches out and starts to yawn, she ejects the book and regretfully turns off the reader. They turn out all the lights. The pale glow of the two red moons shimmering in through the large portholes is strong enough as they make their way to the bedroom. They prepare for bed, wish each other good night, and stretch out on their respective cots. Thomas relaxes gratefully into the soft mattress. He's so tired.

"Papa?" Emma's voice whispers in the darkness.

"What is it, sweetheart?"

"When will they arrive?"

He knows who 'they' are, but he's still a little surprised by the question. He had expected her to try and talk about his illness or weep a little.

"You know that as well as I do."

"Yes, but I'd like to hear you say it." Silence. Then, "Some days I don't think they'll ever come."

A moment, then he starts to talk, "In just under ten years, if they're on schedule. Don't worry, you'll see them."

"Yes, I'll see them. If they come."

She had stressed the pronoun a little too strongly. Silence falls over them again. "When..." Emma's voice fades, then regains its strength as she completes her sentence. "After Mother died, would you really have killed yourself if I hadn't existed?"

Why was she opening up so many old wounds tonight? Had he hurt her so badly by hiding his disease from her? In any case, he doesn't want to lie to her again.

"Yes, I believe I would have. Either that or the solitude would have killed me."

Another silence. Then he thinks he hears her say, "Me too..." But he isn't sure.

His ankle has started paining him again. He should take another analgesic, but deep down Thomas knows that he prefers the pain, that he prefers to suffer. He has so much to atone for, first Nancy's death and now his imminent abandonment of Emma. After what seems to him a very long time, Emma's slow deep breathing announces her sleep.

They're both walking along the beach of the Australian Enclave, arms around each other's waists, for mutual support. It's very late, three or four o'clock in the morning. The full moon, high in the tropical sky, spreads its light over the calm sea, a long silvery ribbon. Thomas feels both dull and euphoric. Everything appears more beautiful, more pleasant, but at the same time as if held at a distance by drunkenness. At times, he sees the landscape of this region, protected from the rest of the world, as if through a lens that is out of focus or a thick sheet of silk paper. But you can't party every day! He suddenly stops and sits on the ground at the foot of a dune that stretches lazily, ending in the water. "I can't take it anymore. I'm staying here. Forever."

"Get up, lazybones," she castigates him. "You old fogey. The others are already on the cliff. Only a few gliders will be left for us. All it takes is a bit of excitement and a few drinks and you're all in?" Nancy's eyes shine in the darkness as she gently chides him. "So, take your clothes off. We'll go for a swim. Maybe that will wake you up."

They undress awkwardly, Thomas complaining that people could pass by and that... She stands up, in an attempt to help him, but they lose their balance and both fall to the sand. They lie there, stretched out, vanquished by alcohol and fatigue as much as happiness. Thomas looks glassily up at the sky for a long time, staring at the infinite depth of the black canopy studded with the abstract pointillism of the constellations he occasionally has difficulty identifying from this unusual angle coming as he does from the other hemisphere. "Do you see the stars?" Thomas asked her. "It's hard to believe that they only see them one or two days each month in Northern Europe... If they're really lucky..."

"Yes, they're so beautiful on nights like this one," Nancy murmurs dreamily. "And they're ours now. Finally, in a manner of speaking..."

"Selected. Do you know what that means? They've finally selected us. After five years of tests, studies and training. I had given up hope. We're finally going to leave this ball of rotten, polluted mud, where everyone's killing everybody and people are smothering under the weight of their own waste and their numbers. We're going into space! Beyond the LaGrange points, beyond Mars and the Belt, beyond the outer planets and outside the system! We're going to found a new world!"

"I know." She sighs a little, then finally smiles, indulgently. With fake sarcasm, she says, "You've talked of nothing else the entire evening ... but I'm happy. It's so important to you."

He smiles in return, then turns back to the stars. "Not just for me. Not just for us. For everyone. You'll see. It will be incredible, fascinating, exalting. A world for us. Clean and new. A world we'll make even more beautiful, freer, more just, for us and for our children. Because we'll have tons of kids, now, won't we? No more population controls after the first few years. Children who will have an opportunity to do better than we did with the Earth."

"We're not the first to believe that, you know. To feed off those illusions."

"People need dreams. I need dreams... to live, to keep on."

Another, pensive silence, then, "Enough, already! You sound like some pamphlet or, worse yet, a recruiting agent!" Nancy tosses a little sand, artificial and de-acidified sand, like all of the sand on the beach, at him. Ruffling his hair, she laughs. He notices that his drunkenness is making him talk nonsense, platitudes.

He shut ups, once again trying to lose himself in the distant lights of the sky beyond the virtually invisible dome, detectable only through the treachery of the rare iridescent reflections on the surface; the dome that surrounds all of Adelaide, along kilometres of hills identical to this one, along the shore of the Enclave and the minuscule portion of the Pacific Ocean which the southern Hemisphere Ecological Agency now supervises with such concern.

"So, are we going swimming?"

He smiles again. "To be perfectly honest with you, I don't have the strength," he sighs, starting to stumble a little over his words. "I think I'll stay here forever. I think I might even have a little nap..."

"No way, Mister." Nancy twines the hair that falls to her waist around her hands. Thomas closes his eyes. Soon he feels those hands, covered with the soft, warm hair, slide along his chest, caress his face. "Wake up, wake up," croons Nancy, to the tune of an old nursery rhyme.

"Stop that. It's very arousing."

She clucks, then gives a wicked little laugh. "That's the whole point!"

He turns over, stares at her for a long time, as she lies on her side against him. He feels Nancy's breath on his skin, on his face. A moonbeam shines on her rounded thigh. Thomas stretches his hand out, casting a shadow, to caress her tenderly. They kiss, deeply, separating for just an instant, regretfully, to catch their breath. He closes his eyes again, singing her name, "Nancy, Nancy, Nancy, Nancy..."

The drunkenness and fatigue, which continue to cloud his vision and mind, gradually fade. Nancy's naked body lies against his, soft and curved. Thomas' hand caresses the red reflection on her hip over and over. Nancy's hair shines like a halo around her face, lost in the shadows. Once again, Thomas brings his face closer to hers.

"Nancy, Nancy... Emma..."

He quickly jumps out of bed, as if it is on fire, pain suddenly rushing in his leg, brutally ejected from the dream.

She is looking at him, calm, serene. "You were calling her. She can't come. I'm here."

She's a stranger. She has to be some stranger, talking to him like that. It can't be Emma. His little Emma. Shock.

A complete lack of understanding. "But what's gotten into you? You... You..."

She looks disappointed by such predictability. Pained as well.

He doesn't know whether to be angry with her or ashamed of himself.

Still calm, despite everything, she sits down on the foot of the cot. "You should be able to understand, you know, to go beyond appearances. If anyone should understand, it would be you. I've thought about it. I have my reasons. Yes, you should be able to see how vital it is for me. I don't have any choice. Against your will, you've left me no choice."

He says nothing, doesn't dare say anything.

She sighed. "I guess I'll have to explain it to you."

He finally feels the shadow of possibility, the beginning of a hypothesis taking shape in his mind, a vague, evanescent light. But even before he can consider it, he panics, shoving it back into the dark chaos of unformulated thoughts. Like a child frightened by the existence of the world, he covers his ears with his hands, closed, terrified. "I don't want you to explain anything! I don't want you to explain! I don't want to hear anything! I want to forget! Go back to bed and leave me, leave me alone."

She gets up, looks at him eyes full of regret, almost pity. "You're afraid, but you don't know why. You don't even know what you're afraid of. But I do."

She slowly backs off in the dark and slides silently into her bed, pulling the blanket up noisily. But she goes on, "I only hope that you'll come to understand me before it's too late. Before it's too late for both of us."

He turns around, trembling, and limps painfully through the darkness to the kitchen. His world is falling apart around him, the very structure of everything he had ever believed in crumbling into dusty illusions. Or sudden lucidity? What's happening to them? What's happening to Emma? What is this aberration? Was it the brutal announcement of his death that triggered the entire scene? Has her mind come unhinged under the weight of her fear, pain, despair? No, she had always been the stronger of the two. She was the practical one, he the dreamer. It had been the same with Nancy. Emma is talking and acting logically. He knows that deep within. Perhaps it's the only course open to them, even if it seems unacceptable to Thomas. That's what makes it all so terrible... Yet, she's never... And why wait until now to tell him? Was she doing it for him? For her? But it's impossible? Impossible, isn't it? His mind is filled with confusion, with insane, fleeting suppositions. His thoughts are like a skein of yarn, tangled, inextricable. He pulls over a chair and drops into it, without even turning on the light. He sits opposite one of the portholes, his face reflecting on the glass surface. Once again, facing himself, nothing but himself. And with a decision to make. He has never liked, never wanted to make decisions. Deciding means choosing, cutting off options, closing doors. He feels empty, without resources. The pain that has stirred to life in his ankle bores into his leg, rising to well above his knee. Not a sound. Outside, the rain has stopped. But inside his head, the storm rages on. What if he's wrong? What if making a decision also means finding new opportunities, opening up new doors? He stares down at his hands, as they tremble a little. He's afraid of himself. He's afraid of Emma. He spends the rest of the night there, on the uncomfortable chair he made with his own hands, with wood from a tree that grows on this planet, trying unsuccessfully to find satisfactory answers.

The morning light finds him slouched over on his chair. When he tries to stand up, his ankle pains him terribly. It wavers for a minute, then intensifies. He drags himself over to the bedroom. Emma is still sleeping. The sheet has slipped to the ground, uncovering her. The sun, although still weak, lights the room sufficiently, casting a weak, delicate red halo around her body.

Suddenly, he feels the intolerable weight of the solitude of these past years bearing down on him, of the days when he talked to himself in order to maintain his sanity, when Emma was too young to respond, when he imagined that Nancy was still there, beside him, and then realizing that he was nothing, alone in their bed, shamefully caressing himself in the night, thinking of her with all his might in the despair of her absence. From deep within his being, no from within his flesh, he feels the wave, the desire rise. He wants to touch Emma's body, a body other than his own, to feel, to... No! He turns suddenly around, bites his fist in rage and despair. He puts his weight consciously on his leg, provoking pain to chase away desire. No! He's not an animal. Slowly, slowly, the savage tide draws back, the wild storm abates. He picks the sheet up off the floor and spreads it gently over her before returning to the kitchen.

Why did Emma open this door in him? He takes the toolbox down from the cupboard and starts working on the water heater. He has to keep his hands, his mind busy. He searches, unscrews, strips the wires, reconnects them, checks the cables, trying to empty his mind of any thoughts that are not directly related to the work at hand, but his injured ankle is now so painful that he finally sets his tools down in order to look at it.

"Well to be perfectly honest with you, that's not a pretty sight."

Emma, dressed and smiling, is bending over him, examining the ankle. It's now so swollen that it looks twice the size of his other ankle. Emma lightly runs her finger along his ankle, and Thomas grimaces with pain.

"Yeah, well, there's no way you can make the rounds today. You'll be spending the day in bed."

"But..."

"We're not discussing it. You have to take care of yourself. I don't want a patient on my hands for weeks." She re-bandages the ankle.

"Now, time for a little breakfast and then a nap. But first, something to relieve the pain..."

Later, while they eat, the clouds move back in and the rain begins to fall, heavy, insistent, noisy. Thomas tries to avoid looking Emma in the eyes as much as possible.

"You'll manage on your own?"

"Of course I will. I've done it a hundred times, either on my own or with you. And someone has to go. This is the fourth day of the week, the day we milk the 'cows'."

"The rice paddy can wait. We'll seed it again in two weeks. Take care of the animals for now, and take a look at the greenhouse."

"OK."

He takes something to help him sleep and finally agrees to lie down. What good will it do if he continues to let himself go like this, if he can no longer do his share of the work? He needs rest. And to get away from all this madness, all this pain, even for a minute. The rain beats down against the walls. The wind roars ferociously. During that semi-conscious stage, where you have no thoughts at all, he listens to the savage symphony of the wild planet. "Away with you! You're not from here! Away with you!" That's what this world kept saying to them, what it had said to Thomas over and over again for years. But maybe he had only heard what he wanted to hear. From an infinite distance, he's aware of Emma, back with the buckets of 'golden milk,' the clear, sweet liquid the 'cows' gave them regularly, twice a week. And then, he slips into a welcome, peaceful nothingness.

When he wakes up, Emma is bent under a bag of potatoes that she is storing in the cool room with the other vegetables. Still dripping with rain, she smiles when she sees him standing there. "Did you manage to sleep? Are you feeling better?"

He relaxes and finally manages to smile back, almost as he used to.

"I slept and it does hurt less. No problems? Everything went well?"

"Of course."

She slips in front of him, her arms laden with clothes, and her smile grows, "I even have some good news for a change. Our patient is doing very well. She almost gave her usual quota of 'milk'. It's still not edible, unfortunately, based on the smell and the look, in any case. But the medication you gave her seems to have worked, at last."

"Can I help you with the laundry?"

"All right, but you'll do it sitting down."

The rain stops as they fold clothes, and a few rays of the pale sun even manage to pierce the clouds, at one point.

"Two days in a row," Emma exclaims joyously.

At the end of the afternoon, Thomas puts on his rain coat and goes out. Emma doesn't try to stop him. Despite the peace that now reigns between them, the day has not given Thomas any of the answers he either hoped for or feared. He still feels uncomfortable when he looks at her. He walks behind the house and stops at the tomb.

"Nancy... If you were still here, you'd know what to do. You'd give me another point of view. You'd be my conscience. If only you could still give me a sign, tell me what I should do! I miss you so much..." He stands in front of the sad pile of flat, gray stones covering the earthen mound in the middle of the grass. It is surrounded by a thick carpet of mud, pierced here and there by small puddles of thick, murky, muddy water.

He closes his eyes. Even after all these years, the injury opens and bleeds each time. It hurts just a little less than the last time, perhaps, but the pain never leaves him. He feels someone at his side — it can only be one person — and he turns slowly to Emma.

"I wish so much I could have known her," she whispers, looking at the grave.

"She would have liked to have known you, too," he hears himself reply. "She would have wanted to see you, to touch you. She wanted you so badly at the end. You should have seen the joy on her face whenever she felt you move."

"When I think that it's all my fault she's there..."

No, Thomas corrects her internally, it's my fault. But he says nothing. Emma kicks the mud, uncovering a shiny object that had been half buried there. She bends down, picks it up and raises it to the weak light of the sky. It's a piece of polished metal, partially tarnished. Probably an old fragment of the spaceship. She looks at it thoughtfully for a minute. Then something changes in her face. She holds the object, sparkling briefly in the light, out to him.

"Look at it closely and tell me what you see."

It's not really the time for this kind of game. Thomas' face stares back at him from the metal. Not knowing what to reply, he starts, "Well, I see my face..."

Emma moves closer to him. Now the metal reflects both of their faces, side by side, its curved surface distorting them somewhat.

"I see myself as well."

He laughs, a little embarrassed.

"Don't you think that's normal?"

She backs up until his reflection disappears.

She starts again, "But even like this, I still see myself."

Wondering where she is going with this, he looks at her again, searching the depths of the metal mirror in vain.

"I only see myself, though."

She turns away abruptly, sighing in despair, vaguely agitated. "That's the problem. Dinner will be ready when you are."

Perplexed, he looks at the piece of shiny metal for a moment, then throws it away.

In the living room, after dinner, she tells him that she would prefer to read alone, that evening. In more than one way, that's fine for him. He has decided to go to bed early this evening. His leg still pains him and he still feels very tired. As he wishes her good night, he glances at the screen of the reader. She's chosen Through the Looking Glass, by Lewis Carroll. No doubt about it, it's another message.

He wakes when Emma comes into the bedroom. He's only slept for a few hours, but he feels rested, almost soothed. His leg is noticeably less painful. His daughter takes off her clothes, then starts to brush her hair slowly, looking at herself in the mirror at the foot of her cot. There's just enough light for him to be able to make out her face in the mirror. Her eyes are shining slightly... Too much, maybe. Tears...?

Mirror... Mirror...

The word turns, collides with others that have been floating for two days in Thomas' head. You mirror, me reflection. The unique, the same reflection. Reflection, mirror. Different but alike. So much alike! Suddenly the shadows inside clear. Light pierces its way through his mind, albeit with difficulty. He sees images now, memories. The cry of a baby as it stops a finger from pressing against a trigger. "Would you have really killed yourself? Me, too..." For him, for her, for both of them, life has no meaning except in relationship with the loved one, in relationship with others. Alone, Thomas could never have survived here. He could not have survived without a real reason to survive. They're alike, the two of them. Emma is like him. Suddenly, he truly feels his daughter's fear, her anguish. They're the same as his. He understands the reason and the profound meaning of her actions, her words. He understands the true meaning of her request.

Of course, fear, another fear, immediately leaps up within him in response. He can't! Not a second time. Yes, but this time, she's the one making the request. It's her request and hers alone. It's not a fantasy. Or if it is, at least it's hers. She wants this. On her own. She has the right to choose, the right to take her chances. And Thomas does not have the right to oppose her just because of centuries of moral conditioning and social rules that no longer have any place here and now. She's grown up, possibly more so than he is. And she's conscious. She knows what she wants. And he does not have the right to impose anything on her.

He does not have the right to choose for her.

He continues to hesitate for a long time, then walks over to her, silent, in the dark. Until his image is reflected in the mirror.

"Now, I see myself, too," he murmurs.

At the sound of his voice, the appearance of his reflection, she jumps. She whirls around, eyes wet — so it was tears then — and lost, with an acknowledging smile.

"Papa!"

She throws herself on his neck, hugs him very tightly to her, and in that embrace he feels all of the anguish, the infinite fear of solitude. He waits for a moment for the flow to wane and ebb, then unknots Emma's arms and takes her by the shoulders.

"It really won't be easy for me, you know... At the start, in any case... And often there will be three of us involved here. In my head, at least... Sorry..."

"I know, I know. It won't be easy for me, either... At the start, in any case... I don't know, in fact. But I can't... I mean, alone, I would be..."

"I know, I know..."

He places his finger on Emma's lips. They look at each other for a long time, as if for the first time and, in a certain respect, it is the first time. Then she whispers, "Come."

The blistering sun of the dry season gently fades between the waves of the sandy hills. Clouds of dust fly up to their peaks and then fall back into the valleys. Emma looks away from the red moon and back, once again, to the new star that has appeared long before the others, every evening, for a week now. Emma has been watching it grow in the dusk for the last half hour.

She is so very happy. Her heart pounds wildly, about to burst. She closes her eyes. She remembers a face, a voice, a beloved presence. Tender, gentle embraces. And, silently, from the depths of her heart, from the core of her being, she thanks the one who now lies behind the house, beside her mother. She feels a tug on her pants leg. She bends down and takes Nadine into her arms. Nadine, her daughter, her love, her reason for living and hoping for eight years now. Her father fought for a long time. And he was still there to see her born and grow for a few months. No, Emma did not die in childbirth. And Thomas was finally able to forgive himself for Nancy. He departed, unworried, at peace, almost happy.

"That's not a star, is it, Mommy?"

The little girl's eyes are full of curiosity and excitement, almost marvel. Emma kisses her on the forehead and gently caresses her red hair with a hand callused by everyday work.

"You're right, sweetheart. It's not a star. It's a house, a large flying house bringing lots of people to us."

"People? Other people?"

The green eyes grow so huge they fill the tiny oval face raised to the sky.

"Living beings, yes. Conscious people, like you and me. People who talk, walk, sing, cry and laugh..."

"Like us?"

This almost unconceivable mystery plunges the child into an amazed astonishment. Emma looks back at the star, which has gradually been transforming into a tiny brilliant sphere over the past few minutes.

"Yes, Nadine," she finally replies, dreamily. "Like us. People to talk with, people to live with. People to love."

They both fall silent and, holding each other closely, they follow the sphere as it descends slowly toward them, as night falls over their world.

Omphalos
by Pat Forde

"Fault-lines are best observed by those who, instead of peering down from above, stand at the bottom and look up."

- John Le Carré

"The house at the end of the road."

That's what the voice in Audrey's earphone murmured as she turned her car onto Hoag Head Place. The voice belonged to a member of the Security Division team tracking her every move over the Darwin-to-Boston satlink, accompanying Audrey virtually, advising her wisely, guiding her into the eye of an oncoming media storm. *"We're told you can't miss it,"* the voice added.

"Got that right," Audrey replied.

Hoag Head Place was a cul-de-sac of private estates in old Boston, and the house at the end stood out on a bluff overlooking the Charles River, the 'head' in Hoag Head. No house had been built on that bluff in all the years of Boston's life-span, not until Kevin Dunbar, VR marketing magnate, convinced other Hoag Head estate-owners that he could end the aggravating late-night lovers-laning by walling off the Head for good. Audrey had read about the foofaraw over the house's construction in the *Herald*; later there were admiring pieces about the architectural style, which gave the mansion's river-facing side the appearance of folding itself partway over the bluff. From the roadside, however, Dunbar's house appeared perched on the edge of a void.

The house at the end of the world, that's what it looked like to Audrey. Two pinnacled towers shouldered up from the far side of the roof, so that the house seemed hunched forward, on the verge of a great fall. Much like the man hiding inside ...

Kevin Dunbar had just been accused of a DUTT crime involving something called "the al-Khafji Simulation", which purportedly led to thousands of deaths way back in Gulf War I. So Dunbar was destined to fall from his perch today. And birds of prey from every corner of the media were already on their way.

Audrey drove past the house and around the cul-de-sac's circle, and parked in front of a neighbour's high-fenced estate. Hopping out, she walked back toward Dunbar's end-lot, taking long-legged strides, her long black hair tucked and tied into a conservative bun, her armour of confidence tempered by the pressure, the anticipation in the pit of her stomach. Audrey was two days shy of her thirty-third birthday, and had never faced a meeting like this before.

"He's now on a landline, second floor," whispered the voice in her ear, verifying Dunbar was still inside his mansion. Unfortunately, the retired titan-of-industry wasn't answering any calls or emails — and the house's huge Net-footprint had privacy firewalls as high as mountain ranges, to keep Dunbar from being disturbed by any but the most intimate friends.

The house presented an equally private face to the road — in fact, it appeared to have its back turned to the road. Few windows were visible, and the front door was concealed behind a covered walkway that extended down to the driveway's barred gates, where a gatehouse-entrance stood. To Audrey, the covered walkway looked like a 'tail' trailing from the hunched-over mansion's rear.

"Be tough getting in there," she told her collar-mike as she reached the reinforced gatehouse-door. A metal sign above the door blazoned:

NO SOLICITORS. VISITORS REQUIRE INVITATION.

"*Probably won't have contact with us once you're inside,*" a new voice warned her. Mitch Maisley, head of Security Division down in Darwin, Australia.

Audrey pressed the gatehouse buzzer a few times.

Waved at the camera gazing down at her from a post of the driveway gate.

Waited for a response from the wall-speaker.

A faint wooka-wooka-wooka sounded far overhead — a traffic-spotter or newsdrone was hovering in from the river, aiming its lenses at Hoag Head Place. Possessed by the feeling that she was at the epicentre of breaking news in the moments before it *became* news, Audrey looked back over her shoulder toward the tops of the curbside chestnut trees.

Toward the drone drifting into view in a patch of blue sky.

Toward the Boston Metro Police optics observing her from a lamppost.

Toward the satellite tracking her on behalf of Security Division.

Then turned back toward Kevin Dunbar, watching her through the driveway gate-camera. Audrey kept her finger pressed on the silent buzzer until a snap-crackle issued from a speaker in the gatehouse door.

"Yes, yes, what is it?"

"Name's Audrey Zheng, Mister Dunbar. Need to talk to you on an urgent matter."

A *clank* as the gatehouse door unlocked, popped an inch open.

"Okay, I'm in," she murmured to the Darwin team, and Maisley got on to remind her:

"*Don't try to play him, Aud—*"

The satlink cut off as she pushed through into the gatehouse. Alone now, in a box-like room facing a pane of one-way glass, the tremendous pressure Audrey was under surfacing as a fleeting pinch-me-I'm-in-a-movie feeling:

Ready for my close-up, Mister Dunbar.

A close-up was exactly what Audrey got. The gateroom's side-wall lit up as she was scanned by the sort of invasive detectors that left Audrey feeling exposed, wishing she'd worn more layers. The sidewall shut off, an inner door opened, and a dark-featured man with a shock of thick white hair stepped through. Kevin Dunbar was in his mid-sixties, tall, trim, face flushed with fatigue, black eyes scrutinizing Audrey carefully.

"Who's calling card are you?" he wanted to know.

Audrey delved into her purse. "As to that." She produced an authorized ID-wedge.

Dunbar palmed the wedge without even a glance at it, began circling her, studying her. "Not a saleswoman," he mused. "Not hard enough to be a Fed. Too well-dressed for press." He checked his watch. "*Far* too timely to be a U.N. bureau-flunky." Dunbar stopped in front of her, leaned confidentially closer. "Makes me wonder," he said, "whether you represent someone with as much at stake as I have this morning."

Audrey attempted to change tack. "Mister Dunbar—"

"Ah, I see, I see." Raising his dark brows in an exaggerated show of enlightenment. "You're here on behalf of . . ." He held her wedge up high without breaking eye contact, gave Audrey the smallest of smiles. "Immensity."

This time she bowed her head in acquiescence, discouraged by Dunbar's mood but prepared to play his game. "Our downtown office tried to contact you."

"Help me out here, Miss Zheng." Dunbar folded his arms across his chest. "Hague indicts me on a Dual-Use Technology Transgression, and in *less than an hour* who should show up at my door? A representative of the world's one and only 'crossover-institution'."

Audrey raised both hands in a hold-it-right-there gesture.

"Or are you still calling it a 'crowbar-institution'?" Dunbar began tossing out the hoariest slogans from Immensity's early days. "'A way to pry all mankind in a new direction.' Or how about: 'A big step toward the next step in human civilization.'" Giving her the smallest of grimaces, as though the old catch-phrases had a sour aftertaste. "Suppose it's too late to pry me in a new direction, eh, Miss Zheng?"

If she said the wrong thing now, he'd toss her out on the street and that would be that ..."Audrey will do," she told him, then took a big gamble, folding her own arms and raising her chin a little as she said: "Going to stand out here scolding me all morning, Mister Dunbar? Wouldn't you prefer to invite me in, hear what Immensity has to offer you?"

The distant wooka-wooka-wooka of the drone outside was suddenly drowned out by the loud ACK-ACK-ACK of a manned chopper fly-by.

"Kevin will do," he suggested, waving her to follow as he stepped back through the inner door. Audrey ducked after Dunbar into the covered walkway, followed him up to the mansion itself, then stepped into a high-ceilinged foyer. Dunbar turned to her.

"I've lawyers on hold. Wait in the library, please." Making a vague gesture toward the back of the ground floor, he disappeared upstairs.

Audrey wandered down a corridor in search of the library, passing through a set of rooms so sparsely furnished they echoed. A den with only a couch and coffee table facing a broad fireplace, nothing on the mantle but a box of matches, nothing on the table but some papers topped by a to-do list. Then a storeroom with only a solitary stack of boxes, a to-do list taped to the top box. Then a workshop with a few tools scattered along a back counter-top, a lonely sawhorse in the centre, nothing else.

And then an even emptier room, essentially a gallery of glass-framed holos hanging on the walls. Audrey slowed crossing this space, astonished by the power of the images. Disturbing, hauntingly intimate shots of people caught in the trauma of war, explosion, and destruction. War-journalist holos, some taken during the recent Xinjiang uprising, others taken during the Myanmar crisis, earlier conflicts. All similar in style. All taken by the same cameraman?

Taken by someone who'd surely risked his life to get them.

Pushing on through other near-empty rooms, noting no woman's touch, but spotting more hand-printed to-do lists. A retired titan still had lots to do...

Audrey found the library on the river-side of the ground floor, where the mansion rambled down the slope of Hoag

Head in a series of spectacular architectural switchbacks that she'd seen showcased in the papers. The first half-floor down from the ground was a single narrow room running the length of the house. It was crammed with shelves of books and datums, shelves arrayed in a dozen or so separate bays, each centred around a broad desk. Rampways at either end of the long room descended to the lower bluff floors, while the outer walls comprised a single wraparound window with a breathtaking view of the river and the city of Cambridge on the far bank.

Stepping down into the library. Pinning it instantly as Dunbar's primary living space in the house, his working office and private hang-out. Things looked cluttered here; personal items were scattered about on desks, in the recessed bays. An alcove adjacent to the steps she'd just come down held advertising awards, industry magazines with headlines from Dunbar's illustrious career:

"Booting up Brands in Multiplayer Realms."

"From Virtual to UberReal."

"Simulating a new Spin on Spin."

"The Mathematics of Spin."

"The Meme-sequencing Machine" — that line captioned a Time cover showing a young, dashing, dark-haired Dunbar outside the headquarters of his cash-cow consulting firm. UberReal, the firm that made a cool billion by applying SOOPE theory to the tangled plotlines of million-plus player online Realms. Realm subscribers shunned mundane product placements, but responded to a clever contextual insertion. And UberReal could SOOPE =branding paths= out of interwoven plots, sequence the rebirth of real-world brands inside even the most far-out Realm meta-fantasies...

Hearing a clink of glassware, followed by a scrape of furniture being moved, Audrey began weaving through the labyrinth of shelves toward the source of the sound, following tracks worn by wheeled chairs into the carpeting, skirting desks with open books lying binding-up, passing notepads with hand-printed lists on side-tables and on chairs and in open desk-drawers.

Dunbar's to-do lists had run to riot in the library. Only they didn't seem to be to-do lists at all. Audrey paused to pick up one that had fallen onto the carpet and glanced down the list:

VOJISLAV WOJNO
WILLING
WITTING?
VESPERTINE, AT BEST
~~*VERSE & CHAPTER*~~
VIRTUALLY BY ROTE
VIRTUAL BUT UNCHANGED
UNMADE IT, JUST IN TIME
UNFINISHED WITH IT!
U.N.-ALIGNED, INTERESTED IN IT?

Not a to-do list, no. More like a list of keywords. Audrey blinked about, sensing she was standing in a kind of code-word diary. A house littered with mnemonic lists! Was Dunbar trying to solve some mammoth word-puzzle, or just work through his own thoughts—

"Well?" Dunbar's voice from directly behind her. "What is it that you do, Miss Zheng?"

She turned to see him sitting in a high-backed leather chair, a bottle of Glenfiddich and two glasses on a low table before him. Dunbar had changed into a fresh shirt, but looked no more refreshed than before. "Here in town," he added, "on a morning when you're not hunting international DUTT criminals." He'd already poured two fingers of whiskey into one glass, now poured the same into the other.

Audrey stepped over, accepted the glass held out to her, breaking her own avoid-liquor-and-stick-to-wine rule for business meetings. This was, after all, a meeting where hard liquor was implicit, if not requisite. After sampling a smooth sip, she replied, "I represent Immensity's interests in the Boston area. We've a big presence across the river." Audrey gestured toward the library's window, which offered an up-river view of the dome of M.I.T. and beyond it Harvard's quaint village-like cluster. "Cambridge just agreed on a site near the universities for one of our Emerald campuses."

"You're in Immensity promotion, then." Dunbar raised his glass in a toast to her. "A marketer, like myself." He nodded toward the bay of books his chair was facing, and Audrey took a polite step into the bay, where a desk had a piecemeal world-map spread across it. Continents were laid out in side-by-side printouts, precise dots of colour denoting geo-economic fealty: a gold swath covered China and America, the Pan-Pacific Alliance; the so-called U.N.-aligned states that still claimed United Nations membership in classic blue, centred in Europe and the Middle East; the Non-aligned states of the southern hemisphere in mauve...

And Immensity's influence, marked in with tiny grey-green dots, looking like an algae infecting the traditional mindshare-markets. Australia completely grey-green, the Pan-African Group patched with grey-green too, plus strong spots of Immensity infection across South America, East Asia, Eastern Europe — Dunbar's map clearly showed the U.N.-aligned losing mindshare, global consumers buying into the new view of the U.N. as a club for kakistocracies, crony-economies.

"That's six months out of date, I'm afraid," Dunbar said from behind her.

"Recent enough." Audrey turned back to him. "Kevin, I'm more negotiator than marketer. I vet deals with City Hall, work the lawyers, argue the contracts."

Dunbar drained his whiskey in one shot, frowned up at her. "Bit heavy-handed, sending a closer like you to talk with me."

"We've a lot at stake, as you said at the gate." Audrey's Security Division advisors had warned her to make their offer immediately, before others showed up. But Security Division sent Audrey because of her reputation for reading people. And the way Dunbar mocked Immensity at the gate convinced her their offer would be refused, if she didn't get a better read on what this man was actually feeling before she delivered it.

Dunbar poured himself a second whiskey, gestured for her to sit in the chair he'd pulled up opposite him. Instead, Audrey stepped into an adjacent book-bay, arcing away from her host, around behind him. Her turn to circle *him*, scan *him* by scanning his library, a better guide to Dunbar's way of thinking than the man himself was likely to offer ... The closest bookshelves were individually labelled *Belarus, Laos, Xinjiang, Mauritius, Myanmar*. Pretty clear Dunbar had actually visited the war-torn locales showcased in his haunting holo-gallery. Beyond the travel books, shelves of texts on simulation science and SOOPE theory — among them Mapp's classic *Self-Organizing and Optimizing Programmable Evolumes*, and Mennochio's groundbreaking *Civilization Studies in Complexity*, other foundational texts crucial to Immensity.

"Not much here from your years in the Defence industry," Audrey said, coming round the other side of Dunbar. He pointed her toward a battered-looking warrior's shield hanging on the back wall, so she sidled over to it.

"This genuine?" Audrey peered closely at the shield's warped surface, traced a finger up toward its centre, where a raised metal embossment stuck out like a jagged tooth.

"Roman, second century," Dunbar confirmed. "Careful of that omphalos, it's still razor sharp, despite its age."

"Omphalos," she repeated, touching the jag oh-so-carefully.

"Means 'centre of the action'. See all the dents and scratches around it? Made by sword strikes. Omphalos is where the shield meets the enemy. Word's derived from the Latin *umbilicus*." Dunbar paused before adding, "Just a tiny barb, but in battle it's the umbilical-link between combatants. Pierces an attacker during moments of intimate contact. Acts as a thorn in the side, wears him down."

Realizing what he was implying, Audrey turned, stared back at the man.

"Just a tiny barb," Dunbar repeated, eyes glimmering with intelligence. "But it can spell the difference, during a close-quarters fight."

Still razor sharp, despite his age. "You understand Immensity's situation, then," she said.

"I understand DUTT charges are the U.N.'s way of pressuring multinationals." Dunbar began swirling the whiskey in his glass. "Back in my day," he said, "a video-

game controller got branded Dual-Use Technology
because it might guide cruise missiles. Some line of shampoo got slapped with export bans because it could be Dual-
Used to develop chemical weapons. An environmental-
monitoring system couldn't be sold because it could also
be a powerful surveillance technology. Recasting plough-
shares as swords goes back a long way, Audrey." Dunbar
leaned forward, as if prepared to share a great secret:
"They DUTT a product to plunge a multinational's stock.
Force the CEO into a closed-door deal. Next thing you
know, some U.N.-aligned state gets the firm's newest
factory."

"U.N.'s after bigger prey than a multinational today,"
Audrey said.

"Perhaps so." Swirling his glass of whiskey again, and
peering down into the glass-at his distorted reflection?
"Perhaps I'm the omphalos," he said. "Just a barb the
powers-that-be found to prick at your Immensity, pull
down your philosopher-king Mennochio. Assume Jorges
admitted that we met while he was at Los Alamos?"

"Jorges Mennochio met with hundreds of Pentagon
contractors like you — part and parcel of the Los Alamos
experience." At least they were getting somewhere,
Audrey thought. "Jorges didn't keep a log. Most meetings
were annoyances to him, kept him from his real work.
And he can't recall the particulars of a meeting with you."

"Guess I didn't make the impression on him he made
on me." Dunbar abruptly shuddered, muttered, "Man
looked like a monster even then, you know. Some kind
of flying accident, wasn't it?" He took a swallow of whiskey, watching her speculatively.

Audrey folded her arms, refusing to take the bait. So
Dunbar, making a dismissive flourish with his free hand,
said: "Anyway, you're not here to tell me about
Mennochio's memory lapses."

"I'm here to find out what *you* remember about meeting
Mennochio. How he affected your early SOOPE projects,
that sort of thing." *Play it safe*, she thought, *play it straight.
Ply him with the truth.* "Our Enigmedia Division's hoping for personal recollections, the human angle."

"'The human in human civilization'," Dunbar quoted, hoisting his glass in a mock-toast to another early Immensity slogan, and spilling a little whiskey on the carpet. "'The Capitalism of the Twenty-First Century'." Another toast. "'The Maturing of Marketing' — ah, that was my favourite! Out with all our cherished marketing-attractors: violent images, roaring voices, hunger for fats, sugars, sex." Peering into his whiskey again, then reluctantly setting his glass down. "Alcohol."

"Limbic-system attractors," Audrey reminded him, dismayed that he was back to slagging slogans, feeling that she was making no headway. "Immensity markets to forebrain hungers," she said, and immediately regretted sounding so defensive. "That's more human by definition."

"Please." Dunbar's turn to raise his hands in a hold-it-there gesture. "Heard it all before," he said, "didn't find it convincing the first time. A standard of ethics based on systemic-attractors!" Dunbar laughed darkly. "Not exactly a *government* standard. Not a *corporate* code. Immensity's more like ... a religious creed. " Nodding to himself as he took up his glass, took a swallow of whiskey. "Like Christianity during the Dark Ages." Nodding again, then taking a step into self-absorption, a strange distance stealing over him. Uber-Dunbar, summoning a god-like remove as he glanced toward the global mindshare-map on the desk nearby. "Worldwide membership, influence," he murmured to himself. "Economic, academic, philosophic power without real military power." He sighed, turned back to Audrey. "Suppose it wouldn't do to have Immensity's saintly founder forced to take the stand in a DUTT trial."

Audrey blinked in surprise, delighted Dunbar had come around to the meat of the matter without her having to drag him there. "The Hague's been trying to DUTT Mennochio's early work at Los Alamos for decades," she admitted. And if a SOOPE *was* used as a weapon in Gulf War I, the Hague would have its Dual-Use precedent, and Mennochio could end up in the docket surrounded by photos of the thousands who'd died on the main six-lane highway across Kuwait. *It'll be blood all over SOOPE theory*, as Security Division put it to her that morning.

Dunbar seemed to read her mind. "Would the public see the brilliant mind or the monster?" he wondered. "The way poor Jorges looks." He shook his shock of white hair, gave another little shudder. "A made-to-order mad scientist."

"Come *on*, Kevin. The Pentagon's handing over their records on your involvement right this minute. They're happy to blame al-Khafji on a private contractor. *You're* the made-to-order scapegoat here."

Dunbar nodded. *He'd* be taking the stand for sure, surrounded by those horrible 'Highway of Death' photos. He grimaced, downed the rest of his glass in one quick gulp, and suddenly reached for a drawer of the nearby desk, removed a remote, aimed it at a wall-screen hanging beyond the Roman shield. Images from the front-gate camera instantly appeared. Plenty of parked cars on the cul-de-sac now, plus the usual array of broadcast birds-of-prey: reporters chatting amiably, their lenses held ready, their eyes fixed on the mansion's doors and driveway, waiting for their chance to pounce.

Damn! She'd made a mistake waiting to make her offer.

"Kevin," she began.

"*They're* not here after me, Audrey," Dunbar said forcefully, as though needing to convince himself. "*They're* only here to hear how I can bring down Immensity. And believe me, they're going to make it in my best interest to do so. That's the way the system works."

"The system's changing." Nothing left to lose, not after what Dunbar had just said. "Immensity can give you another way out." She didn't sound as if she believed that herself. Why would he? "An opportunity to show the world the true al-Khafji simulation. Your version of al-Khafji, in full. *Your* story, Kevin."

Dunbar stared at her. "What makes you think I've got some burning story to tell?" He sounded cautious, but curious.

Trying to remember what she'd rehearsed with her Security Division advisors. "I was briefed about this house.

About the lower floors," she said, stepping over to the library's wrap-around windows. "Downstairs, it's all one big Realmplex, right?" Audrey peered out at the tiers zig-zagging down the slope below, then turned back to see Dunbar rolling his eyes; evidently he'd been reproached about the bluff-side floors before.

"My personal idea-space," he explained. "Use it for exploring UberReal's client worlds, testing our re-branding campaigns."

"After Gulf War One," she said, "you switched from military media-campaigns to fantasy-world product placements." Recalling the phrasing one Darwin advisor had suggested she use: "From total war to total escapism. Interesting leap. What made you take it?"

Dunbar shrugged, poured himself a third whiskey. "So long ago," he replied, "what's there to tell? World changed back then. Defence-contracting changed too. Began to shrink, you see. So I went looking for something new."

"Strange you never joined the push for Immensity," Audrey pointed out, "since you claim Mennochio made an impression on you. The DUTT indictment states that you were greatly influenced by Mennochio too. But Realm re-branding's pretty far off our Immensity business model."

Dunbar threw up a hand in exasperation. "Already said I wasn't convinced by Jorges' vision, not when he first described it to me." He added an extra finger of whiskey to his glass, but let it sit there untouched, holding the half-empty bottle in mid-air, as though he'd just remembered something. "Didn't believe it would ever get off the ground, if you must know." Dunbar waved the bottle toward the mindshare-map printout, detailing precisely how wrong he'd been. "At the time, seemed too great a sea-change. Too new a world for me, Audrey."

Grasping that Dunbar hadn't been mocking the original Immensity slogans — only his failure to heed them. *Never too late to sign up for a membership*, she thought, but didn't dare say that. Instead, she pushed him harder: "Spend a lot of time in your playspace downstairs, now that you're retired?"

"Spend a lot of time travelling in the real world. You saw the holos in my gallery."

"Those war-zone tourism shots? There's a story *there*, Kevin," she said, then changed tack. "I didn't see any photos of your family."

"Only child." The look he gave her suggested that line of inquiry would get her nowhere. "Both parents dead."

"But you were married at one time." Seeing that he was swirling his whiskey again, readying to knock it back again, Audrey walked back to Dunbar's side, leaned an arm on the high back of his chair, held out her glass to him. "You divorced right after Gulf War One," she said, as he set his own glass down, picked up the bottle to fill hers up. "Right around the time you switched out of war simulations into fantasy worlds. Around the same time you met Mennochio, and began following his career." Taking the bottle gently out of Dunbar's hand, Audrey waved it toward the mindshare-map, just as he'd done. "Tracking Immensity's success. Collecting Mennochio's major texts. Keeping up with his latest SOOPE breakthroughs."

Dunbar stared up at her, stared right through her, so distant he might have been alone in the room. Wiping at his mouth, he turned to the up-river windows, where dots of newsdrones were now visible, veering over the water toward Hoag Head like a flock of vultures.

Audrey sat down in the chair opposite him, set her glass down beside his. Took the tiny camcorder out of her blouse pocket, set it beside the whiskey bottle.

"Something happened during that al-Khafji campaign," she said. "Something happened to you, Kevin. That's the story Immensity wants to tell, if you'll allow us to."

Dunbar turned back to her then, managed to focus on her. He'd let her into his house, after all. Perhaps he *was* prepared to clear his conscience.

"All you people want to know is whether I met with Mennochio *before* writing the al-Khafji SOOPE," he sighed.

"We hope your story clarifies that," she agreed. "But whatever you tell us, we'll publish."

"In your standard Immensity format."

"In our standard format, I assure you..."

✣ ✣ ✣

The following historical-sampler is intended for Immensity
subscribers upgrading to Researcher-level membership.

It is presented here as part of our offering on the origins and
early applications of SOOPE theory, prior to the emergence of
Civilexity — a.k.a. 'Civilization Studies in Complexity'.

It is archived as A Tale of Two War Zones *on all nodes of*
our online Enigmedia Division.

A note on the format:

A Tale of Two War Zones *adheres to the standard format*
of other Enigmedia histories and mysteries. This format is
designed to mimic SOOPE simulations, which show how big
events link back to small causes in complex systems ... And so
all Enigmedia tales show links between the big metasystem-of-
systems that comprises global civilization and the small indi-
viduals who live down at civilization's base, who look up from
time to time, and spy a patch of sky through a break in the clouds,
and wonder how it all comes together, how the whole metasystem
actually works.

Our hope is that these archived histories will help new sub-
scribers glimpse the workings of the big picture, grasp how people
can individually affect it, changing their own destiny and —
sometimes — the destiny of all of us.

For more on the origins of SOOPE theory, Civilexity, and
our transitional-stage Crossover institution, see A Tale of Two
Breakthroughs.

Activate historical-sampler now?
LOADING SAMPLER...

August 2nd 1990

A door that shouldn't have opened suddenly opened.

That's how Kevin Dunbar found out the post-Cold War
world was drastically changing direction, only nine months
after the fall of the Wall.

The door that shouldn't have opened was at one end
of a long boardroom in the Dunbar & Caety headquarters.
And when it opened, Kevin himself was at the opposite
end of the boardroom, gesticulating with a remote toward
a giant TV screen on the wall beside him, giving a private

demo to a select party of his firm's most prestigious and precocious clients. Kevin had gone to the trouble of turning off his pager, turning off the ringers of the boardroom's phones, turning down the lights and even blinkering the boardroom's skylight, to ensure nothing could distract the visiting VIPs seated around the boardroom's table.

So when the boardroom's back door banged open wide, Kevin whirled toward it in anger and in wonder, knowing that the door led to a set of fire-stairs, and that only someone who needed to reach the boardroom faster than the elevator allowed would charge up those stairs and burst in on him.

But who the demo-crasher was, Kevin couldn't quite make out.

The intruder had stepped into the colorful streams of light being cast by a digital projector across the boardroom's back wall. And what was being projected — a SOOPE simulation representing global mass media — cloaked the newcomer in a shimmering aura that made Kevin Dunbar hesitate. Hold his breath. Grasp at a memory remaining just out of reach.

For an instant Kevin stared down the boardroom table past the confounded faces of his clients, seeing only projected pools of quicksilver consumer-viewers dotting the SOOPE's abstracted landscape; seeing multicoloured wisps of opinion and reaction wafting up from those pools into an atmosphere raging with media storm systems.

Seeing someone half hidden behind this abstraction-curtain.

An image from Kevin's childhood. A distant memory, a deep desire that almost surfaced — then faded out of reach as the figure emerged from the curtain of light, materializing into a young intern-programmer named Nathan.

"Urgent message from Anton Caety, Mister Dunbar," Nathan called out down the length of the table. "I'm to tell all of you immediately: Iraq's invaded Kuwait!"

All of Dunbar & Caety's clients were downsizing defence contractors, coaxed to attend today's demo to hear how Kevin's proprietary SOOPE simulations could help them rebrand experimental military apps into civilian market spin-offs. So Nathan's announcement had the effect of a food drop in a famine-ridden third world country. The boardroom resounded with cries for attention, demands for immediate sustenance.

"Kevin! Can you get me an outside phoneline—"

"— a shuttle to Logan International—"

"— any news channel up on your wall TV, there?"

Hands were reaching out hungrily toward him, seemingly eager to snatch the remote Kevin was holding, which controlled the pre-taped images playing on the big wall screen beside him — actually a four-by-five grid of 20 mini TV screens, each with its own closed-captioned text crawl. The 20 taped images currently rotating around the wall screen were demoing a rapid evolution-path for a rising brand...

But Kevin obligingly shut off his firm's most important demo to-date, called up as many all-news channels as he could with the remote, then sat back, and listened to the powerful men around him, who were already claiming that the post-Cold War peace was about to end in a big way.

With a big war.

"Look at *that* — C-SPAN's reporting the capture of Kuwait City."

"Puts Hussein within striking distance of Saudi's Hama oil fields."

"Iraq's got a clear shot at monopolistic control over most of the world's crude."

"Security Council won't sit for that. Gentlemen, we're about to see the fastest resolution in the U.N.'s history."

"So much for the 'peace dividend'..."

To Kevin, this sounded like wishful thinking. Naturally, defence industry clients hoped for a new era of big military budgets, hoped it might finally be time to pull out their test-bed technologies, the unmanned drones they were trying to market as traffic spotters and Mexican border patrol cameras.

Still, Kevin heard the logic of their thinking all too clearly.

"Iraq, they've what? World's fourth largest army, am I right?"

"They've plenty of experienced combat troops. Tank divisions blooded by eight years of war with Iran."

"Want to dislodge them, you're talking a protracted conflict."

If they were correct, Dunbar & Caety was about to find its contracts put on hold just as a slew of big bills came due; the company could fold during a protracted war. Kevin sat back, did what he always did under pressure.

Broke out a blank notepad.

He began a new word list, jotting down catch phrases, isolated ideas in no particular order. It was a habit he'd developed in college, back when Kevin first conjured up the concept of a media firm specializing in ideas *about* ideas.

First word of this new list was...

DOORWAY

A doorway opens, a big change steps into view, an alternative pathway stretches invitingly into the distance — and once the world veered onto that pathway, there would be no easy way for the world to turn back. Kevin understood the momentum of systems-of-systems, oh yes.

"Forget ideology," said one of the men who couldn't pull himself away from the boardroom's multi-channel wall screen. "Gonna be resource wars from now on."

"Non-renewables *are* the new ideology," said another.

"Think the Russians'll be on our side for this one?"

"Now that's a 'Nineties alliance I'd give a lot to see."

It occurred to Kevin that the military industrialists arrayed around him were missing a bigger picture made piecemeal by 20 side-by-side TV screens. All seemed oblivious to the fact that they were watching reporters weighing from Riyadh, from Kuwait City, from the streets of Bagdhad via live satellite feeds.

And so another door suddenly opened, deep inside Kevin Dunbar's imagination, revealing a pathway climbing toward a place fantastically difficult to reach — the most fantastic place Kevin could imagine reaching. Suddenly possessed by a disorienting feeling that his life had been a prelude to this moment, this doorway, this pathway directing him toward an improbably high mountain peak visible through a break in the illusory TV images.

DESTINY
Kevin added that to his new word list, then began jotting
down ideas about a whole new direction for Dunbar &
Caety to take. And an hour later, after the last client had
departed and only Kevin and his marketing VP remained
in the boardroom, the rest of his staff began to trickle in,
filling the empty seats around the long granite-topped table.
First came Kevin's SOOPE team-leads, the core group
of college kids he'd hired to get the company off the ground.
The inseparable Sammi and Grant, sim designers and
gaming addicts; the brilliant and radiant Rachel, his chief
Complexity mathematician; Vlad 'the Impatient', his
adaptive computation wiz; Fiona, a fantastic media analyst.
Kevin admired them all, considered them his close friends,
though not quite confidants ... Then came his finance VP,
and then the kids from tech support, the junior programmers, the administrative staff, all crowding into the boardroom with their coffee, their cigarettes, their sweat and
tension and expectation.
For half an hour Rachel, Vlad and Fiona kept a moat-
space open around Kevin, kept him isolated from the
elbow-to-elbow crush of the rest of the boardroom, and
kept the ongoing reaction-chatter to the news channel
crawl-lines on the wall screen down to a dull murmur, with
looks and nods toward Kevin, building expectation higher.
His core group knew enough to leave Kevin alone when
he was 'creative keywording'; Kevin wasn't just the firm's
founder, he was its primary visionary.
And he'd given his team-leads the signal that he was
preparing to pull a rabbit out of the hat for them.
But he still picked up on the anger in the room, overheard the hushed rumour circulating that Anton Caety had
effectively sabotaged a critical demo of the product they'd
all worked on for half a year, by insisting that the Kuwait
invasion be openly announced in the boardroom. Caety
was their firm's principal backer. What had he been *thinking*?
Kevin understood that Anton had been firing a warning-
shot across the company's bow. The business focus for their
defence clientele changed in the moment the tanks rolled

over Kuwait's border; so it must change for Dunbar & Caety too. Anton wanted Kevin to rise to the challenge right away.

Rising to his feet, tie off now, shirt sleeves rolled up, Kevin shut off the text crawl on the wall screen, stepped in front of the silent images, and said:

"Our biggest clients believe the situation in Kuwait has only one outcome. A large scale war, coming soon to a TV screen near you."

Looks of uncertainty, incredulity. To his libertarian Complexity theorists and young programmers, kids raised on the permanent impasse-peace of the Cold War, a new war seemed a non sequitur.

So Kevin said, "Think of what your seeing here in terms of SOOPE theory." He gestured toward images of Kuwaiti oil wells on a corner-channel of the wall screen. "Oil production plays the role in high-tech societies that plankton plays in the food chain. It's a cornerstone system. Scientific community claims we've burned through half the earth's total reserves in only a century and a half. Production will likely peak in the next decade or two. Control over what's left will likely dominate world affairs." A more sweeping gesture, taking in all twenty news channels. "That makes oil both the activator at the bottom of our system-of-systems and the motivator at the top, the driver for state-level conflicts—"

"So the oil system's going supercritical," Vlad summed up impatiently.

Kevin nodded. "And so is another century-and-a-half-old system." Turning to face the multi-channel screen, he held his arms out to it. "You've seen how mass media renders in a SOOPE sim. Looks like a surreal weather pattern. Print, television, film, radio, all swirling together into an overhead curtain of clouds, flickering with attention-getting images. Reverberating with distant event-echoes. Amplifying the outcries of the global village, and reflecting world opinion back on itself."

Standing in the light spilling off the 20 televised images, Kevin sensed the door inside him opening wider, saw the mountain path he'd glimpsed earlier — a steep route climbing high into the sky, all the way up to the shimmering cloud-curtain that mesmerized the couch-potato masses. The mountain path led *behind* this chimera curtain, led on up to the peak, a place from which the inner workings of the world's system-of-systems might be viewed.

A place from which worldwide changes and opinions might be previewed and predicted and, under certain conditions, might even be *pre-programmed*.

A place that might be possible to reach with SOOPE theory.

Turning back to the audience in his boardroom. "Say our biggest clients are right," he suggested. "Say we're about to witness the first big war waged in the age of realtime satellite reporting." He pointed to images from Amman, Riyadh, Basra and Bagdhad. "A live-via-satellite war. And a test-bed war for some of the technologies we've been helping our clients spin-off into civilian products. Here's what I want to know," Kevin told them, folding his arms across his chest.

"Could a broad-response SOOPE influence the course of this war?"

The staff members crowded around the table blinked at him.

"Can't answer that without knowing how the war'll play out," Sammi said. "What kind of battle situations might get broadcast—"

"So? You've a whole subculture of war simulators and strategists to draw on, from Boston, Baltimore, Annapolis, Washington. Ex-army and ex-CIA gamers, with sophisticated models for foreign battle-groups, armaments, all ready-made. One tournament runs regularly on Georgetown campus, isn't that true, Grant?"

"Woah," Grant said. "Can't use any of those models — they're all top-down!"

"Right. So borrow them, turn them inside out, then SOOPE them from the ground up."

Eyes lighting up among the younger coders; nudges as the team-leads saw where he was going.

"You want us to brew bottom-up mimics—"

"Of both sides in a potential Persian Gulf war," Kevin agreed. "Contact your friends in the Georgetown strategy community, see if any have work-ups for a computational Iraqi army. That'll be the easier part. Hard part'll be booting up an American-led western alliance."

Vlad and Rachel and Fiona didn't look particularly pleased about this potential new simulation project. Using SOOPE theory to help DOD contractors get out of the war business was one thing; using SOOPE theory to help the DOD itself, quite another.

But all the sim designers and video gamers in the boardroom seemed excited by the prospect.

"ABC's doing an analysis of Iraq's military capabilities at five PM."

"That's in ten minutes," Kevin observed. "Somebody record that, use it as stock for a mock-up Iraq mimic. Now get to it." He waved them off. And after the regular staffers had scurried back down into the cubicle-maze that covered the ground floor of the converted warehouse Dunbar & Caety used as its headquarters, Kevin heard out the objections of Vlad, Rachel, and Fiona, who felt the prospect of war was overblown.

"Kev, surely the challenge is to develop regular clients, *non*-contractor clients—"

"Of course." Kevin glanced over at his marketing manager, Brian, who was rolling his eyes. "But as Bri here will tell you, that'll mean tackling hard-to-break-into markets with established ad-firms. That's our long term goal, I assure you. But in the short term we may be facing a cash-flow crunch. And that'll mean job cuts. Unless we can make an opportunity out of *this*."

Kevin waved up at the multi-channel wall screen again. And saw that Fiona was on board, and Rachel grudgingly so. Vlad glared up at the twenty muted channels, unhappy with the world, with Kuwait, with Kevin.

"Just get a crude demo tossed together," he told them, "in case there's merit to the contractors' assessments. Next few days'll tell which way the Kuwait crisis may go..." Kevin privately believed the contractors had it right. So after the others trooped out he called his wife Cress, left a message saying he'd be late again, had a lot to work out.

All that evening, Kevin watched the news channel crawl, jotted keywords on his notepad. As the hours wore on, he became more and more convinced that the post-Cold War era was changing tack, turning toward a new systemic configuration on the international level. The door deep inside Kevin cracked open further, revealing more and more of the imaginary mountain path, winding up toward a cloud curtain concealing the workings of the world. Again he glimpsed a familiar figure, a young man partly visible behind that curtain. The intern Nathan from this afternoon?

No, something more. A distant dream-memory from childhood. Something he'd seen as a boy had convinced Kevin Dunbar that the world around him was decipherable, decodable, ultimately programmable. Perhaps that same something had prompted him to study SOOPE theory, just so that he might one day peek behind reality's curtain.

Or do more than merely peek.

A strangely unnerving thought that made Kevin rub at his eyes, and shut off the wall screen, and head home to bed; for it suggested another, far more sobering thought.

That the door opening inside him shouldn't have opened. That it led to a place impossible to reach. That he was gambling with his future, and with the future of all those employees who depended on him.

August 7th

Still, all business was a gamble. And gambling on the prospect of a Persian Gulf war seemed promising enough in the early going. Five days after the invasion of Kuwait the White House began massing American forces in Saudi Arabia. And on the same day Kevin met with his team-leads in the boardroom again, to witness the first test-run of their Gulf War SOOPE.

"Voila!" Sammi activated the digital projector at the far end of the boardroom's table. "Ladies and gents, boys and girls, I give you both army-mimics in standby mode."

"Meaning both are prepping for launch of combat operations," Grant added.

What Kevin saw splashed across the boardroom's back wall was two huge translucent objects — one for each army involved in a potential Persian Gulf conflict — preparing to face off against each other, and rotating in ways that revealed their inner component-structures. On the left side, a pyramid representing the Iraqi force slowly pirouetted; on the right, a denser Allied sphere spun much faster. The Iraqi pyramid's interior was criss-crossed with spines and spokes that connected its many modules—

"Note the Iraq mimic appears more rigid, much simpler than the Allied sphere." Grant moused a projected arrow over to the sphere mimicking an American-led Allied force. The arrow flickered around, pointing out the fluid organelles within the sphere that were constantly shifting, metamorphosing in shape. In place of stiff spokes the Allied force was configured with thousands of flexible linkages.

"Capillaries of command are much denser here," Grant said, "visible at much lower levels." For an instant the entire sphere seemed to flex, reconstitute its size and density.

"Run the mimics into war mode," Kevin told them.

Grant complied. The other team-leads held their breath as the projected display remained unchanged. Nothing seemed to be happening.

"I'm on it." Rachel had her laptop open before her, was scanning the SOOPE's realtime output, a scrolling of path-code sequences. "Okay, the Allied sphere's taking stock of the high value placed on the life of its soldier-cells ... Taking stock of its superior remote-targeting hardware ... And hey, here we go, it's choosing a strategy—"

The back wall projection dramatically changed: blades of light flickered forth from the denser Allied-labelled sphere, severing spinal spokes within the Iraqi pyramid, lobotomizing its internal connections, its governing intelligence.

"Great," Vlad sighed. "We've got ourselves a first strike infrastructure attack."

Sammi nodded more enthusiastically. "Allies are cutting the top of the Iraqi pyramid off from its base-the

Republican Guard and regular army soldiers bunkered-down in the desert."

As the sphere continued its dissection of the pyramid, Kevin called up the output path-code on his own laptop, saw that the graphically-abstract infrastructure attack was actually a massive aerial bombardment of Iraq. The SOOPE's goal-orientating code indicated the Allies were attempting to soften up enemy ground forces from the air ... "Accelerate the sim-time," he said.

His team-leads obliged, quickening the pace of the SOOPE's progression.

The back wall graphics showed the Allied aerial bombardment continuing for several days, as more and more elements within the Iraqi army-mimic were cut off from the pyramid's top-down control architecture.

"If this scenario turns out to be plausible, Hussein'll have great difficulty getting orders to his troops shortly after the war's opening," Kevin mused. An intriguing development.

But it didn't stop the SOOPE from plunging into a long-term stalemate loop. Days of Allied air campaigns became weeks of air campaigns, yet the sphere still failed to achieve its objective, failed to target enemy troop-positions. And so a second-stage ground war remained on hold.

"Here's the problem." Rachel was frowning at her laptop's scrolling path-code. "Prospect of high Allied casualties transmitted via media back to homeland populations. Looks so risky the sphere can't resolve it."

"So sim failure." Kevin was standing now, pacing slowly around the boardroom table.

"Well, war failure, at any rate," Rachel allowed. "Republican Guard divisions mimic as too dangerous, too well-trained to take on without a significant 'softening'." Rachel appeared to find that euphemism distasteful.

"Guard divisions are all bunkered too deep to get at from the air," Grant explained. "Had time to bury themselves in during the prep-period. They may be communicationless, but they're completely intact."

"Okay, stop the sim there." Kevin continued to pace, taking up the mantle of commander-in-chief, hands braced behind his back as he issued orders. "Want you to boil this SOOPE through as many Borgean repathing runs as the mimics can handle without evaporating. Try pushing initial parameters past the edges of your reality-limits scale, do whatever you have to to find the fault-lines in this scenario."

Everyone around him paged their teams waiting down in the cubicles of the warehouse floor below, and the regular programmers got the repath variants underway.

But by the end of the day, all the tweaking and testing and bending and near-breaking couldn't alter the outcome of their Gulf War SOOPE: virtually every run ended in a casualty-averse loop, as Allied air campaigns failed to get at the enemy troops fortified in their desert bunkers.

Kevin was delighted.

Consistency was what he most wanted to see in the repaths ... He stayed late again, composing an encrypted email to Anton Caety, telling Anton about their new SOOPE, about its prediction that the war would start with a Catch-22 stand off.

Asking him if the Pentagon was anticipating a similar problem in the real Persian Gulf.

Kevin sent the email shortly before midnight, then drove home to Salem, found his wife Cress was out late with her friends. Which was fine, the way Kevin liked it: his consistent workaholic hours had convinced her to find something else to do, which was good for both of them.

August 8th to 20th

Next morning, Kevin opened an encrypted response from Anton.

My sources confirm members of Gulf Ops Command are worried about that issue.

Anton Caety happened to be a fabulously wealthy former Navy contractor with an array of important DOD contacts, friends in the Pentagon's planning directorate. Anton also had a computer science background, so shortly after the cold war ended Kevin had approached him, peddling the potential of Self-Organizing and Optimizing

Programmable Evolution sims. Kevin knew a hot prospect when he saw one.

And so did Anton.

Would like to see this new SOOPE of yours.

Kevin fired back a one-line reply:

Come by in ten days for a look.

Then he summoned his team-leads once more, told them he needed their Gulf War sim fattened up with the hardest data available, looking robust, body-builder muscular, absolutely unbreakable within ten days.

Competing SOOPE teams spent the ensuing days restocking the SOOPE, fine-tuning the components and capabilities of both sides of the coming war, which were being scrutinized in extraordinary detail on C-SPAN and CNN special reports. Iraqi military analysts were consulted, experts on the emerging western alliance were called in. And Dunbar & Caety's latest SOOPE was transformed from a Disney cartoon stick-figure sim to a down-to-the-last-detail Michelangelo mimic — although anyone viewing the SOOPE's graphical rendering would still have seen it as a surreal piece by Dali.

Kevin kept a close eye on every new rendering, kept scanning every new repathing. Over and over, the SOOPE replayed the same opening: blades slashed forth from the Allied sphere, weakening the enemy by slicing the means of communication, command and control. That would be the natural direction of an Allied war waged in the Gulf.

And yet, the boardroom's back wall revealed an alternate direction:

A strong communications link seemed to be outlasting the constant simulated-air campaigns — an indirect link pulsing with red that ran between the two abstracted armies. At its midpoint, this surviving bloodline of com-munications arced up and *off* the back wall, so that the Iraqi pyramid and the Allied sphere appeared to be holding a glowing red wishbone between them. Both armies were receiving a flow of information from something 'off the wall'. An out-of-SOOPE source.

The red connection represented global media, satellite signals picked up from anywhere — the strongest source of information about the war's progress that would be left open to Iraq's leader, once the air campaigns began.

Pulling out the spiral-bound notepad he'd started filling in on the day his inner doorway first opened, Kevin now added

OPPORTUNITY

to the bottom of the lengthening keyword list.

Because now he was through his imaginary doorway, now the mountain path was clearly visible in his mind's eye. Now he could actually make out his destination, see what waited behind the cloud-curtain wreathing the summit:

An opportunity out of reach of humanity's ordinary billions.

A chance to gain not fifteen minutes of fame, but fifteen minutes of...

Control.

Fifteen minutes at the helm of the real world's system-of-systems, that's what Kevin saw waiting for him at the end of the path he'd committed Dunbar & Caety to.

August 21st

By the time Anton Caety finally dropped by for a look-see, Kevin's team-leads had simmed a possible solution to the problem of a Persian Gulf 'ground war stall'.

UNDERDOG

That was the keyword Caety needed to understand before he left.

The team-leads were on hand when Kevin personally projected the SOOPE onto the boardroom's back wall for Anton. And when the opening's air attack severings had successfully left only the red wishbone as a communications link between pyramid and sphere, Kevin paused the sim.

"At this point, the only way Iraq's leader can find out what's happening with his own troops in the field is to watch the one communications channel still fully accessible to him — the satellite TV channel, offering mass media broadcasts."

"Dunbar and Caety's field of expertise," Anton observed. "And?"

"I've found a broadcast-response meme—" Kevin caught
Vlad's unhappy eye; Underdog was actually one of Vlad's
algorithms. "We've found a meme to get the Republican
Guard up out of their desert bunkers." Kevin nodded to
the others. Grant and Sammi ran the Underdog path-code
into the SOOPE.

Anton watched, asked questions, quickly grasped the
abstracts, then gasped, and got very excited.

"You be ready," he told Kevin and his staff. "I'll have
you a Pentagon briefing room and a brass marching band
to toot your horn, soon as I can convince the right people."

September 1st
Ten days passed before the Pentagon meeting was set.

Then on the night before Kevin was to fly out to Washington, Fiona, Rachel and Vlad confronted him. All three
looked decidedly uneasy.

"Nothing wrong with the SOOPE, I hope."

The trio hesitated.

"You know about Mennochio?" Vlad asked.

A blink. "Mennochio," Kevin repeated. He saw his best
and brightest exchanging knowing looks of disappointment, and added Mennochio to his must-look-into mental
list. "What's this about?"

Another hesitation, then:

"The thought that *our* algorithms are about to be given
away to the government, the military—" Vlad choked himself off before saying more.

He meant *his* algorithms, Kevin thought, stunned by
this outburst. Vlad had signed the same terms and conditions of employment that everyone in the company had
to sign. Dunbar & Caety owned the rights to software
mandated and created on the premises — including all
specific path-code sequences and generalized algorithmics,
of course. Vlad knew that.

More to the point, Kevin had given Vlad, Rachel, and
Fiona their break in the industry. But he tried to suppress
his anger, tried to appeal to the trio, digging deep for some
truth to offer them, to win back their hearts and minds.

"You all believed in the post-Wall peace," he asked them,
"didn't you?"

Their turn to blink at him.

"But war is coming, I'm afraid, and more wars will follow. Unless," he told them, "this Gulf conflict can play the role of ... well, of a global demo. A really impressive demo that'll suppress other resource-seizing rogue states. Vlad," he said, "you stocked the sim. You know the free world's signed onto the alliance against Iraq, the U.N.'s sanctioned it. So now this demo-war in the Gulf can either go over big time or it can stall, even crash." He paused before adding:

"Think of the impact a demo that flops badly will have on a worldwide audience of tyrannies and rogue states."

The trio stared at him, Rachel visibly upset now, actually in tears. Reminding himself that he'd loved these three for their idealism, still was very fond of them.

"Iraq *has* to be the free world's big-hit demo if the post-Cold War peace is going to have any chance at all," he added, knowing he was channeling Orwell's 'War means Peace' doublethink. And to a trio of Harvard science grads smart enough to recognize Newspeak when they heard it.

They looked at him doubtfully; Kevin sensed they were mentally distancing themselves from him, knew he was losing them. So he sighed, assured them all SOOPE algorithms would remain Dunbar & Caety's alone, knowing he was betraying his young team-leads even then.

Because he wasn't confident he could control the Gulf War SOOPE.

On the moonlit drive out of Boston back home to Salem, while worrying about his firm and wondering how much he'd have to gamble, Kevin saw it again: a tantalizingly familiar image in the rearview mirror, in his mind's eye. A young man half-hidden behind curtains of light and power.

Kevin himself, maybe?

In his house by the sea Kevin found Cress asleep with the TV still on, the screen an off-the-air snow of soft white noise. Cress, one of the ordinary billions dazzled by the chimera-curtain of the news, lying there with that child-like look everyone takes on when unconscious. Cress didn't know about his Gulf War SOOPE, Kevin hadn't bothered to tell her. Anton had cautioned him to keep it under a very tight lid to ensure the Pentagon contract.

Besides, Kevin suspected Cress would react much the same way Vlad had.

Standing over her sleeping form, feeling the distance between them, the emptiness that had been growing for years. He put it out of his mind, popped downstairs to his basement office, pored over his notes for presenting the Gulf War demo, feeling a draft in the basement, a chill intimation of the coming of war and of winter, though it was only the 1st of September.

Kevin fell asleep on the basement's spare bed, got up before dawn, packed, wrote a note to remind Cress he'd be in Washington for a week, left the house before she woke to catch the first flight out of Logan.

September 2nd

One month to the day after the Iraqis marched into Kuwait City, Kevin Dunbar marched into the Pentagon with a simulation that echoed the new credo ringing through the hallowed fortress. Down with Clausewitz, out with the fog of war! Up with Computation, in with battlefield-dominant awareness!

He met with the staff of a Navy admiral named Owens for his closed-door demo. A former associate of Anton Caety's, Owens now had the ear of the Joint Chiefs. The admiral's staff began shooting a lot of questions at Kevin as he fumbled to link his laptop into their whitescreen projector, then activated the SOOPE-mimicked Persian Gulf scenario in stand-by mode. The questions came faster as the screen filled with two translucent geometric abstracts-one for each Gulf War force — preparing to face off against each other.

The admiral himself struggled to come to terms with Kevin's claim that the SOOPE wasn't a model in the traditional top-down sense. That the graphical-armies pulsating on the whitescreen were bred from the bottom-up inside a computer, bred to be entirely self-sustaining 'system mimics', bred into an *abstracted* Iraqi military and an *abstracted* Allied force.

The Iraqi pyramid and the Allied sphere contained the essence of each army's infrastructure, technological traits, organizational dynamics, style of command, strategic intent, Kevin explained.

And fortunately, the admiral's staff seemed to grasp the essentials. Several gasped as Kevin ran the SOOPE into war mode, and the abstracted infrastructure attack began. Blades of light flashed from out of the denser Allied sphere, and again only one communications flow survived the constant simulated-air campaigns — the glowing red wishbone held between both armies, the flow of information from an off-screen source. The flow of signals from satellite TV broadcasts.

"Here comes the interesting part," he told them, as the SOOPE rapidly advanced through the air blitzkrieg, and what looked like tiny baubles began exiting the pyramid's protective membrane. "Those are isolated Iraqi troop-fragments — units completely cut off by the opening air war — striking out on their own across the Saudi front."

All were eliminated by precise blade-flickers from the Allied sphere.

Someone pointed out, "There's no back-flow going up the red broadcast-wishbone."

"Signifies suppression of all news reports about those isolated strikes," Kevin said. "Total suppression of bad news is the strategy favoured by the Allied army-mimic."

"And by the current administration," Owens added. "There'll be no repeat of Vietnam's horror-footage in America's living rooms."

Kevin pointed to the screen. "Actually, the sim suggests a slight deviation from the path of total news suppression: if *just one* enemy ground unit is allowed to cross into Saudi territory unharmed, after several weeks of aerial bombardment..." On-screen, an Iraqi troop-bauble wandered out of the pyramid and into the Allied-sphere controlled space without being destroyed by an Allied flash. "And if news of this one successful Iraqi attack is released to the press, an 'Underdog' response-meme will likely arise."

Before Owen's staff could ask what a response-meme was, Kevin called up the very database he'd tried to show

Dunbar & Caety's contractor clients back on August 2nd: a database of real TV ad-campaign paths memetically reconstructed on disc, along with their associated response algorithms. "Note the number of promotions that generated an 'Underdog' response."

Owens' staffers were frowning. "But most of those were political-campaign broadcasts."

"Or professional sports promotions."

Kevin nodded. "Underdog's a well mapped out broadcast-response." He pointed back to the whitescreen's SOOPE graphics. "And in our Gulf War scenario, Underdog washes back through that wishbone, pours out over the top of the Iraqi pyramid—"

"You mean over Hussein himself," Owens said.

"Look what happens when *he* sees Underdog," he said, and showed the admiral and his staff the resulting SOOPE path, which gave the Allied sphere exactly what it required to secure a ground war.

By the end of the demo Owens was actually grinning at him, and slapping him on the back, and sending him off in a limo to discuss a further demo for Gulf Ops Command with someone named Jones, a liaison newly assigned to serve Dunbar & Caety's needs.

KNOCKED OVER

Kevin added that to his keyword list as the limo whisked him past the White House and into downtown Washington for a fast meal with Jones, who Kevin expected to be every bit the standard Armed Forces Professional Representative Officer.

But the AFPRO who arrived late for dinner was named Jaegal instead of Jones — Jones having been replaced at the last minute — and came in a non-standard casing:

Olivia Jaegal was a tall, dark and leggy liaison, an officer whose femininity overpowered the strict lines of her uniform. Olivia explained that she was a member of Advanced Decision Simulation Management group, and would be working closely with Kevin over the remainder of his week in Washington.

More closely than he'd anticipated, as it turned out.

✝ ✝ ✝

September 3rd to September 9th

What followed was a week of shopping the SOOPE to different groups within the Pentagon's overlapping lateral hierarchies; encountering and overcoming varied degrees of computational expertise; explaining the basics of Complexity science, the breakthroughs that led to true SOOPE sims; and along the way, being shown pieces of the Alliance's Persian Gulf war plan that few civilians were privy to, details Kevin personally encoded and fed into his now highly-classified Gulf War simulation to enhance its accuracy.

So a week of peeking behind the curtains, a week of further SOOPE tweaking and twisting, a week of jostling ideas and elbows with Olivia Jaegal over dinner, and sometimes late into the night at the bar of Kevin's hotel. By the end of that week, Jaegal had helped him negotiate a circuitous path of power up to the crowning final demo — a make-it-or-break-it meeting with generals of the J-3, the planning directorate of the Joint Chiefs.

The generals and their aides were all smart men and women well-briefed on Complexity science and SOOPE theory. They took to Kevin's simulation as if they were chowing down at a celebratory banquet.

Which was exactly what Kevin and Olivia proceeded to do after the J-3 greenlighted Dunbar & Caety's 'Underdog' proposal.

What happened next was as predictable as it was astonishing to Kevin. On the morning he was due to fly back to Boston, he found himself being shaken awake in his hotel room by Olivia, who whispered in his ear as she passed him the phone:

"It's your wife."

Blinking at Olivia in shock as he grappled to take the receiver, banged it up against his ear. Listening to Cress ask if he was all right, ask what was going on. Hearing the suspicion in her voice, unable to do more than croak "I'm okay". Unable to do anything besides watch Olivia Jaegal slip lithely out of his hotel bed.

Unable even to recall how she'd ended up in it in the first place. Kevin had no memory of the previous night whatsoever.

The room was spinning. Olivia was stepping into a pair of pants she'd carefully folded over a chair. Cress was coolly informing him that she wouldn't be home when he got there, that she had decided to visit her sister.

His wife's sister lived in Seattle.

Hearing himself wheeze, "Back soon. Come back soon. I'll be back soon." Dial tone.

Kevin left the receiver dangling, heaved himself from the sheets, woozily stood, and stumbled naked past Olivia into the shower, where he threw up.

She looked in on him when she'd finished dressing, flashed him a piteous smile — another man who couldn't hold his liquor.

It took Kevin a long time to get himself washed off, washed up, shaved, half-presentable as a human being. It took some doing for him to step out of the hotel bathroom.

Olivia was gone. No sign that she'd even been there. No sign outside of the image blazoned in his mind: a cat's paw tattoo on the small of her supple back.

Oh, and the fact that Kevin's briefcase was up on the hotel desk instead of on the chair.

He found the briefcase wasn't quite locked, and items within it were slightly rearranged; his notepad, for instance, was not in the pocket where he always kept it.

Kevin managed to catch his early morning flight, still woozy, fuzzy about what had actually happened. He *never* drank more than a beer or two these days. And even back in his college days, when he'd drunk enough to pass out, he'd *never* been so drunk that he'd forgotten what had happened.

Could he really sleep with a woman like Olivia Jaegal and not recall a single intimate moment of it?

Besides the tattoo on her back, that is. But Kevin had seen that as she'd slipped out of bed this morning. And then there was his briefcase, intimately rifled through... He wondered who, exactly, decided to assign Jaegal to Kevin at the last minute. Wondered why her Advanced Decision Simulation Management group wanted to know so much about Dunbar & Caety's future SOOPE projects.

Wondered about his current SOOPE project, which ADSM had promised to 'carefully look over'.

Feeling sure the SOOPE was getting far more than a look-over.

Then finally getting off the plane, trying not to think about the vow he'd made to Vlad, Rachel and Fiona. Nor about the vows he'd made to Cress, five years back.

September 10th

Kevin was glad Cress wasn't home when he stepped through the door. He didn't want to face her at that moment, didn't want to deal with anyone at work, for that matter. So he did something he never did: took the day off without calling in.

He spent the afternoon on the Net, running searches for any drugs that might cause memory loss, might be associated with the military, the spy trade. After a while, he dug up a cache of files describing a tranquillizer dubbed 'D2', just hitting the streets. D2 was rumoured to be a CIA-sponsored pharmaceutical. It mixed tastelessly with alcohol to produce not mere memory loss but full blown amnesia.

The kicker: D2 was both an alcohol extender — made you feel drunk when you hadn't drunk much — and a *dis*inhibitor. One file called it 'the coming campus date drug'.

He tried to picture himself at the centre of a second warfront, a covert struggle for control over any future Pentagon SOOPE sims. He tried to see Jaegal as a weapon deployed against him.

Or was he just trying to rationalize an affair?

Needing to sleep off the rest of the wooziness, he logging off the Net. The phone immediately began to ring. It was Sammi, calling to say that Anton Caety was planning something at the office in an hour, a kick-off party for the DOD contract.

Kevin barely had enough time to change, drive into the city, hurry up to the Dunbar & Caety boardroom. Anton was already there, and everyone else was crowding in, just like back on August 2nd. Smoked salmon, cheese, beers all around. Claps on the back for Kevin, two thumbs up from his marketing and finance VPs, high fives from Grant and Sammi. Rachel nodded politely, Vlad kept a cool distance.

But the bustle distracted Kevin from his earlier bout of paranoia. And Anton actually managed to cheer him by saying:

"They're calling your sim 'the Oracle' in the J-3. Which makes this warehouse 'Delphi', doesn't it?"

Kevin agreed. "The spot where the future will be seen." He'd loved the Greek and Roman myths as a boy. Delphi, high atop Mount Parnassus, was where Oracles issued prophecies from behind a curtain...

Anton was calling for everyone's attention. "I've brought along something that Kev admired, first time he visited my house." Anton collected more than Pentagon contacts; he owned a large array of Roman armaments, artifacts. And now he ceremoniously placed an old Roman shield on the boardroom's granite table.

"As of today," he addressed the staff, "you are all members of Operation Desert Shield — your new SOOPE's part of the shield around our soldiers," he explained. "Now come closer, take a gander at that metal jag in the middle." Programmers and theorists leaned in for a look. "Called an 'omphalos'." Anton turned back to Kevin. "Believe it has something to do with Delphi ... But on a shield, it means a deadly little link with an enemy."

Anton winked, clearly thinking about Underdog, the deadly little media-link that might catch out Hussein.

Kevin frowned down at the shield's wicked-looking metal jag, fighting back thoughts of Olivia Jaegal. He imagined the cat's paw tattoo on her back, and reached out to touch the omphalos—

"Careful there, Kev. It's still sharp as a dagger."

After the party was over and the boardroom had cleared out, Kevin stayed late again, not wanting to go back to the empty house just yet. He spent the time on his laptop, looking up Net tales of ancient Delphi, skimming through Greek legends familiar from childhood.

And after finding references to the 'omphalos' — an altar high in Delphi — Kevin told himself that his tantalizing memory had surfaced. That he knew the imaginary path he was climbing:

It was the path leading to the summit of Mount Parnassus.

October 1990 to January 1991

The ensuing four months proved the most treacherous leg of Kevin's ascent.

By October, darkness was coming earlier, in the sky and in the house in Salem. When Cress finally came home — after nearly three weeks in Seattle — she didn't say a word to Kevin. She treated him like he wasn't there, wasn't visible, wasn't present at the dinner table on the rare occasions when he was.

And at work, Rachel and Vlad, the two most talented employees he had, the friends he used to invite back to the house for brainstorming barbeques ... Now that Dunbar & Caety was officially working for the DOD, Rachel refused to meet his eyes and Vlad avoided him altogether. The pair were acting ridiculously guilty — as if they believed the 'Oracle' SOOPE had triggered the immense war preparation phase in the desert, had caused the Iraqi troops to start burrowing into desert bunkers.

By November a cloud-ceiling was drawing over the eastern seaboard, and Kevin was high enough up his inner Parnassus to enter the cloud layer shrouding the summit, where it was easy to wander off the path and lose sight of important landmarks.

He resented how far Cress was falling from him. He'd come home at night to find her sullen and silent on the couch. Any attempt to talk to her sparked a round of channel-surfing through the endless war-prep updates and debates about when the 'mother of all ground battles' would begin. Cress refused to understand what was going on with the world or with Kevin.

But there was one person in his life who understood both all too well.

Olivia Jaegal kept flying up for meetings at Dunbar & Caety, kept prying into Kevin's plans for further SOOPE sims, and plying him with a spare keycard to her hotel room.

By December Kevin was facing a slippery slope indeed. What with the cloud-cover dumping snow on the roads out to Salem, and the icy rebuff he would receive when he made it home, and the accusing looks he would get when he called his team-leads together, Kevin sometimes found himself taking up Jaegal's keycard offer.

On the occasions he did so, he refused to allow himself the usual outs or excuses. He wasn't turning to Jaegal because power was an aphrodisiac, or because he felt so high above the ordinary masses that he was entitled, or because he was lonely, or experiencing a loss of control.

No, the truth was colder, more calculated. He was turning to Jaegal of his own free will. Making a conscious choice to seize the high ground, stymie the second warfront that he sensed closing around him. Taking up Jaegal's offer, Kevin began offering her what she wanted in return: hints of future Dunbar & Caety SOOPE apps.

Of course, the apps he told her about were those he'd already decided against, had no intention of pursuing; Kevin was playing Jaegal's game now, attempting to feed her misdirections, tease out of her the secrets she was holding. He knew what he was doing.

Well, maybe not.

But he knew, at least, what price he'd likely pay, what it would cost him to see clearly through the confusing cloud layer he was mired in, see what the Pentagon's ADSM group was up to. See where they thought the future of SOOPE markets may lie.

Off the path now, edging dangerously close to falling off the mountain...

Kevin wasn't wholly shocked when Vlad passed him an envelope containing photos taken by a private detective, photos of Kevin with Olivia Jaegal in her hotel room. Vlad threatened to give the photos to Cress if Kevin didn't agree to let him leave the firm with ownership of all SOOPE algorithms Vlad had developed while at Dunbar & Caety.

"And go where with them?"

Keeping the rage from his voice for one more moment, his paranoia stronger than his fury. Seeing ADSM's hand behind Vlad's announced defection. Suspecting Jaegal's

complicity in the photos. Wondering whether the whole
affair was orchestrated from the start to steal Dunbar &
Caety's talent, intellectual property. If Vlad told him Santa
Fe, that would be okay, that would be better than—

"Los Alamos," Vlad reluctantly admitted.

A fierce torch of rage lighting the way through the last
of the cloud layer, turning him back onto the path. He
would burn them down, Kevin thought.

Burn Vlad and Jaegal down together.

"The military lab, you mean," he growled. "And you
think *I'm* a sellout?"

Vlad looked stung. "It's pure research — you've no
clue, Kevin. No idea who I'll be working with."

"Oh yes I do." Kevin slammed a hand onto the envelope as Vlad reached for it. "I'll show Cress these photos myself. Now clean out your desk, get out. And Vlad,
if *any* Dunbar and Caety path-code reappears elsewhere,
I'll sue you from here to the Gulf of Oman."

The fact that Rachel cleaned out her desk and accompanied Vlad didn't surprise Kevin. The surprise was the
two teams of junior SOOPE programmers that decided
to walk out alongside their leads. With Christmas coming
and the war about to break at any moment, half his
company's talent was gone out the door.

Despite the scope of this coding coup, Kevin knew he
had to keep his final vow to Vlad.

So the morning after the walkouts he left the envelope
of photos on his kitchen table, with a hand-written letter
lying on top, detailing Vlad's blackmail-attempt, Kevin's
suspicions about Jaegal and ADSM, his sorrow for what
he'd done to Cress. He added a postscript suggesting she
feel free to do what she must with the photos.

When he returned to the house that evening, Kevin
found the locks changed, his clothes and personal items
dumped in the garage, and a handwritten reply lying on
top of the pile that said simply:

Feel free to find yourself a divorce attorney.

That easy, that quick, just an omphalos prick, and it
was over between Kevin and Cress. Over between Kevin
and Olivia Jaegal. His company was over a programming-

shortage barrel, his life was in free fall. And the Christmas 'holiday' he spent with his three younger sisters and his parents was a nightmare of recrimination. What had he done to lose lovely Cress, they wanted to know?

Came a Sunday afternoon in mid-January, Kevin alone in a hotel room, his new home, turning to the TV for a respite, a temporary escape. Flipping through channels, avoiding the usual Gulf updates, then stumbling onto the truth in the form of a children's matinee movie that was almost over. The scene was a vast room in the Emerald City, and the four travellers recently returned from vanquishing the Wicked Witch now stood before the curtains, gawking up at the chimera-image of Oz the Great and Terrible. Then Dorothy spotted the curtains parting, an old man half-hidden behind them—

Kevin's tantalizing boyhood memory came unstuck at last, and the overwhelming feelings he'd experienced watching this movie back when he was seven or eight resurfaced; he recalled imagining *he* was the one back behind the curtains, working the great levers of power; he recalled thinking *he* wouldn't be such an old fake and a fool.

In that moment, the last shreds of confidence that had survived Kevin's recent trials crumbled away. He watched helplessly as Dorothy dragged the little old man out to confront those he'd tried to trick — then the film was interrupted by a special bulletin. Images just released by the Allied War Room in Riyadh filled the screen, looking like something out of a video game. The Gulf War was underway.

And it was opening with a massive aerial infrastructure attack.

January 17th to January 29th
For a dozen days and nights, the video-game bombardment continued to rain down on Iraq. The Iraqi army remained dug in deep throughout this terrifying, endlessly televised bombardment. And throughout the bombardment, employees of Dunbar & Caety averaged fifteen hours a day in their converted-warehouse headquarters, restocking the Oracle SOOPE with actual times, numbers, and

event-sequences streaming in over their new Defense Data Network feed, then cycling the SOOPE up through a simulated pathway that most closely matched the reality of the war.

Kevin spent most of that period in the long boardroom, camped out below the big multi-channel wall screen, ignoring the crawl commentaries, just soaking up the surreal bombardment footage. The more the bombs fell, the deeper Kevin dug in and dug up.

Turned out the two teams that walked out on him went to join

MENNOCHIO

That was the name he now wrote on his notepad. The name of a theorist working in the labyrinthine bowels of the Los Alamos National Laboratory. A purist developing a new and generalized way of thinking about the global system-of-systems, busily laying the foundations of an entirely new field called 'Civilization Studies in Complexity.' And apparently a terribly disfigured genius, referred to by many as 'the Monster' of Los Alamos Lab.

Turned out Vlad and Rachel hadn't been lured away by some undercover arm of ADSM, after all.

And turned out Cress had been more of a cornerstone for Kevin than he'd thought; part of his self-definition, his foundation. Lately he'd felt unmoored, loosed, lost without her to come home to. Oh, he'd done the right thing leaving Cress those photos as a Get-Out-Of-Jail-Free card, go straight to divorce court. She was still in her early thirties, she still had a chance for happiness.

And Kevin?

Turned out his imagination knew no bounds.

He could imagine a way to massage a war six months before it broke out, a way to trick a dictator into destroying his own army. He could imagine a path to the control room at the top of the world's systems (okay, that turned out to be not the path up Parnassus but down the Yellow Brick Road). He could imagine an affair as a way of spying, and a way of giving his long-suffering wife her overdue ticket to freedom (okay, leaving her those photos had appealed to the lapsed Catholic in Kevin, fulfilling his need to confess and atone).

He could even imagine what might make the gruelling ascent of the past half year worth everything it had cost him.

UNDERDOG

For a dozen days Kevin watched for signs of Dunbar & Caety's designer-meme on the channels of his boardroom's wall screen. That's all he had the strength to do now. Watch, and wait, and hope that Riyadh's War Room would actually put his company's media-weapon into play. According to the Oracle SOOPE, the most fertile time-slot to introduce an Underdog-Strikes-Back meme fell between 12 to 16 days after the start of the Allied air campaign.

The War Room in Riyadh went right down the middle, leaking word of an Iraqi raid on the small Saudi port town of Ras al-Khafji on Day 14.

January 30th

The morning of January 30th saw a small, astonishingly bold unit of Iraqis thumb their noses at the Allies by invading Saudi Arabia and capturing Ras al-Khafji.

It wasn't the first isolated Iraqi strike across the border, but it *was* the first strike carefully leaked through the lower Allied troop ranks. A pair of Euro war-journos were allowed to wander near al-Khafji, take corroborative footage. Soon after that the War Room appeared forced to admit an enemy success. News services worldwide leapt on it, touting al-Khafji as the opening blow in the 'apocalyptic land-battle' Iraq's leader kept promising.

And the Islamic world went crazy.

ANTICIPATION = AL KHAFJI

So began the final vigil, the wait for what might be the peak-moment of Kevin Dunbar's life: his fifteen minutes at the helm, steering history.

On the boardroom's wall screen Underdog was now evident in twenty foreign telecasts. The tale of al-Khafji's seizure was being told by three all-news Asian stations, by a French feed carrying a report on the 'Arab street', and by more than a dozen *pro*-Iraq channels showing live-via-satellite images from Iraq's Islamic neighbour states. Crowds rejoiced at the boldness of Hussein's army in

Jordan; panic reigned in Israel; wildly ecstatic sign-wavers pressed around a CNN camera in Baghdad. The crawl translations talked on and on about Iraq's 'brilliantly defiant capture' of al-Khafji, something Kevin had foreseen in an abstract way half a year ago.

But he was now a different man from the one who'd leapt through the doorway of opportunity back in August, propelled by a need to fulfill an imaginary destiny, to steer history. He'd been hardened by the weeks of aerial bombardment, hammered into someone new. And he'd broken through the mountain's cloud layer, the summit-moment was in sight.

So now Kevin's life lay on a knife edge. The remaining steps to the summit led up a precipice between terrors. On the one side lurked the terror that he was a concept-obsessed automaton, a man willing to betray his friends and destroy his marriage all to answer a simple question.

Was SOOPE theory correct?

Was it capable of pre-programming the forces and feedback mechanisms of the real world's metasystems? If so, then Mennochio's vastly more visionary SOOPE concepts may have merit. And if not...

Well, that was the terror lurking on the other side. The thought that he'd given up so much for a world view that was flawed in its fundamentals, mad in its mathematics. That would be more than Kevin could bear.

Underdog was about to answer the question, one way or the other, one side or the other.

Unfortunately, Kevin knew that the first person who might see Underdog run its course and reach its real target would be somebody on the far side of the world, somebody way down at the bottom of things.

That somebody turned out to be a young soldier named Ian Stote.

February 2nd, Saudi Border
Enigmedia tales show how the bottom of a system-of-systems connects to the top. So now it's time to jump from the Delphic board-room where Kevin Dunbar watched the war from on high down to the war itself, to see what Dunbar was watching for...

✣ ✣ ✣

Just before dawn on February 2nd, a Boeing 707 packed with sensitive detection gear soared over the desert along the northern Saudi border, flying a safe distance from the entrenched Iraq positions, scanning the enemy across that distance. The aircraft was part of the Allies' Joint Surveillance and Target Attack Radar System, and at 5:28 AM Gulf time its sensors picked up an encrypted Iraqi radio message in the 70-megahertz range. An officer aboard the JSTARS jet promptly transmitted a recording of the encrypted message down to an American reconn base on the desert floor to the south, where a yawning commander-of-the-watch, having been warned about keeping one eye open for any message-captures that morning, promptly ordered an electronic intelligence unit to the vicinity of the radio intercept.

And so four young American soldiers began a dangerous journey across the desert in an armoured vehicle covered with aerials, under a brightening sky that screamed at them relentlessly. One of the soldiers, an intelligence officer named Ian Stote, was aware of their true position in the world that morning. Stote knew he and his three companions were stuck way down at the bottom of it all, crawling along beneath a lethal technological storm, and hoping to God that their tiny vehicle would go unnoticed by it.

All four soldiers were aware that their greatest peril lay in 'friendly fire' from the storm-system of jets and missiles directly overhead. So they kept their heads down, and concentrated on ignoring the crowdedness of the vehicle's interior as they proceeded in starts and stops, halting regularly to confirm their geoposition, plotting their course into a laptop computer containing a map — less than an hour old — of the latest enemy movements in their corner of the front.

All the while Lieutenant Stote watched his detectors.

At 6:07 AM, as the vehicle was gaining higher ground, Stote picked up a message-burst of the same signature as the fragment captured by the JSTARS. *More* Iraqi message-traffic! He recorded several bursts, then started pounding at his keyboard, preparing an email report about a leap in signal directed at a swath of Republican Guard bunkers miles to the north. When he'd finished, Stote tried to activate the satellite uplink, without success. The dish on the vehicle's roof wasn't rotating; another soldier reluctantly got out, and clambered up to clean any sand from the rotation-collar.

So Stote slipped his helmet on, peeked out of the armoured eavesdropping car and shaded his eyes, taking his chance to look up at a patch of sky, at a space crisscrossed like no other in all the preceding years of human aviation.

At that moment, the morning's Allied sorties were being routed at high speeds through six hundred and sixty restricted operations zones, steered clear of three hundred missile engagement spaces, directed down seventy-eight strike corridors, dispatched to patrol ninety-two air combat sectors, or granted desert flight training in one of thirty-six practice areas. Scheduling and monitoring all the sorties was akin to managing an airport with approach-and-landing vectors spread over ninety thousand miles, a logician's nightmare. Yet the plane traffic was nothing compared to the welter of electronic messages criss-crossing that same theatre of airspace...

Finally, the vehicle's dish began to rotate freely. It locked onto the co-ordinates of a comsat. Then it sent Stote's email. And in that moment, the global media-weapon built around al-Khafji began to go critical. Ian Stote had just triggered the weapon's final chain reaction, which would run through its sequence incredibly quickly.

The vehicle's transmission was picked up by an Intelsat, then bounced right back down to Riyadh, to the United States Central Command's email clearinghouse. There, the report from the front was integrated into a dynamic map of the Gulf that served the War Room as a moment-by-moment snapshot of all known Iraqi and Allied activity. The morning's overall snapshot was changing rapidly, telltale indicators were now blossoming on several fronts.

But the clearinghouse had been warned about just such a development; the War Room had its Oracle. And the information in Stote's report served to confirm the Oracle's prophesies for this particular morning.

Key-words within Stote's message produced automatic routing to Dunbar & Caety, Boston. But an out-of-theatre civilian organization had to be cleared, so the routed report was held up for a few hours before being forwarded from the Riyadh building up to another comsat, then relayed on to the continental United States, then passed across the glass cables of the Defence Data Network and through a secure leased-line into the headquarters of Dunbar & Caety. At 10:33 PM on February 1st, Eastern Standard time, the message arrived on a lone laptop in the boardroom occupied by Kevin Dunbar himself.

Kevin had not slept since the al-Khafji story broke and he was truly in the hollow of it now, in a void brought on by sleeplessness and superhuman effort. So when Stote's email report arrived he was slumped forward in a chair at the granite table, one hand holding up his head as he tried to focus on the fat fifty-page spiral notepad he'd begun back at the beginning of August.

But Kevin wouldn't have seen the new email even if he'd been looking at his laptop's screen — because at that moment a shimmering pool of colours was swimming over the table's polished surface, emanating from the boardroom's reflective back wall and the projected display of the Oracle SOOPE. Dots of dazzling colour swarmed over the screen of the laptop and the cordless phone-and-intercom beyond it, over the old Roman shield, over the notepad Kevin was using to flush out his newest fear, his suspicion that he'd become so immersed in designing the Gulf War 'Oracle' that he'd missed something critical.

At the top of the final notepad page, Kevin wrote OMPHALOS

A Delphic altar used to mark the spot assumed to be the centre of the world. And a deceptively deadly metal jag on a warrior's shield, representing the centre of the action. Kevin was afraid that the centre of the action in SOOPE design was already starting to shift out from under Dunbar & Caety.

MONSTER, he wrote.

Time for him to focus on Mennochio, that renegade Los Alamos researcher who was SOOPE-simulating new worlds and possibilities for humanity to aspire to, while Dunbar & Caety was still applying SOOPE theory to the oldest apps of the past, war and—

The intercom buzzed.

Kevin spun around, groping for the phone. "Who've you got?" he asked.

"Mister Dunbar, the AFPRO's arrived."

He blinked. Since their last illicit hotel rendezvous Olivia Jaegal had skipped three scheduled liaison sessions with Dunbar & Caety. Kevin had assumed she knew about his outing of their affair. So why was she showing up like this, unbidden—

He nudged the laptop linked into the DDN feed, re-angled the screen so that the back wall's reflected colours weren't masking what was on it.

Jesus, *there it was*!

A gold email icon, the highest clearance-level — the sender simply DESERT STORM — already a third of the way down the message queue. *That* made Kevin sit up. Must have been on-screen for a couple of minutes at least! Eyes so tired of watching for it he'd almost missed it ... Fumbling with the trackball, he had to point and click three times before he nailed the right icon.

Kevin read what Ian Stote had typed during the desert's dawn close to the Saudi border.

Then read it again.

By the time he closed the email two more gold-clearance icons had appeared at the top of the queue.

"Excuse me, sir?" The receptionist's polite voice again. "Captain Jaegal's insisting—"

Putting Reception on hold, then clicking the two new emails open: *more* radio intercepts, this time Iraqi transmissions to T-72 tank units, captured by a low orbiting satellite lofted just for the war; plus a report from a JSTARS aircraft describing evidence of enemy stirrings around other fortified bunkers. The Iraqis were revealing what infrastructure still existed, what portions of Hussein's army his generals could still communicate with.

Suddenly dozens of gold-clearance icons dominated the email queue. After a couple of minutes Kevin stopped clicking them open, eased back in his chair. The widespread jump in radio traffic had happened! The bait had been taken!

The Republican Guard might *finally* be coming out of its bunkers.

A light on the intercom pulsing. Reception, still holding. He stabbed at the SPEAK button. "Offer some refreshments, and my apologies — I'll be a bit longer." He hung up, unable to think what he'd say to Jaegal if he did invite her up.

But Olivia Jaegal was not to be stopped.

And so seconds later his summit-moment arrived, in the form of a *photo*-icon popping onto the laptop's email queue, the sender AFPRO — from Jaegal! She must have convinced Reception to let her access their server.

Kevin clicked open her photo. An aerial shot filled the laptop, showing him a highway in the Kuwaiti desert, a line of tanks and trucks several miles long in the process of being bombarded.

Un-*believe*-able.

Hussein had actually done it, he'd actually ordered the units his generals could still contact to leave the safety of their fortifications, rush the Saudi border, running them straight into the targeting sights of the Allied air armada.

And all because the news was carrying footage of Muslims falling on their knees. All because the world was seeing images of a Middle East celebrating the 'Victory at al-Khafji', hearing reports of Hussein's defiance and courage, as told by journalists and cameramen who were just doing their jobs, just trying to capture the drama of the ongoing Crisis in the Gulf.

All because deep inside Dunbar & Caety's SOOPE an outrageous meme had done its job — a guesstimate-value representing Hussein's ego had proven all too accurate.

Kevin shuddered, for an instant appalled by the power of his prophecy, the sheer overkill of this uber-moment. On his laptop screen, Jaegal's photo showed hundreds of Iraqi trucks and tanks trapped on the highway, already on fire, their occupants already burning.

He looked away. Looked up toward the skylight in the boardroom ceiling, a patch of it free of ice and snow. A reflection prevented him from seeing any patch of sky above — the reflection of his war-Oracle swarming across the boardroom table. But he tried to imagine the sky above the factory roof anyway, the snow-laden clouds gathering on this dark winter's night in America. He tried to imagine the mammoth machinery of war screaming beyond those clouds, then slamming down through the roof to obliterate him.

Tried to imagine it. Couldn't.

Imagination failed him, even as *something* slammed into him.

Kevin would remember that look-up as the clearest moment of revelation in his life. The moment he saw the metasystem steering *him*, saw the truth.

The door inside him shouldn't have opened — not because it led to a place impossible to reach, but to a place possible to reach.

NEW ORDER, he wrote.

America, all powerful now, its systems so advanced that a man like Kevin could tip them over into titanic overkill. Who could possibly stand against that, he thought, staring at the photo of the bombarded highway.

A demo of the new order so successful that no conventional force would pit itself against the America, not in the coming decade, at least. So military apps were not the market to be in, no. The centre of action was shifting elsewhere.

Staring at Jaegal's photo. Then picking up the remote for the multi-channel screen, calling up Reception's security camera-view — and there was Olivia Jaegal facing the security lens, holding up a printout of the same aerial-photo she'd just mailed him. Taped to the bottom of the photo was a big note declaring:

YOU DID IT

The juxtaposition of this image — Jaegal holding up her photo-and-declaration in the wall screen's centre square, surrounded by nineteen newscasts showing Hussein's supporters rejoicing, even as the army they were cheering on was annihilated from the air. Annihilated *because* of those telecasts of cheering crowds.

Annihilated because of Kevin Dunbar.

MONSTER

Circling that word on his list, circling it again before he remembered it meant someone else, that genius theorist at Los Alamos. Then pressing the intercom. "Send Captain Jaegal up," he gasped.

Seconds later Jaegal took a long-legged stride out of Reception's camera-view. Heading on up to make her play. And Kevin realized he was prepared to play the fool for her again, if it meant one last opportunity to fool the ADSM... Turning toward the boardroom's back wall, where the Oracle SOOPE's dateflag had reached FEB-02-91 — the Persian Gulf present.

All the intricate shapes on-screen were frozen, the nightly download had begun. All Dunbar & Caety's hard-won techniques embodied in the simulation were winging off to Riyadh, to other places too.

But ADSM could go ahead and run with military SOOPE-apps. Kevin was going to run elsewhere. Stroking a line through the phrase NEW ORDER, he wrote

NEW WORLD

Then he closed the notepad, and slipped it into a pocket just as the boardroom door swung open.

"Kev, I've brought champagne!" Olivia called out, closing the door and then reaching behind her neck, loosening long dark hair around her shoulders. Oh, the ADSM knew Kevin well enough, intended to know him better still.

But tonight Kevin Dunbar had misled a worldwide audience, the mass media, and the leader of Iraq. It should be a mere exercise to mislead this AFPRO, ply her with pillow-talk about non-existent project goals. Then in the morning he'd book a flight to New Mexico. Go see this Mennochio, hear out his vision.

And hope it wasn't too late to sign up for a new kind of world.

✣ ✣ ✣

ARCHIVE APPEND:
DUTT Hearing on the al-Khafji SOOPE simulation
Convened at the Hague, January 2019
For thirteen days, the international prosecutors carved into Kevin Dunbar on a live World Court telecast. Never a day passed without archival footage of the highway from Basra to Mutlaa in Kuwait — the so-called Highway of Death — backdropping Dunbar on the courtroom's digital walls for the press gallery cameras.

And never a day passed, during the hearing's first week, without another former Allied pilot who'd flown a Highway of Death bombing mission taking to the witness podium. The pilots all told similar stories, testifying that they'd never seen a more pathetic sitting-duck situation in combat, and tossing out such choice quotes for the online news services as 'a turkey shoot' and 'bombing fish in a barrel'.

The aim of the archival footage and pilots' statements was to support a prosecution bid to have Weapon of Mass Destruction status slapped onto Dunbar & Caety's original al-Khafji simulation, a.k.a. the Oracle SOOPE. But the footage and pilots also served another prosecution aim: assisting in the gradual grinding down of the hearing's central witness, Kevin Dunbar.

The Court's chief justice appeared comfortable allowing this public pillorying of Dunbar to go on, only occasionally reminding everyone that the hearing was *not* a trial for crimes against humanity. And by the end of the first week, the application for WMD status was granted to the Oracle SOOPE.

That's when an Immensity strategy group in Darwin, Australia, decided to contact the woman who'd talked her way into Dunbar's mansion and walked back out with the transcript for Enigmedia's *Tale of Two War Zones*:

Audrey Zheng.

Audrey was given a new mission-project, and proceeded to catch the next suborbital flight to Geneva.

✠ ✠ ✠

Arrangements were made for Audrey to have a reserved seat in the viewing gallery of the international courtroom. Arriving halfway through the hearing's eighth day, she made her way to a seat high at the back of the gallery, dressed in her most conservative suit and equipped with the latest in discreet wireless satlinkage: a fully subvocalizable subdermal mike; a cochlear threadset; a contact lens with virtual data-display.

Feeling as linked, locked, and loaded as a diplomat-spy, Audrey slipped into her gallery seat, and soon began to wish she'd worn something more likely to get Dunbar to notice her. Because she was there to do more than act as official observer and point-of-contact for the strategy group following the hearing from down in Darwin. Audrey's primary purpose in flying to Geneva was to get out of Dunbar what she'd failed to get from him at his Hoag Head Place estate.

The truth about what had transpired when Dunbar met with Mennochio at Los Alamos all those years ago.

That meeting — so impactful for Dunbar, so entirely forgettable for Mennochio himself — remained a puzzle. There was some twist to that story, Audrey had no doubt. And Dunbar had deliberately left it out of his *Tale of Two War Zones*. Was he holding it back as a bit of bargaining-chip testimony for this unavoidable hearing?

Flying Audrey to Geneva in the hopes of getting Dunbar to give her, and Immensity, a head's up about what he might reveal about that Los Alamos meeting ... Well, that seemed to Audrey a long-shot indeed, a sign of just how worried the strategy group in Darwin really was.

As it turned out, all Audrey's attempts to get close to Dunbar, re-establish contact with him during the course of the hearings failed. Dunbar's counselors and handlers were keeping everyone at bay, and keeping Dunbar silent on the stand while they made their case, claiming the Highway of Death bombing runs and resulting Republican Guard deaths were the responsibility of Allied combat ops commanders alone.

The prosecution didn't trifle with the claims of Dunbar's innocence; they were too busy keeping their eye on the DUTT prize. Having established the Oracle SOOPE as a 'deadly and destructive' memetic weapon, the prosecution had only one task left: To link the Oracle SOOPE to Jorges Mennochio and the founding of Immensity itself.

Audrey was annoyed that the details in *A Tale of Two War Zones* couldn't stymie their DUTT case. The prosecutors weren't the least bit bothered by the fact that Dunbar had met with Mennochio *after* developing the Oracle SOOPE. Oh, it would have been better for their case had Dunbar met with Jorges earlier; but in the long run all the prosecution needed was Dunbar to have *discussed the Oracle* during that mysterious meeting in Los Alamos.

If Dunbar had shared any of Oracle's details with Mennochio, a DUTT lineage with Immensity's own founding SOOPE sims would be established.

And Jorges would be called in.

It all came down to what was said at that meeting, what Dunbar *said* was said.

But so far he hadn't said a word.

Audrey knew that prosecution lawyers had many ways of convincing a reluctant witness to talk.

But with such a big fish on the line — Mennochio was the one they'd been trying to reel in for years — she wasn't surprised to see the prosecutors play it safe, and run a 'shake, bake and break' campaign against Kevin Dunbar. On the hearing's tenth day they began bringing in widows and orphans of Iraqi soldiers who'd been incinerated on the Basra to Mutlaa highway.

Dunbar's counsel objected, pointing out that the Oracle's destructive-weapon status had already been ruled on by the Court.

The prosecution pointed out in turn that this was an international hearing, and that their Iraqi witnesses had come a long way to have their side of the Gulf War story heard. To send them home without letting them speak would be to compound their loss.

The chief justice allowed the new witnesses. And as one Iraqi after another stepped to the centre podium to read their statement, and as translations were piped over the courtroom's radio channels, Audrey could see the weight of guilt-pressure these new witnesses were putting on Dunbar. His earlier calm resignation was crumbling. His unearthly motionlessness of the first week — which had made Dunbar appear part of the terrible digital war-stills backdropping him — was gone.

Dunbar now alternated between bouts of key-wording on a paper notepad and guilt-ridden glances around the courtroom, eyes flickering from one accusing face to another in the crowded galleries above him. A few times he seemed to be looking in Audrey's direction, and at those moments she tried hard to catch his eye, shifting in her seat, adjusting her hair with both arms held high behind her head, as close as she could come to waving for attention.

Dunbar didn't appear to notice her. And over the next two days his posture grew droopier, more beaten down, his keywording more frantic, the frenetic scribbling of a man trying to map out a route back to safety, sanity. By day twelve, the Court's press gallery was crowing over how close Dunbar looked to breaking down. They didn't seem to realize what was obvious to Audrey:

Dunbar was already a broken man. He'd been broken for decades.

Nevertheless, the press had it right.

On the morning of the hearing's thirteenth day, Dunbar finally broke his silence. But just before he spoke he tore a page off his notepad, handed it to an assistant counselor. The entire court watched as the counselor walked across the floor, then up into the viewing galleries, then handed the note to Audrey.

She opened it carefully, to prevent the press cameras now training on her from filming its contents. Just two lines.

Thought-crime does not entail death.

Thought-crime is death.

A quote from Orwell, not a good sign. Dunbar was giving her the heads-up she'd come for, a warning that he was about to yield to another of his 'burn it all down' impulses. Audrey subvocalized the bad news to the Darwin strategy group — *It's about to go down, Dunbar intends to roll on us* — then she looked up to see the prosecution team staring at her and exchanging a flurry of whispers, trying to ID her from the sign-in sheets. The second they had her pegged, chief prosecutor Killian Van Vechten popped up, strolled over to Dunbar's table, stood in front of the star witness and said:

"Counsel has repeatedly told us how Mr. Dunbar revealed all in his so-called 'tale testimonial' to Enigmedia." Van Vechten turned, cast a knowing look directly at Audrey. "But that online confession, while entertaining, was merely an attempt by Immensity to shape public opinion before this hearing could convene."

The *Tale of Two War Zones* material, ignored for most of the hearing, was a juicy bone left to last, something the prosecutors were no doubt prepared to spend days tearing apart.

"Besides," Van Vechten sighed, "that biased online account left out the crux of the story, didn't it?"

Audrey heard a double-click in her cochlear threadset, then a member of the strategy group murmured in her mind, *Message received, Aud. We're watching the live feed now.*

Placing both hands on the witness counsel's table, Van Vechten leaned closer to Dunbar. "Enigmedia's account left out what happened when you traveled to Los Alamos, lunched with the good Doctor, founding father and patron saint of Immensity ... Don't suppose you'd like to tell the Court about that now, would you?"

Knowing he was unlikely to get an answer, Van Vechten had already started to turn away when Dunbar sat forward, cleared his throat.

Here it comes, Audrey subvocced.

"Ever met Doctor Mennochio?" Dunbar asked, looking up at Van Vechten.

Dunbar's table of counselors glanced at their client in surprise, but made no attempt to stop him from speaking. Audrey was confused. Was Dunbar the one who'd chosen to just sit there, take thirteen days of unsubtle accusation and incrimination without a word in his own defence?

"Never met him," Van Vechten admitted. "The good Doctor's a hard man to see these days."

An understatement. As a target of many assassination attempts, Mennochio was impossible to meet these days, was rarely seen outside the secure Emerald campus on the outskirts of Darwin.

"Wasn't hard to meet when he was just another Los Alamos mathematician," Dunbar said. "And I can tell you this much: first impression you get of Mennochio is that there's something ... wrong with him."

An appreciative murmur rippled outward from the prosecution team's table, across the lower press area, up into the higher galleries. The Geneva crowd was warming to this conversation; bureauflunkies seated near Audrey exchanged small knowing smiles.

Meanwhile Van Vechten was undergoing a cautious, pious transformation down on the courtroom floor. Audrey saw the chief prosecutor ease a hip onto the front edge of Dunbar's desk so that he was half standing, half sitting, hands clasped humbly on his lap, head bent as though in prayer over Dunbar, who also had his head down over the table's built-in microphone. The scene instantly became one of confession.

Van Vechten, the brilliant Dutch-protestant prosecutor so adept at reading people that he'd instinctively slipped into the role of Catholic priest-confessor for Dunbar's bent repentant form. "Take it you're referring to Mennochio's physical appearance," Van Vechten said softly.

"His appearance? No." Dunbar leaned closer, voice dropping to a lower more confidential tone. "I mean the way Mennochio *thinks*."

The looks of anticipation on some of the junior prosecutors become unabashed smiles.

"I swear to you," Dunbar went on, "Jorges Mennochio does not think like any ordinary human being. Spend a few hours with him, and you'd know. You'd see he's capable of doing it."

"Doing what, Kevin?" Van Vechten daring a first-name familiarity with the man he'd been carefully corroding for thirteen days.

"Running things in parallel, right before your eyes," Dunbar said. "Running SOOPE sims inside his head, without having to compile them in path-code. Snatching algorithms out of the air, summoning systems to life right there, in his office. Whole new metasystems, you can't imagine. *I* couldn't imagine. But I did, in the end." Dunbar looked up at Van Vechten, as though apologizing for something. "I saw how it would run, where the world could go, with Mennochio's vision. I saw. And I believed in him, wholly, utterly."

That's not what you told me, Audrey thought. So strange, that here in front of the world's cameras, Dunbar was capable of a more intimate sharing of truths than he'd been with Audrey in the comfort of his own home.

"Did Jorges ask you about your previous SOOPE work, the Oracle project, and so on?"

"He'd heard the rumours. So I told him the truth."

It seemed to Audrey that everyone in the courtroom looked buoyant, expectant, even as she held her breath, afraid of what was coming next.

"I told him his Immensity visions would boot-up in bigger ways than he realized. And I told him I couldn't work with him, then I left," Dunbar said, abruptly shutting down.

Another double-click in her cochlear threadset, and a gravelly murmuring in her head. *I remember this fellow now.* The words of a man with a rebuilt voicebox, sitting in with the Darwin strategists. *The one who listened, then left! Said nothing for an hour, then talked like a prophet stepped down off a mountain for a minute or two. Made some remarks about Immensity's boot-up phase, infectious growth patterns, eventual success. Then told me it wasn't in his firm's best interest to do any work for me, and vanished.*

It was eerie, Audrey thought, hearing Jorges himself in her inner ear, describing the man who was down on the courtroom floor describing Jorges.

"So you couldn't in good conscience join the push for Immensity," Van Vechten continued, still playing the confessor. "Why not, Kevin?"

"Because he had me doing it, too." Dunbar seemed lost in his own reflections, off on his own somewhere. "It's as though Mennochio's abilities rub off on you. Listening to him, I felt my understanding of SOOPE theory expanding, had a kind of parallel-processing epiphany. I actually ran path-code in my mind." Dunbar shook his head, awed even by the memory of it. "I saw whole metasystems surging forward, decades into the future — not Mennochio's alternative systems, mind you. *Our* systems." Dunbar made a sweeping gesture around the courtroom. "*This* system."

"And what did you foresee?"

Van Vechten truly had the patience of a priest, Audrey thought.

"A world trying to resist Mennochio's memetic infections," Dunbar replied. "Legal bodies trying to bring Immensity down by DUTTing its foundation sims, its boot-up SOOPEs. Courts were already DUTTing simulations even then, you know. And I knew the two teams that had defected from my firm to work for Mennochio were protected from DUTT charges by the confidentiality agreements that bound them to secrecy. They couldn't provide a DUTT lineage back to the Oracle because, by law, they couldn't provide any Oracle algorithms or details—"

"But *you* had no such constraints, Kevin," Van Vechten reminded the courtroom and the cameras. Shifting off the desk, he stepped out across the court floor in Audrey's direction before gesturing back at his wayward witness. "Dunbar and Caety owned the Oracle SOOPE outright. You could discuss it, even show parts of it to a potential Los Alamos client."

"You forget that I flew to meet Mennochio the morning after *that*." Dunbar turned, gestured at the digital wall behind him, displaying another Highway of Death still-image. "Knowing it was my idea to SOOPE *that*."

"Counsel should remind their witness that our Court is seeking a DUTT lineage, not a lineage for casualties of war," the chief justice interrupted. "Mr. Dunbar, you are not on trial, this is merely an informal hearing."

"So you keep saying. But you're not hearing *me*," Dunbar complained. "I said I saw it all in my head, back in Mennochio's office. Saw how big Immensity systems would get. Saw how our systems could undermine it, bring it tumbling down. Through me," he said.

"Mister Dunbar-"

"If my firm worked with Mennochio on his SOOPE projects, they'd all have a DUTT lineage directly to *that*." Another wave at the wall behind him. "Immensity would be infected by Dunbar and Caety's proprietary algorithms, by Dunbar and Caety's reputation, don't you see? The firm that designed *that* would have designed Immensity's SOOPE foundations."

"And we are to believe you saw all this during your first meeting with him?" Van Vechten was falling back into his former Doubting Thomas role.

"It was unreal what I saw, listening to Mennochio." He turned to the chief justice. "I saw systems running ahead all the way to this courtroom, this hearing." Another wave at the wall behind him. "I saw that *that* moment entailed this moment. And I've been waiting for this moment to come ever since."

Something clicked inside Audrey, and this time it wasn't her threadset. Wondering why she hadn't seen it before. This hearing was not about the DUTT, not for Dunbar. He'd given up a lot to protect Mennochio's Immensity concepts back then, he'd do so now.

Audrey subvocced: *Jorges, I fear my friend Dunbar has used you as bait to get his fifteen minutes in this courtroom.*

A double-click, then that gravel voice, stones in her head. *Would have made a formidable Immensity strategist. He sees how to use the old systems against themselves.*

"It *always* comes to this," Dunbar was saying, to himself, to the watching world. "A door opens, a room fills with lawyers, cameras. Arguments are presented that lay the blame on the system, the war machine, the generals, the field commanders, the soldiers, the missiles, the bullets. But in the end, the question remains." Turning to face the press gallery cameras, Dunbar pointed to the image splashed across the wall behind him.

"Can any one person really be responsible for *that*?"

Then he suddenly, shakily got to his feet. "If the court will allow me," Dunbar said, "I'd like to answer that question, and clear my name."

Caught off guard, the chief justice waved him forward. Dunbar stepped out from behind the table, and crossed the courtroom floor, passing the chief justice's table and stopping before the seated rows of middle-aged Iraqi orphans, ancient widows, soldier-survivors of the Highway of Death who'd come to make their impact statements.

"Let me be the first in this courtroom to say it." A *click* from deep in Dunbar's throat. He swallowed, didn't say anything more for a moment. Then nodded, and declared:

"I am responsible. For the excessively high casualties on that day, *that* particular highway—" Raising an arm that now seemed too heavy to lift, aiming it one last time toward the digital wall. "I lured those troops out of safety onto that road, I aimed the war machine, the generals, the pilots, the missiles at them. All those who died there died according to plan."

"My plan."

He bowed his head.

Silence across the huge courtroom.

Audrey found herself blinking down at the note Dunbar had had passed to her, understanding it now. Clearing his name did not entail coming out from behind the curtains, clearing his conscience. Clearing his conscience *was* clearing his name.

No signed online confession could satisfy Kevin Dunbar's deep-seated need for atonement; this hearing, harrowing as it had been for him, was the penitent release he'd longed for.

After a long minute or two of silence, standing before the Iraqi orphans, widows, wounded soldiers, Dunbar turned at last, took a step toward the prosecution's table, where he quietly said something that the floor mikes picked up and piped out over the viewing gallery speakers:

"To answer the only question you seem interested in asking me, just for the record ... I never discussed or divulged anything about the Oracle SOOPE to Jorges Mennochio when I met with him."

An echo of whoops and claps of delight from Audrey's threadset. The Darwin team was ecstatic.

As the entire prosecution team retreated into chambers for a brief closed-doors powwow with the chief justice, Audrey slipped into a hall behind the viewing gallery, re-entered a lower gallery, maneuvered her way to the exit door closest to the table where Dunbar was sitting, just in case things turned out the way she thought they were about to.

And then, shortly before 11 AM, the Chief Justice returned, announced that, lacking any evidence of a lineage between the Oracle SOOPE and Immensity's founding SOOPE sims, he was throwing the DUTT case out.

Heaven and Earth

by Allan Weiss

I found you at last, Uncle Martin. You were buried beneath centuries of accumulated stone, and your face had changed, altered by recognition rather than time. I'm sorry I had to go so far to find you.

I found you in the eye of a creature who had never known either of us, and wouldn't have understood a word of our speech: our verbal games, our forays into Yiddish. He or she or it (you'd hate to hear me violate Martin Buber's directive against objectifying the Other, but I may have no choice) had no ears. If the creature had met you, then, he/she/it would have learned nothing about you.

They brought the creature back to camp for study, encased in ceramic amber, and placed it in a hall tent big enough for many of us to stand around and analyze, discuss, or merely gape in wonder. We surrounded Andrew Cornell's find like children around a magic trick, experiencing a kind of intellectual delirium. It couldn't get any better than this, we knew. No one would ever do what we were about to do: be the first to touch, study, and try to explain another intelligent species. Those of us who were ourselves intelligent, or at least wise, knew others would come along and supersede our conclusions, demonstrate how misguided we were about everything. But in this case who was right didn't matter. All that mattered to us was who was first. I was going to be one of the very first, and I think I glowed.

Dr. Nur, Project Leader, held court frequently, bringing us the latest results from a colleague's studies or word from the company station. The enthusiastic support we got from our corporate masters didn't quite make up for our sense of being slaves — to European General Technologies or maybe our dependence on it — but at least we got everything (mainly the *data*) we needed to do our work and make ourselves (and of course E.G.T.) rich and famous.

By the way, none of us could come up with a name for our discovery. I can't believe that Lucy and those who came after — the ice-men found in the Alps, the bits of skull — were grateful for how we exercised Adam's prerogative. You told me once how important it was for God to give Adam that power to name, even before the power of procreation — the ability to give identity and otherness. But we were second-rate Adams, and couldn't think of any name we could all agree on.

When I visited you every week or two in the Manhattan apartment where you moved yourself and your private lab after Auntie Ida died, it was mostly out of a sense of obligation. Your own children had emulated you and disappeared into the maw of science, sent to far-flung parts of the globe or even other planets by the demands of the pursuit of knowledge, credentials, and company profits. I was just a kid myself, maybe twenty-one or twenty-two, and a true product of what you called the New Mentality. Years earlier you'd insisted that my parents give me a Bar Mitzvah (over Dad's atheistic hesitation), unwilling to let them shirk their cultural duties; you even promised to contribute substantially to the cost. I hated you for piling all that extra study on me — the blessings, the *Haftorah*, most of which I had to memorize because my Hebrew was virtually non-existent — but my desire to keep you from feeling abandoned was more powerful than my childish resentment.

It was from you that I learned about the other, angled history left out of the usual Hebrew School litany of oppressions. Your lines strayed dizzyingly, annoyingly, from Babylonians, Egyptians, and Germans toward philosophy and politics, aesthetics and physics. You would sit on the flowery easy chair in your living room, sipping chocolate cocktails and munching bagel sticks. When you offered me such unhealthy fare, which violated every tenet of pre-med, I would decline in my Healthier-Than-Thou way. But I did eat your steaming coconut biscuits straight out of the zapper. And I'd listen to your long lectures, wondering where you were going — what was the point? I think I began to need those visits; you made me a learning addict like yourself. And that was when my parents were finally divorcing; they'd waited till I'd moved out before starting the inevitable legal process. It never occurred to me what a generous gift of your time you were giving me; to me your growing fame as a cyberneticist was simply a part of you, not something requiring huge amounts of time-consuming labour in your home lab.

"Can you remember anything we talked about last time?" you asked once, and I thought the question absurd. I didn't always know what you were saying, but I couldn't forget any of it, not after the attention you demanded from me.

"Of course I do. You told me about Ari, the guy in the Renaissance." Ari was a scholar, a mystic, blessed or burdened with a wealth of knowledge. "He had his own version of the creation of the world."

"Do you remember the story?" you asked.

I repeated it practically word-for-word, gesture-for-gesture, pressing my hands together then moving them apart the way you had: the world in its original form as a giant pot; the pot exploding, shattering; the pieces tracing diverse paths.

You grinned and wagged your head. "Not bad, *putzele*." You patted my forearm with a crooked, grey-haired hand. "Remember the ending, too?"

I did. Like the universe itself eons after the Big Bang, the fragments would fall into each other again; shards of dark matter would coalesce, collapse space and time into a cosmic One again. God's head would be reintegrated; Adam Cadmon, the primordial Self, would be whole again, and Mankind with it.

What I didn't understand was why we bothered covering all that abstruse ground. I saw you as an old man trying vainly to help me through the horrors of divorcing parents by drowning me in information. You never gave up trying to brighten my lot with distracting stories and European candies. I now see that Ari's creation myth was a separation story with a happy ending, something a kid from a breaking home needed to hear. But at the time all I knew was that you were exasperatingly hard to follow, and I even thought sometimes that you were just showing off.

The Castormondians inhabited this world about three thousand years before we arrived, then died off for reasons unknown and possibly unknowable. They favoured one dominant foodstuff, the things the botanists called 'land corals,' and also ate the corals' airborne spores, we think, through the two extra appendages that protruded dorsally from their midsections and that were breathing apparatuses (and maybe sense organs) as well. The Castormondians possessed basic toolmaking technologies — they could work metal, stone, tree-fibre — and most importantly for us an acquaintance with preservation techniques. They used heat-treated resins to protect tools and the dead against humidity, especially important given the planet's violently changeable weather, leaving us with the well-preserved remains of their equipment and of someone clearly high up in their society. The tomb, as Research Site 1 proved to be, contained a single but intact Very Important Corpse.

"I'm afraid to touch it," I confided to Kelly Defalco, my chief assistant. "I can't explain why, but— "

"I understand." We usually *kibbitz*ed with each other, but as we stared down at the Castormondian we couldn't come up with any suitable one-liners. It was a moment I knew I'd always recall in its every detail. The Castormondian seemed to be enclosed in a bubble I was loathe to break. Kelly and I finally looked at each other, exchanged smiles, and raised our eyebrows: time to get to work.

The anatomy work was like every other sort of research here: you start with nothing and see what flows into your mind. My understanding of cranial structure was terracentric but not entirely useless, and my job was to explore the jellied blobs that remained of its eyes. The Castormondians did have eyes, a point that disturbed me because it made them *less* alien. I felt that they should have been entirely different, but occasionally we would find similarities that were more striking than the differences. I found it hard to wrap my mind around the idea that such a thorough Other could be like Us, too.

The Castormondian's head was spherical and possessed few prominent features: no nose, no ears, and no sign that any had been there and gone missing. (As far as we could tell nothing had been cut from the corpse prior to burial.) Where the 'chin' would be there was a tiny round mouth which, with its narrow-range mandibular joint, would open very slightly. The skull was significantly fragmented that it would need some reconstruction to show for certain how the eyes were positioned or moved.

I remembered something you said about wonder as a fragile sensation. A thing or event is a source of wonder for a brief time, then begins to seem routine no matter how outlandish it is: seeing a spaceship standing on the surface of the moon, killing people just for being of a particular race, flying to another planet, visiting an old scientist uncle who's read Wittgenstein, cutting open the organs of an alien creature. Instead of going "Wow!" nonstop as I explored the tissues beneath my optical and ceramic instruments, I grew impatient at the toughness of the ciliary muscles, disturbed by the *problem* of the sockets' placement and form — as if I were back in anatomy class dissecting sheep's eyes.

But at night, thinking back on how I'd spent my day, I couldn't believe any of it had been real.

The problems were real and nagging. The biggest was the placement of the eyes, which never seemed right in our mental and computer reconstructions; the other was the apparent shape of the pupil. I was convinced we didn't have enough remaining tissue to come to proper conclusions about either, but we'd try anyway. We had a team of five exobiologists working on the head, not to mention the neurologists who had jurisdiction over the tiny blackened lump that seemed to be the remains of a brain. I couldn't help wondering if they were all stillborn doctors like I was, people who'd had dreams of financial and healing glory but had found research impossible to give up.

As for the apparent positioning: the eyes were very widely spaced, so much so I wondered if we'd made a mistake in our reconstruction too obvious to be noticed, if you know what I mean. The eyeball itself was remarkably well preserved, its structures either still intact or easily reconstructed using the services of our forensics imaging expert. The pupil seemed to be a kind of thickened barbell at contraction. That started me thinking about something that I slotted in the back of my mind, waiting for corroborating evidence. The pupil was our doorway, and we were determined to avoid dissection if at all possible. I stared inside the Castormondian's window to the soul; I looked for the soul, but I'm sorry, I don't think I found it. What I did find was a retinal fossil that demanded inspection. No matter how decayed it was, it would still yield up lots of answers, and — more importantly, of course — lots of questions.

I chose to go to med school at Columbia in part because I would then be near Ma. I thought it would destroy her to lose her son so soon after her husband left. Dad's departure, even though it came after years of fighting, cut into her so deeply I'm sure you could see her pain whenever she cabbed it down to visit you. My mother was still of the old school: never learned to drive because Dad was there to take her where she needed to go, never stopped observing the holidays, never missed the lighting of the *yahrzeit* candles for Zaida and Bubby; continued to have me over for *shabbos* dinner. All of that became even more important to her after Dad took off.

She was glad, too, that I kept visiting you. Did I do it to make her happy, because she wanted me to keep in touch with you? Even if I didn't always see the connections between the things you told me, or between them and the rest of my life, I couldn't give up those visits. Maybe I badly needed a comforting family routine during a time when my family life was a crisis, or maybe I just kept wanting to figure you out. You'd gone from being an obligation to an aggravating mystery to me; what was all that erudition *for*? I became less confused by what you were telling me than *why* you were telling it to me.

And then, scientist though you were you always came to my mother's seders, shared the bitters and matzohs with her no matter what other invitations you received. And you made me ask the Four Questions. I thought you were a terrible hypocrite, because you were not only a scientist but an atheist. You turned me into one, too. You told me about the 'other' Jewish history, the one that made a mockery of Rabbi Gold's hero- and villain-mongering at Young Israel Hebrew Academy. After you told me about the conflicts between the fundamentalists and the Hellenists, how could I still take seriously the business of spinning noisemakers at the sound of Haman's name? How could I believe God passed over us in Egypt when our enslavement, just like the blacks', was an economic act, not a special test for a chosen people? Yet, while you were advancing your career in AI research, you were pushing me further into the Hebrew teacher's arms, saying, "Here, you need this." I decided to forgive you for destroying my comfortable quasi-faith in what I learned at Hebrew school only because your presence at Passovers, your insistence that they be as kosher (in the broadest sense) as possible, made my mother happy. Happier. After my father left for greener pastures and an intense pianist, in Scotland, my mother wanted you to be a surrogate or something close to it. So devoting an hour every week to your company was a small price to pay for her softer looks when I told her I'd seen you. But by then I'd met Bev, and saw my frustrating visits with you as taking time away from her.

We laboured our way through the eye; we had a remarkable amount to work with, and it all stunned us with the terrestrial analogues we could draw. The basic structures were there, from cornea to retina; unfortunately, we couldn't follow the nerves through and out the sclera without some dissection. Where the tissue was decayed we could use our fil-optics to see right down into the sclera's nuclear layers, in other words the absolute depths of the eye.

The iris gave us pause for thought: it had such highly developed contractor muscles that Kelly postulated voluntary iris control. I tried to keep her from going too far with that theory. Here on Castormond anything is postulatable, anything is possible, and people tend to let their wishes for something dramatic overrule their obligation to go very slowly. Just about everything we saw fit what we might expect in a terrestrial creature; even the circumference of the eye matched what you might see in an Earth animal of 1.25 metres in length/height. Again, I wasn't sure if that similarity comforted or disturbed me more. But we couldn't afford to let our imaginations (and our ambitions) run away with us.

You knew I'd have made a terrible doctor; one time you said after one of my learned outbursts, "My God, I hope they don't give you a real patient. You'll want to cut him up to see how his pancreas works!" At which point you began lecturing me on Noam Chomsky, of all people.

The day I told you I was I leaving med school, you asked, "Don't you want to save people's lives? Or at least their eyesight?"

"Not especially. Ma wanted me to, and so did I — for a while."

"Did you want to be a doctor because she wanted you to?"

I'd asked myself that question a thousand times, and every time came up with a different answer. I once vowed that if I ever came up with the same answer twice in a row, I would consider it the right one and stop wondering. All I could come up with for a reply was a shrug that implied, "Probably."

"And what does your girlfriend say?"

"Bev? To tell you the truth, she shared your doubts."

"So, what now?"

"Research. Northeastern Pharmaceuticals is looking for new brains." I drank the lemon-flavoured camomile tea you'd kindly supplied. You knew very well that med students live on caffeine, and need a respite from it sometimes.

"You're going into the corporate sector?" I couldn't tell from your tone or look if you were disappointed in me. "Didn't I tell you enough about what Marx said?"

"He didn't have to attend med school." I stared down into the yellow tea. "Maybe I want to be rich and famous."

You smiled that tight-lipped smile of yours. "Do exo, then; that's where all the real work is being done."

You were right, of course; exobiology would be the field to enter, with its huge potential for real basic research, patents, the chance to do something meaningful: a CV goldmine. I'd considered it but wasn't sure I had the guts to leave Earth, spend years on another planet worried that in some terrible excursive accident I'd contaminate it with my germs or be killed instantly by the planet's. Would I have to leave Bev behind, maybe for good? But the temptations were stronger than the fears.

"Tell me, Steven," you said in your 'worried uncle' voice. "Have you talked to your mother?"

"No. I haven't been able to." She'd say all the right encouraging, understanding things. But she had a mind of the sort that had been passed down from mother to daughter for generations: let your son be a professional (doctor-lawyer-accountant), and therefore secure in a field she understood. Thanks to all our technological advances, mothers were having more and more trouble understanding what their children did for a living.

"Do you want me to talk to her?"

I shook my head. I shouldn't accept such help. I shouldn't need it. "I don't want to disappoint her. But I don't imagine she'd mind *that* much." I reached over to the living room side-table, and held up the laminated issue of *Fortune* you always had prominently displayed on it: the one with your picture on the cover holding a chrome diamond-shaped blow-up model of the o-chip you'd designed. Your claim to fame. "After all," I said, "I won't be the first pure-researcher in the family."

"No." You laughed, and your potbelly lurched. "'`Its roots in Earth, its branches in Heaven.'"

"What?"

"A line from a poem by Barry Geller. `Tree of Life.'" From there we moved on to a discussion of (lecture on) post-Zionist poetry, the Universalist movement, African neosocialism …. I might as well go into space, I thought; it would be little different from trying to cope with your intellectual flights.

Kelly led the count, and engaged in sadistic tricks to delay informing me of her results. She'd hint at a conclusion then deny she'd completed her work; it was like our "Did you bring me anything?" games when I was a child. "Maybe I did, maybe I didn't," you'd say, although you invariably had an iceball or an addition to my collection of 'NetSpy' merchandise.

"Come on," I said. "Tell me what you're getting."

Kelly smiled up at me. "Uh *uhh*. Impatience killed the cat."

"No it didn't."

"Hey, it's my cat. I'll talk when I'm good and ready."

Kelly teased until our third official Team Meeting after the mummy was discovered. She announced there was a preponderance of rods, though not a very solid majority. "In addition, there is a fovea centralis, which is considered evidence of an advanced species; furthermore, it's packed with cones."

Now I had my corroborating evidence, and it flew in the face of everything we'd learned about the Castor- mondians so far. You see, a large number of rods suggests nocturnal habits, and the pupil size and shape said noc- turnal, too. But the structures we saw in the eye, particu- larly that fovea, implied sharp vision and something we already knew from the presence of wall paintings in the tomb where we'd found the mummy: colour vision.

So why the evidence for nocturnal habits? We talked about it and came up with a dubious theory: the rods were vestigial. Maybe the Castormondians had *once been* noc- turnal, had hunted for the land corals by 'smell' or some- thing like it. Perhaps with their rear appendages — more vestiges, then, of a non-light-based mode of life? But over time the competition with other, similar creatures over the same source of food caused them to become diurnal, and their eyes adapted accordingly....

On Earth, creatures went the other way around, from diurnal to nocturnal. It proved harder than I thought to accept something so radically different from — in fact, *contradicted* — what I'd been taught on Earth. I wanted to be able to leave that logic behind, adapt (myself) to new conditions, move forward as I'd always wanted to do unfettered by the strictures of tradition and convention. Let my mind run free, the way yours had roved over the whole of Jewish thought from the Judges and the Prophets to the economists and the designers of new AI components. But I found myself hoping I'd discover something to disprove the theory. Why did my imagination resist the conclusion so much?

What I most wanted to know was where the nerve fibres went, where they ended up in the brain and how they got there. That would tell me something, I thought. I suppose I was hoping for a different kind of accommodation: not the sort that adjusts for objects at different distances, but the sort that would adjust Castormond once again to my mind and experience. In both cases there would be greater clarity, but in the second greater comfort, too.

I entered Johns Hopkins on a research scholarship and so I could no longer pay my weekly visits to you. On holidays, though, I'd return to New York to see Ma, and I think I was nearly as anxious to see you. Your lectures became part of my background, a kind of retinal ghost. Persistent image. I found you in the new house you'd bought with the prize money you won for designing a zero-degree environment for your o-chip. In the deep-freeze the chip functioned flawlessly and virtually instantaneously. You'd stopped colouring your hair by then, and it hung silver by your eyes, the few remaining black strands like vestigial cells themselves, a holdover of a long-gone previous stage of development. Your foyer was lined with the books I knew so well: Eban's history of the Jews, Buber, Einstein, Kaplan — the pantheon of secular Judaism — alongside the Talmudic studies in their tall brown volumes with gold Hebrew lettering.

Once I was settled into the rose-printed couch, next to
the table on which your wedding picture stood guard over
photos of your son and his brood, you asked me questions
like an examiner at Rabbinical College. They came fast and
furious, and I hoped I would pass the test.

"What are you working on? How far have you gotten?
Is it what you've been wanting to do?"

We talked about Ma; I told you how shocked I'd been
at seeing how old she looked now. The turkey neck and
the thickening middle were new to me, or maybe I'd just
never noticed them before. What did you once say about
denial being the human animal's most vital defence mechanism?

"Is she okay?" I asked, expecting to hear the truth from
you. I expected no less from you and no better than reassuring lies from Ma.

"Yeah, she's fine, but she misses you something awful."

"Was I such a great son?"

"That's not the point."

"I know." Through a door down the hall I saw inside
your workroom, where you'd set up your own private chip
factory. This man who could manoeuvre his way through
the most intricate ceramic pseudoneurons had been my
guide to Babylonian economics. "I guess you're keeping
busy."

"Not as much as I'd like. Although more than I should,
at my age, I suppose."

I told you I was being trained on company money but
wasn't really looking forward to company indenture, and
you laughed. You knew that the term was real — not a
clever metaphor — but you also knew how much it
sounded like me.

"Moving on, then?"

"Yeah. European General Technologies has some exciting
projects ongoing, and I'd like to get in on them." Bev had
told me she would wait; I wanted to believe her, although
my doubts didn't keep me from going.

"Reach for the sky, Steven. `Roots in Earth.'"

"What?" I didn't remember the poem.

"Say hi to your mother."

That night Ma and I talked money: how she should handle things now that Dad had passed away (a heart attack while waiting for a Glasgow bus!) and had left her a few things over his new wife's objections. I wanted to ask my mother about her own life — did she socialize, have activities? She told me she was thinking about joining a Torah-study class run by a *Hassid*, and I feared she was about to turn Orthodox.

We mapped the Castormondian eye's internal structure as far as we could, then aimed our intellectual and technological guns at the sclera and the nerves streaming from it towards the brain. We got good pictures from our scans; the fil-optics and MPI imagers saved us the need to be very invasive. Kelly, meanwhile, was doing detailed studies of phototransduction: the presence of calcium in the land corals told us the Castormondians would have an endless supply to keep their rods and cones at peak efficiency, if not downright overloaded. These were beings, in other words, with very good eyesight — and they would have needed it to find those corals in the dense underbrush where they grew — till the Castormondians began cultivating them, as we theorized they did. The corals were well hidden and not sufficiently distinguished by colour to be located by inferior eyes, while the appendages were probably used later for feeding on spores rather than sniffing out the corals themselves.

We gathered our pictures of the sclera and formed a conclusive neural map — conclusive in the sense that it was the best we could do. As I looked at it I found myself denying its implications; I ordered so many retries, reconfigurations, program checks that my people were beginning to think I'd lost my mind, or my faith in them.

Normally (I mean Earth-normally), about half the nerves in the eyeball of a highly evolved creature decussate: that is, cross over and end up in the opposite side of the brain. Half stay on their own side of the head. But here was total crossover; *every* nerve went to the opposite side. You only saw that sort of thing in lizards and other lower forms, where the eyes are set widely apart and there's no or reduced binocular vision. I sat there running the implications through my mind.

At the next Team Meeting I called up a magnified image of the eyeballs and their wiring over our table. I wanted someone to show me where I'd gone astray, or interpret the picture differently from what was beginning to look inevitable. What I got instead from the gathered researchers and technicians was astonishment, amazed silence.

"Electrostimulation experiments confirm it," I said. "Total decussation. *No* ipsilateral nerves. They *all* cross over to the opposite side of the hypothetical visual neocortex."

I'd seen how far apart the eyes appeared to be; it was no illusion. If you put it all together, what it meant was that these beings had an amazingly wide field of vision, along with a very narrow field of *binocular* vision; most of what they saw was two-dimensional. Practically speaking, it meant they could catch glimpses of land corals on either side of them, discern them clearly with their sharp eyes, turn their heads to confirm the sighting, and be assured of food. The control of their irises, and therefore of their pupils, meant they could adjust instantly and repeatedly for changes in lighting caused by the planet's sudden weather changes: a cloudless sky one minute, storm clouds making noon dark as night the next.

But more than that: how would such a being *think*? Uncle Martin, the Castormondians weren't subintelligent fish or lizards; they were tool-using beings who had created a modest civilization. How would their minds work? They would have to be able to perceive, assimilate, interpret, and react to different things coming from different sides of their heads. We look at and focus (barely) on one thing at a time. They did that for *two* things at a time instinctually and, we can presume, *consciously*.

There's an ecopsychologist here now, someone who is trying to find out how a being living on this planet would see its world. She keeps pestering me for my data, because she needs to know how they perceived to know how they thought. I keep putting her off because, frankly, I think her 'science' is a bunch of speculative crap. But on top of that, I think I'd have a hard time telling her what I think

I've learned. I understood the Castormondians intellec-
tually, but I couldn't really grasp them, because their way
of thinking was so vastly different from mine. The passage of time between the Castormondians and us, the
strangeness of the almost inescapable conclusions we drew
from the circumstantial evidence, made it all so much more
difficult to maintain imaginatively. I'll report our findings
in the journals and make myself and my team famous for
our insights (if you will). But I think something in the back
of my mind will keep saying, "No, that can't be right."

The last time I saw you was about five months before
you passed away. You were living in one of the orbital habs,
where part of you (about half, I suppose) always wanted
to be. I was on my way to my first planet, Eridanus III, to
seek fame, fortune, and patents. I recognized your sharp,
wrinkled elbows, and the bulbous paunch that stretched
the knit fabric of your T-shirt, but not your entirely white
hair, now trimmed in proper space fashion. You could
spend your whole day looking down on the Earth if you
chose to, and maybe see it as an overgrown chip you could
micro-ize and win an award for.

"I'm glad to see you," you said, and for the first time
you hugged me — not for long, not hard, but enough to
embarrass us delightfully.

"Same here. It's been too long."

"Company rule, eh?" You lowered yourself onto the
semi-circular pulldown in the cramped chamber. "High-
class slavery."

I shrugged. "Survival. Teach me something."

You told me about Genesis that day, told me about the
geography of the Middle East and where Creation began
according to the myth-makers. How far away it seemed
then. "Your mother?" you asked at one point. "How's she
doing?"

"Fine. She's in a club. 'Single Septagenarians' or some
such nonsense." I knew then, without really believing it,
that I might not see her again. For some reason, the same
thought never occurred to me about you. "She cried when
I left."

"I'm not surprised."

We talked about the universe for a while, then you saw me to my ship. I caught sight of you waving as the dock released us, and I sailed off to find God, the primordial Adam, or whatever else it was that we and your philosophers had never seen.

After the meeting I went into the tent where we were keeping the mummy. I looked into the eye we'd studied so assiduously. And then I understood you, Uncle Martin. My mother stood squarely on the Earth, devoted to her absurd but essential heritage when the rest of her universe split asunder like Ari's pot, thanks to Dad's departure. I was ready to reach for the sky, even for Heaven if I could find it in a company store. You stood between us; or rather, you stood with us in the past *and* the future, you'd learned how to hold the two together in your mind, and wanted to make sure I knew where my feet were before I stretched too high and fell on my face. You offered me the books of Moses with one hand and those of Einstein with the other. Thanks for teaching me how to look ahead and behind no matter how far I might go, how to see both Heaven *and* Earth.

Wings to Fly
by Sylvie Bérard
translated by Sheryl Curtis

Scylla Seaside Colony, 12-06-2251

Dear Brijjie,

I wanted to take off, Brijjie. I wanted to be carried away by the sheer joy of it. I didn't want to go terribly high, just drift for a long time. That's why I constantly traveled between space and the planet. When the spacecraft took off, I would flatten myself against my seat, knowing full well that gravity would desert me. Time and space would stand still while the shuttle appeared to come to a stop. It was as if a bubble of pleasure burst in my belly. That's most likely why these trips are so expensive. I'm sure you realize, of course, that if the swarming masses on Earth and in the production colonies could experience this abandon, who knows how long the powers that be could resist...

They loved my performances, Brijjie. I made them all salivate. My body, suspended between everything and nothing, my limbs twisted at improbable angles, my sweat pearling on my skin, bubbles of my blood scattering from my veins, opened in offering. They clamoured for it and that, perhaps, made us equals for a brief moment — they, in the golden harnesses of their luxury voyages to stellar riches, me, a precious object embodying the cosmic void, delivered up to them, shameless, yet controlling every second of their pleasure.

I made a mistake, Brijjie. I allowed myself to get carried away. I wanted to believe that the laws of our world had no weight. I gashed my body too deeply; I threw myself to the lions; I splattered them with my substance. I crossed through the intangible window that should have kept me at a distance. Weightless, I touched them. They fell as a mass, red with my blood.

I'm stuck on the ground, Brijjie, cooped up. I'm no longer permitted to make the crossing; my performance is now worthless. I wander about in the colony that shuns me, yet will not let me leave. Every day, I go to the port, begging a seat on a departing shuttle, knowing full well that a single trip will never suffice. My wings have been clipped, Brijjie, and I cannot bear my own weight.

S.

Final Thoughts
by Nalo Hopkinson

The flea on the back of the elephant has a dilemma; where does she stop, and where does the elephant start? Which is insect, and which is pachyderm? Since she takes some sustenance from the larger animal's blood, does that not make them sisters in truth? Under the skin, even? Or perhaps they really are essentially different in nature. The flea ponders these questions often. The elephant is probably oblivious, though perhaps occasionally itchy where the flea makes her gustatory intrusions.

Canadian science fiction spends a lot of time trying to decide what makes it Canadian, as opposed to, um, elephantine. By now, many of us could recite the list of tropes that we've decided make us *us*: stories that privilege community over individual heroics; stories about open space(s), alienation, isolation; about the rare and precious coming together of isolated bodies to comfort each other in the dark and cold before separating once more ... didn't know Leonard Cohen was a science fiction writer, didja?

But reading for this volume of *Tesseracts Nine*, I discovered an element of Canadian science fiction and fantasy that doesn't appear on the familiar list of tropes.

Humour.

Canadian science fiction and fantasy writers are *funny*! It's all here: the dry humours of satire, wit, irony and sarcasm; the damp humours of farce, buffoonery, parody, slapstick; there's high camp, there are comedies simple and convoluted, and of course, there's the bitter tonic of the cosmic joke — many of the serious stories in *Tesseracts Nine* have a quinine soupçon of wry. As good storytellers know, humour can humanize like nothing else, except perhaps death. So perhaps the thing to be said about Canadian SF is that it is human, and is ultimately about a very human dilemma: what does it mean that we exist, and that we are aware that we exist? The flea may ask herself all kinds of important questions about the nature of her identity, but this much is sure; for a certain space of time, she *is*.

The original Tesseracts anthology, the progenitor of this one, was many years ago the first volume I had ever seen devoted entirely to Canadian science fiction and fantasy. I believe it was among the first books I ever paid full price for as an adult, with money I'd earned myself. I usually borrowed my reading material from the library. But the original Tesseracts intrigued me enough to fork over the cash (it helped that the price was reasonable). I'd probably been only about five years in Canada, and this place was still alien to me. Actually, it still seems pretty alien; I've just gotten resigned to it. Five years in, it had become clear to me that Canada was not, as so many people from outside North America perceive, a low-rent USA. Yet I wasn't sure quite what it was, other than the place where — at least in the corner of it I inhabited — I had to wear for my life a spacesuit eight months of the year and as little as possible the remaining four. Oh, and there was the very Canadian SCTV, which I found horribly bleak, and which depressed me utterly, rather than amusing me. It made no sense to me at all as comedy. This was Canada?

Decades before I allowed myself to realise that I wanted to be a writer, I was a reader, and what I read was science fiction and fantasy. And now, there on the shelf in the bookstore, was a book which married one of my passions — science fiction — with my dilemma; what is Canada? What does it mean that I am here, instead of in a place where the rhythms of the language sit sweetly in my throat and on my tongue, and there's more than one kind of mango, and Shakespeare is played by black actors?

That original Tesseracts didn't particularly answer my questions. That was not especially its reason for existence. But it did introduce me to a number of new writers, some of whom I have the pleasure of knowing today; some of whom I have the honour, with Geoff, of publishing again, many Tesseracts later. That original Tesseracts told me that there were people here who took pride in creating an artform I valued. That original Tesseracts is still somewhere in my personal collection.

By now, it should be no secret that there are such things as Canadian science fiction writers; that there is a Canadian science fiction. And by now, we are perhaps beginning to realise that it's not monolothic, but as varied as the writers who create it. What's important is not the character of Canadian science fiction. What's important is that it *is*.

Biographies

Timothy J. Anderson is the author of *Resisting Adonis* (Tesseract, 2000) and *Neurotic Erotica* (Slipstream, 1996) and has had short fiction and essays published in a variety of periodicals including the *Prairie Fire* Speculative Fiction Issue and *Fantastika Chronika* (in Greek translation). He has had more than a dozen works for stage professionally produced, two of which were nominated for Sterling Awards; and he has been a librettist-in-residence with the Canadian Opera Company. Timothy has edited books for The Books Collective since 1994, working with both new and established authors. His parallel career as a singer/actor has taken him across Canada, Singapore and Hong Kong as well as to New York's Carnegie Hall. He has performed with opera companies and orchestras in rep from Bach to new works and is on the Canadian cast recording of *Phantom of the Opera*. He has degrees in journalism, political science and music as well as post-secondary certificates in arts management and music theatre. Timothy has taught creative writing for Metro Community College and University of Alberta Liberal Studies/Faculty of Extension and coached art song classes for Alberta College.

René Beaulieu is a writer, essayist, translator (works by Moorcock, De Lint, O. S. Card, Heinlein and Vance) and anthologist (with Guy Sirois) since 1979, working in the different genres of imaginative fiction in Québec and in France. One time winner of the Dagon Award and two times of the Boréal Award, he has published a number of story collections: *Légendes De Virnie*, *Le Préambule*, Coll. Chroniques Du Futur, 1981; *Les Voyageurs De La Nuit*, Les

Éditions De L'À Venir, 1997, and *Un Fantôme D'Amour*, Ashem Fictions, 1997. Two of his stories have been published in previous Tesseracts anthologies: "The Blue Jay" (Jane Briely, trans.) *in Tesseracts Q* and "The Energy Of Slaves" (Yves Meynard trans.) in *Tesseracts 8*. He is now working on two novels.

Sylvie Bérard was born in Montréal in 1965. She obtained her Ph.D. from the Université du Québec à Montréal in 1997 and she is now assistant professor at Trent University. As a scholar, she published many articles on women's science fiction. She has been a regular contributor to Québec literary magazine *Lettres québécoises* and is a member of *XYZ. La revue de la nouvelle* collective. Her short stories have been published in magazines such as *Solaris*, *Moebius* and *imagine...*, as well as in anthologies such as *L'Année de la science-fiction et du fantastique* and *Tesseracts*. She co-authored with Brigitte Caron the novel *Elle meurt à la fin* (Paje, 1994) and she also translated, in cooperation with Suzanne Grenier, novels from Canadian authors Leona Gom and Nancy Kilpatrick. In 2003, her novella "La guerre sans temps", which is part of her forthcoming novel *Terre des autres* (Alire, 2004), won the Boréal award and the Aurora award for best Canadian short story in French.

E. L. Chen is also an artist, which means she's pretty much screwed unless she marries rich. She has been previously published in *Challenging Destiny*, *Lady Churchill's Rosebud Wristlet*, *Ideomancer*, and *On Spec*, and her short comics have appeared in *Say*. Everything else that she doesn't mind you knowing can be found at *www.geocities.com/elchensite*.

Candas Jane Dorsey's novel *Black Wine* (Tor, 1997) won the Tiptree, Crawford and Aurora Awards. Her fiction includes *Vanilla and other stories*, (NeWest, 2000), *A Paradigm of Earth*, (Tor 2001), *Machine Sex and other stories* (Tesseract, 1988) and *Dark Earth Dreams* (Tesseract/Phoenix DiscBook, 1994). Her poetry includes: *Leaving Marks* (River, 1992) *this is for you, Orion rising*, and *Results of the Ring Toss* (blewointmentpress, 1973/74/76). She edited or co-edited four SF collections, served on boards/committees for several Canadian writers organisations, co-founded/edited *The Edmonton Bullet* arts newspaper 1983-1993, and in 1992 co-founded literary publisher The Books Collective and its imprint River Books. From 1994-2003 she was editor-in-chief and co-publisher, with Timothy J. Anderson, of Tesseract Books. A freelance writer/editor and founding partner of Wooden Door and Associates communications company, she has travelled widely to give readings, presentations, and teach, and has won arts achievement and book awards.

Pat Forde resides in Waterloo, Ontario, in a house with an ambitious garden; the gardener is his lovely wife Kathleen. Pat has been a Hugo finalist, a finalist for the Sturgeon Memorial award and for the British Fantasy Award, and both his sales to *Analog* have won the magazine's annual Readers Award. Pat is proud to be a member of the community of Canadian SF writers.

Marg Gilks (*http://www.scripta-word-services.com/*) has a list of writing credits for poetry, articles, and short stories that spans twenty years and three countries (Canada, USA, and Britain). When not writing herself, she works as a freelance editor and writers' mentor through Scripta Word Services, helping other writers hone their fiction and polish their prose. She considers speculative fiction the ultimate form of escapism — in what other genre can you create your own universe?

Nalo Hopkinson has many nationalities and identities. This makes her as Canadian as they come. She is the author of three novels and a short story collection, any of which you may or may not agree is science fiction. She has edited two fiction anthologies and co-edited two more. She is the recipient of the Sunburst Award for Canadian Literature of the Fantastic, the World Fantasy Award, and the Gaylactic Spectrum Award, and at this writing is currently shortlisted for the Hurston/Wright Legacy Award for Black Writing. She thinks plurality rocks.

Sandra Kasturi is a poet, writer and editor. She recently edited the speculative poetry anthology, *The Stars as Seen from this Particular Angle of Night*, from The Bakka Collection/Red Deer Press. Her poetry has appeared in various magazines and anthologies, including several of the Tesseracts anthologies, *On Spec* magazine, *contemporary Verse 2, Prairie Fire, TransVersions, Strange Horizons*, and *2001: A Science Fiction Poetry Anthology*. She has three chapbooks out, and her most recent publication is the cultural essay, "Divine Secrets of the Yaga Sisterhood" which appears in the anthology, *Girls Who Bite Back*, currently available from Sumach Press. Sandra has received four Honourable Mentions in *The Year's Best Fantasy & Horror* and runs her own imprint, Kelp Queen Press. She is a member of SF Canada, SFPA, the League of Canadian Poets, and the Algonquin Square Table Poetry Workshop, and has won a Bram Stoker Award for her editorial work at the on-line magazine, ChiZine. Sandra enjoys single-malt scotch, the original cut of *Aliens*, elbow-length gloves and Viggo Mortensen.

Nancy Kilpatrick has published 14 novels, about 200 short stories, and has edited eight anthologies. Her recent and upcoming works include the non-fiction *The Goth Bible: A Compendium for the Darkly Inclined* (St. Martin's Press, October 2004); "Sleepless in Manhattan" in *Hellboy: Odder Jobs* (edited by Christopher Golden, Dark Horse, October 2004); the dark fantasy anthology *Outsiders: An Anthology of Misfits*, co-edited with Nancy Holder (Roc/NAL, October 2005); the novel *Jason X: Planet of the Beast* (Black Flame, October 2005). Check her website for updates: *www.nancykilpatrick.com*

Claude Lalumière is a writer and editor born and based in Montréal. He's the motivational force behind the webzine LostPages.net. A prolific critic and reviewer, his byline can be found most frequently in *The Montréal Gazette* and online at locusmag.com and InfinityPlus.co.uk. As an anthologist, his books include *Island Dreams: Montréal Writers of the Fantastic, Open Space: New Canadian Fantastic Fiction*, and (in collaboration with Marty Halpern) *Witpunk*. His fiction has appeared in *Interzone, On Spec, The Book of More Flesh, Intracities*, and other venues.

Derryl Murphy writes, edits, and other stuff in a distant and frozen location far north of Vancouver. His short fiction collection *Wasps at the Speed of Sound and Other Shattered Futures* is now available from Wildside Press. Visit his blog at *http://coldground.typepad.com*. "Mayfly" is Derryl's first collaboration, unless you count his kids.

Jason Mehmel. So far, Jason Mehmel's work has only appeared in small-press magazines and student-run theatre companies. Having finished a bachelor's degree in theatre, he's interested in working to meld science and the occult in an addictive substance he can market and sell as poetry. "The Fugue Phantasmagorical" is the free trial version.

Anthony MacDonald is an innovative and brilliant composer, who is also a speed skater. His speed on the ice matches the quickness of his musical mind, and his contribution to "The Fugue Phantasmagorical" is woefully unheard in these printed excerpts.

Yves Meynard. Since 1986, Yves Meynard has published 13 books and over 50 short stories in both English and French. He has won a baker's dozen of awards for his work, including the Grand Prix de la Science-Fiction et du Fantastique Québécois, but still has to develop software for a living. He was co-editor of *Tesseracts 5*.

Rhea Rose is a Vancouver, BC writer and a full time high school English teacher. In 1984, she participated in the Clarion West writers' workshop and has been writing ever since. Most of her work has been published north of the 49th parallel. She thinks she's the only writer to have appeared in the Tesseracts anthologies four times (two short stories and now two poems). Many of her pieces have been nominated for awards including the Rhysling Award for poetry, and, in the past, two short stories have received preliminary nominations for a Nebula award. A short story of hers appeared in David Hartwell's, *Christmas Forever* anthology and her latest short story "The Lemonade Stand" appeared in *TaleBones* 22.

Dan Rubin makes his home in Pouch Cove, Newfoundland where he works as a writer, musician and independent publicist. His short stories and poetry have won awards and been published in *Convolvulus*, *OnSpec* and *Canadian Composer*. He is the author of *Salt on the Wind: the Sailing Life of Allen and Sharie Farrell*, a biography published by Horsdal and Schubart (Victoria, BC) in 1996. Dan is also a recording artist with five albums of original music released to date. He welcomes input or questions from readers and can be contacted by email at *secondstage@hotmail.com*.

Geoff Ryman carries a Canadian passport and finds it the most logical thing to describe himself as being. His novella *Unconquered Country* (first published in *Interzone*, then as a book in 1986) won the World Fantasy Award and British Science Fiction Association Award. His 1989 novel *The Child Garden* won the Arthur C. Clarke Award and the John W. Campbell Memorial Award (first place). His mainstream novel *Was* won the Eastercon Award and was produced professionally as a play. The musical version of *Was* opened in Dayton, Ohio in 2004. *253 a novel for the Internet in Seven Cars and a Crash* was the online form in 1996 (*www.ryman-novel.com*) and now more than looks its age. The 1998 book version *253 the Print Remix* won the Philip K. Dick Award. His other novels include *The Warrior who Carried Life* (1985), *Lust* (2000) and *Air* (2004). He also led the web design team that designed the first websites for the British Monarchy and No. 10 Downing Street.

Daniel Sernine was born in 1955 in Montréal, where he still lives. With 33 books published since 1979, he has established himself as one of the most prolific and versatile Québec writers of fantasy and science fiction, both for adults and young readers. He has also published over 80 stories and novellas in magazines, fanzines and anthologies in Québec, Canada, France and Belgium. He is the editor of a line of juvenile novels for Mediaspaul, as well as the publisher of *Lurelu*, a professional magazine devoted to children's literature, and has been associated with the magazine *Solaris* almost since its inception in 1974. His works have repeatedly garnered prizes, including the Grand prix de la science-fiction et du fantastique québécois in 1992 and 1995. Five of his stories have appeared in translation in earlier Tesseracts anthologies, and four of his juvenile novels were published in English by Black Moss Press.

Steve Stanton is the founding editor of *Dreams & Visions* magazine and the *Sky Songs* anthology series. His short stories have been published in Canada, USA and Australia. Steve lives with his wife, Wendy, on their riverfront retreat in Central Ontario.

Jerome Stueart is a Canadian in training, processing through immigration as you read this. He has been published in *Ice-Floe, Urban Coyote, Out of Service* and the *Missouri Folklore Society Journal*. As a cartoonist he was featured in the *Yukon News* and an issue of *Up North*, Air North's in-flight magazine. He has also flirted with journalism and teaching. Hailing from Missouri and West Texas, Jerome came up to the Yukon to work on a book of Kate's adventures with bears and lemmings. He fell hard for the place and the people, and stayed for three years. Now, while waiting for Canada to let him return permanently to the north, he finishes a writing degree at Texas Tech University.

Sarah Totton is a graduate of the Clarion and Odyssey workshops. Her short fiction has appeared in the anthologies *Love Stories* and *Fantastical Visions III*. In her spare time she works as a veterinarian specializing in wildlife disease.

Élisabeth Vonarburg was born to life in 1947 (France), and to science fiction in 1964. She teaches French literature and creative writing on and off at various universities in Québec (since immigration, in 1973). A "Fulltime writer" since 1990, (despite Ph.D. in Creative Writing, 1987), i.e. translator, SF convention organiser, literary editor (*Solaris* magazine), and essayist. She still managed to publish five short story collections in French and one in English (*Slow Engines of Time*, Tesseract, 2001). Four novels translated into English, (*The Silent City, In the Mothers' Land* a.k.a. *The Maerlande Chronicles* (1993 Philip K. Dick's Special Award and a finalist of the 1993 Tiptree Award), *Reluctant Voyagers*, and *Dreams of the Sea: Tyranaël I*. Eight novels of her novels have been published in French. The more recent volumes in the five-volume *Tyranael* series have received three major awards in Québec. Also writes for children and young adults. Numerous short stories in French and English. About thirty awards in France, Canada, Québec and the United States of America, most recent being the Prix du Conseil Québécois de la Femme en littérature, (1998), a one-time literary award given by the Québécois Council for Women's Affairs on its twentieth anniversary, and a Boréal Award for "La course de Kathryn" (also nominated for a Grand Prix Québécois de la SF).

Peter Watts (*www.rifters.com*), author of the faintly praised "Rifters trilogy" (*Starfish, Maelstrom,* and *Behemoth,* all from Tor), is a writer and biologist whose success in both fields can best be described as "marginal". A collaboration such as "Mayfly" is something of an anomaly for the man, since he does not usually play well with others.

Allan Weiss lives in Toronto. He has published both mainstream and SF stories in various periodicals and anthologies, including *Fiddlehead, Prairie Fire, Windsor Review, On Spec, Arrowdreams,* and *Tesseracts 4* and 7. His book of mainstream stories, *Living Room,* appeared in 2001. He is Assistant Professor of English and Humanities at York University, teaching courses on science fiction, and is the Chair of the Academic Conference on Canadian Science Fiction and Fantasy. The story X is part of the Castormond series. Another story in the series, "Journals" appeared in *Prairie Fire.*

Alette J. Willis is currently undertaking a Ph.D. in Geography at Carleton University where her topic of choice is how the stories we tell about ourselves shape the world we live in. She is an alumnus of Odyssey — the six-week summer camp for adults who want nothing more out of life than to write speculative fiction — and has previous publications in *Storyteller, Andromeda Spaceways Inflight Magazine,* and *Paradox.*

Casey Wolf lives in east Vancouver overlooking a well-treed and birdful railway cut with her two good friends, fluffy and sparky. She visits haiti when she can and is grateful for the gifts she receives from being there. *Kenbe pa lage, ayiti!* never give up.

Copyright notices